PRESERVING WILL

THE ALIOMENTI SAGA
BOOK 5

ALEX ALBRINCK

PRESERVING WILL
By Alex Albrinck (www.alexalbrinck.com)

ISBN: 1494498464
ISBN-13: 978-1494498467

http://www.AlexAlbrinck.com
alex@alexalbrinck.com

Cover Art by Karri Klawiter (http://artbykarri.com)
Interior Design by Alex Albrinck

Dedicated to my family
Who teach me every day about unconditional love

CONTENTS

ACKNOWLEDGMENTS

Many thanks to my family; you have all provided incredible support throughout the writing process. There's no way I could have finished writing these books without your love and support.

To all of the authors who have, unknowingly, shown me that my dream of writing and publishing my novels needn't remain just a dream: Thank you.

Sixteen-year-old Will Stark sat in the back seat of the family's four-door sedan, twiddling his thumbs. Thus far, everything about the day had gone well. They'd gotten out of the house without incident, and he'd soon complete a major life milestone.

But history suggested his parents would find a reason to deny him that accomplishment.

As long as he could remember, he'd been treated, not as their beloved only child, but as some type of disease to eradicate. Only public opinion prevented them from leaving him on the side of a road somewhere and forgetting he'd ever been born, and he wasn't sure how much longer he'd be able to rely on that type of pressure to keep his life… minimally tolerable.

He knew the smart move was to stay quiet, to let events play out, to talk about this later, after they'd gotten home, or even a week from now. But he couldn't avoid asking, and had the haunting suspicion that this conversation would be the trigger to changing this positive experience into one he'd rather forget.

He cleared his throat.

Rosemary Stark, seated in the passenger seat, whirled around, her eyes full of loathing. "What do you want? We're taking you to get your driver's license. Isn't that enough?"

"Thank you for that," Will replied, his voice quiet and timid. Most people would be startled at his mother's tone, for Rosemary presented a sweet, gentle persona in public. The public didn't see this side of Rosemary, though.

His mother nodded, as if his apology had appeased her wrath, and she started to turn away.

"But," Will continued, "once I'm able to drive myself around, I'll need to get a job."

"You're not getting a car," Richard Stark snarled, glaring at his son from the rear view mirror. "We've discussed this."

"I'm not asking you to buy me a car," Will replied.

"And we can't waste time driving you around, so getting a job is out of the question," Rosemary added. "Don't we provide you enough as it is? You get an allowance, and…"

"If I get a job and can walk or ride my bike to and from," Will said, speaking quickly, "I can save up the money, buy my own car, buy my own gas, and then nobody would need me to drive anywhere."

"There's the insurance cost, however," Richard said, in a tone that was both cold and bored. "Are you accounting for that in this plan of yours?"

Will nodded. "Of course. The insurance cost goes up whether there's a car in my name or not, so…"

"What?" Rosemary whirled on him once more, eyes blazing. "I was under the impression that insurance costs only kicked in if there's a car registered to you."

"My friends at school said that the insurance costs for their families went up as soon as they became registered drivers," Will replied, his voice fading. The conversation, as he'd feared, was veering off course, and not in his favor. Just as it always did.

Rosemary directed her gaze back at her husband. "Did you know that, Richard? Did you know that this boy's going to cost us more money when he gets his license?"

Richard glanced in her direction. "The boy didn't see fit to tell me, either." His eyes flicked briefly in Will's direction via the rear view mirror. "Thought you'd spring that little surprise on us after the test was over and the damage was done, did you?"

"No!" Will shook his head in protest. His hands pressed against the seat, and his knuckles turned white as he gripped the edge in his desperation and despair. "I thought you already knew. It's why I want to get a job, so that I can help pay for the increase…"

4

"Help?" Richard interrupted. "Help? You'll be fully responsible for those increases as soon as they begin. Thought you'd drop something like that on us when you know full well my hours have been cut back, how tough times are, and…"

"I never tried to hide anything!" Will snapped. Then his face fell. "I mean… that's not what I… that didn't come out right."

Rosemary snorted. "It didn't come out right? You're trying to con us into an extra expense that you know we can't afford, and you have the gall to sass us when we catch you?" She glanced at Richard. "There's only one way to punish the boy."

Richard nodded. "I'll turn around up ahead."

"What…. what do you mean?" Will asked. But at only sixteen years of age, life had taught him to anticipate exactly what his father meant.

"You're not getting your driver's license," Richard hissed. "And that's final. When you've saved up enough money to fund the increase in insurance costs, and your own gas money? Then we'll talk."

"But I can still get a job, right?" Will asked. "I can walk, or ride my bike, or…"

"No, I don't think so," Rosemary told him. "It's too dangerous to be walking or riding your bike around at night."

"So… you'll drive me, then?"

"No, I don't think so," Richard replied. He glanced at his wife, who nodded at him to continue. "I think you need some time to learn your lesson, boy. It's not right to lie to your parents."

"But I thought…"

"Nobody cares what you think!" Rosemary snapped. "You're not worthy of having an opinion. Remember?"

Will winced as if slapped, and his head drooped, crushed by the latest disappointment in his life. Sometimes, he wished it would all just end.

Rosemary shook her head. "Seth never would have given us this kind of trouble," she muttered. "It should have been him, not Seth."

The single tear escaped Will's right eye and slid down his cheek, and he turned to face out the window. He wouldn't let them see him cry.

But even in his despair, he felt something. A tingling

sensation, a strange sense that someone out there, someone he'd never met cared about him. It might not make up for his parents' apathy and antipathy, but anything helped. His life might not have meaning to those who'd brought him into the world, but maybe, just maybe, it would have value for others.

He'd be happy to make a difference for just one person.

The car swerved, and he slammed into the door.

"Look out!" Rosemary screamed.

"I see them!" Richard shouted. Will snapped his head forward and leaned to the middle of the car. He could see the men loafing around in the middle of the street.

Will heard the horror in his father's voice. "The brakes are out! I... I can't stop the car!"

"Richard, do something!" Rosemary screamed.

"I'm trying!" he shouted. In the last act of his life, he glared at his only living child with complete loathing, a look assigning blame for the accident underway.

Will saw it. But he had no time to dwell on that final look of disgust.

Richard swerved right to avoid hitting the men in the road, a sense of incredulity forming as the car accelerated, even as he tried to activate the parking brake. The car slammed into the guardrail with a sickening thud, with a force sufficient to snap the seatbelts of the car's occupants. Richard and Rosemary hurtled forward into the dash, heads slamming hard, their deaths occurring in an instant.

Will, held in place by some miraculous force he couldn't explain, was the only survivor of the initial collision, the only one conscious and able to experience the shock as the guardrail fell away, as the car slowed just enough to teeter on the edge of the road, dangling precariously.

Will wondered if he'd be able to escape and survive... and then the car tipped over the edge and plummeted to the street forty feet below.

I
Assignment

1995 A.D.

They moved through the lightly traveled hallway, their footsteps echoing in the absence of people or material to absorb the sound. Purified, oxygenated air wafted against them as they walked, feeling more like a natural spring breeze than the forced, stale air one might normally find indoors. As she walked, the young woman observed the construction and layout with a practiced eye. The young man accompanying her presented a casual air, walking with his fingers laced behind his back.

"We have one room set aside for teleportation at present," Joshua said. "It's been sufficient for our needs until now. But with the increased Alliance presence in this part of the world, we're starting to see...collisions."

Ashley nodded. "We had the exact same issue at South Beach, and Sahara's just now implementing the procedures necessary to resolve the problem. There were too many travelers vying to use a finite number of safe teleportation landing spots."

She'd arrived here not long after she'd finished a six month stint at Sahara, the underwater Alliance port city off the southern tip of Africa. Her expertise in designing a teleportation traffic management system for the heavily-utilized South Beach location was being put to use in the lesser-used ports. Collisions—incidents in which multiple people tried to teleport to the same spot at the same time—were avoidable catastrophes. And as their presence in the Eastern hemisphere grew, the Alliance preferred to meet the challenges of increased teleportation traffic in a proactive manner.

"How do we fix the issue here?" Joshua asked.

Ashley considered. The current teleportation hub was a single room of modest size. It featured unique objects teleporters could use to travel into the space. The problems were obvious to her experienced eye. "I can answer by explaining what we've done at the other facilities. First, we took a single large teleportation room, much like you have here, and divided it up into a number of smaller rooms. The room you have today is large enough for a dozen people, for example; you'd do well to divide it up into seven rooms. That's what we just did at Sahara, by the way. Once the smaller rooms were built out, we painted each a unique color of the visible spectrum. Red, orange, yellow, blue, violet, and white."

Joshua frowned. "That's only six rooms. You skipped green and indigo. And white's not really part of the spectrum."

Ashley sighed. "Purple and indigo are similar in appearance and could be confused. To fix that issue, we substituted white for indigo."

Joshua acknowledged his understanding with a nod. She wasn't providing a science lecture; they were looking for easily distinguishable colors. "What about green?"

"The green room is a larger room than the others, able to accommodate multiple travelers at once. We *had* seven single-person teleportation rooms, but we found that recruiters would try to teleport in with one or more recruits, and…"

Joshua laughed. "Squish. I can see where that might be a problem."

Ashley wrinkled her nose. She didn't find the idea of teleporting three people into a room smaller than a human telephone booth amusing. Painful? Yes. Amusing? Definitely not. "The green room is larger, able to hold at least three people. More, if there's sufficient space."

Joshua stroked his chin, nodding. "I think I'm beginning to see the logic here. The six smaller rooms provide unique teleportation targets for individual travelers. The larger green room provides a landing spot for someone coming in with one or more recruits. It would also provide space for those bringing in weaker members of the Alliance who might not be able to teleport far enough on their own." Joshua frowned. "Do people…just pick their favorite color and teleport there?"

Ashley shook her head. "No. We did try that for a while. People would pick a random color and pop in. However, certain colors got picked at a much higher rate than others. Then people would try to pick *unpopular* colors. There aren't a lot of simultaneous teleportation efforts, mind you, but there were enough that we'd get two people coming in at the same time once a week, and the high percentage of collisions helped us realize that we needed to take an additional step." She stopped walking. "We used the example of reservation systems—say, for hotels—from the human world and applied it to the problem."

Joshua cocked his head in interest. "Go on."

"With hotels, they maintain a schedule of which rooms are in use and which are not…and more importantly, *when*. If someone calls looking for lodging, they can determine quickly which rooms are available during the requested dates. It's similar to what we're dealing with here, but the timelines are far different. With a hotel room, people might call hours, weeks, or months ahead, and they'll stay anywhere from a day to a week. Here? If someone calls in, they need to get here *immediately*. And they only need to hold the room for a few minutes."

Joshua nodded. "So the solution you've developed requires people to reserve the teleportation rooms."

"Correct," Ashley replied. "We have volunteers sit in a central space with visibility into each of the teleportation rooms. The volunteers are typically people who are new to the Alliance, familiar with Energy but not yet strong enough for long-range teleportation or work on the Outside. We keep two people in that observation room at all times. Everyone traveling to the Outside now has a comm link. We provided specific comm links just for those on duty. If someone needs to teleport, they activate the connection to the comm units at the observation desk."

"I've heard about that," Joshua said, nodding. "I'd heard that concept, having a single link for emergencies, was developed for the Defense Squad."

"It was," Ashley agreed. "But, thankfully, it's only needed once or twice a month for that purpose. Instead of connecting to the nearest Defense Squad, the comm system now lets us contact the people on duty if we need them. The request to teleport comes in, the person taking the call gives them a room color, and…"

"And they teleport in without concern of collision." Joshua rubbed his chin. "I can see where that will be helpful for us here as we get more traffic." He frowned. "Why two people? And what if they assign the same room at the same time?"

"Excellent questions," Ashley replied. "We keep cards matching the colors of the rooms on the desk where the volunteers sit. When a call comes to one of them, they take the card on top to indicate that they're reserving that room. Once they've communicated the destination to the caller, the card remains in front of them, color-side down, until the room is available for use once more. At that point, they flip the color side back up and put it on the bottom of the stack. It's not complicated, but it works."

"Simple is often the best approach," Joshua agreed. "And why two people?"

Ashley's eyes took on a distant look. "Emergencies can happen." She took a sip of the sweet fruit drink Joshua had supplied. Emergencies took many forms, from calls of nature, to the events she'd experienced back in South Beach… and the time she'd met *him*.

Seventeen years earlier, she'd been sitting at the volunteer observation desk she'd helped establish when the call had come in. Judith, one the Firsts, had been gravely injured, and Eva needed to teleport her in to get the medical attention the woman required. Archie had assigned them the green room, and had immediately intervened when he realized the extent of the damage. Eva had been knocked unconscious from the massive Energy expenditure, and Judith was slowly dying from her injuries. Archie had notified the medical teams of the severity of Judith's situation, and had ensured Eva had a place to rest and recover, before returning to his duties. Had Ashley not been there as well, no one would have been there to handle the three rapid teleportation requests that came in while Archie dealt with the life-or-death struggle.

Had Ashley not been there, she wouldn't have met a man who'd not hesitated to help two women in their time of greatest need.

She'd not seen Archie since those days, but they'd gotten to know each other quite well during their shifts. Their time together hadn't lasted long enough. Once his initial six-month shift had finished, he'd headed back to the Cavern, further developed his skills, and had headed Outside. While she'd remained at the Cavern, developing deep expertise in modern human computing technologies, he was off on missions in New Zealand. He'd have to come through Coral Beach on his way back to the Cavern. It might be childish, but the knowledge that he'd be there at some point had been a key factor in her acceptance of a request by Joshua to visit the undersea port to offer her particular expertise.

Coral Beach bore strong similarities to the South Beach and Sahara ports she'd already lived in. Like the other sites, it was built beneath uninhabited landmasses, and the port's exterior was covered with a variety of substances the Alliance had created as part of its never-ending fight to avoid discovery by Aliomenti and human alike. Human radar scans wouldn't find the port, or the submarines arriving and departing each day. If someone happened upon the port city and looked directly at it, they'd still see nothing. The port was invisible.

The interior provided hints of a unique personality to this particular transportation hub. They'd pumped a scent resembling eucalyptus throughout the complex. A handful of enterprising youngsters—Energy-wielding children who'd been born in the port to parents stationed here on duty—had confiscated miniaturized cameras and microphones, teleported to the Sydney Opera House, and planted them inside. They'd been punished by their parents for their actions—until they showed how the orchestral music could be played live throughout the port city as a result. Coral Beach sent a sizable anonymous donation to the Opera House each year.

Ashley flicked her eyes at Joshua. He'd matured a lot since his teenage prank, having gone from "vandalizing" a human landmark to providing day-to-day operational leadership of the undersea city. He was still a bit rough around the edges, but he'd live for centuries, giving him plenty of opportunity to mature.

She took a deep breath, inhaling the eucalyptus scent, and took another sip of her drink. "What is this, by the way?"

"Pureed koala."

She spat the drink out and fixed him with a glare as Joshua howled with laughter.

"I'm joking, of course. It's a mix of fruits native to a handful of the nearest islands. The combination creates an effervescing effect in the mouth that I find intriguing. And it tastes quite sweet. Do you like it?"

Ashley looked at the cup's contents closely. "You're sure there's no koala in here?"

"Positive."

"Then I love it." She took another sip. "Would you like me to talk with some of the construction engineers about making the structural changes?"

He shook his head. "The construction part I can handle. But we'll need help on the comm links and establishing the schedule for the volunteers who will handle the calls."

Ashley nodded. "I can do that."

They were ready to head back toward the central section of the underwater city when the door to the teleportation room opened up. Eva, the woman who'd teleported Judith to safety nearly two decades earlier, emerged. She was a tall, regal woman with platinum blond hair and a face that made it clear that she wasn't one to trifle with.

"Hello, Eva!" Joshua said, unable to keep the surprise from his voice. "To what do we owe this honor? I didn't know you were working in this part of the world."

"Hello, Joshua," Eva said, grasping the man's hand. "I am enjoying the beautiful background music you arranged years ago."

Ashley snorted as Joshua's ears turned pink. "I...ah...thank you?"

Eva's mouth turned up in a slight smile. "I am here to speak to Ashley. May we be excused?"

Me? Ashley wondered why the ancient woman was looking for *her*. Nobody seemed to know exactly how old Eva was, but the rumors had her at over one thousand. Ashley hoped she looked that good as she approached her own millennial birthday.

Joshua nodded, and after he shook Ashley's hand and thanked her for providing her insights, the two women walked away.

"I... have to admit I have no clue as to why you've come to see me, Eva," Ashley said, glancing at the other woman.

Eva gave a faint smile. "I am relieved to hear that."

They moved through a handful of people just heading in

from one of the submarines while Ashley tried to make sense of Eva's reply. As she considered, Ashley caught sight of a familiar face in the crowd. "Archie!"

The man paused, turned around, and stared. "Ashley? Is that you?"

"Excuse me, Eva," Ashley said, as she trotted over to Archie. The man stared at her with a bewildered look on his face. "This will take only a moment."

Eva followed.

"It's been a long time, Ashley," Archie said, and he smiled. "It's good to see you."

"And it's great to see you, too," Ashley replied. "Where are you headed?"

"I just finished up my Outside time, so I'm going to spend a few days here and then head back to the Cavern to decide what to do next. What about you?"

"I'm here to help Joshua update their system of teleportation rooms. There are some changes we made at South Beach that should really help them. They have a single large room and no one to coordinate the comings and goings. Oh, I almost forgot… Archie, have you met Eva? We were just talking when I saw you."

Eva inclined her head with a smile. "We have met. Archibald ensured I had a comfortable bed in which to sleep after we helped our friend Judith a few years back."

Ashley blushed. "Oh, I'm so sorry. How could I forget?"

Archie held out his hand to Eva. "It's good to see you healthy once more. What brings you to Coral Beach?"

"I arrived so as to deliver a message of extreme importance to two people, but I only expected to find Ashley present," Eva replied. "I am most fortunate that you have arrived, Archibald, as you are the second person I seek."

Archie blinked. "I'm sorry?"

Ashley glanced at Eva. "You have something to tell *both* of us?"

Eva nodded. "Let us help Archie store his belongings and meet at the lower level restaurant. I will deliver my message there."

They met in the lower level restaurant twenty minutes later. The restaurant specialized in seafood, but the choice of cuisine wasn't its best-known feature. The exterior walls and floor in the restaurant were created from a transparent material and offered an unobstructed view of the sea life swimming around them. Over time, they'd developed a simple, non-toxic chemical which illuminated the area around the restaurant, providing an ethereal view of the outside in an area where little sunlight reached. While the views were impressive, many residents and visitors found it difficult to eat when a shark swam directly at them. The restaurant was nearly empty for that reason.

And that was why Eva had suggested they meet there. She wanted privacy.

After they'd placed their orders, Eva considered for a moment before beginning her comments. "I said that I came to bring a message to both of you, and that is true. But with no context, the message will seem laughable, and you may doubt my veracity. I shall therefore begin with a question. What do you know of Will Stark?"

The two of them glanced at each other, surprised. "He's old, and was one of the founders of the Aliomenti," Archie replied. "He lived in the original North Village before all residents other than Adam and the Leader of the Aliomenti died in a tragic accident. I know that you lived there as well, so you're probably better able to answer that question than me."

"He was responsible for a lot of the innovations the Aliomenti experienced, usually far before the general human population became aware of and used those ideas," Ashley added.

Eva nodded. "Have you ever wondered how it was that Will so often arrived at these insights and innovations, so far ahead of others in both human and Aliomenti communities?"

Archie shrugged. "He's a genius?"

"I will agree with that," Eva replied. "Genius should have limits. Yet we have a man who invents electricity and computers three centuries before Franklin flew his kite. He built a self-navigating submarine when most still struggled to pilot boats with rudders and sails on the water. He made advances in commerce that put the Aliomenti on the road to a level of wealth the world had never before seen, even in the hands of the most powerful of monarchs. Seeing advances in one area driven solely by one man would be staggering. But in *all* of them? It should be impossible. So I ask again: why was Will Stark so far ahead of his time?"

Ashley's look of puzzlement was shared by Archie. "I don't

know. Why does it matter?"

"The answer to that question will shape your combined futures. That is why it matters."

"Why?" Archie asked. "What does the source Will's genius have to do with my future?" He looked at Ashley and paused. "Wait. With our *combined* futures?"

Eva studied both of them. "It is good that you are already seated. What I am about to tell you is known only by a very select group, only those who need to know. Before I reveal this information to you, I must therefore have your solemn vow to never reveal what I will tell you to another."

Their suspicions were raised. Secrets were frowned upon in the Alliance. The fact that they were being asked to swear never to reveal a deep mystery about Will Stark felt counter to the group's ideals. But they trusted Eva, and curiosity won out. Both of them nodded their consent.

"I know the true secret of Will Stark's genius. The secret is this: he was born just three months ago."

Both of them stared at her. "Come again?" Archie said.

"Will Stark was born at the start of this year. 1995."

Archie laughed. "That's impossible. Seriously, what's the big secret?"

Eva said nothing.

"You're serious, aren't you?" Ashley's face was full of doubt and confusion.

Eva nodded.

And then Ashley understood. "You're saying he was born... *now*... and then went... *back* ....to the beginning? That's why he had so many ideas? Because they weren't new ideas to him. They were memories, historical facts."

Eva nodded. "Precisely."

Archie snorted. "Oh, come *on*! I can't believe you're actually falling for this, Ash. She's pulling a prank on us." He snapped his fingers. "Joshua, the guy who runs this port... he's a pretty big prankster from way back. He's probably in on it."

They paused while their food was delivered, each taking the time to savor a bite of perfectly grilled salmon. Eva took a sip of water before responding to Archie's comments. "I assure you, this is no joke. Will was born three months ago. He will become a very successful businessman in the human world. He will marry and have two children. Before his second child is born, he will be found by the Hunters and attacked."

Archie rolled his eyes. "Let me guess. Our newborn Will ends up married to the Shadow, right?"

Eva nodded. "That is correct."

Archie laughed and glanced at Ashley, stunned to see her look of acceptance at this news. "You're truly buying this?"

Ashley gave him an exasperated look. "Archibald, have you forgotten your skills? Scan the woman, determine if she's telling the truth, and stop acting like an utter fool."

Eva smirked.

Archie sighed, and trickled Energy into Eva, assessing her thoughts and emotions. When he stopped, he wore a look of shock on his face. "She's... she's... she definitely *believes* it to be true."

Ashley smacked Archie on the arm. "It *is* true, moron. Now shut up and let the grownups talk." She stabbed at a piece of salmon. "You mentioned that Will's secret of success would have something to do with our futures. Can you elaborate?" Her eyes widened. "Are we supposed to help send him... back?"

Eva shook her head. "Not directly. That will be a job for others." She took a sip of water. "There is a machine back at the Cavern which can display targeted memories with perfect accuracy. We can record those and watch them. When Will told a few of us his secret—and yes, we had our own initial doubts, just like Archibald— we used that machine to record his memories of the future. That is because Will's survival of the Hunters' attach that day is the epochal event in our very history. If the Hunters succeed in killing Will— which they want to do because he confesses to violating their Oath against reproduction—then none of us would be here. He *must* survive. He *must* be rescued. And he *must* be transported to the past."

She hesitated. "We wondered how we would protect him until that moment. He is born to very human parents and has no Energy skills. His name and likeness are those of a man the Hunters have known for centuries. They would not mistake him for another. And thus, he's at risk during this time. True, the Shadow will be with him the final ten years before his transport. But until that moment, before the time of the attack—what happens then?"

"Why can't the Shadow handle it?" Ashley asked. "She's

powerful enough to deal with the Hunters."

"The Hunters and Assassin do not know the Shadow exists, for her true identity is one the Leader of the Aliomenti would be most interested in learning. Will has fought to ensure she has never needed to use Energy near the Hunters, and we do not wish to give them a signal for tracking purposes. When the Hunters arrive that day, they will believe her to be the human wife of the ancient Will Stark. She will be targeted for death. The Hunters will come away from the attack believing the Assassin was successful in his murderous mission. That must not change."

"Wait a moment," Archie said, raising his hand, and then lowering it sheepishly. "They'll *believe* the Assassin was successful?"

Eva nodded. "Will is rescued by the Alliance, and they take him to the distant future to train him in Energy skills, and to provide him with advanced technology to help him survive his journey. During that time in the future, his memories show a run-in with the Leader, the Hunters, and the Assassin. The Hunters make it clear they think his wife and son died in the attack, because they taunt him about his loss. That means the Shadow *cannot* use her skills to destroy any of them. That memory from the future is one of the reasons Will always argued strongly against invasions and attacks. He knew those we would most want to destroy are meant to survive."

"You mentioned we were involved in this somehow...?" Archie prompted.

"Yes," Eva replied. "In our reviews of the memories Will provided, we observed those with whom he interacted: those living in the Alliance community in the very distant future, as well as the humans living near him in his community. That community is both large and private. Five homes exist inside the walls that surround it. One of those homes is owned by the Starks. One is occupied by a very human couple, with only the woman surviving until the day of the attack. And the other three are occupied by current members of the Alliance, all in disguise as older, wealthy humans."

Ashley whistled. "And...we're one of those couples?"

Eva nodded. "The memories—which you will be able to see in the Cavern—give an idea of your role in human society. Peter and Judith, two of our Firsts, live there as well. And Aaron, another First, lives in the fifth house."

"That sounds like a great bunch of neighbors," Archie said,

finally warming to the news.

"Wait a moment," Ashley said. "You said there were five families living in the neighborhood. The Starks. A human couple. And three Alliance couples. One of those couples is the two of us. One of the couples is Peter and Judith. But you didn't mention who in the Alliance is with Aaron."

Eva merely smiled.

II
Illusion

1995 A.D.

When she woke, Hope's eyes refused to open, crusted over with the remnants of the tears she'd used to fall asleep the previous night. She considered staying in bed; life was something she didn't want to deal with at the moment. Yet she knew the people living in the Cavern needed her right now, perhaps even more than she needed them. They needed to see the brave face she wore, the decisiveness and determination to continue to advance the goals of the Alliance. They weren't a one-person organization, doomed to wither and die with the loss of their founder and leader. Their own ideals demanded they continue on, continue to thrive, and continue to live with the same zest they'd shown before.

If she let them see or sense how much Will's loss had shattered her, though? That might all end. And that was the one thing Will would never want. Or forgive.

And so she saved the tears, the agony, and the tremendous sense of loss for her times alone in the house they'd shared for centuries, crying herself to sleep each night. It was only by the sheer force of will she'd developed over centuries of facing life's greatest challenges that she adopted a stoic, even cheerful image in public, concentrating on restraining her emotional Energy so as to keep

19

everything running smoothly and moving forward.

Today was a new chapter in her life after Will. It was the first time she'd venture Outside since news of Will's loss had arrived months earlier. She'd looked forward to such journeys in the past, for she was almost guaranteed to have a "chance" run-in with Will during her travels. And if not? She still knew that he was out there, somewhere, and that they'd be reunited at some point in the future.

Now? She had no such assurance.

Well, that wasn't quite true. In fact, she'd see Will this very day. She'd told everyone she was scouting a young man, someone she believed would make an excellent member of the Alliance in a few years.

The infant Will Stark would indeed be just that, and so much more.

In many ways, seeing six-month-old Will would be the ultimate form of pain, the reminder that this infant was the only Will Stark now, the only one she'd ever see again. She'd have the tortuous role of watching her husband grow from newborn to man, and have him for only a few years before he set off to rescue her from the mental and physical torture that was her childhood.

Will's own childhood would be no picnic, either.

"His parents wanted a daughter, and *only* a daughter," Adam had explained. Somehow, he'd managed to be present at Will's birth, a feat he'd not bothered explaining. "They'd planned out every bit of their lives, Hope. They'd marry, have a son, then have a daughter, invest heavily, retire when their youngest—their *daughter*—graduated school and was self-sufficient, and then travel and dote upon their grandchildren. They'd written the story of their lives ahead of time, and expected life to give them exactly what they demanded. When Will was born… well, what they'd demanded from life could no longer occur. They could never seem to accept the fact that they still had two healthy children, and that nothing about their plan needed to change. They couldn't accept life's minor alteration to their plan, and the shock and frustration at the realization that life could tell them no…it's materializing as hatred for Will. I'm convinced that if the hospital hadn't intervened, if they'd not called and told the babysitter that they'd be coming home with their son… I dare say they would have left Will behind. Or worse… they might have taken him home and neglected him to the point that he wouldn't survive." He shook his head. "It was awful. I injected him with some Energy, some protection, to help him deal with what I fear will be a childhood spent being unloved and told he's worthless and unwanted."

Hope had nodded. "He told me a few times that his childhood was very difficult. Now we know why."

It was that thought, the idea that the infant Will might be in danger, that motivated her to action this day. She climbed from the soft, warm bed, forcing herself not to look at the spot Will used to occupy. She stretched, using a bit of Energy to loosen her stiff muscles. After a quick shower, she packed clothing suitable for a woman spending time in the United States in 1995 into a backpack, shrugged the pack onto her back, and walked out the door and into the Cavern.

Three centuries earlier, the hidden, underground city known as the Cavern hadn't existed. The space had been empty, devoid of all life, and lacked even a trace amount of air to breathe. Will had located the empty space within the Antarctic landmass, along with the access tunnel, a passageway starting thousands of feet below the ocean's surface. He possessed a vision and a degree of persistence that seemed more supernatural than the accomplishments achieved with the Aliomenti and Alliance. That vision had been more than fulfilled. If they'd teleported someone into the Cavern today, the visitor would swear they were outdoors in a tropical oasis, not inside a rocky cave buried under miles of rock, snow, and ice.

A slight breeze caressed her cheek, and reflexively she put her hand to her face. She knew that fans had been embedded in the rocky walls forming the Cavern's exterior, but it *felt* real. The air was fresh and clean, more heavily oxygenated than the air they'd breathe Outside, and there was faint hint of some unidentifiable scent that lifted her spirits. The grass and plants lining the path she traveled were real, grown from seed harvested from similar plants now native to the Cavern. The sound of rushing water greeted her ears, and moments later she crossed a footbridge spanning a modest river. The water was deep enough to enable boat travel; the bridges were designed to sense foot and river traffic, and would rotate aside to allow boats to pass in safety.

A rumble of distant thunder sounded, producing reverberations in the ground as she walked. The winds increased in speed gradually, starting to whip her dark hair about. A single raindrop fell on her head, and she couldn't help but laugh. Who could imagine an artificial thunderstorm happening three miles below the most desolate and deadly land on earth?

As the rains increased in intensity, she thought of the man who had, and her mood rumbled like the thunder surrounding her. Nothing would stop her from protecting him as long as she was able. There were so many who owed their very existence to his courage and imagination.

Hope bolted toward a small building along the path toward the center of the city, her motion off balance as she tried to move with the bag on her back. The building was a small food distribution facility, one where residents could make smoothies, and she looked around to see if anyone was working. Most functions in the Cavern were automated. Food production and preparation happened without human intervention… unless a human *wanted* to intervene. Complete automation meant everyone could work at the projects and activities of their choice; if no one wanted to work at a smoothie bar, the bar would still function without issue.

"Hello?" Hope called. "Is anyone working here today?"

"One moment!" The voice was sprightly and full of enthusiasm, and the Energy reaching her told Hope the speaker was a neophyte. The young woman emerged a moment later, beaming as she recognized Hope. "Shadow! What a pleasant surprise!"

"Hello, Samantha," Hope replied, smiling. Few knew her real name, and even fewer knew her birth name. Arthur's obsession with finding and capturing Will had been legendary; they'd little doubt he'd employ a scorched earth policy if he learned his only daughter lived. And so Hope, who'd lived in the shadows for centuries, was known as the Shadow inside the Cavern, her true identity hidden for the safety of all.

"I've been experimenting with some new combinations that have been quite refreshing," Samantha explained. She began selecting fresh bits of fruit and vegetables. "Apples, bananas, and some mango, along with some greens. Interested?"

Hope nodded, suddenly famished. "That sounds delicious. Thank you!"

She watched as the young woman bustled about, clearly enjoying the work. It wasn't something Hope had seen Outside. The humans living there rarely engaged in activity that was both productive—enabling them to meet their basic survival needs—and in line with their true passions. It made for many lives of quiet desperation. She hoped that she, or her children, might one day help alleviate that sad reality. Perhaps the vast fortune Will would accumulate in the human world could be put to work helping people live out their passions, with less concern about having a place to live or food to eat.

Samantha chopped and blended the ingredients together, and then handed Hope a frothy mix. "It's one of the new recyclable cups, by the way. There are bins scattered throughout the city for disposal."

Hope took a sip, and her eyes closed as the sweet flavor raptured her tongue. "This is absolutely delicious. Thank you so much!"

Samantha beamed. "My pleasure."

The storm subsided; the random rainstorms rarely lasted for long during the day. "I'll be heading out. It was good seeing you, Samantha."

"Likewise, Shadow."

The rainwater was absorbed into the walkways and into the underground drainage system. She maneuvered through the center of town and headed toward the beach and the end of the exit tunnel, enjoying the post-storm freshness to the air. She continued to sip on her smoothie as she walked, keeping her eyes open for one of the bins used for the disposal of nano-based dishware. Alliance research into miniaturized machines, robots, and building materials enabled them to create cups, plates, and cutlery that never had to be washed. Once used, the discarded items were dropped in bins that disassembled them into their component nanomaterials, and those were recycled into new dishware the following day. After finding one of the specialized bins, Hope finished her smoothie with a loud slurp, and dropped the cup inside. The cup disintegrated.

She lifted her eyes toward the beach in time to see Eva materialize in front of her. The older woman had just returned from a trip to Coral Beach. "Eva!" Hope called. Eva had once been like a second mother to her, and she felt a strong attachment and fondness for the woman.

Eva saw Hope and returned a warm smile. "Hello, Shadow. Are you leaving soon?"

Hope nodded as the two women approached each other and embraced. *How did it go?*

Very well. Our second target arrived just as I did, and I was able to speak with both of them. She has some work to finish there, and then they will both return to the Cavern for further briefings on the project.

Hope raised her voice to a normal speaking tone. "I am. I have some interesting possible Alliance targets that I'm following up on. And…" She paused, feeling herself choke up, and forced herself to steady her voice. "I… just need to spend some time away from here."

Eva's face clouded, and she reached out to squeeze Hope's arm. "I wish that I knew the words to make the pain leave you. The best way to preserve and honor his memory is to continue the work of the Alliance in the world."

Hope nodded. "I agree. That's what he'd want, more than anything else." *I'm going to go check on him.*

Eva's eyes widened at the thought, exhilarated at the idea that Hope knew where a living Will was hiding, before the actual meaning of the words registered. *You are going to see the infant Will.* There was a tremendous sense of disappointment at the telepathically transmitted words, and Hope winced inwardly at the renewed sense of loss the words triggered.

Eva then nodded in response to Hope's spoken words. "Then that is what we will do. I wish you a safe and productive journey Outside, Shadow."

"Thanks, Eva."

Hope teleported into one of the subway pods used to move Alliance members between the Cavern and the undersea dock where the fleet of submarines rested, pulling the backpack into her lap for the journey. One of the docked vessels, a replica of the original *Nautilus*, was for her exclusive use. The original had been retired and sat hidden beneath the sea at a location that only Hope knew. That was the destination she set for the new *Nautilus* as she teleported aboard. As the vessel set out at a high rate of speed, invisible to the human eye and all artificial sensors, she checked the supplies. She found several days' worth of frozen meat—mostly fish—along with fresh fruit and vegetables harvested from the Cavern's automated farms. The on-board juicer would enable her to create fresh juices as desired, and the craft would create all the fresh drinking water she might need. The submarine, with its highly-developed air purification systems, could serve as her home for weeks, or months, if needed.

She grimaced. Living underground for two months without seeing the light of day? She knew just such an experience awaited her in 2030. The difference? In that instance, she'd have her son there to keep her company.

The rear of the craft boasted the most notable enhancement over the original *Nautilus*. The shuttle craft attached to the exterior was the most advanced flying transport vehicle the Alliance had yet created. Spherical in shape, the craft used gravity to power movement in all directions, including vertically—and did so invisible to the human eye and all human sensors, including radar. The all-purpose craft didn't boast the long-term cache of supplies of the submarines. The underwater vessels stored volumes of food, clothing, and water, whereas the all-purpose flying craft were intended for short-range transport in the water, on the ground, or in the air. She'd use the submarine to reach the outskirts of Young Will's home town, and then take the shuttle craft the rest of the way.

Everything about the sub checked out, and Hope ordered the computer to plot the second leg of her journey to the United States for use after her initial side trip. That second trip, the official one, would take her through the Atlantic Ocean, then the Gulf of Mexico, up the Mississippi River, and then traverse the Illinois River before she made the remainder of the journey in the flying transport craft.

The thought of her final destination made her think of Will.

Adam had been quite certain that the wound inflicted by Porthos had been fatal. He had no protection from such a wound, either. Will had taken a sword splitter—a vest that displaced the atoms forming a sword around the intended victim—but Adam reported that Will had taken it off before moving to meet the Hunters. He'd fully expected he might die on that trip, and the loss of the vest, and Adam's fury at the hypnotized traitor in their midst, had convinced Hope and many others in the Cavern that Will was dead.

She thought of Eva, though, of her questioning of Adam. Had Adam actually seen Will die? No; Will had teleported far away, based upon the massive wash of Energy the teleportation effort had produced. Did Porthos go after Will? No, the Energy expended would put Will beyond even Porthos' Tracking senses.

She felt the flicker of something inside, something she'd not dared allow herself to feel often since Adam's crushing announcement. *Could* Will still be alive? And if he was... where had he gone? Why hadn't he contacted them?

The last was the easiest question to answer. All clues extracted from Will's memories, all communications from the "diaries" sent back in time with Will from the distant future, said Will didn't exist after that encounter with the Hunters. Nobody had seen him, nobody knew if he was alive. Will was someone very bound to his perceived duty; if he was alive and wasn't supposed to be, then he'd figure out a way to stay hidden. He'd still find a way to do good, to be the change he wanted in the world. But they'd never know. Not even her.

But he had to go *somewhere*. Adam's description of the events that day suggested he'd traveled a long distance from the island housing the Aliomenti Headquarters and casino. That meant he'd had a target in mind, and probably had picked out his spot before he'd ever left to go to the island.

In her rare moments of quiet hope, she'd thought through that scenario, the one where Will *had* survived and traveled into hiding. It didn't take her long to figure out the most likely spot he'd visit. It was a spot only she knew. But that knowledge was a double-edged sword, for it gave her the chance to confirm her worst fear, to end all wishful thinking that he'd survived. She might arrive there and find Will's body. But she'd know for certain he was dead, then, and the closure might well be for the best.

But she might also learn that he was alive, that he'd survived that attack after all.

She glanced at the map showing the submarine's course, watching as the craft moved toward a set of coordinates in the middle of the Atlantic Ocean. The new *Nautilus* was travelling to the final resting place of the original.

It was Will's style. He wouldn't compromise her by letting her know ahead of time his plans, for her emotion at his supposed death might not be genuine. It had happened from the very beginning, when he'd not told her Eva had survived Arthur's literal backstabbing, for he'd not wanted to put on her the pressure of maintaining a false mask of grief. Yet he'd set things up so that she would be the only one who *could* learn the truth, and she could do so at any time.

She was on her way there now. But until the journey ended, she could do nothing but wait.

Hope spent as much of the trip sleeping as her body could manage. Single-person journeys like this were a mental challenge, for she missed the companionship to be found on the full-sized submarines carrying dozens of people. There were books aboard the vessel, and she took the opportunity to read. Human imagination fascinated her, and she enjoyed the science fiction and fantasy worlds authors crafted with nothing but words, marveling at the degree of accuracy with which they'd predicted the advances that the Aliomenti and Alliance had already achieved in their visions of future and foreign worlds. She'd read, nibbling on bits of baked fish, sipping away at the sweet nectar of blended fruits and vegetables, enjoying the comfort of the mattresses that always made her feel like she was sleeping on air.

And then, suddenly, it seemed, she was there, as if she'd teleported the craft the distance rather than sailed it for thousands of miles beneath the ocean waves. She had a copy of the original Nautilus' remote, and used it to trigger the vessel's exterior light. She saw it: the brief flash illuminating the otherwise dark undersea world.

There was no time like the present. She took a deep breath and teleported aboard the remote craft.

The air smelled stale, reflecting the fact that no one had been aboard for months—or far longer. She looked around, listening, trying to sense if a living man was aboard, or had been aboard recently. She listened with higher senses as well, trying to find a hint of Will's Energy aboard the boat.

She found nothing. No Will. No body. No hint of Energy. No sign that he'd been aboard this vessel at any point in time in the past year.

That made no sense. This was the only place he could have gone, where he'd be safe in terms of masking the Energy burst of his teleportation arrival, and where he'd have the isolation he'd need to recover from his injuries. It was the only location that made sense when paired with the amount of Energy expended upon his departure from the island.

She sat down a moment, thinking about the man once again.

His every action had been calculated to keep her safe, to

protect her from even the possibility of danger from Arthur. He'd insisted she be called the Shadow in the Cavern. He'd discouraged her use of Energy in the presence of the Aliomenti, not because she couldn't hold her own, but because he didn't want Porthos having anything he could use to Track her. Everything was done to protect her and ensure that she survived to meet Young Will, and that together the two of them would bring Josh and Angel into the world.

The children.

Something suddenly snapped clear in her mind, something that had nagged her about one of Will's memories, something she'd never before been able to articulate, but which she now saw with perfect clarity. She scavenged around the submarine, locating several sheets of paper and a pen, and ran several calculations. When she finished, she wrote a note to a man who might not be alive, but whom she was certain would come through this ship at some point in time if he still drew breath.

Hope teleported back to the new *Nautilus*.

She'd not answered her key questions about Will's survival and possible whereabouts with any certainty.

But her realization about the children, and the note that realization enabled her to leave behind, gave her more hope than she'd had in months that everything was happening exactly as it was supposed to happen.

III
Redemption

1996 A.D.

"They are here."

Clint looked up as Eva walked into his home, her heels thumping loudly on the solid wood floors of the old manor house. The house had been built more than a century earlier, and though it lacked many modern amenities, it fit Clint's needs perfectly. Most critically, it was highly isolated from large human populations, giving him the opportunity to practice his Energy skills without fear of observation by those untrained in its usage.

But Clint didn't expect to live here long.

"How much time do you think we have?" he asked.

"I doubt they will wait long," Eva replied. Her voice was grave. "After Will was lost to them, they will wonder as we do if he has survived. They have spent time healing their wounds, but I believe they will now step up the frequency of Hunts. If Will is gone, they believe such efforts will drive a stake through the heart of the Alliance. If Will survives, the increased abductions of his friends may draw him out of hiding."

Clint nodded, his eyes distant. "They'll use us as bait to get their true target."

"Precisely. In this case, we are well-prepared for the attack the Hunters and Assassin will launch."

29

Clint looked at her. "Are you *sure* you want to do this? It wouldn't be difficult to leave. I don't want you getting hurt."

"Someone must test the sword splitter," Eva replied. Her tone left no room for argument. "I have some experience in being stabbed by murderous fiends and living to tell the tale. That makes me the ideal candidate."

Clint remembered the story, often told within the Alliance. Before the Aliomenti were named, they were a group of people living in a village built in a forest. Eva had challenged the power structure of the village—dominated by the same man who commanded the Aliomenti today—and had been banished. As she'd been escorted from the village, Eva had been stabbed in the back and left to die. Will had anticipated the attack, and his quick action had saved Eva's life. She owed Will her very existence, and was willing to take a chance of her own, following his recent example.

Clint sighed. "Should we cancel the party, then? I don't want to get any humans hurt if the Hunters should choose to pay us a visit."

"No," Eva replied, thoughtful. "The crowds will make the Hunters' task more difficult. If they come to the party, they will need to be discreet in their efforts to lure you to capture and me to my death. There will be witnesses, too many to silence without drawing attention to themselves. If we cancel suddenly, just as the Hunters have arrived, they may begin to suspect the degree to which we are able to track their movements. No, it is best to let the party proceed as planned, and to exercise appropriate levels of caution throughout the festivities."

Clint had moved to the small town a year earlier, after "officially" severing ties to the Aliomenti by withdrawing significant amounts of cash from Aliomenti-affiliated bank accounts. He'd also planted the tracking chip extracted from his body in a location that left no doubt about his contempt for his former "family." That meant he'd be on a watch list, certain to command a visit from the Hunters.

That was what he'd wanted. And he'd worked to make certain they moved him to the top of that list.

Eva had arrived in town not long after Clint, using the name "Eva Elizabeth Lowell" as a pseudonym. The name would mean nothing to the Hunters, but word that they'd killed Eva Elizabeth

Lowell would undoubtedly haunt Arthur.

Or had the self-proclaimed Leader forgotten them, two of the women who'd died at his wish and command, so many centuries earlier?

"Miss Lowell" had used Energy to alter her usual appearance. She now looked less like a regal woman in her early forties and more like an emaciated, haunted woman in her late twenties. She'd arrived in town complaining that she suffered from a terminal illness, which explained her unhealthy appearance to the local human population. A chance meeting with Clint had occurred, and not long after, doctors in the area proclaimed her to be in perfect health. She'd let slip in several social situations that Clint had healed her, and word of the miracle had made its way back to Aliomenti Headquarters.

Just as they'd intended.

The Aliomenti had recognized the ability to solve two problems by retrieving Clint. A traitor would be in custody to receive his just punishment. And the only beneficiary of Clint's Energy largesse would soon be dead, his departure ensuring that no more humans escaped the ravages of terminal illnesses through his efforts.

The Aliomenti had no idea who Clint truly wished to help… or that they were walking into a trap to ensure he could do just that.

Photos from recent encounters between the Alliance and the Hunters showed that the gash under Athos' right eye had never healed. Will had somehow poisoned the blade, and all efforts to stitch the wound closed had failed. The wound originally held pods of nanos, highly specialized versions that would track down captured members of the Alliance and eliminate the Dampering effect of the prison cells holding them. Once Energized, they'd receive a message from the machines providing an image usable as a teleportation target. Alliance members hiding on the island housing Aliomenti Headquarters would help them into an undetectable flying craft that would carry them back to the Cavern.

The plan had gone smoothly, perfectly, save for one thing. Will had insisted on being the one to plant those escape-enabling nanos on Athos, had insisted on proving that he didn't fear taking on the Hunters directly. He'd done so because he'd been baited into believing that people saw him as one like Arthur Lowell, a man content to let others do the difficult, dangerous work while he remained a spectator. It was a taunt that had cost Will Stark his life.

31

And Clint was the one who'd made those comments.

The fact that he'd been in a type of trance at the time didn't matter to him; Clint owed it to Will and the rest of the Alliance to make up for what he'd done, and there was no better way to do so than getting back on the inside, helping captured members of the Alliance flee. He knew the names of the escapees and the dates targeted for their rescue, and would have specialized technology with him to assist them in their escapes. He didn't know how long he'd be in that prison, but given the depth of his remorse, he suspected his self-imposed penance would last for a very long time.

Clint had scheduled a party that night for Halloween, a human holiday in many countries, where adults and children alike would dress in costume. Children would visit their neighbors, make comical threats, and be rewarded with candy for their efforts. Clint had always considered it a strange way to celebrate, but for purposes of fitting in, he went along with the pageantry.

He'd hired a professional crew of decorators and caterers for the event, along with two plainclothes police officers to enforce the guest list. As Clint's parties were already legendary in the small town, he needed to strictly enforce admission to avoid overcrowding the house... or worse, running out of alcohol. Nothing seemed to anger humans more than learning that the free liquor was gone.

He provided the list of guests and a sample invitation to both guards, who positioned themselves at the front and rear doors of the house. "Make them show a photo ID, and ensure the name matches a name on the guest list. Everyone was instructed to bring the invitations that were sent to them. The cards have small RFID chips inside. Scan the cards with the wand; if the light turns green, the invitation is legit. That means that if the light is green and the name is a match, they're allowed to enter. If not? Send them away."

"Don't worry, sir," the guard at the front door told him. "No one will get in unless they've been invited."

If only that was true, Clint thought. He wondered what would happen if one of the guards told the Assassin he wasn't permitted inside the house, and shivered.

He and Eva retired to their bedrooms to change into their costumes, and Eva took the time to redo her hair and makeup in line with the newly-buoyant public image she'd created for Miss Lowell. They both emerged a short time later, and Clint complimented Eva on her costume.

Eva smirked. "Are you referring to the outfit, or my magical youthening cream?"

Clint smiled. "Whatever answer would make you happy."

Eva patted him on the arm. "You are a wise man."

The caterers arrived and began setting out the entrees and snacks, and the bartenders arrived shortly thereafter with an assortment of sodas, wine, beer, and liquor, including a large selection of bourbons from the nearby distilleries. The disk jockey arrived, and it took him several trips to his passenger van to haul in the hundreds of CDs in his collection. He set up his speakers and stereo equipment, put on a mix CD of popular music, and began looking for Halloween-themed songs in his collection.

Once the guests started to arrive, Clint forgot about the Hunters. The house vibrated in time with the bass from the speaker system the disk jockey had wired together, and the noise of the music and dozens of voices left everyone with little choice but to lean close and shout in order to be heard. His nose wrinkled as the smell of alcohol and sweat began to fill the entire house. The sweet scent of the drinks and candy must have attracted flying insects; though Clint didn't see or hear them, he was certain he'd been bitten a few times.

He looked up from a conversation, suddenly feeling the Energy permeate the room, and spotted Porthos. The man was dressed in costume, and it was clear he'd been intent on sneaking up on Clint without detection. Clint snorted inwardly. Porthos must believe he was the only one capable of sensing Energy use in his vicinity.

Clint scanned the room without turning around, his skin feeling the slight tingle from the Energy behind him. Athos and Aramis were there, not yet in his line of sight. Somehow, he hadn't seen them enter the house or sensed them in the crowd. That was concerning. If Aramis approached him without detection, the Hunter could immobilize Clint. In this setting, people would think Clint had gotten drunk, had started to pass out on his feet, and then comment how great a party it was.

They had him surrounded, trapping him in the place of his choosing, and he'd failed to put up even a modest defense. He needed to reverse the situation, and could think of nothing better than ruining their anonymity... to a degree.

"D'Artagnan!" he called out, loud enough for everyone to hear him over the music and chatter. He fixed his gaze upon Porthos, and the crowd turned to look at the Hunter dressed as a pirate.

Porthos scowled, and Clint could sense Eva's internal laughter at the Hunter's discomfort.

He traded barbs with the Hunters, but became aware that Eva had started moving. He flicked his eyes around as the insults escalated, unable to locate her. He could only assume that the Assassin had arrived, and, as part of the plan, Eva had left the house with him.

He didn't dare risk communicating with her telepathically. Not with Porthos standing in the same room. He'd need to trust that she could take care of herself... and that the sword splitter would work.

Porthos artfully ended the intensifying—and public—verbal banter between Hunters and Hunted, and the party resumed in earnest, the guests deciding the confrontation was nothing more than a staged act between old friends. As the party resumed, he expected the Hunters to try to close in on him, pinning him in the house, until Aramis' deadly grip rendered him helpless.

Instead, they left.

That worried him. The Hunters were certainly not going to leave town, not without him. It could only mean that they were planning to wait until the party ended. A minor bit of panic arose; the Hunters were horribly efficient at their work. If they believed they could return to retrieve him later...

It was ironic. He meant to be captured, wanted to be captured, and yet every instinct in him fought against his capture. His mind told him to run now, to ramp up his Energy Shield and sneak away in a car driven by a guest. Yet how could he? If they'd left, they'd certainly expect him to do just that. And that meant they'd ensured that option wouldn't work.

He wondered if Will had gone through the same type of emotional conflict a year earlier.

Thirty minutes later, Clint felt extremely sleepy. As a man in unnaturally good health, Clint normally had no issues remaining awake and fully alert far later than this. He felt a chill. Had the Hunters somehow gotten a sleeping potion into him? He glanced down at the drink he held. Others drinking the same beverage showed no ill effects. If they'd not used the drink to get the sleeping potion in him, then… how?

His hand slapped the side of his neck in realization. Those hadn't been bug bites earlier. He'd been so preoccupied with the party that the Hunters—Shield-free—had walked close enough to give him injections. Clint cursed himself for his lack of attentiveness to his surroundings. Getting caught unaware by the Hunters—when he *knew* he was being Hunted—was an amateur mistake. He should have been keeping an eye on Eva, not missing Hunters sneaking sleep serum into him.

Clint's legs felt weak, and he began to sweat as if the temperature in the house had suddenly risen twenty degrees. The thundering bass from the music was creating a huge ache in his head, and made him feel wobbly on his unsteady legs. The overpowering smell of the various types of alcohol, normally something that didn't bother him, was making him feel nauseous. The serum the Hunters had injected into him was starting to take full effect. He excused himself, and began to make his way outside, where the cool, fresh autumn air awaited him.

"Fire!"

Clint whirled toward the sound of the voice. The disk jockey alertly stopped the music. "What? Where?" He could feel the tension in the room, from guests worried that the fire was in the house and they'd struggle to escape.

"The barn—the barn where the horses are kept—it's on fire! I can see it from the front porch!"

He knew, then, where Eva and the Assassin had gone. He hoped he'd pick up a hint of Energy from her, letting him know she was alive.

Clint was pushed aside as guests rushed to the front of the house, trying to get a view of the fire. Realizing he'd never get out that way, Clint staggered his way through the suddenly empty room to the back door, limped down the stairs, and worked his way around to the front of the house, hanging on to the railing and leaning against the side of the building to keep himself upright.

The barn was engulfed in flames, and even in his fatigue he could feel the heat from this spot, hundreds of yards away. Eva had lured the Assassin there, away from the crowd of humans, and allowed him to "execute" her. The Assassin, as he so often did, set the building containing his victim ablaze, eliminating all evidence of his crime.

He squinted, using his enhanced sight. And he saw it—the glint of gold from the tiara in Eva's costume, faint in the limited lighting, low to the ground... and moving. She'd survived.

He sighed inwardly, the relief spreading through him. But he had a job to do.

"The horses!" Clint shouted. "We need to get to the barn and check on the horses! They're trapped inside!"

Spurred on by their love of the animals and an irrational lack of fear of the flames, the guests raced toward the barn—and dodged out of the way as the dozen horses Clint owned raced by in the dark, illuminated by the sun-like blaze behind them. Clint wondered how Eva had managed to free the animals before her "death." Or had the Assassin done that?

"We'll need to chase them all down," Clint shouted, somehow able to construct a plan even as his body wanted to shut down and sleep. "There are fences surrounding the property. The horses can jump them, but they may calm down once they're far enough away from the fire and elect not to make the effort. All of them will have bridles in place. Approach them carefully, talk in soothing tones, and pat their muzzle. Then take hold of the reins and lead them back."

The guests took up the challenge and spread out, none of them bothering to ask *where* the horses should go upon retrieval. The barn was gone. Clint didn't worry about their oversight, because he'd be gone before they tracked the frightened animals down.

Clint felt the Energy presence of the Hunters now, and knew the men were waiting to get him alone, away from his guests. The public confrontation earlier had served its purpose; the Hunters wouldn't dare subdue him in the presence of the horde of humans who could identify them to the local press. But Clint would oblige their desire to isolate him. He moved past the barn, away from the house, and once he was certain he was beyond the sight of his human guests, he broke into a jog. The burst of adrenaline from the fire and the impending chase lessened the effects of the sleep serum; he felt more alert now than at any point in the past hour.

Aramis materialized in front of him, and Clint sensed Athos and Porthos finish their own teleportation jumps behind him. Aramis reached out the hand that would immobilize him through the Energy Damper. But Clint slammed an elbow into Aramis' arm, knocking it aside, and teleported five miles away. Given the effects of the drug—which adrenaline could overcome for only so long—he doubted he'd last many more hops.

Before he'd had a chance to catch his breath, they were there.

It was the *modus operandi* of the Hunters. In addition to their unique gifts, the Hunters were some of the most powerful teleporters in the Energy world. With Porthos' Tracking skills, they'd force their prey to teleport to avoid the Damper, again and again, until at last the victim collapsed from exhaustion.

Moments later, Clint was prone on the ground, his face nestled into the cool, fragrant grass, and he doubted he'd ever be able to move again. His Energy stores were drained, and the energy in his physical body was depleted by the lingering effects of the serum. He offered no resistance as the Hunters moved him to a rental car, and then into a transport craft with a Dampering cell. The craft was no better than an ancient relic by Alliance standards—there were few inertial dampeners in place and the air was warm and stale—but Clint offered no protestations about his predicament. He acceded to the demands of the serum and slept.

When he woke, sunlight burned down on him from the large window inside his cell. With the artificial Dampering restraining him, he was no flight—or teleportation—risk, and the inclusion of the window allowed prisoners to view the freedom they'd lost through their capture. Ocean waves frothed below him, and he tried to imagine the sound of the water's movement. The plane began its descent, and he saw the monolithic black marble Aliomenti Headquarters. Aboveground, he knew, the building served as the world headquarters for the international banking business that provided and expanded the great wealth of the Aliomenti. Below the surface, however, the Aliomenti worked in their labs and housed their prisoners.

That prison level would be Clint's new home.

The plane touched down gently and taxied into the hangar at the foot of the building. As the engine purred down to a quiet roar, the Hunters unlocked the cell and hauled him out. Aramis held one of Clint's arms to maintain the Damper, while Porthos took the other. Athos led the way down the steps, and the group made its way to an elevator that carried them to the sixth underground level. The interior was dark and uncomfortably warm. Athos held his palm to a door, and after a light turned green, he pulled it open. Porthos and Aramis hauled him inside, saying nothing.

Clint was paraded through walkways lined on both sides by cramped Dampering cells. The faces inside were worse than lifeless, for while they maintained the youthful appearance enjoyed by all ambrosia users, their Energy had been drained from them. The long-term prisoners here had lost all hope. Those lifeless eyes and empty faces turned to watch him. It was disheartening, but it furthered Clint's resolve. He would help all of these people escape.

One face, though, bore a different appearance. It was very subtle, and Clint doubted the Hunters had noticed. But there was a small spark in the man's eyes, as if his Energy was suddenly, inexplicably, returning, and the man was quite certain he was imagining the sensation that had been absent for so long.

Clint knew better.

The pods of nanos Will had unleashed upon the prison level via the gash under Athos' right eye were comprised of a material that nullified the Dampering effect of the prison cells. Freed of the Dampering, an Energy user's stores would gradually replenish. Clint suspected the man would need more time before he'd allow himself to accept the truth, before he'd be confident enough in his recovered abilities to teleport outside. Clint would do whatever he could to help when that day came.

They reached cell 66 and the Hunters hurled Clint inside. Already deprived of his Energy, Clint didn't notice anything different within the cell. He knew he'd be unable to teleport right now, but then again, he wouldn't need to do so for quite a while.

Athos moved straight to the door of the cell. "Where is he?"

Clint frowned. "Where is... who?"

"Will Stark."

"Sorry, Will can't come to the phone right now. Please leave a message at the tone." Clint added a rude sound effect to the end of his snide comment.

Athos blasted Clint with a burst of Energy that knocked the prisoner off his feet. "Where. Is. Will. Stark?"

Clint glanced around. "Why? Are you expecting him? You're not very good party guests, by the way."

"I *stabbed* him," Porthos snarled. "He should be *dead*. He should have died on the spot that day, and we'd have his body to show the sniveling cowards of the Alliance that the great Will Stark is no match for the Hunters. But instead, he teleported away, farther away than even I could track. Tell me the truth: is Will Stark dead?"

"I certainly hope not."

He felt the outside Energy grip him and pull him to the door, and Athos clapped a hand to Clint's forehead. "Where is Will Stark?"

"No idea."

Athos roared and shoved Clint to the back of the cell. "He doesn't know." He turned to Aramis and Porthos. "Now what?"

"We keep asking," Porthos replied, "until we find someone who *does* know the answer."

"And then we'll track him down," Aramis said, glancing at Porthos. "When we do? It won't go well for Will Stark. We won't take it easy on him this time."

"I'm sure your scary words terrify Will, given your dominant historical performance against him."

The Energy seized him again, slamming him into the front of the cell and then hurling him to the back once more. It hurt, but the taunt was worth it.

"We'll stop by tomorrow to finalize the length of your prison term, Clint," Aramis told him. "It's safe to say you'll be here for many decades, and you'll spend that time watching as we fill these cells to capacity."

Clint just smiled at him, and the Hunters walked off.

Clint let the anti-Dampering nanos embedded in a cut on the inside of his leg out, and felt the relief as his Energy stores rebuilt. He couldn't let them grow *too* much—Porthos would notice—but a small taste of his own Energy each day would keep him full of hope.

And he'd use that hope to encourage everyone here on their escape day.

Aramis believed the prison level would change, believed the Hunters would continuously and dramatically expand the number of captured Alliance members housed in these cells. Aramis was right, in one sense. The prison level *would* change dramatically over the years.

The cells would be emptied, and the prisoners would be free.

Clint would ensure that it happened. He owed the late Will Stark that much.

IV
Parting

2010 A.D.

Pages were turned in rhythmic fashion, filling the living space with the sound of paper scratching against paper. Adam found himself mesmerized by the descriptions of a dozen different types of data encryption and a comparable number of data storage systems. Humans might not have reached the sophistication they'd achieved within the Alliance—after all, the Energy users had been storing data for centuries—but their imagination in this space was impressive.

Adam's role had been the most difficult to find in the recordings of Will's memories. They'd finally located him, indirectly, in a brief series of conversations Will and Hope held with their estate attorney. They'd referenced a secret third party, working in the background without public scrutiny or pressure, someone with veto power over the disbursement of the family fortune in the event of their deaths. Will had noted to Hope on the drive home that his data storage and security lead would be an ideal candidate for such a role.

Hope had nodded, the movements exaggerated. "He's the first man I thought of for the role, because as much as you talk about the man, I feel like I've known him for… *ages.*"

Will had found the exaggerated statement confusing. But for Adam, Hope, Eva, Aaron, and the others, it was enough. She'd

40

referred to the candidate as the "first man," and they realized it could only mean Adam.

They knew Adam would need to stay close to Will and Hope, and have some reason for living in and around Pleasanton. Hope hadn't given a name to the man, which suggested that Adam would take on a pseudonym in his work with Young Will. He would manage something related to data storage and security, whatever that meant. He'd need to get proper training and human credentials in the field, and ensure that his name and reputation reached the ears of Young Will.

Adam never worried that the subject might burden him mentally; after three hundred sixty-five years of living, he'd mastered the art of learning new and complex subjects. His greatest worry was that he'd find the subject dull. As he'd immersed himself, however, he found it to be just the opposite. The topic fascinated him. On each trip Outside, he picked up stacks of books on the subject, quizzing himself relentlessly, until he could talk at length about the differences in mirroring technologies, explain multiple encryption approaches, and opine about the strengths and weaknesses of major and minor players in the industry. He was, in short, fully prepared to walk into a college classroom and enter a prestigious, challenging program of study, despite not having a strong academic record he could present. The relentless self-study would, along with a future degree, prepare him for a human career that would bring him to Will's attention in the future.

As a student preparing to enroll in college, Adam was required to fill out a myriad of forms related to financial aid. He'd declined to do so, because he had no need for such aid. He'd inherited his father's fortune, and had combined that wealth with his own to build a truly massive estate with large cash reserves. He glanced at the costs of tuition, room and board, books, and various activity fees, though, and wondered exactly how people without his vast savings could afford the cost. He sighed. Perhaps one day the Alliance could figure out how to solve that particular problem. For the moment, though, he was grateful that he'd notice the expense of his education about as much as most would notice a penny dropped into a fountain.

He sighed at the distraction, and used the opportunity to perform a time check in relation to his current Cavern-related work.

Like most working here, he rarely concerned himself with the precise hour of the day. Time was largely meaningless, creating a low-pressure environment that helped those in the Alliance to thrive in health and mental growth. The outdoor ambient lighting simulated day and night to provide the Alliance members living there with natural alterations of light they'd find in the world outside. Most kept the standard skylights in their home's roof open to the "sun" to provide such basic life event timing. Adam typically did as well, but today, he needed the clock to tell him when to perform a check on the success of his own secret experiment. And the skylight was closed to prevent anyone from seeing what he was doing.

The quest had begun fifteen years earlier. Adam had been present at the birth of Will Stark, a man he'd considered a great hero and friend. Few members of the Alliance knew Will Stark was born in the year 1995, something they'd reasonably think impossible for a man all knew to be centuries old long before that year appeared on calendars. But Will would be rescued from certain death twenty years from now, rescued in a time machine that would eventually make a one-way trip to the distant past with Will as its sole occupant. He wasn't sure why he'd done it, why he felt like he needed to be there. But in the end he became a witness to history, able to see the humble and tragic beginnings of the man who'd made such a profound difference in the world, who had been a friend to Adam's own father, and who had helped the younger Adam understand his place in the world.

And while there, Adam had witnessed something none of Will's memories had revealed, something Will himself had never known. He'd made a promise to the infant Will that day, a promise made with the understanding that no one else could ever know what he was doing... or why. Today, after over a decade of work, Adam might finally see his promise fulfilled. The clock gave a gentle chime, and Adam marked his place in the textbook and rose from his seat, shivering slightly as he moved.

His house was unusually cool, a fact most explained by noting that Adam had lived much of his life in northern climates and preferred less tropical temperatures. It was far warmer in the bunker where the experiment had been in operation since that day in 1995.

Adam had gotten the idea for the bunker under his house from the memory videos they'd recorded with Will. During one of the sessions, they'd asked where Hope and young Josh had gone when they'd disappeared. Will explained what had been related to him through his future contacts: Hope had teleported sufficient amounts of rock and dirt from beneath their house within the walls of De Gray Estates—the name of the community Will would build and where he and Hope and Josh would live—to permit the creation of a secret bunker reachable only by teleportation. There, she and Josh had lived until media furor surrounding the inferno had died down, and they'd emerged to begin their new lives.

Adam had chosen to work the farms in the Cavern since his arrival, and had used his profession and frequent daily visits to those farms to discard dirt and rock two pocketsful at a time. With the space cleared, he'd built walls, piped in breathable air from the house above, and set up basic lighting. He'd never known what he'd *do* with his secret lab; he'd built it simply because the idea held a mysterious appeal to him, the completion giving him a sense of accomplishment. Perhaps, he'd mused, it reminded him of the natural underground caverns hidden beneath the salty lake and valley of the island the Aliomenti had called Atlantis.

The bunker remained an empty amusement until he'd returned that day from witnessing Will's birth.

He hadn't returned empty-handed.

Will's birth had been one of the most emotional events he'd ever witnessed. No one, not even Will or Hope, had known Will was a twin, that his sister had been stillborn, and that even in the womb Will had tried to pull her to safety. Adam, posing as an intern to explain his presence in the delivery room, had been tasked the unhappy chore of disposing of the dead child's remains.

He'd left with both blood samples from Will's parents—a gift he'd provided Hope in the event Old Will ever emerged and they found a need for that clean blood—and the infant's body. Before leaving, he'd whispered a promise to the sleeping infant Will, promising that he'd do something to help the sister Will himself had tried so valiantly to save.

It had been a foolish promise. Adam had no power to bring the dead to life. The tiny girl was gone, and he'd been a fool to promise to do something for her. But he was true to his word, taking the infant's body with him as he hopped into the flying transport craft that would take him back to the Cavern. If he failed to keep his promise, it wouldn't be for a lack of trying.

He planned to store the remains in a refrigeration unit he'd built in the bunker. But he found, to his shock, that they weren't remains at all.

The little girl's heart was severely underdeveloped, and the lack of pulmonary strength had prevented the physicians' sensors from detecting her pulse, brainwaves, or other signs of life. Adam, cradling the infant in his palm, had been shocked on his return journey to feel the tiny body move. The movement was faint, but he'd sensed it, and knew it wasn't just his hopeful imagination at work. There'd been something else there: an emotion, a striving to live and survive. In that instant, overcome by an emotional presence far stronger than the tiny, dying body in his hands, Adam became a man possessed. The child lived, though barely.

He had a chance to keep his promise to Will. He would save her, and let her live the life nature tried to deny her.

He'd accelerated his flying craft past the mandated limits, setting off thunderous explosions behind him as he exceed the sound barrier, slowed to enter the ocean water at less-than-suicidal speeds, and accelerated forward once more through the water until he teleported into a shuttle pod already halfway to the beach inside the Cavern.

The passengers had been surprised at his sudden appearance, highly irregular in their experience. No one teleported to an already moving pod. Their faces asked the unspoken question.

"I… I *really* need to use the bathroom," he said.

Everyone squirmed away from him.

He teleported directly home at the instant the pod reached the beach, heading straight to his private bunker. He hooked her up to a respirator, worked feverishly to aid her heart's efforts to beat, injected a highly nutritious solution into her blood stream. Then, and only then, did he begin to work on her.

Her will to live was powerful, an urge she voiced in the telepathic communications the two of them held over the course of the years Adam worked to give her the life she so desperately wanted. Adam fed her with a near-constant stream of Energy, adding in what nutrition he could devise to feed into her body and brain. He managed to keep her in something like a coma, her body always motionless, struggling not to grow but just to live, while her brain, fed by the nutrition he injected, developed as well as it could in the limited physical space available. Adam thought of nothing else as he wandered among other residents of the Cavern, but in a city filled with people doing research of one form or another, finding someone immersed in thought was nothing unusual. Few paid him any attention.

During one of his outings, he spotted Aaron, and remembered the work the man had done with cloning. That gave him an idea. He would clone limbs and organs for her, regenerating the parts that failed, until he found success, bringing life to her body so that she could live and grow as any little girl should. But while her spirit was strong, Adam wondered if he'd be able to find an answer, to mold a body that would live, before that indomitable will began to crumble.

Thus far, he'd been working for more than a decade. She hadn't quit fighting. And though he'd taken short trips Outside to maintain appearances, neither had he, obsessing over her cure more than anything else.

Adam had run into the same problem with cloning that Aaron had long experienced and never resolved: the short lifespan of the bodily cells generated via the cloning process. Individual limbs and organs didn't seem to suffer that fate; Judith's regrown arm, for instance, still functioned perfectly decades later. Yet when he pieced individually cloned organs and limbs together into a new body, those body parts suffered the fate of full clones. It was a sort of reverse symbiosis, where putting multiple, long-lived cloned parts together limited the survivability of each.

He'd hit upon his newest hypothesis only a month ago, stunned he'd never thought of it before. If the cells were dying… why not infuse them with a fruit that eliminated the effects of aging upon human beings?

The latest cloning effort would be complete in just a few minutes, and Adam had no interest in waiting longer than necessary to see if the regrown limbs and tendons and organs showed the signs of health and permanence he'd sought for so long. It wouldn't be the first few minutes that would matter; they'd gotten through plenty of first hours or first days. It would be that first week, two weeks, and first month that would tell him if his experiment had been a success.

A knock sounded at his door. The vibrations shook him deep

inside, as if amplified far beyond their normal volume level, and Adam was startled from his thoughts. He glanced at the door and sighed inwardly.

"Come on in, Eva."

Eva opened the door and walked in, nodding in his direction. She glanced at the textbook sitting on the table as she took a seat. "You are still studying for your role. You are taking no chances."

"Will Stark sets high standards for the people he hires."

"You will not be working for him immediately. You must first…"

"Go to college. Yes, I know," he replied. "As best we can determine, by the time I come to Will's attention I'll have years of experience in this field, and may need to feign deep levels of experience even before I start my official studies."

Eva nodded. "I understand." She looked around. "I was under the impression you would be leaving today."

Adam nodded. "That's the plan." He glanced at his bed, where a set of luggage sat empty. "At some point I guess I'll need to pack, won't I?"

"I came to offer my assistance."

Adam shook his head. "I can handle that on my own, thanks."

Eva cocked her head. "Is something bothering you, Adam?"

"Not at all. I've just… lost track of the time. I really should get started on my packing, shouldn't I?"

Eva paused for a moment, and then nodded. "You missed our status call. I suspected you might be distracted by your final preparations for your departure. Everyone reported that all is well, that they are in place, and their roles are developing as expected."

Adam nodded absentmindedly. He was in charge of keeping everything on schedule for the events of the year 2030, but now he'd need to leave the centralized hub of the Cavern. It was difficult to think of something beneath Antarctica as the central hub of an operation that would concentrate itself in a few of the United States, but that had been the case. "Good to hear." He arched an eyebrow. "Speaking of people with current roles Outside, what brings you here?"

She shrugged. "It is apparently fashionable for women in my position to have some… what do they call it… plastic surgery?" She snorted. "My people tell me that I must get my nose altered. I told them to tell me what they think my nose should look like and I will go to my own doctor." She arched an eyebrow. "It is convenient that such procedures are expected to keep the person out of sight of the public for a few weeks, so I am using the time to come here to the Cavern and visit." She stood up. "I sense that you prefer to pack for your own journey without assistance, and I will respect your wish. It was good to see you again, Adam."

Recognizing that he'd been a poor host, Adam stood and gave her a hug. "It was good to see you as well, Eva. I... guess I'm just nervous about heading back Outside for an extended period once again. It's been nothing but short trips for the past few decades." He smiled. "Tell Aaron I said hello."

"I will do that," Eva replied, smiling back in a manner suggesting all was forgiven. She headed out the door.

Adam teleported to the underground lab before the door finished closing.

The air was over-oxygenated, optimized for the infant whose body he'd been desperately trying to rebuild for over a decade. Adam flipped a switch, and the ambient light came on with a level of intensity reminiscent of twilight, bright enough to see in, but not bright enough to harm sensitive new eyes. The lights generated a slight humming noise.

The girl rested in what he'd dubbed her "bassinet," the top of the cloning machine he'd built in the center of the room. His primary living quarters were cold, not because he'd grown accustomed to the cooler air of northern climates as popularly believed, but because he diverted huge amounts of power and nearly all of the warmer air in his home into the underground bunker. It was a sacrifice he was willing to make. The "bassinet" top was closed at almost all times, and the air he pumped inside was even more purified and oxygenated than the air in the larger room. A nutrient rich paste and pure fluid were fed into her body through tiny feeding tubes, tubes that he frequently moved from body parts dying to body parts living. He'd built a specific tube to directly feed her brain, the one part of her body that had never faltered. He'd set that up early on; he wanted to ensure that, even when he was away for several days, her brain had no chance to suffer a fatal event.

At this point, if the girl died, Adam wasn't sure he'd want to survive. Not even if it meant the failure of the plan to bring about Will Stark's future survival. Her life and survival had become his own personal, private mission.

He'd been accustomed to her body looking, literally, like death: tiny, unmoving, pale, and sickly. Today, her appearance literally took his breath away. Her skin was smooth and pink, and her chest rose and fell rhythmically as her budding lungs processed the air inside the bassinet. Her eyes were closed, and her face, so often scrunched in an expression of intense pain, was peaceful, the face of a cherubic child sleeping. Her arms and legs twitched, testing muscles and ligaments and tendons, daring to expend the energy needed to move.

Her breathing was inaudible inside the "bassinet." But the steady pulse on the heart monitor broke the silence of the lab and brought tears to his eyes. This was *different*. This was *it*. He knew it, knew it to the depths of his very soul, knew that this child would finally, truly, live.

Adam moved to a chair against the outer wall, sat down, and let the relief and joy spread through him. He reached out to her mind. *We've done it. I'm certain of it this time. You'll finally be able to live a true life.*

He could feel the joy pour from her. *I can feel it as well. There is no pain, no sense that my body is failing.* Telepathy meant he could have a conversation with someone who, physically, had the body of a newborn. Her mind had continued to develop, and he talked to her in this fashion about the world in which he lived, his studies, and anything else she found interesting.

Adam rocked back against the wall. This must have been what his father had experienced. Like him, the elder Adam had been taken with a helpless young child, had given an inordinate effort to help that child live, and had protected her against any who might do her harm until she was able to defend and take care of herself. His father had many faults, but when he felt the call to protect, nothing would prevent him from accomplishing his goals. That relentless drive to protect those he chose was a trait he was glad he'd inherited.

He had a problem, however. The child his father had protected, now known as Hope, had two parents, parents well-known in her home village. He was the only one who knew this child's parentage. Even if he said he'd just been trying to perfect the cloning process and had succeeded, others would want to know *who* he'd cloned... and why Adam had opted to perform his research in private when cloning had been a topic of interest to the Alliance for decades. Will had never been told he'd had a sister. In fact, Young Will was now considered an only child after the tragic death of his brother five years earlier. At no point in the videos of Will's memory had they found any indication that he had a sister, living or dead. And he, Josh, and Angel had never referenced a sister in the diaries sent back in time to provide guidance until they'd developed the ability to extract Will's memories.

Why? Why hadn't they mentioned her?

Had she died at some point in the future? He truly believed she was viable outside the artificial womb he'd constructed for her. The thought that she'd perish in the future, becoming a nonessential bit of information to Will Stark and his journey through the past... he shook his head. He wouldn't, couldn't, allow that.

If he wouldn't allow her to die, then he must assume she'd lived. And if she'd lived, there must be some reason he'd seen fit to keep word of her existence from Will.

Had he kept her true identity a secret from Josh and Angel as well? This infant, strange as it might seem, was their aunt, the sister of their father. Wouldn't they have every right to know about her?

And then he remembered it, a brief conversation he'd seen from a memory Will relived for them, the moment he'd learned that surly Fil and sweet Angel were brother and sister. Will had turned to Adam and asked if the man was their cousin. Adam, curiously, had offered a faint smile, and a comment that he was happy Will hadn't asked if Adam was their uncle.

He'd thought his comment from the future had been a mere amusement when he first watched it, an opinion reinforced by the fact that he'd run his hand through his eternally thin hair, as if poking fun of his appearance and his seemingly advanced age. And to Will, who at that time hadn't realized he was two centuries into his own future, talking to people centuries old, the comment had been just that, a self-deprecating joke.

Adam now wasn't so sure it *was* a joke. Had he sent himself a message from the future, in the same manner Hope had used to provide a clue to the nature of his future job? Why, specifically, state that he was glad Will hadn't asked if he was their uncle?

Was he perhaps giving himself a clue that the children's *aunt* lived, in secret?

He couldn't be certain of the full meaning of the message just yet. For now, though, he'd keep her survival—and more importantly, her identity—a secret.

That survival would prove a difficult secret to keep. She'd grow, need more food, and need the freedom to move around. She couldn't move around, though. Not here. Not in a place where people would know from her very thoughts the very scientific nature of her origin. Not where a simple blood test would reveal her parentage and very famous sibling.

But he couldn't keep her caged like some animal. The solution would need to come to him... somehow.

With a sigh, he teleported back to his main room—and froze.

"Your emotion was a bit strong, Adam," Eva told him. "You will need to learn better control if you mean for the girl to live and keep her existence a secret."

Adam stared at her.

"Very little happens around here that I do not detect. I try to avoid listening, but many people shout to my sensitive Energy ears." Eva sighed. "How long will you need, before you are confident the girl will live?"

Adam's jaw dropped. "How... how long have you known?"

"One does not approach the Cavern as if one is a meteor crashing to Earth without drawing attention, Adam. I have known the entire time. And yes, that knowledge does include her ancestry."

"Why not say anything, then?" Adam asked.

"I suspect it was for the same reason you are looking to remove the girl from the Cavern. There is no indication from our various sources of intelligence about the future to suggest anyone knew she existed. That may change; perhaps we simply said nothing to keep Will from learning the truth, whatever the reasoning for such a decision might be. But it is apparent to me by various bits of logic that this girl will not be raised here in the Cavern."

Adam sighed. Oddly, knowing someone else knew—and ostensibly approved—of his actions, and understood his current concerns, was a relief. "I feel a tremendous bond with her... and yet I realize that I must take her away, and soon." He shook his head. "What's wrong with me? Why am I not fighting to find a way to keep her here?"

"Perhaps you recognize that a home here would be no home," Eva replied. "Her parentage would not long remain a secret, which would prematurely reveal the truth of the origins of Will Stark to an audience far too large to keep silent in in the face of future Aliomenti threats. She would grow up with unfair expectations in terms of Energy ability and leadership skills. She would be far better served growing up elsewhere, with periodic checkups by the very few who know her true story."

Adam glanced at her, realizing that she meant to relieve him of the burden he most feared. "You mean to take her with you when you return from your supposed surgery, don't you?"

Eva nodded. "I do. Humans have orphanages, homes for children who have lost their parents, and I intend to place her in one and ensure her treatment there is exemplary. I will likewise ensure that her eventual family is composed of people we would be proud to invite to join the Alliance. And I will tell you where she is at all times so that you may check in on her as you see fit." She placed a comforting hand on his shoulder. "Do not fret, Adam. You have done a wondrous thing. It is time to let go, and to let this girl live the life she is meant to live… a life only possible through your Herculean efforts."

Adam said nothing for several minutes. He finally looked up and nodded.

"You did not answer my original question, though," Eva added. "How long will it take you to ensure she will live outside the artificial womb she resides in today?"

"Two weeks," Adam said, after a moment's consideration. "I need two weeks."

Eva nodded. "You recognize that you will miss the start of your schooling if you remain here that long."

Adam dropped his head. "I hadn't thought of that. But I won't leave her until I know for sure. If something goes wrong, I'm the one best suited to attend to her."

"I agree," Eva replied. "But it is also a well-known fact that you were planning to leave for your next trip Outside *today*, to meet the admissions director at your chosen university and plead your case for admission, since you are, by the records they have, one without a high school diploma, and thus do not qualify for admission through normal channels. You will lose one year of schooling for her, a price I am certain you are willing to pay. However, you must devise a plan to explain your failure to depart as scheduled to those living here, and it must be a plan fit for public consumption."

Adam thought about it, came up with his plan, and grimaced. "I know what I must do, Eva. But I'd prefer you were not here to witness what will transpire. You will be as surprised as others when it happens. As you should be."

Eva nodded. "I shall depart, then. We will speak again in two weeks on this subject."

She left, leaving Adam alone with his thoughts of the large hammer in his laboratory.

It would hurt.

But she was worth it.

●●●

Two weeks later.

Adam expected the knock at the door this time.

Eva walked in and shut the door behind her, glancing at the cast covering Adam's lower right leg. He sat in a large, stuffed chair with its back facing her at an angle, his damaged leg propped up on a stool.

"Why the leg, if I may ask?" Eva's tone indicated she was not questioning his choice, merely curious about his thinking process.

"A bruise or a strain wouldn't prevent me from traveling, not with the way we heal. A break or a ligament tear in an upper limb couldn't reasonably keep me here, either; I could still travel, and I'd be able to head to campus and meet with the admissions director without much issue, outside some initial pain tolerance concerns." He glanced at the leg propped up on the couch. "The leg, though? As badly mangled as it was, even one of *us* couldn't heal quickly. And if I showed up there in this condition? The humans would wonder how someone with a leg broken in three places, with an injury that ought to require surgery, could possibly heal so quickly." Eva could see his shoulders rise from behind as he shrugged. "I did talk to the university, though. They're willing to let me enter next year after interviewing me and recognizing that, even without a high school diploma, I could still test out of most any subject and start my collegiate career as a sophomore. With that performance, and the ability to pay cash for tuition, they'll wait for me as long as necessary." He paused, and in the midst of the obvious pain, his facial muscles moved as a smile covered the face Eva couldn't see. "Most importantly, all of it cleared me to remain here as long as needed."

Eva pulled a chair out from the table with an audible thud on the wooden floor and sat down. "The performance to sell the accident was masterful as well. I cannot imagine the pain."

Adam grimaced, remembering. He'd needed to shatter the bone before leaving his home. He couldn't get the leverage with his arms, and so he'd used Energy to swing the sledgehammer into his shin. The pain had been incredible, but he'd managed to hold the screams inside. Teleporting to the nearest bridge, he'd started to walk across—an action that drove an additional surge of pain that nearly paralyzed him with agony—before allowing his foot to slip between the side slats, trapping his leg. He lost his balance and fell awkwardly. A sound clip of a huge branch snapping, played through a hidden music player and speaker, had left no doubt to those watching that the slip and fall had snapped his leg, in three places as it turned out.

He'd refused the advancing nano-sized surgical robots for treatment, asking that he undergo surgery. He wanted his recovery to be human-like, for he'd need to go Outside again soon, and the story of his shattered leg and recovery would be one he could then share with humans he'd meet. The successful surgery involved inserting pins into his leg, stabilizing the bone and allowing it to heal. His leg would heal faster than any human even *without* the added assistance of nanobots. But his goal had been accomplished, even if it had been at the expense of his pride and a not insignificant amount of pain.

He nodded at Eva. "I suspect I'll endure future snide comments about my clumsiness as a result, but I'm fine with that."

She paused, and then asked the key question: "How is the girl?"

In answer, Adam rotated the chair to face her.

The infant was swaddled in tightly bundled blankets and slept soundly. Eva only then noticed the soft cooing noises she made as she slept.

Eva wiped the tear that had formed from her face. "You have performed a miracle, Adam. I hope you are proud of yourself."

He nodded. "When are you leaving?"

"As soon as possible," she replied, with a heavy sigh.

Adam had expected it, and looked down at the sleeping child. "My friend will take you to your new family now," he whispered. "I want you to remember something. I will always know where you are, and what you are experiencing. My friends and I will always protect you from any calamity. One day, perhaps, when you are older… I hope that we can be reunited. Until then, though… you are in the best possible hands." He wiped a tear from his eye with his free hand, and grudgingly handed the child over to Eva.

As Eva left, as he allowed the tears of grief to fall without shame, he couldn't help but wonder if he'd done the right thing.

V
Alone

2011 A.D.

It would be one of the pivotal events in Young Will's life.

The crash that would claim the lives of Richard and Rosemary Stark, the accident that would leave a sixteen-year-old boy an orphan, would occur this day. Will's memories of the event were vivid, clear, full of the sounds of screaming and compacting metal, the scent of gasoline and oil and fire and fear, and the emotion of a boy wondering how he'd survived—and if his life would, tragically, be better for being left all alone in the world.

With the event so powerfully embedded in Will's mind, they were easily able to locate a memory in which Will read a newspaper article about the event. The article gave the date, time, and location of the crash. The sentence that attracted everyone's attention noted the young survivor asking how it was he'd survived a crash that had killed both his parents in an instant and left the family automobile a crushed mass of gasoline-soaked metal. The team had exchanged looks at this news, and all of them, including Will, reached the same conclusion. Will had survived unharmed because he'd had help.

Alliance help.

The crash would start atop an overpass protected on both sides by a steel guardrail reinforced with cables, and end on the road below. The guardrail had been inspected just days earlier; a mechanic had performed routine maintenance on the car a week prior, and everything had checked out in perfect condition. Yet the brakes had failed as Richard Stark tried to stop the vehicle. The guardrail, the same guardrail that had prevented a dozen similar tragedies in the past two decades, had loosened upon impact, and the Starks' car had plunged to the road below. In the minds of the human authorities, neither the accident nor the survival of the teenage boy in the back seat could be explained. Young Will was told, repeatedly, that it was all a terrible accident, that it shouldn't have happened, and that every bit of available evidence suggested that it *couldn't* have happened. Human error wasn't to blame.

The newly orphaned Will Stark had chosen not to sue any parties involved, much to the chagrin of the dozen lawyers hounding him to file charges. When asked to explain his decision, Young Will had given his characteristic shrug. "My parents are dead, and no court decision can bring them back." His voice tinged with a hint of sadness. "My last memory of them now is one of them screaming. I have no interest in reliving that experience for a trial that can have no benefit to me."

The nightmares had continued throughout the past millennium, often jarring Will awake from a deep sleep, leaving his skin damp with sweat, shaking as the haunting memories consumed him. Reliving the experience for the Project 2030 team had been oddly therapeutic for him, for reasons he couldn't explain. And it allowed him to consider alternative explanations for the tragedy.

"The number of coincidences—newly installed brakes and freshly inspected guardrails both failing at the same time—led to a great deal of speculation about foul play." He drummed his fingers on the table they sat around, each watching the memory video on a holographic screen in front of them. "It was true that I didn't want to relive it, didn't want to go through something that had no possible benefit to me. People told me I'd make a lot of money, which didn't interest me. It would be like trading my parents for a check. And as… imperfect as they were, in later years I would have happily given away my fortune to have them back, to make peace with them. No, my private reasoning was that I *did* believe the accident was no accident. I had no idea if my parents had enemies, but if they did? Those enemies had managed to stage a car accident that couldn't be explained. If they could do that, surely they could silence an orphaned teenager." He shrugged. "I didn't want to die."

Adam had steepled his fingers together, his face taking on a look that all of them found disquieting. Will faced Adam, arching an eyebrow. "Say it, Adam. I've wondered the same thing as well. So... might as well put the theory out there for discussion."

Adam sighed. "What if it wasn't an accident... and *Will* was the target?"

The words had chilled them all. Had the Aliomenti discovered the secret of Will's origin, and decided to eliminate him at the beginning, before his vast Energy skills made such attempts impossible? Was it something handed down from on high by Arthur Lowell, Leader of the Aliomenti, an order to seek out Young Will and eliminate him from the pages of history before he could become a threat?

Will drummed his fingers again, with more aggression, and Energy sparks danced off the wooden surface with each contact. "I don't think Arthur ever had a clue about me. And I don't think his initiation tactics would allow anyone else to present such a theory to him. It would mean that someone was better than him, that someone had figured out something about me that Arthur had never realized despite our centuries spent together. The Hunters would have been told if Arthur suspected I was only thirty-five at the time of the attack and likely an Energy neophyte, and it was clear they were stunned at my lack of skill."

"That doesn't eliminate the possibility that this was an attack orchestrated by Aliomenti leadership, though," Adam replied. "Let's say that Arthur realizes that there are people in the human world called Will Stark, and wonders if you might hide in plain sight, as it were. He might tell his minions to kill everyone with that name, making it look like an accident, and report back when they're done." He cocked his head. "The only way they might fail is if the targeted Will Stark had our help, and that would *certainly* be of interest to Arthur. But think about it... if you failed in that effort, would *you* tell Arthur Lowell?"

"Fair point," Will conceded. "And as much as I'd like to dismiss the idea, it makes too much sense to do so. We have to approach the event assuming foul play initiated by the Aliomenti. I don't know of anyone else who would target me at that age—and I certainly have no recollection of my parents having the type of enemies who'd stage an accident like that to kill them."

Eva waved her hand. "What if it really *was* just an accident?"

"We still need to have people there to protect Will," Hope replied. "No human could survive a crash and forty foot plunge to a concrete road below." She glanced around, her gaze settling on Adam. "This new insight, though, means we need to be prepared to deal with an Aliomenti presence."

"We'll need two teams at the site, each with a different focus," Adam decided. "One or two people will need to provide an Energy shield of some kind to protect Will from the crash itself." He glanced at Hope. "Is it safe to assume you want to be part of that effort?"

Hope nodded. "Like you could keep me away." She shot a fierce, protective glance at Will, who smiled.

"Good," Adam replied, a faint smile on his face as well. "I think we also need to have at least five others in position—invisibly—watching for any Aliomenti lurking around the crash site. If we see them there loosening bolts or tampering with the brakes… we'll know how it all happened, but we have to let them finish the job." He nodded a sympathetic glance at Will. "Sorry."

Will shook his head. "I understand. No need to apologize."

Adam nodded, and then turned his gaze to the woman seated to his right. "Eva, this is the type of effort the Defense Squad typically handles. They need to let the Aliomenti present—however many there might be—sabotage the car and guardrail. And then they need to swoop in, subdue the perpetrators, and take them to a safe house for questioning." He thought for a moment. "We may need to alter their memories as well. No point letting Arthur and company learn there's someone getting an extra bit of help, especially someone with that particular name."

Eva nodded. "I will assemble a team to patrol and monitor the site."

Eva had kept the promise she'd made years earlier. Three invisible craft hovered above the future accident site, watching and waiting for the hint of Energy that would announce the arrival of one or more Aliomenti saboteurs. Hope piloted a fourth solo craft, monitoring the Stark household. She'd planted small cameras, microphones, and GPS devices within the car; which would enable her to track the vehicle and ensure she protected Will during the upcoming collisions.

The team had leveraged a pair of submarines to travel the bulk of the distance from the Cavern, using the underwater vessels to haul the reconnaissance craft they now used to observe in invisible silence. Hope checked the time. She still had a few minutes before the Starks would emerge to begin their fateful trip. Though the air was breathable in the flying craft, the purification systems weren't quite to the same standards as those in the submarines. She'd been out of fresh air and sunlight for more than a week, and decided to enjoy a brief excursion outdoors. She piloted the vessel down into a thick grove of trees near the house and teleported to the ground just outside the craft.

She allowed the early spring sunlight to touch her skin with its warmth, felt the caress of the cool breeze that whispered through the trees, felt the handful of twigs lining the ground break beneath her feet with sharp snaps. Hope closed her eyes and inhaled a deep breath, allowing the familiar sensations of nature to calm her nerves in advance of an event that would traumatize the teenager who would one day become her husband. She could see his childhood home through a gap in the trees. His beginnings were humble, indeed. While the Starks weren't poor, they were far from wealthy. Will attended public schools, wore second-hand clothes, and did not own a mobile phone—a device that would become ubiquitous in the next five years. Will Stark certainly hadn't become the richest man in the world building upon the successes of family who'd come before him and left him a vast fortune with which to start.

Hope's wrist communicator vibrated. The sensors she'd planted had detected the family leaving the house, commencing their journey to the local Department of Motor Vehicles so that sixteen-year-old Will could take the test for his driver's license. With a sigh, she teleported herself back inside the invisible aircraft and floated into the sky. After locating the green four door sedan via her tracking sensors, she put the craft on autopilot, allowing the vessel to match the movement of the car below. Hope needed to focus her attention on the passenger in the back seat. She was solely responsible for protecting Will, and she'd do so by surrounding the teen with a thick Shield of Energy. That Energy expenditure was dangerous, however. The longer the Shield existed, the greater the chance that any

Aliomenti in the area would sense the Energy burst. She needed to track the car and the conversation to ensure that she knew exactly when to activate the Shield.

Will sat in the back seat of the car, looking glum, hardly the reaction one would expect for a teenager heading to take his driving test and enter a new stage of his life. His parents, Richard and Rosemary, made idle chatter in the front seat, oblivious to the presence of the young man in the back. Will looked nervous, but cleared his throat. Richard glared at him via the rearview mirror, and Rosemary turned to look at him. The loathing felt for their son was clear in their eyes.

"What do you want?" Rosemary snapped. "We're taking you to get your driver's license, aren't we? Isn't that enough?"

"Thank you for that," Will said, his voice timid and quiet. Rosemary nodded once, and then turned away from her son. "But once I'm able to drive myself around, I'll need to get a job, and..."

"You are *not* getting a car," Richard said. "We've discussed this."

"I'm not asking you to buy me a car," Will replied.

"And we can't waste time driving you around, so getting a job is out of the question," Rosemary added. "Don't we provide you enough as it is? You get an allowance, and..."

"If I get a job and can walk or ride my bike to and from," Will said, speaking quickly, "I can save up the money, buy my own car, buy my own gas, and then nobody would need to drive me anywhere."

"There's the insurance cost, however," Richard said, in a tone that was both cold and bored. "Are you accounting for that in this plan of yours?"

Will nodded. "The insurance cost goes up whether I have a car just for me or not, so..."

"What?" Rosemary whirled on him once more, eyes blazing. "I was under the impression that insurance costs only kicked in with a car registered to you."

"My friends at school said that the insurance costs for their family went up as soon as they became registered drivers," Will replied. Hope detected the softening of his voice; the boy was clearly worried about the direction this conversation was heading.

Rosemary directed her gaze back at her husband. "Did you

know that, Richard? Did you know that this boy's going to cost us more money when he gets his license?"

Richard glanced in her direction. "The boy didn't see fit to tell me, either." His eyes flicked briefly in Will's direction via the rearview mirror. "Thought you'd spring that little surprise on us after the test was over and the damage was done, did you?"

"No!" Will shook his head in protest. His hands pressed against the edge of the seat, and his knuckles turned white as he gripped the edge. Hope could feel his desperation and despair. "I thought you already knew. It's why I want to get a job so that I can help pay for the increase…"

"Help?" Richard interrupted. "*Help?* You'll be fully responsible for those increases as soon as they come in. Thought you'd drop something like that on us when you know full well my hours have been cut back, how tough times are, and…"

"I never tried to hide *anything!*" Will snapped. Then his face fell. "I mean… that's not what I… that didn't come out right."

Rosemary snorted. "It didn't come *out* right? You're trying to con us into an extra expense that you know we can't afford, and you have the *gall* to sass us when we catch on?" She glanced at Richard. "There's only one way to properly punish the boy."

Richard nodded. "I'll turn around up ahead."

"What…. what do you mean?" Will asked, his sixteen-year-old face marked with a crease of worry that told Hope he knew *exactly* what they meant.

"You're not getting your driver's license," Richard hissed. "And that's final. When you've saved up enough money to fund the increase in insurance costs, and your own gas money? Then we'll talk."

"Then I can get a job, right?" Will asked. "I can walk, or ride my bike, or…"

"No, I don't think so," Rosemary told him. "It's too dangerous to be walking or riding your bike around at night."

"So… you'll drive me, then?"

"No, I don't think so," Richard replied. He glanced at his wife before his eyes flicked to the rearview mirror and Will's quivering image. "I think you need some time to learn your lesson. It's not right to lie to your parents."

"But I thought…"

"Nobody cares what you think!" Rosemary snapped. "You're not worthy of *having* an opinion. Remember?"

Will winced as if slapped, and his head dropped. Hope's heart broke. She wished she could hug him.

Rosemary shook her head. "Seth never would have given us this kind of trouble," she muttered. "It should have been *him*, not Seth."

Hope could almost hear the tears rolling down Will's face. The sense of devastation would have overpowered her if she'd been flying the craft at that moment, would have caused her to crash the vehicle, and she was grateful, yet again, that they'd worked so hard to build autopiloting features into everything they built.

That was another innovation Will had insisted upon.

Hope used her sleeve to wipe the tears from her eyes.

The sensors began to beep once more, and Hope snapped to attention.

The three Aliomenti neophytes were there. Two stood in the middle of the otherwise empty road, positioned so as to force Richard to swerve to his right to avoid them. The third stood near the guardrail. Hope could feel the tiny trickle of Energy, the physical intoxication, the sense of new power gone to the heads of men clearly unready for its responsible use. This was no effort or directive planned from the top. It was, instead, three men figuratively and literally drunk on their ability to murder those they considered their inferiors without detection, without repercussions, randomly choosing to do so to the first unfortunate souls that came along.

This was no planned murder. Will had been orphaned in an act of stupid cowardice.

Hope felt a slight sense of shame when she realized that she might well have chosen not to save the lives of Will's parents, even if history said they'd survived. The scene she'd just witnessed in the car left in her a smoldering anger towards her in-laws that even the passage of centuries would fail to quench.

She tapped the radio. "Three bogeys at the scene."

"We see them as well, Hope," Eva replied. "Will needs a Shield right now."

Hope reached her Energy into the car below, forming a thick shield of Energy around Will's body. The hopelessness and despair of his situation traversed the link between them, nearly overpowering her Empathy sense. Hope shook her head, clearing her mind. She then pushed back, using the Energy Shield to surround Will with positive emotions, impressing upon him a sensation of being loved fully, of acceptance, a belief that his life was one worth living. She filled her Energy with a sense of purpose and destiny, of an overwhelming and powerful belief that Will was one destined to change the world for the better, to improve the lives of millions, even billions, of people… and to be the truly special person in the life of at least one. She could feel his emotions turning, sensed the feeling of pride and purpose beginning to overwhelm the powerful sense of neglect and worthlessness he'd lived with his entire life.

And then she felt him lurch.

"Look out!" Rosemary screamed.

"I see them!" Richard shouted. Hope could feel his rising desperation. "The brakes are out! I… I can't stop the car!"

"Richard, do something!" Rosemary screamed.

"I'm trying!" he shouted. In the last act of his life, he glared at his only living child with complete loathing, a look that said he knew who he'd blame for the accident.

Will saw that look.

Hope ramped up the push-empathy Energy levels. She didn't care if she was caught at this point. She couldn't let Will be lost to the despair he felt in this instant.

He had no time to dwell on his father's look. Richard swerved right to avoid hitting the men in the road, a sense of incredulity forming as the car accelerated even as he tried to throw the parking brake on. The car slammed into the guardrail with a sickening thud, the force—with the Energy assistance of the Aliomenti saboteurs—sufficient to snap the seatbelts of the car's occupants. Richard and Rosemary hurtled forward into the dash, their heads smashed on impact. Their deaths were instantaneous. Will, held in place by the loving Energy cocoon of his future wife, was the only survivor, the only one conscious and able to experience the shock as the guardrail fell away, as the car slowed just enough to teeter on the edge, dangling precariously. Will had just enough time to consider offering a desperate prayer that he could climb out of the car to safety before the car tipped over the edge.

Will's scream tore through the microphones, the scream one of terror, the sound of one who watched as a life never truly lived came to a sudden end. She could hear his thought and promise, one made as the car began its descent.

If I survive this, I will marry for love and make my wife and children happy and proud of me. I will make a fortune so that they never lack for anything. And I'll help everyone I can so no one ever feels neglected and unloved and unsuccessful like I've felt my whole life.

It was a strange quirk of telepathy that the recipient's mind translated emotions and pictures into words. Will's mind had no time to formulate three sentences of distinct thought in the seconds it took the car to hit the concrete road below; he had no time to consider the meaning of the words as the sedan crumpled like an accordion, crushing the bodies of his already-dead parents and smothering his own Energy-protected form with twisted shards of metal. Yet the emotion behind it was genuine. Will had reached a point in his life where what he'd *experienced* in his life was the direct opposite of what he *wanted* from his life. It took a near-death experience to free him to articulate those realizations into thoughts, thoughts he'd later write down and carry with him at all times to remind him of the promise he'd made. Had his parents survived, Hope realized, Will's relationship with them would have changed dramatically.

It took Will nearly a full minute to realize that he'd somehow survived both the initial crash—surprising—and the forty foot drop—impossible. He looked around, and his acceptance of his parents' deaths was instantaneous. He didn't see their crushed bodies, just enough mangled metal and shattered glass to realize that whatever miracle saved him hadn't been extended to those who'd given him life. Hope remembered that Will once told her that they'd effectively been dead to him for years, had treated him as a worthless waste of space, and that their deaths had, paradoxically, finally freed him of their mental tyranny and allowed him to live.

She finally understood what he meant. And in truly understanding, she had a deeper insight into the man she now impossibly loved and respected more than she ever had in the preceding thousand years.

"Hope, is Will okay?"

She blinked, snapping herself free of the emotion-based connection with Will. "He's fine, Eva. Did you capture the villains?"

"We did." Eva's voice was confident, inflected with a subtle touch of annoyance, as if the question suggested doubt that her teams would apprehend the perpetrators. "We will be returning to the safe house to incarcerate the criminals and extract what useful information they may possess. When finished, we will ensure that they find themselves waking from their alcohol-induced sleep with no memory of this day... and terrible headaches that we will be certain to exacerbate. We will see you there when your business here ends."

Hope smiled. Eva knew she'd want to stay with Will through to the end of the ordeal before leaving him.

She kept the Energy Shield up, flooding him with feelings of confidence and purpose. Emergency crews arrived, sirens blazing, men and women approaching the scene with horror and a realization that no one inside the crushed green hunk of metal lived, that their purpose was to secure the guardrail and reroute traffic. They saw the first flicker of flames near the crushed car, and moved quickly to douse those flames to prevent an explosion which might injure one of them or destabilize the supports for the overpass. Hope could feel the intense heat of the flames through Will, and could feel the drop in temperature and relief of all those gathered as the flames winked out of existence. Hope shuddered; he'd have another fire to deal with in twenty years, and he wouldn't escape that one without burns as he had this time.

She watched as the machine known as the jaws of life pried the mangled wreckage apart, heard the crews shout immediate and resigned recognition of the deaths of the driver and passenger seat occupants, and felt Will's peaceful acceptance of their official loss. She felt the air flow in as the machine pried the metal away from him, heard the shouts of surprise through his ears, the stunned recognition of the rescue crews when they found Will not only alive, but without significant injury. The metal had bent away from him upon contact with the Energy Shield; it looked to the rescue workers as if a series of freak coincidences had resulted in metal colliding with metal, providing a protective barrier around the teenager in the back seat rather than a tortuous death. They had no explanation for Will's lack of injuries from the impact of the collision and fall, though, save for a little-believed theory that the metal cocoon had acted as a type of shock absorber.

One shrugged. "He *was* wearing his safety belt."

"Maybe we can get him to film a public service

announcement recommending their usage."

They argued about whether the safety belt made a difference in this instance, but in the end there was no other explanation to offer. Miracles and Energy Shields weren't accepted explanations for survival in reports written by humans.

"I guess you have someone up there watching out for you, huh, kid?" one of the medics told Will after giving him a clean bill of health.

Will could do nothing more than nod. But he did glance up, and his line of sight happened to catch the spot where the flying craft hovered. Hope smiled.

A family friend took Will back to the empty house that night. As the only surviving child of Richard and Rosemary Stark, Will inherited their entire estate. His parents had taken out a second mortgage to finance trips the two of them took over the years. They owed more on the house than it was worth. When Will sat in the church pew a week later, as his parents' friends mourned a loss he himself did not feel, he did so knowing that the burial costs would exhaust the entirety of his parents' assets.

He was orphaned, penniless, and homeless. His country was trying to dig its way out of an economic recession that fought death as vigorously as he had in the car crash. Hope knew from Will's own memories that things would get far, far worse before they ever got better. And yet she knew that even against such long odds, all alone in the world, Will Stark would succeed. The emergency worker was wrong. Will Stark didn't have just a single guardian angel watching over him, enabling to survive, to become the man who'd lead the recovery a desperate nation needed.

No. Will Stark had an entire Alliance behind him.

VI
Student

2011 A.D.

He'd looked like a man in his early forties for centuries. Today, Adam would take on the appearance and moniker of a nineteen-year-old college freshman.

The fortyish-looking man entered a stall in the restroom within the university student forum, tuning out the peculiar aromas assaulting his sense of smell. He removed an object from his backpack that looked like a small wad of aluminum foil, attached an end to the inside of the stall door, and pulled. The shiny material turned reflective as he stretched it out, and in a moment, with the edges affixed to the door, he had a private mirror to use to perform his personal cosmetic alterations.

He'd learned the basics of Energy-based appearance alterations centuries earlier, and Hope, who'd gone through more pseudonyms and appearances than anyone else, had offered him tips to ensure that he aged appropriately. If he retained his nineteen-year-old face for decades, people might wonder what was going on. Hope told him that wasn't the biggest error.

"Once you've aged in public, you can't rejuvenate your appearance," she told him. "Your efforts must look natural. People will accept efforts to mask signs of aging—hair coloring, cosmetic surgery even—but they'll know how you've made those types of changes. If you truly look young again, though, if people can't figure out what you've done? You'll never be able to use your new image in public again, because no lie you provide as an explanation will give people answers they can believe."

Those types of errors—a failure to age, the risk of rejuvenation—were a core reason why trips Outside typically lasted less than twenty years. Adam would need to carefully manage his public appearance and his true appearance for the next two decades. With everything he needed to manage and monitor during that time, an appearance slip would be an unfortunate but predictable error.

Ashley, who'd founded a series of technology companies over the past decade, had developed a day-by-day image aging computer program. Adam located a second small wad of material that looked like plastic wrap, and stretched the material out over the mirror. The plastic wrap was a single purpose computer, designed to display the image of his new face as it should look on that day, naturally aged. By overlaying it on the mirror, he could see his current appearance and the proper image at the same time, and adjust his appearance as needed, matching whatever subtle change might be suggested by the program.

When Adam removed the image computer overlay moments later and looked at his new reflection in the mirror, the change was striking. Gone was the fortyish-looking man with the brown eyes and thinning brown hair. He now sported thick, dark hair and blue eyes, and his skin had smoothed to match that of a man not yet out of his teens. He nodded at his new reflection. He made faces, pinched his skin, and ran his hands through his hair. He even popped a piece of sour candy into his mouth, forcing himself to watch the expression in the mirror change as his body shook and shuddered with the tart taste. Each action, odd though they might seem, was designed to train his mind to recognize the new appearance as his, not that of a stranger. By the end of the strange series of actions, he had cemented the image of his new face in his mind.

After rolling the plastic wrap and aluminum foil up and stuffing them into his backpack, he flung the bag over his shoulder, wrinkled his nose one last time at the aromas emanating from the nearby stalls, brushed his new, longer hair off his face, and walked outside. He blinked as bright sunlight assaulted his eyes.

The college he'd elected to attend specialized in his chosen technology field, and had the added advantage—from Adam's perspective—of being small. While larger schools, boasting tens of thousands of students and faculty, would make it easier to blend in, it also increased the risk that someone from the Aliomenti was there looking for recruits or defectors. His chosen school was in the northwestern portion of the United States, far away from the Aliomenti Headquarters, and far from those locations where most search efforts commenced. The Aliomenti had lost the strong work ethic his father and Will had described from the early days, when the very first Aliomenti worked with their hands, taking pride in improving their skills. Today, getting their hands dirty, literally or figuratively, would appall their leadership. Traveling beyond the scenic coastal areas of a country—especially when it required lengthy travel from Headquarters—represented a level of effort the Aliomenti would avoid if at all possible.

Adam smiled inwardly. Their laziness made his job that much easier.

He glanced at the paper in his hand and read his class schedule. With the year off due to his accident, the school had the opportunity to assess which of its many prerequisite courses he might skip after demonstrating mastery of the subject through a series of examinations. Drawing upon the life experiences earned over his three centuries of life, Adam had breezed through the exams, earning the right bypass the introductory, prerequisite courses and jump directly into the core classes for his degree. Adam signed up for the maximum number of courses the school would allow during his first semester. He had no intention of developing an active social life, and his centuries of healthy living and Energy skills enabled him to work long hours with little sleep. The registrar had noted that the school's base tuition covered only a finite number of credits, and that Adam would need to pay up front for the extra courses. Adam had paid without hesitation, for the amount was a trifle to him. His checking account, set up under his pseudonym, was well-funded by the standards of any American college student, but it was an amount he'd never miss.

He found a campus map and used it to locate the building where his first class of the day would occur, studying the sign with deep interest. It was an unnecessary exercise, for Adam had memorized the campus layout, room numbering schemes, and the locations of the offices for each of his classes, professors, and teaching assistants before he'd arrived at the school. He thought it would be something expected of a new student on campus his first day, and thus he'd done it in an effort to seem normal to any who might be watching. He wondered if by trying to act normal he might stand out in a manner he was trying to avoid.

Adam reached the building five minutes the class started and slipped inside. The air was ripe with the anticipation of a new semester, triggered by dozens of students trying to find their classrooms while simultaneously flirting with each other. Adam wandered into the large first floor lecture hall and found a seat in the middle of the back row next to a gangly man with red hair and freckles.

"Is this seat taken?" Adam asked.

The young man looked up, glancing at Adam with cobalt-blue eyes. "Not at the moment."

Adam sat down, dropping his backpack on the floor. "I'm Cain," he said, turning to offer a hand to the young man next to him. As he said the name aloud, his earlier mental training kicked in; he truly *believed* he was Cain Freeman.

"David," the redhead replied, completing the handshake. The freckles and youthful face left Adam wondering if David was even eighteen years old.

"You a freshman?" Cain asked.

"Sophomore, actually," David told him. "Tried to test out but wound up having to take most everything standard last year. What about you, Cain?"

He recognized the effort to remember a name by repeating it in conversation. "I'm a freshman, David. I was supposed to start last year, but I had a bad accident right before my first semester was supposed to start. Recovery took too long, so I waited to start until this year. I guess it helped to have nothing to do but sleep and study; I took the tests and passed all of them."

David let out a low whistle of appreciation. "Well done, Cain. I think you can call yourself a sophomore as well, then." He grinned, wrinkling the freckles on his face. David pulled a notebook and a pen out of his bag and set them down on his desk. "Have you picked a major yet?"

Cain nodded. "Information technology. I think data storage and security is going to become critical in the future. You?"

"Biotechnology. Minor in robotics. Same reasoning, actually."

The professor entered the room, and Cain took an instant dislike. The man had no interest in being there, considering teaching underclassman a waste of his valuable time. But the department head required professors to teach classes, and so the man was here, begrudging the students in the room every second of the class. He had a mandate to be here and teach, but that didn't mean he had to give his students his best effort, and Cain knew the students would likely suffer for the lack of preparation and interest.

He turned his attention from the disinterested professor to the student sitting next to him. "That's an interesting combination."

David nodded, his face lighting with enthusiasm. "I've been reading about subatomic building materials for a few years. I think we can use those structures, and robotics built on a similar scale, to deliver medicines directly to cells and increase their effectiveness."

Cain nodded, thoughtful, as he considered the idea. "That sounds fascinating, actually."

David nodded in agreement. "Robotics with that level of sophistication will require a great deal of computing power, probably more advanced than anything available now. I still need to understand the basics, understand what the trends are, and understand how I might be able to take advantage of everything going forward. And then... I have to figure out how to miniaturize it all to a degree never before attained in human history." He grinned, scrunching up his freckles. "Nothing like a great challenge to motivate you, is there?"

Cain inclined his head. "Indeed." He paused a moment. "If you don't mind my asking... how old are you, anyway?" He gave a faint smile. "Sorry for asking."

David laughed. "Don't worry about it. I get asked that a lot. I'm nineteen. I just look a lot younger than I am."

The professor's projected voice reverberated through the room, and the feedback from the microphone sounded like a klaxon inside the lecture hall. Cain covered his ears, but David hadn't even flinched. The redhead noticed Cain's attention. "I had this guy for a lecture last year. He starts every class doing that, says it's to wake us up." He reached up and pulled out earplugs as the feedback stopped.

"I've learned to come to class prepared."

Cain winced. "I'll keep that in mind." He paused a moment, as the professor rambled on about the goals of the class. "Any other insights on this guy?"

"He hates teaching, so ignore the lecture. His class materials and handouts are outstanding, though. He bases part of your grade on attendance, so the best bet is to sit in the lecture hall and study the handout notes and ignore him. He doesn't ask or answer questions." He held the earplugs out. "I recommend using these the entire class period."

Cain nodded, rubbing his painful ears. "I'll keep that in mind."

David put the plugs back into his ears. Moments later, a pair of teaching assistants moved through the lecture hall, handing out thick packets of papers. David took one and handed the stack to Cain, who passed the remainder on to the next student. He scanned the materials and found David's assessment to be accurate. He risked using a bit of Energy to shield his ears and focused on reviewing the printed materials.

He felt the vibrations in the floor of the lecture hall as the class session ended, and removed his own virtual earplugs as he began to pack his supplies away. He turned to David to offer thanks for the guidance on the professor along with a generic farewell. But David was already gone.

The remainder of the day passed without incident. Cain's other courses were held in room-sized classrooms with far more interaction between teacher and pupils. Students groaned about the homework assignments due at the beginning of the next class, which puzzled Cain. He expected his homework from the six classes he'd attended during the day to take less than an hour to complete. Then again, he reminded himself, he had a few centuries of experience in focusing himself upon a task with such ferocity that he finished those tasks in what seemed an instant. It was one of the reasons he'd opted for a single occupancy dormitory room. A young adult would be startled and possibly frightened by his intensity. And he didn't want them to have a chance to learn his most deeply held secrets.

Later that evening, with his assignments completed, Cain wandered around the small campus for an hour, watching the students as they mingled. Conversations ranged from current romantic interests, to complaints about professors and homework assignments, to speculation about the weekend's football game. Cain realized he'd need to learn about the most popular sports in the area so that he could speak intelligently if engaged in conversation on those topics. He headed to the student union and bought a slice of pizza to take back to his room for dinner. After centuries of subsisting primarily on food prepared to maximize health and nutrition, he found the smell of the greasy, doughy concoction disgusting. When he reached his room, he locked the door behind him and stared at the pizza. After several moments spent steeling himself at the potential horrors the food might trigger in his body, he finally took a tentative bite. The mix of artificial substances and processed foodstuffs set off every manner of rejection system in his body, and it took a significant amount of self-control to avoid being sick. He fought through it; if he was to mingle at all, he'd need to be able to consume a common college food staple without gagging.

At five minutes until ten o'clock that night, his alarm sounded. It was time to restore his appearance to that of Adam for the evening's activities. He repeated the process from earlier in the day, but needed no overlay of his birth image to recreate his original appearance. Though he'd never forget his true self, his abilities, or his mission on behalf of the Alliance, he'd need these few minutes each day to reset, just as he'd need time each morning to resume his role as the human and aging Cain Freeman, teenaged college student.

Adam activated his tablet computer and launched a special application that he'd built himself. The app set up a highly secure video chat room, impenetrable except for the few members of the Alliance with copies of the same app. The apps had a self-destruct feature; if the owner of the tablet failed to launch within a few minutes of the predefined meeting time, the app would delete itself and all traces of its existence. They could get the app back, but only if they returned to the Cavern to reimage their machines. Even Adam, the author of the app, couldn't restore his app while Outside.

He launched a second app, one designed to produce a specialized form of white noise in the room. It acted as an impenetrable bit of soundproofing; even if Adam shouted, no one outside the cone of silence generated by the app could hear him.

Within moments, a checkerboard pattern of faces appeared on his screen. Hope. Eva and Aaron. Graham. Archibald and Ashley.

Judith and Peter. All except Hope were in their current human world disguises, faces suggesting ages ranging from mid- to late-forties. All had connected for the Project 2030 status call, slated for this time once each week. Most of these calls were brief; they'd long since learned to dispense with idle chatter and focus only on mission-critical information and developments that needed to be shared with the group. All of them, save for Hope, had human appearances to maintain, and long periods spent in isolation talking into a tablet computer would raise suspicion.

"Good evening, everyone," Adam began. "Cain Freeman's first day of class was uneventful. He should be able to graduate without issue in three years or less, and be well-positioned to join Will Stark's future enterprises on schedule."

"We traveled through Pleasanton over the weekend," Eva announced. "It is a very quiet place, with a small population and little industry to provide employment for the population. Aaron and I both made comments about wanting to live in such a quiet town in the future."

"Frank completed his chauffeur training and is scheduled to take tests over the next two weeks," Graham told the group, using the pseudonym provided by Will's memories. Graham would one day serve as the driver who'd help uncover the horrors unleashed by the Assassin. "I should have plenty of experience developed over the next few years, and will be ready to work with the VanderPooles when the time arises."

"We started another Internet company a few weeks ago, using the proceeds from selling our first technology company before the market crash in the year 2000," Archibald said. "We suspect this one will provide the cash flow to enable us to buy an estate in Hope and Will's future community." He nodded at Ashley. "Ashley has started reading up on nanotechnology and is making noise about the important role for the devices in her vision of the future. We believe the investments and initial statements will position us well to start a nanotechnology research firm in a few years." He smiled at Adam. "We'll probably need someone to secure our intellectual property if you're looking for work at that point."

Adam laughed and nodded.

The group was efficient with their reports, and within five minutes they were done. Everything was going according to plan. So far. "Thank you, everyone. Eva, if you don't mind, I'd like a private word with you."

After a flurry of farewell messages, everyone signed off, and Aaron stepped away from the screen and outside the soundproofed cone of silence. The conversation would be private. "Any news on the girl?"

Eva nodded. "Yes. She was adopted by a couple living in Pleasanton. That is why I insisted we alter our route to go through the town. We did need to start making comments about Pleasanton as a possible future residence, and that is how I convinced Aaron to make the detour."

Adam blinked. "You put her in Pleasanton?" He felt a lump form in his throat.

"We will all live there for a time, Adam. I will live there for years, giving me adequate means to check on her without raising suspicions. It is a small, sleepy town at the moment, one the Aliomenti would never consider checking. It was the ideal location for many reasons."

Adam nodded, only now appreciating the foresight. "Did you… were you able to check on her? On the adoptive parents?"

"No. Traveling through a quaint town is not terribly suspicious; stopping to query the head of the orphanage there about the fate of a specific child would initiate curiosities we do not want aroused."

Adam nodded. "Understood. Thanks, Eva." He terminated the connection.

It was the pinnacle of frustration for him; after more than a decade of preserving her body through repeated cloning of organs, bones, and tissues, a time during which only her brain had remained unchanged, after that final breakthrough when he'd ensured her body would live and grow and develop… after all of that, he'd been forced to watch her leave. She'd grow up human, raised by human parents, away from the Alliance and away from him. He could only hope she'd have better luck with her adoptive parents than those that gave her life. Richard and Rosemary Stark hadn't set a high bar in that regard.

Adam drummed his fingers together, considering the idea that popped into his head. It was crazy. But he had to know. With Eva's message, he'd struggle to sleep until he knew the little girl was in good hands.

He made his decision, and moved quickly before he changed his mind.

After donning a hooded sweatshirt to hide his Adam appearance, he left his room, allowing the door to close and lock behind him. The students in the dorm would think nothing of it; they'd think Cain had simply gone out to join one of the many late night parties taking place in dorms and houses around campus.

Nothing could be further from the truth.

The single-person invisible flying craft was floating between the canopies of two large trees outside the campus. Adam walked there at a brisk pace, hearing his footsteps first slap against the pavement, then crunch gravel, then whisper through the soft grass beneath him. He glanced around, testing first with his human eyes and ears, and then with his enhanced Energy senses, to ensure no one was nearby. Once he was certain he was alone, he teleported into the vessel.

The ship sensed his presence, activating the interior cabin lighting and intuitive flight control interface. A map showed his current position; Adam zoomed out to show a larger portion of the United States, slid the map to his left, and zoomed in on the tiny city of Pleasanton. He tapped on the screen twice, confirmed Pleasanton as his destination, and set the ship's autopilot to move toward his destination at maximum velocity. Within moments, the craft was hurtling eastward at a speed well in excess of the sound barrier. Adam closed his eyes; the auto-pilot would give him the opportunity to take a short nap.

In what seemed like seconds, he was jarred awake by a beeping sound announcing his arrival at his destination. He caught his breath, sat up, and glanced at the screen. The map showed that he'd reached Pleasanton, and a few voice commands for the ship computer soon had the vessel hovering noiselessly over the orphanage. Below him, children slept, dreaming of being part of a family. Adam would need to get in, find the information he needed, and leave, all without drawing the attention of the children or the adults who cared for them.

Adam sighed. He had no choice. He'd need to risk using Energy.

Adam closed his eyes and pressed his sense of sight inside a floating, baseball-sized globe of Energy. The globe floated in front of him before exiting the craft. It was as if he was the one flying outside, dipping down through the cool night air before phasing noiselessly through the front door. The globe enabled Adam to traverse the first floor until he found a sign identifying the office for the orphanage. That was what he needed. He floated the vision globe into the office and scanned the room, getting a good mental picture of the layout despite the darkness. Satisfied, he recalled his Energy, then teleported directly into the room.

Adam allowed his eyes to adjust to the darkness, letting his mind clear so that every creak of the aging building didn't set him on edge with the idea that someone was moving toward him. He glanced around. The office desk sat in the center of the room, and the walls were lined with filing cabinets. He glanced at the computer monitor and keyboard on the desk. That would be the fastest way to find the information he needed. A quick tap of the mouse revealed what he'd suspected. The machine was password protected. With a sigh, Adam glanced at the plethora of filing cabinets. He'd need to look through the paper files, which would both make noise he couldn't afford and use time he couldn't waste.

He lit a small Energy light and scanned the labels of the cabinets. He needed to find a list of recent adoptions. Eva hadn't told him the name the girl had been given, nor had she supplied the names of her adoptive parents. He'd need at least one of those to be able to check in on her. Eva didn't want to think her name; Aaron would hear the thought and become suspicious. He'd gotten the only clue to her identity and location he'd get. It would need to be enough.

He stepped toward the first set of filing cabinets. They were labeled alphabetically, which wouldn't help Adam without a name. He continued scanning, hoping to identify cabinets with files on recently processed adoptees.

Adam looked up suddenly, his senses on alert. He slid the drawer closed, extinguished his Energy light, and phased into invisibility.

The door to the office opened with a startlingly loud creak. A woman's hand reached inside and flipped on the light.

"Whoever you are, I have a gun!" The voice, spoken in barely more than a nervous whisper, echoed into the empty room. The weapon entered the room first, followed by a skittish woman in a thin gown and robe. Her light brown hair was wild and frizzy, and her eyes were wide with terror, as if she expected an attack at any moment.

When the attack failed to materialize, she stepped into the room, waving the gun back and forth at the shadows. Her eyes scanned the space, looking at closet doors and at the desk with the computer. She moved slowly, ripping open each of the three closet doors with the gun outstretched, and closing them as each space proved empty of intruders. She bent down to peer under the desk in a similar fashion, and found the space vacant. She stood back up and looked at the desk. Her eyes focused on the mouse, and she frowned. She pushed the mouse slightly, re-centering it atop the floral pattern mouse pad. Adam shook his head.

Finally convinced that she'd imagined the sounds of an intruder, the woman left the room, shutting the door behind her. Adam waited a moment, and as he'd expected, she burst back into the room a moment later, gun at the ready, expecting the intruder to have materialized after thinking themselves safe from further detection. But the woman still found nothing. Shaking her head, she flipped off the light, exited the room, and closed the door behind her.

Adam waited five minutes, using all of his senses to ensure that no one else would intrude. Finally convinced, he phased back into solid form and glanced at the room. His eyes moved back to the desk. If the adoption had been finalized recently, the paperwork might not yet be archived into one of the file cabinets along the wall. He moved to the desk and opened the single file drawer, finding only four folders inside.

The third one held his answers.

Her picture was there. She would physically have reached eighteen months of age, far larger than she'd been when he'd turned her over to Eva. But there was no denying the face, the eyes, and the sparkle the green eyes expressed even in a still photo. It was *her*.

He glanced down at the bottom of the paper, making a mental note of the address and names scrawled there. He put the papers back into the folder, taking care to ensure they were stacked evenly and stored in the precise middle of the folder, in line with the preferences he'd seen from the orphanage director moments earlier. He shut the drawer, extinguished his Energy light, and teleported back to the craft. Within seconds, the auto-pilot was transporting him toward the house a few miles away.

He appeared in front of the house for just an instant before phasing invisible. It was a simple ranch house, with a neatly trimmed lawn and a single, older model car parked in the driveway. He walked up the drive to the front door, glancing at the hand-carved wooden sign identifying the family inside.

Adams.

He smiled. The family's surname seemed a positive omen.

He moved through the door into the house and glanced around. The home had only two bedrooms, and he found the girl asleep in the smaller room, nestled in her crib under a warm blanket. Her breathing was steady, rhythmical, and perfect. It was a beautiful sight to see. She was finally whole, able to live and grow. Unable to restrain himself even in his intangible state, Adam reached out to brush a hand across her cheek.

The little girl's eyes opened, revealing the green he recognized from centuries of association with her older brother. She looked directly at him, though he was invisible and non-corporeal, and emitted a squeak.

He jumped back, noiselessly, startled that she'd been able to sense his presence. Had he frightened her?

Within seconds, Emily Adams was in the room, followed closely by Paul. She picked up the little girl, and Adam couldn't contain his joy. They were attentive parents, well attuned to her needs, and he could ask for nothing more. His work here was done.

As he moved silently out of the room, he could hear Emily comforting her new daughter. "Shh... it's okay, sweetie. Mommy loves you. Daddy loves you. You'll be fine, sweetie.

"Go back to sleep, Gena."

VII
Protection

2016 A.D.

"This thing makes me look fat, doesn't it?" Will Stark scowled as he spoke, but there was a slight hint of amusement in his eyes.

"Sir, I don't think that's something you should be concerned about," Lance Maynard replied. "I'd also remind you that my job is ensuring that you remain alive and functioning. I consider winning fashion awards in celebrity gossip magazines a secondary concern."

Will snorted and thumped his torso, feeling the thick padding of the bulletproof vest. It was the lightest weight, thinnest model Lance could find, and even so, Will felt almost claustrophobic with the vest on. He could already feel the sweat building inside his clothing, even here in his air-conditioned office. With a sigh, Will glanced at the giant of a man who led his security team. "Do you really think people will try to shoot me, Lance?"

Lance didn't flinch. "It is my job to assume and prepare for the worst, sir, and recommend actions to counter all possible nefarious plans of others." The man's eyes were steady, calculating; even now, he was looking for threats to their safety. "I've never lost a client, Mr. Stark. I have no intention of breaking that streak with you."

Will nodded. "I appreciate your concern for my well-being, Lance." He shook his head. "I'd hoped to spend my twenty-first birthday doing something other than being fitted for a bullet-proof vest, though."

"Happy birthday, Mr. Stark," Lance replied. "I hope this gift is an unnecessary tool in reaching your next birthday, and many more after that."

Will nodded, clapping the man on the shoulder. "Thanks, Lance. Let's go."

Maynard led three other heavily armed men into the elevator shaft. As ex-military, the men weren't subject to the new statewide ban on all firearms for private citizens, and through them Will would enjoy a level of protection not available to most citizens. His first business had generated sufficient income and wealth to afford such protections—and, ironically, it made such protection necessary. Will would have preferred to live his life as any other young man heading off to his job each day. Comments directed at him during his commutes suggested his safety was at risk from those interested in robbing him or doing him harm. As the general economy worsened and the taunts become more frequent and vitriolic, Will had finally lost his nerve and taken action. He'd hired Maynard's team of personal security specialists. Today, that decision had resulted in Maynard fitting Will with a bullet-proof vest he was to wear in public at all times.

So much for normalcy.

Will's story had become the stuff of legend. Penniless and orphaned at sixteen, he'd lived with guardians the next two years before setting out on his own. He'd worked overnight and weekend shifts, scraping together enough money each month to pay rent on a tiny apartment, subsisting on the most basic of foods. In those difficult times, he'd hit upon his business idea, a company that would use information technology to bring the costs of medical care down dramatically without sacrificing quality. Investors had considered his ideas impossible to implement, with no hope of ever achieving profitability. But Will had persisted, and one kindly man had gifted him a small bit of money, with no requirement that he ever be paid back. It wasn't much, but Will made it work. That man's investment in Will had paid huge dividends, and Will had seen his net worth top one billion dollars just before his twenty-first birthday. He'd offered stock to his investor, but the man had refused.

Will made it a point now to follow that man's example with his own newfound wealth.

His company employed hundreds, and hundreds more had jobs due to his "cash infusions" to passionate entrepreneurs. Many of those entrepreneurs had insisted on giving Will an ownership stake in the form of stock *after* his investments helped those new companies achieve profitability, and Will had accepted those gifts. He'd made it a point to never accept such offerings before those companies became profitable, because he knew from his own experience that those businesses needed time to develop without having to worry about paying dividends to people like Will who didn't need the money. Will now earned as much from the dividends from those unrequested gifts of stock in the companies he'd funded as he did from his own business. The costs of medical care, which had been doubling every five years, were experiencing the first reduction in the rate of growth in decades. With enough time, the technology would bring significant reductions in actual costs, not just in the rate of growth.

His company had accomplished a great deal, but it wasn't enough, though. Not yet. The long running recession and economic stagnation was deeper than he'd feared even three years earlier. Economists were now predicting as many as thirty years of economic depression, claims simultaneously derided by those politicians in power and seized upon by those seeking to supplant the majority. Will feared they were arguing for the right to drive a ship into an iceberg. His only hope was that his company and the investments he'd been making could limit the damage, and plant the seeds that would grow and help restart the economy after the inevitable slowdown began in earnest.

Many seemed to appreciate his efforts; several popular Internet blogs asked why there weren't more people like Will Stark, men and women using their own success to lead others to similar outcomes. Those same blogs, though, were filled with the comments of people who expressed their disdain for Will Stark. He shouldn't charge for his services. He should give more away, especially to causes dear to the hearts of those posting. His successes were nothing more than self-aggrandizement, his investments performed for pure publicity. Will Stark was a menace who needed to be stopped.

Permanently.

Will had found Lance Maynard's company and had been impressed with the experience he and his team brought. Will wanted to hire a firm permitted to use firearms in his defense, not because he wanted anyone shot, but because he thought an armed security team might be a deterrent to those wishing to permanently silence him. According to the laws of the state and his home town, no one save his security team should have a gun, yet armed robberies were on the rise. The sight of the weapons the men openly carried gave him a calm that was worth every cent he paid them.

●●●

Michael checked the calendar once more. According to the memory videos, this was the day on which the first assassination attempt on Will Stark would take place. In reliving the memory of this day, Will noted that he been stunned he'd survived the attack, as if some unseen force had saved him. That memory had prompted knowing looks all around.

The Alliance would be present at the scene of the attack, and would need to intervene to ensure Will's survival.

Michael led the team responsible for ensuring that Young Will survived the assassination attempt that would take place this day, providing a hidden complement to Lance Maynard's human security team. Michael had two advantages over Maynard's team: Energy and advance knowledge of the nature of the attack. Michael was hampered by the fact that no part of what he was about to do could look, to an objective observer, like some type of divine intervention. His efforts would prove only partially successful, for though he'd survived, Will referred to this event in the same hushed tones reserved for the accident that claimed his parents' lives.

He tapped on the microphone on the aircraft's control panel. "Do you have him in range, Shadow?"

Hope's face appeared on a corner of the screen now dominated by an image of Will Stark's surroundings. "I do, Michael." They'd agreed to avoid using Hope's name in the event any Aliomenti happened by; the less they gave away about the true identity of this man and his future wife, the better.

"In Will's memory, the attack happened when he was about five steps from the limousine," Michael reported. He touched a spot on the screen, and a faint impression was left behind, visible on Hope's screen as well. "Roughly there. We need to ensure that our protections are in place before he reaches that spot."

Hope nodded, a gesture visible on Michael's screen. She'd have responsibility for shielding Will from the upcoming onslaught of bullets; Michael would ensure that those responsible for the attack would struggle to escape before being gunned down by the surviving members of Will's human security detail. "I've enhanced the vest he's wearing; anything that hits that vest will bounce off him. How do we make sure the bullets only hit the vest, though? We can't have people saying they saw bullets bounce off his face. That's what worries me. They won't all aim at his chest. How do we redirect bullets without being obvious?"

Michael sighed. "I'll figure it out. Somehow." Four gunmen would spring out of the shadows, opening fire at Will. Three of Maynard's men would die, and Maynard himself would suffer minor wounds. Will, protected by his security team, would suffer a broken rib and minor scrapes, but would be otherwise unharmed.

Michael would adjust the aim of the four gunmen, adjusting the trajectories of their weapons at the source to ensure the bullets hit the bullet-proof vest. Hope had him protected as well, and would ensure Will suffered nothing more than superficial damage from the bullets. They suspected that plan would keep Will alive from the four assassins, while maintaining their secrecy. But there was a problem.

Neither Michael nor Hope was sure how they'd maintain those defenses and deal with the *fifth* gunman.

● ● ●

The security team led the way out of the office building. Maynard looked around, weapon held in a posture of calm alertness. Will stepped out after two more men followed Maynard, blinking in the bright sunlight. He held a hand up to shield his eyes. The fourth guard followed Will. Will should have felt safe and secure, despite the verbal threats that had never manifested as anything more than mere words. He was surrounded by an efficient fighting team, men prepared to sacrifice their lives on his behalf, men who would ensure something as simple as walking to his limousine was uneventful.

But he felt anything *but* safe and secure.

The hairs on the back of his neck stood up. He felt like he was being watched, and the sensation crept down his spine. A bead of sweat dribbled down his back, generated only in part by the heat the vest kept inside his body. It was paranoia, no doubt, triggered by the fact that he was now constantly thinking about the possibility of an attack.

He shook his head. The paranoia was going to consume him. He had to live his life, not give in to the fear.

Maynard moved to the door of the limousine and opened it.

Will's mind barely registered the sight of the gun barrel aimed directly at his face before the shot was fired.

●●●

"*Gun!*" Hope screamed. She focused on Will's face, slathering it with Energy, protecting it from the close-range impact of the bullet. It was too late to adjust the aim of the gun emerging from the limo or alter the trajectory of the projectile.

"Watch out for the others!" Michael shouted. He unleashed additional tongues of Energy at the three additional gunmen who emerged from shadows of the building, behind the security detail and Will, just as those men opened fire on Maynard's team.

●●●

The explosion as the gun fired was the loudest sound Will had ever heard. At such close range, it was louder even than the crash that had killed his parents. The bright light blinded him, and he felt himself knocked backward, falling toward the ground as other flashes of light and explosions erupted around him. The pain was intense, an aching sensation centered near his ribs.

Was this what death felt like? A bright, blinding light, a tremendous amount of pain, and a sensation of falling backward?

His head hit the concrete and he lost consciousness.

●●●

The three assassins nearest the building trained their weapons on the security team and opened fire as the first gunman emerged from the limousine and fired at Will from point-blank range. The close-range shot knocked Stark to the ground, and the remaining bullets tore into the bodies of the three guards working for Lance Maynard. The men fell to the ground, screaming in pain, their blood reddening the concrete sidewalk. The smell of copper and gunpowder filled the air.

The assassins adjusted their sights as they stalked the survivors, aiming at the young billionaire lying on the ground, and pulled their triggers again.

This time, the guns jammed.

Maynard had been knocked to the side and to the ground by the opening door, and thus had been spared the onslaught of bullets. Now, with his ever-present calm, he rose to a knee and fired his weapon with brutal efficiency upon the four assassins. Within seconds, all four attackers lay dead on the ground, joining the three members of Maynard's team.

It was only then, only after seven men died, only after the explosive and rapid discharge of bullets, that Maynard heard the screams around him. Pedestrians and passers-by had nearly been caught in the crossfire, and were terrified that more was to come. All eyed his weapon and fearsome gaze in horror.

Maynard ignored their terror, instead holding his weapon at the ready, turning quickly around, searching, alert to any indication that a secondary force sheltered in the shadows, prepared to ambush any survivors of the first attack. He saw nothing. Finally satisfied the threat had been neutralized, Maynard flipped the safety on and holstered his gun.

Only then did the pain hit Maynard. The door he'd opened had exploded into him, kicked into him by the gunman inside the limousine just before the assassin opened fire. That had hurt. The blood and stinging pain in his shoulder indicated he'd been struck by at least one of the bullets. The fall to the ground had been awkward, and he'd severely twisted his knee, possibly damaging ligaments. Gritting his teeth, Maynard limped toward Will, expecting the worst. The gun had been pointed directly at his client's face. Will was most certainly dead, his head splattered on the concrete.

But Will's face was intact. He was breathing steadily. Maynard winced as he lowered himself to the ground next to his client and checked Will's pulse. Slightly elevated, indicative of the shock he'd experienced, but otherwise fine. His skin showed only minor scratches from the fall to the concrete.

Maynard stared at the man. He'd seen the gun aimed directly at Will's face. The attackers were well-trained, professional. There was no possibility that the shooter had missed his target—Will's face—at point-blank range.

Yet he *had* missed.

Maynard touched Will's face. There was nothing there but skin; his finger left a faint discoloration on the man's cheek. No bulletproof material protected the man's face. He glanced down at Will's shirt, spotting the tear in the clothing. Somehow, in a manner Lance Maynard couldn't explain, the bullet intended for Will Stark's face had instead hit him in the chest, striking the bulletproof vest Maynard himself had helped the man don only minutes earlier.

He lowered his face into the ground so that no one could see the scowl on his face, couldn't see the anguish of the betrayal he himself had suffered after accepting the huge contract to arrange the death of Will Stark.

Someone had sold out Lance Maynard, after Lance had sold out Will Stark.

He'd been approached by the mysterious stranger not long after Stark hired his team. The fee offered had been enormous, impossibly large, and Maynard had doubted the sincerity. But the man explained who he worked for, in a circuitous manner, and Maynard had realized that the group had both the means *and* the motive to offer Stark's own security chief the amount necessary to turn him. Maynard felt no emotional attachment toward Will Stark. Will was another person with the means to pay Maynard's extraordinary fees, and Maynard carried out his contracted duties. Emotional attachments were to be avoided; they led you to make mistakes, mistakes that would cost clients their lives and, more importantly, Maynard his reputation. Emotional attachment would lead him to feel a sense of loyalty, and loyalty might cause him to decline generous counteroffers that came with a none-too-subtle hint that Maynard was expected to accept… or else.

With this hit and associated payment for its successful completion, his professional reputation would no longer matter. He'd not have to worry about emotional attachments to clients like Will Stark. Maynard would be able to retire to a life of luxury he'd never before imagined possible. He'd accepted their offer. One third of the money had arrived as promised. Maynard used it to hire his hit squad. He'd play his role, and even convince Stark to wear a bulletproof vest, as the team had been instructed to aim for vulnerable regions where the vest offered no protection. He fed the hit team information on Stark's schedule that day, where the limo would be parked, where they could lurk until the attack commenced.

Something had gone wrong, though. Very, very wrong.

The plan was straightforward. The hit team would intercept the limousine, execute the driver, and park in front of the office building. One man would remain inside the vehicle, in the rear cabin where Will Stark normally sat. The others would exit the vehicle for the seclusion of various nooks and alleys near the office building. Maynard would lead the security team from the building to the limousine and open the door for Stark. The man inside would eliminate Stark with a head shot. The three in hiding would then emerge and shoot the remaining bodyguards. Maynard, defended by the open door, would fire a few errant shots at the assassins before the shooter in the limousine would shoot Maynard in the leg. The assailants, their faces masked, would flee. Police would find untraceable ammunition casings on the crime scene. Maynard, the lone survivor, would be exonerated. He'd receive his medical treatment, attend Stark's funeral, shed a few tears, and then depart for his new life of luxury in a tropical paradise.

But the man in the limousine had *missed*.

Somehow, an expert marksman had missed a man standing only two feet away. Somehow, guns maintained in prime condition by firearms experts and sharpshooters had jammed after firing only one round each. One of those bullets had even hit Maynard rather than one of the guards.

There were too many witnesses at that point. If Maynard did nothing, suspicion would—correctly—fall upon him. If he didn't shoot back when the attackers' guns jammed, his reputation would be shattered. And with his failure to complete the hit "requested" by the powerful group, he'd need to find new work. It meant one of the men he'd hired had sold *him* out, betraying the betrayer. Maynard made his decision in an instant, and had eliminated each of his co-

conspirators, playing the hero in the eyes of the terrified crowds, taking out the men who'd tried to kill Will Stark.

There was no other way to explain the failure of their plan.

He wouldn't be getting his additional money, now; that much was certain. He fully expected to receive a visit demanding repayment of the initial amount in exchange for his life.

In fact… the man who'd approached him, the man who'd offered the small fortune to eliminate Will Stark… he could easily have paid off the hit squad as well. Take out all of them. Including Maynard. No loose ends. No cash outlay for successful completion of the mission.

That was the danger of this game. You could never trust anyone willing to be bribed… or to resort to extortion.

He glanced up at the crowd that gathered nearby, who were gasping at the site of the dead men. More than one person looked nauseous at the sight of the carnage, and the smell of vomit mixed with the tangy scent of blood pooling on the sidewalk.

One of the people in the crowd recognized one of the men lying on the sidewalk. A murmur spread through the crowd. People whispered the man's name, offered their non-professional and untrained opinions as to his physical state, and mused as to the impact on the country of the young entrepreneur's assassination.

Someone pointed at Maynard and shouted a question. "Will Stark… is he… will he survive?"

Maynard glanced once more at the man's steady breathing, marveled at his continued existence, and nodded.

People in the crowd breathed deep sighs of relief. "I wonder if we'll ever know what happened," someone said.

Maynard shook his head. "I doubt it," he muttered. Nobody could hear him.

Nobody could see the transformation that occurred inside him, either, one triggered by the realization that the role of mercenary was one destined to end in his own eventual demise. And for the first time, he felt guilt over an effort to take a life. He felt guilty about the men dead at his feet. And most of all, he felt ashamed… ashamed that he'd been willing to orchestrate it all for money. He couldn't explain it, but somehow, the fact that Will had escaped with not just his life, but only minor injuries, told him this man was destined for greatness beyond even what he'd already achieved. That great man trusted Maynard with his life.

From this day forward, Maynard vowed, it would be a trust he would deserve.

●●●

Both Michael and Hope were breathing deeply, emotionally drained by the sudden explosion of violence directed at young Will Stark over the course of a minute. They'd reacted on instinct, as prepared as they could possibly be from the memories Will had shared a quarter century earlier. Watching a recorded memory wasn't the same thing as living through it, though. Watching a memory had no impact on whether Will survived the attack; their actions today, though, had helped save Will's life.

Or had they?

"Did you… save him?" Michael asked. His face, still occupying a corner of Hope's viewscreen, remained flushed, but his breathing had started to stabilize.

Hope shook her head. "Did you?"

Michael shook his head as well, and they both realized the implications.

Someone else had helped them that day.

"Perhaps Will had some latent telekinetic ability that redirected the bullet?" Michael offered. His tone suggested he knew the idea was illogical.

Hope considered that. "I suppose anything's possible. Whatever it was, though, or *whoever* it was… we have to accept the fact that what was done saved Will's life. I don't know that I got my Energy positioned in time to block that bullet… or if there was enough there *to* bock it."

She was overcome with the emotion of the statement, the realization that she'd reacted too slowly. *Had* her efforts been in time? She'd never know. She could go back and watch the recording of Will's memory again, determine if she'd been the one to deflect the bullet from the gun aimed directly at Will's face, yet she didn't want to watch a memory knowing it might show that she'd failed in doing her job.

Michael waved a hand in the screen. "Shadow, you must focus. Do you sense we have anything further to fear from the fifth gunman?"

Michael had been trailing Will that day, the day when Lance Maynard had slipped away and met the shadowy figure who'd offered millions to orchestrate the murder of Will Stark. But Will had never learned of the attempted betrayal; his memories showed Lance Maynard to be loyal and devoted. That inconsistency between observed fact and recorded memory made Maynard, the "fifth gunman," a wildcard on this day. Had history changed?

Or had Maynard, watching his target survive a perfectly executed hit, made a split-second decision to change sides and not fight whatever force had saved Will? It was a practical decision, but it still left open the possibility that Maynard might one day betray his employer again if the opportunity arose.

Hope considered this, and shook her head. "I sense he's no further threat; that experience changed him. We need to do a deeper scan to know for certain." Her eyes hardened. "The experience with Clint means we can never be too careful."

Michael shivered. "You don't think the Aliomenti had anything to do with this, do you? That would be a troubling development."

"I don't know," Hope admitted. "The thoughts I picked up from the security chief suggest his attack was motivated solely by money, not a desire to serve the Aliomenti's long-term plans. And in reality, if the Aliomenti realize who Young Will actually is, and recognize that he's no threat to them, they aren't going to concern themselves with subtlety. They'd have the Hunters flash in, grab him, and teleport him to a transport craft before Will would know what happened. No, I think this man's motivation was an excessive amount of money and fear for his own safety. It's the potential retaliation by those who hired Maynard that concerns me. If he believes those who set him to this assassination attempt will come after him, he may even now look for an opportunity to kill Will to protect himself."

On the screen, Michael nodded slowly. "I'll stick close to Will, then, at least until you're able to handle that full time. It won't be long now, will it?"

Hope smiled. "Not long at all. Just keep him alive until then, okay? I don't want to lose him. Again."

Michael nodded. "You have my word, Shadow."

VIII
Employment

2018 A.D.

Cain Freeman walked into the nondescript building carrying nothing more than a printed report. He had an interview today with Ashley Farmer, the founder of a company called Nanoscience, Inc. Ashley had learned of Cain through her business network and had asked him to come in and talk about a potential full-time role with the new company.

There was no reception desk. He found a few basic plastic chairs in what he believed to be the lobby and, with no way to announce his presence, sat down to wait. He glanced around. His research into both company and founder revealed a belief that capital was best spent on people and the tools needed to help them succeed, rather than posh office space and ostentatious furnishings. The office for the research and development company looked like it was housed inside an old factory… and, in fact, it was.

At precisely ten o'clock, a door opened and a mature woman with slightly graying brown hair emerged. Everything, from the hair on her head to the trim business suit she wore, was impeccably clean and in order. He noted her quick appraisal of his appearance and grooming, and detected the faint smile of approval at the recent trim of his hair, his cleanly shaved face, and his freshly laundered shirt and suit. Her eyes flicked to the report in his hand, which was the idea.

"Mr. Freeman?"

He rose from his chair and walked to her, his hand extended. "That's me. I'm Cain Freeman."

She accepted the handshake with a firm grip. "I'm Ashley Farmer, Mr. Freeman. Please, come in." She motioned him into her office and shut the door behind them. He remained standing until she motioned him into one of the cloth-covered chairs near her desk.

Ashley Farmer wasted no time with preliminary conversation. "Mr. Freeman, I've invited you in today because our company is working on a new and highly proprietary technology, and I need to ensure that what we discover and develop here *stays* here until such time as I choose to release information, prototypes, or final products to the general public. In other words, I need my data and information secured tighter than a high security prison. My personal network of business contacts tells me you're something of a phenomenon, and that you're the best in the world at doing exactly what it is I want to do. Your recent move from a contracting role for multiple companies, to an expression of interest in securing a full time role with one company, coincides perfectly with my interest in hiring someone with your skillset."

He nodded. "The timing is indeed fortuitous, Ms. Farmer. After years of doing contract work, I've come to believe I can be most productive if I'm able to focus my attention on a single organization at a time. Once I made that decision, I refused new contract work opportunities and allowed existing contracts to expire. That has enabled me to look for something full time." He smiled, an expression of complete confidence. "I'm hoping that *this* is that something."

Ashley ignored the leading comment. She gestured at the document Cain held in his hands. "I noticed the report you've brought has this company's name on the cover. Is that something you wished to show me?"

He nodded. "This is something I do for all potential clients. The most dramatic way to show the need to implement security— whether through me or others—is to see concrete evidence that current security is insufficient."

"We take security here quite seriously, Mr. Freeman," Ashley said, a tone of warning in her voice. She frowned and crossed her arms.

"It's not sufficient to take it seriously," he replied. "Those seeking to defeat your security to access your proprietary and sensitive information are only interested in what loopholes you've left for them to exploit. Good intentions do not provide protection from malicious intent and adequate skill."

Ashley sighed. "That's understood. We've established firewalls to protect our internal networks and physical security to prevent unauthorized entry. No one will crack our security."

"You don't actually believe that, though," he replied, and his voice was quiet. "If you did, you wouldn't have called me." He placed the folder on her desk and pushed it to her, the paper scraping against the wooden surface in a manner that clearly jolted her. The office suddenly seemed extremely quiet.

Ashley Farmer reached out slowly and opened the report to the first page—and gasped.

Cain Freeman kept his expression neutral. The page showed the latest schematic for producing the company's most prized piece of new technology, a miniaturized sensor capable of detecting and orienting on masses of cells with a specific protein pattern. The company's most popular product—a miniaturized robot able to move along a preprogrammed path using claw-like feet—would one day be combined with this new technology, with the startling potential to allow nanobots injected into the bloodstream to seek out and travel to cells with specific disease patterns. If they succeeded at that merger of technologies and products, they'd work on additional "modules" to allow the "nanobots" to perform specific tasks upon reaching diseased cells—including injecting medications directly into unhealthy cells to promote healing.

That was the future.

At this moment, Cain knew, Ashley wasn't worried about the future combination of products, because the man seated across the desk from her had defeated her security systems and stolen her company's most ambitious research efforts.

She worked to regain control of the interview. "I should have you arrested for theft," she snapped.

"But you won't," Freeman replied. "You won't, because you need to understand *how* I got that diagram… and more importantly, what you could have done, and could do in the future, to prevent others like me from doing the same."

Ashley stared at the diagram, not trusting herself to refute his charge.

"The loophole I exploited is described on the remaining pages of the document," Freeman said. "And there are other loopholes I could still use to extract the same information without your permission or knowledge. If we choose not to work together, you have in your hands the blueprint to fix the most glaring security hole; you'll stop ninety percent of information thieves with those recommendations. And working through that process may help you identify other gaps as well. In what I intend as a good faith gesture, I have, on the final page, included a signed, notarized, personal pledge to be cease any further intrusion efforts should we choose not to work together."

Ashley snapped her focus back to him. "There's no need to engage in *further* efforts if—"

"I have no further copies of the diagram. That's also part of the signed pledge. No one else has or will discover that diagram through any of the efforts used to produce this report."

Ashley took a deep breath. Cain thought it was clear she was debating whether to trust the pledge of a man who had committed the information equivalent of breaking and entering, but at the same time he'd provided instructions on how to fix the gap. She didn't suspect she had much choice *but* to believe him.

She finally spoke again. "That's a very impressive demonstration of your skill, Mr. Freeman. And given that demonstration, I don't have much choice but to trust your word as stated in the signed pledge." She paused. "I admit I'm intrigued, though. We've had several private assessments of our security, all of which proclaimed our systems impenetrable. Your demonstration shows me that there's more we need to do, *far* more, and I can think of no one better to lead those efforts than the man who cracked the supposedly impenetrable network." Ashley Farmer offered him a wan smile. "When can you start?"

"No bartering over compensation packages or other terms of employment?" he asked, arching an eyebrow.

"I suspect you'll demand a king's ransom," Ashley replied. "But you've shown me today that my company's intellectual property is at risk, and if I can't protect that intellectual property, this company will not survive. Given that, I will agree to demands commensurate with a *modestly* wealthy monarch."

He laughed, reached into his jacket pocket, and pulled out a single sheet of paper. "These are my terms." He set the folded sheet of paper on her desk and slid it halfway across.

Ashley eyed him with great curiosity. Her hand moved atop the paper, and she slid the form to the edge of her desk, her wedding ring scraping the wooden surface as she did so. She didn't remove her eyes from Freeman until after she'd picked up the paper and unfolded the document. She scanned the terms, and then looked at Freeman once more. "I'm... surprised, Mr. Freeman."

He shrugged. "I think long-term, Ms. Farmer. My contract work allowed me to save enough money to live off of for several years, so I do not need a large salary. This company is relatively new, and I suspect its most prosperous times are yet to come... but only if it survives long enough to reach its potential. Public records indicate that all employees—including you, Ms. Farmer—receive only modest salaries. I've no desire to work for a company in which my gargantuan salary leads to an exhaustion of funds before the company reaches its peak. No, it's better for everyone that you pay me a modest stipend today and shares of future profits." He drummed his fingers on her desk. "This company has the opportunity to be the next great success story, Ms. Farmer, much like what Will Stark has done. I want to be part of making that a reality, rather than the one who caused it to crumble into oblivion."

Ashley set the paper down on the desk and stood, a movement Freeman matched, and she held out her hand. "I like the way you think, Mr. Freeman. Welcome aboard."

Freeman shook her hand. "Thank you, Ms. Farmer. I look forward to a productive working relationship. Should I report for duty on Monday?"

Ashley nodded. "That would be perfect. I'll alert our human resources department that you'll be starting. You'll need to spend time completing paperwork, set up your working space, get access to our network..." She chuckled. "Well, you can probably handle that last bit without any help." Cain Freeman smiled.

Ashley motioned him to the door and walked him out to the lobby, where a gangly young man with red hair and freckles sat waiting. "Thank you for coming, Mr. Freeman. Mr. Richardson?"

The red-haired man glanced up and nodded. "I'll be with you in just a few minutes."

She turned on her heel and went back into her office, shutting the door behind her.

Cain glanced at the red-haired man sitting in the chair. "David? Is that you?"

The man looked up, and his face lit with recognition. "Cain! It's been a while since we traded notes about inept professors." His eyes flicked toward Ashley Farmer's office. "How'd it go?"

"We talked. It was a productive conversation."

"She recognized your genius and hired you on the spot, then?" Richardson asked, grinning.

Cain couldn't help but smile. "Something like that." He nodded at his former college classmate. "I take it you're for an interview as well."

David nodded. "They're looking to do here what I've wanted to do for years, what I told you about since that first day in school… or, at least, they're the company best positioned to do so." His hand gripped a small vial with a stopper. "I think I've reached the limit of what I can do on my own. With the resources, here, though? The sky's the limit." He smiled an impish grin. "And I think Ms. Farmer will be interested in something I've been working on."

Cain chuckled. "Knowing you, it's a cure for cancer, but it *only* has a ninety-eight percent cure rate."

David's smile matched the one Cain showed earlier. "Something… not quite like that. But still interesting."

Cain looked thoughtful for a moment, as he'd been hit with a wave of telepathic and emotive messages from Ashley Farmer. Both Cain—Adam's present Outside persona—and Ashley had known this day would come, and both had done their best to keep the interview natural. Ashley hadn't told Adam anything about the office, nor had she mentioned anything in status reports about what they'd worked on. Adam, for his part, didn't mention that he'd hacked into the corporate network after about thirty minutes of focused effort. It was fair to say Ashley had been far more surprised at the events that had just transpired.

The idea she'd proposed in that thought wave—outside the sheer shock at the skill he'd displayed—was one that gave him pause. Their credo—to be the change you wanted in the world—had long been seen as one to be carried out using Energy skills. Nudge a person toward a specific idea, help someone recover from illness or injury, move money into ventures promising to advance the human condition in some manner.

Ashley noted that the original Aliomenti, like Will and Eva, had been far more hands-on in their efforts. They didn't invest money; they learned and perfected crafts to make better products and materials and eventually saw those approaches move naturally into human society. Were they missing out on the chance to do something similar now? If Adam, as Cain, could dedicate his focus and considerable abilities to learn into becoming so dominant in a field or technology, they could change things for the better directly, rather than working through humans from the shadows.

It was something worth pondering.

David eyed him curiously. "You okay, Cain?"

Cain blinked a few times, and then remembered what Cain had said a moment earlier. "Sorry. Just trying to figure out what it is you're going to do that will undoubtedly wow Mrs. Farmer."

David eyed him, and then nodded. "I'm planning to grab lunch nearby after my interview. Want to join me? I'll tell you about my interview if you'll tell me about yours."

"Deal," Cain said.

At that moment, Ashley Farmer emerged from her office. She seemed surprised to see her two candidates chatting together, and Cain smiled. "David and I sat through a few college classes together several years ago. We were just reminiscing."

Ashley allowed herself a smile. "I'm glad the two of you were able to catch up." She nodded in David's direction. "If you're ready, Mr. Richardson?"

The lanky man nodded. After a firm handshake with Freeman, he followed Ashley into her office.

Cain remained seated in the plastic chair in the lobby. Once the office door closed, he pulled out his smart phone, plugged in a set of headphones, and put the buds in his ears. To any observer, he was simply listening to his favorite music.

In reality, he'd snuck in to Ashley's office before she'd arrived that day and planted a camera and microphone. He'd cheated there, using teleportation to break through the physical security, and wouldn't use anything found that way as part of his security cracking efforts. He hadn't been convinced he'd use the equipment at all. But he was intrigued by what David would discuss, and thus elected to eavesdrop.

"Thank you for agreeing to interview me, Ms. Farmer," Richardson said, as he took the seat she indicated with a wave of her hand. His manner was one of casual calm born of supreme confidence.

She nodded. "What can you tell me about yourself, Mr. Richardson?"

He pulled the small vial from his pocket. "I fear my biography is decidedly uninteresting, Ms. Farmer. But given what your company is looking to do, I thought you might find the results of my tinkering the last few years to be of interest."

He pulled the stopper out of the vial and spilled the contents on her desk, and Ashley jumped back in her seat in shock at the sheer brazenness of the act.

Nothing came out of the vial.

Ashley was perturbed. "Mr. Richardson, what is the meaning—?"

Richardson held up a hand. "Watch." He pointed at the desk, at the spot where he'd "poured" the contents of the vial, and then leaned down until his face nearly touched the surface. "Hello."

Ashley looked at the redheaded man, disbelief on her face. She'd never seen more bizarre behavior. "Mr. Richardson, I must ask again—."

"Look," he repeated, pointing at the desk once more.

She looked. Her jaw fell open for the second time in as many interviews. And Cain Freeman, watching from the outside lobby, sucked in his breath as well at what was happening on her desk.

The previously invisible particles poured from the bottle came together in larger and larger clumps, dancing across the wooden desk, attracted to each other by some unseen force. Ashley seemed to stop breathing and her eyes went wide, watching the bizarre and amazing display before her.

When the particles stopped moving, they'd formed the letters to the word "hello," a word that now appeared to be written in a streak of black ink on the surface of her desk.

It was bizarre. It was impossible. It was brilliant. Cain grinned. He'd known his old friend was brilliant, but he'd no idea he'd made so much progress with the miniature devices.

Ashley had been mesmerized into open-mouthed silence. The man before her had done what her team still struggled to do, even after years of effort and millions in investments. After what seemed an eternity, she looked at him and said the only words that came to mind. "When can you start?"

David smiled, the gesture exaggerating the freckles dotting his face. "Well, I need to figure out how to terminate my apartment lease back home, find a place to live here, and move everything in… Can I start a week from Monday?"

She nodded, still in a daze. "Of course."

David grasped the end of the letter "h" on her desk and lifted the entire string forming the word off the surface. He dangled the end inside the vial he'd used earlier, and allowed the particles to fall safely inside before putting the stopper back in the opening. He dropped the vial into his pocket before glancing back at Ashley. Cain couldn't help but snort. It was definitely a good idea to clean up the boss' desk after you write on it with a nano-bot magic marker.

Ashley shook her head. "That display shows that you've figured out how to fix our most vexing problem, how to get the tiny bots to move in relation to each other. Those bots of yours… they have to be aware of each other, have to know how to move in relation to each other to form patterns."

Richardson shook his head. "They have some intelligence, but they aren't *that* smart. What you're suggesting is that those bots could form that word with any of the bots in any location within the word string. They don't do that, not yet, anyway. Right now, bot number one is always next to bot number two, and the two will seek each other out until they join up. Each bot is intelligent enough only to move to correct its position relative to another bot. In other words, if I lose one bot, the rest wouldn't know to close the gap. And they're not able to form other words unless I do a lot of reprogramming." He shrugged. "There's a lot of improvement I'd like to see made, because I think these can be used in construction, or in medical devices, or other ways I can't even think of right now, if I can get a more intelligence into them. I just don't have the resources to make the next step."

Ashley nodded. "I think we can help you there. If we give you the right materials and supplies, can you help *us*? Can you help us figure out how to fix them and make them work?"

David nodded, his freckled face spreading into a grin. "Of course. That's what I do. I fix things."

•••

Seeing the interview nearing its end, Cain Freeman ended the video and audio feeds, pocketed the headphones, put his phone away, and walked outside to wait for his former classmate. He didn't have to wait long. Moments later, David stepped into the bright sunlight and breathed a sigh of relief. Cain chuckled inwardly. David was relieved that his demonstration had gone well. Ashley Farmer didn't know—yet—that David had run through his demonstration the previous night—and that it had failed miserably. She didn't know he'd been up the entire night trying to figure out what had gone wrong, and had been within minutes of calling to cancel the interview. He'd found the problem just in time, and the actual demonstration had gone as well as he could have hoped.

Now he needed sustenance.

Cain waved at David, attracting his attention. "How'd it go?"

David grinned, an expression that reached his deep blue eyes. "She offered me a job. It looks like we'll be coworkers, Cain."

Cain offered a hand, and David shook it. "Congratulations! Ready to get some lunch and tell me about it?"

David nodded. "Absolutely. I... forgot to eat breakfast."

Cain laughed. "Late night?"

"You have no idea."

Cain, of course, had more than a mere idea about the accuracy of the statement. He slapped his new coworker on the back. "I heard there's a nice diner up the street. I'll drive."

David nodded, and followed Cain to the rental car. Minutes later, they pulled into the parking lot of a small restaurant with a simple name: "The Diner." The decor inside was reminiscent of a 1950s restaurant: booths with plastic-covered cushions for seating, stools lining the front counter, a menu dominated by burgers and thick milkshakes. The restaurant wasn't crowded despite the lunch hour, and the two men slid into opposite sides of an open booth.

"Have you found a place to live yet?" David asked.

Cain shook his head. "Not yet. Nanoscience paid for my

flight and a hotel room for the interview. Now that I'm going to be working here in Pleasanton, though, I guess I need to find an apartment. You?"

David shook his head. "I'm in the same predicament. I did some checking, though, and found an apartment building on the outskirts of town. It's relatively cheap and there are a couple of units available."

Cain nodded, appreciating the forward-thinking—and positive—research the other man had performed. "Let me know the address. I'll definitely take a look."

Cain heard the approaching footfalls, an audible indication that their waitress was nearing the table. He watched as David's attention was distracted. Cain watched his dining companion's face light up, the undeniable sight of a young man seeing a beautiful woman. Cain turned to look at the target of David's affections… and frowned.

He turned back toward David. "I'm pretty sure she's already taken, David," he whispered.

David sighed. "I don't doubt it," he whispered. "But a guy can dream, can't he?" He smiled at the woman as she reached their booth.

"Good afternoon, gentlemen," the young woman said, in a voice so very familiar to the disguised Adam. "My name is Hope, and I'll be taking care of you."

IX
Encounter

2020 A.D.

Will stared out the window of the limousine carrying him from the airport to the hotel. It was twilight, and the rainstorm reduced the scant remaining visibility to near zero. The loud thudding of the raindrops helped him realize that he'd see little at the property today, even if new construction work hadn't gotten underway.

The weather pattern was similar to the one that had sent him through Pleasanton a year earlier. Powerful storm cells had diverted his private plane from its intended landing in Columbus, forcing them to touch down instead at the small, isolated airport in the southeastern Ohio town. With fuel supplies for the private plane low, and refueling stations unable to meet their demands, his entire entourage of security personnel and assistants had been forced to stay the night at the sole hotel they could find. His people had complained bitterly about the "inadequate" accommodations, accustomed as they were to luxury hotels with exquisite furnishings, room service, and an on-site concierge. They'd groused as they'd hauled their own bags through the blinding rain into the small rooms, bickered over who would sleep on beds instead of cushioned chairs in the shared accommodations, and were aghast at the limited choices in cuisine. All of the men and women considered it the worst night of their lives.

All of them, that is, except one.

Will felt alive in this sleepy little town, felt a joy in his existence, a joy he'd not felt in... well, ever. It was because no one living here had the slightest idea who he was. No one begged him for—or demanded—money. No one wanted his autograph. And no one seemed interested in taking a shot at him or his people... not with a gun, a camera, or words.

What would it be like to live in a place like this, every single day? To not feel as if each step might be your last? To be a normal man who could drive himself to work? To be able to shop at a grocery store without the event becoming a public spectacle?

Perhaps, in a town like this, he could meet that special someone, the woman he believed was out there, waiting for him, a woman who'd want him for who he was, not for the checkbook he possessed.

Will had insisted that they spend the next day in the little city, and as they drove around, he absorbed the atmosphere of the place as if it was the very stuff of life itself. He eyed the dilapidated buildings as if seeing valued antiques, the roads in all manner of disrepair as if they possessed some hidden charm. When the crew drove by a heavily wooded tract of land on the outskirts of town and he spotted a "For Sale" sign, Will knew he needed to act.

He hired a man to travel back to Pleasanton the following week and negotiate the sale of the land on Will's behalf. The giddiness and sensation of safety he'd felt in Pleasanton dissipated after they'd returned home—likely due to the twelfth attempt on his life—and he envisioned a fortress built on his new property. One portion would house his business empire, and the remainder would be dedicated to a gargantuan private residence with state of the art armed security protecting him and the other occupants. An architect was hired to turn his vision into blueprints.

Two events changed his thinking.

Further reflection on the design concept helped him realize that he had no interest in having his private and public lives so intimately mingled. The ability to walk from his house to his office held appeal when compared to an hour long commute. Yet it meant he'd never truly be away from his work, or the people he employed. The decision was made and the revised concept sent to his architect.

The property would be for his personal residence only. The added space gave him far more interesting options.

The second event was the passage of the thirty-first amendment to the Constitution. After many horrific armed attacks in public places—including the many attempts on Will's life—the new amendment modified one of the original ten. Firearm ownership by private citizens was no longer a protected right, but rather subject to any limitations local and national legislatures might see fit to enact. The ink was barely dry on the newly passed amendment before state legislatures passed, with near uniformity, laws limiting firearm ownership to police, military, and militia members only, charging heavy fines and imposing prison sentences to those who chose to resist rules to surrender firearms to local authorities. As often happened with such legislation, it was an open secret that monetary contributions to the right people would result in exemptions and grace periods for influential individuals.

Will's private security team was denied a waiver. Faced with the prospect of long prison terms, they felt compelled to turn in their weapons. They now protected Will by increasing the number of guards surrounding him at all times, and Will's longing for a simpler life—one where he didn't wear a human strait jacket—intensified.

The impact on the design of his new home was significant. They'd envisioned decorative walls with a large, round-the-clock, armed security team preventing access by those who might engage in harmful activity inside. The structure itself would now provide the sole defense. Penetrating the walls would be such an expensive and dangerous prospect, even without the threat of being shot, that no one would bother making the effort.

Will held the tube with the plans for the gargantuan estate in his hands. He saw a sign for a restaurant ahead, with the simple moniker of "The Diner." Suddenly famished, Will asked the driver to pull in.

Lance Maynard looked at him from the opposite side of the limousine cabin, frowning as the vehicle pulled off the road into the restaurant parking lot. "What are you doing, sir?"

"I'm eating dinner. It's late, and I didn't eat lunch today."

"You'll recall, sir, that I had inquired about lunch while you met with the architect, and—"

Will held up his hand. "I'm not blaming you, Lance. I'm

merely stating the fact that I'm hungry and would like to have dinner here."

Lance's mouth twitched. "You want to eat... here." His scorn toward the restaurant, and the people working there, was evident in the condescending tone of the words.

"I'm not asking *you* to eat here, Lance, in a place so clearly beneath you."

Maynard's face reddened slightly. "I'm merely looking out for you well-being, sir. We've no verification if the food here is safe, or if the patrons... are... well, trustworthy."

Will rolled his eyes before fixing the security chief with a glare. "I've changed my mind, Lance. I'm ordering you, and the rest of the crew, to eat somewhere else. Anywhere but here. I'll go inside by myself, look over these plans, and enjoy a nice, greasy burger without any of you needing to expose yourselves to small town cooties."

Maynard sat up, rigid. "I made no such statements, sir." He kept his tone just a shade below angry, trying to work deference to his employer into the anger he felt at the accusation of arrogance.

"Not in so many words, no." Will shook his head. "But your malevolence toward this town and everyone who lives here couldn't be any more apparent if I could read your mind."

Maynard opened his mouth to protest, and then sighed in resignation. "I suppose there's no changing your mind, then?"

"No. Hand me the umbrella and take the rest of the crew someplace else. Meet me back here when you're done." As he opened the door into the driving rain and raised the umbrella into the storm, he couldn't resist one final dig. "If all of you behave, I might even treat you to ice cream later." And he slammed the door shut behind him.

He fought his way through the buffeting winds and rain, finally pushing the door open and ducking inside. Despite the umbrella, he was drenched, and he shivered as the cold, conditioned air brushed against his skin.

"Leave it by the door, please."

Will glanced around, spotting a middle-aged woman in a waitress uniform looking at him. "Leave... what... where?"

"Leave your umbrella by the door. We don't want you tracking the water inside. There's enough moisture around just from drenched clothes, but rest assured… we won't ask you to leave *those* by the door." Her matronly eyes twinkled with well-intentioned mirth.

There was at least one chuckle at her comment, and Will, to his surprise, blushed crimson. He added his umbrella to the pile and glanced around. There were perhaps a half dozen other patrons there, each isolated physically and mentally from the others. Will recognized the soft tones playing over the speaker system, a song popular back in the 1960s, and he found himself humming along.

The woman who'd spoken to him earlier led him to a booth in the corner, pointing to a door a few feet away. "The men's restroom is right there, sir, if you'd like to try to dry off a bit."

Will nodded, leaving his architectural drawing tube on his assigned table. Maynard would have been horrified, certain that someone would steal the plans. Will doubted it, and didn't like the man's bias against those from smaller towns. Will had so disliked *something* about the plans that he almost wished someone *would* steal them. And it wasn't as if the architect couldn't print new copies of the plans at any time.

Will dried himself using paper towels and the heated air dryers as best he could, and emerged a few moments later. The tube of diagrams was still on the table, right where he'd left it.

Of all the times to be proven right in his judgment of people…

Sighing, Will realized he'd have to look at the plans. Again. And realize he didn't like them at all. Again. And realize he couldn't explain why. Again.

He popped the cover off the tube and slid the plans out on to the table. The documents weren't large; they were general-purpose sketches showing the concept the architect had devised based upon her interpretation of Will's specifications. Will scowled at the documents and at his inability to articulate what was wrong with them. His mood wasn't helped by the fact that he was hungry, and that the smell of the greasy, tempting food filled his nostrils.

"You look preoccupied. Would you like me to come back later?"

Will glanced up… into the most startlingly bright pair of blue eyes he'd ever encountered. He was momentarily speechless, lost in eyes that seemed to go on for eternity.

He shook himself internally, trying to regain his focus. "No, no, definitely not. I'll need all the nourishment I can get to help me fix what ails this." He gestured at the plans in front of him. "I haven't looked at the menu, but if you serve a giant, messy cheeseburger with lots of toppings, fries, and a chocolate milkshake, I'll have that."

She smiled and patted his arm. "You try to beat some sense into those papers and I'll be back with reinforcements."

She walked off, leaving Will reeling. Her touch had been like an electric spark against his skin—but it was pleasant rather than painful. Her hair was cut just below her shoulder, tied back in a ponytail to adhere to food service guidelines, and was such a bright blond color that it appeared to be a heavenly white.

Will blinked at the thought. *Heavenly?*

He shook himself, physically this time, and focused on the diagrams. But her eyes kept looking back at him from the papers. Sighing, he lowered his elbows to the table and rested his head on his hands. He'd never get this done if he spent so much mental energy thinking about a woman he'd never before seen in his life. And she was young, too; her face suggested she was several years younger than Will. She was off limits, to be sure. She was far too beautiful to be interested in someone like him at any rate.

Focus, Will! The words were bellowed inside his head, but they had no effect.

"Who won the battle?"

She was back, balancing a tray with a perfectly made chocolate milkshake and a cool glass of water. "Not me. I can't win the battle, let alone the war, if I can't identify the enemy's weakness."

She laughed. "You have a spot in mind for this tasty drink?"

Will nodded, sliding the plans closer to the window and gesturing at the vacated section of the table. She sat the milkshake and glass of water down in the cleared space—and then, to his shock, sat down next to him. "What are we looking at?"

He turned and looked at her. Her skin was clear and smooth, like porcelain, and her brow was furrowed in a manner suggesting a deep level of focus and concentration. He wanted to impress her for some reason, and mustered up a witty response. "Uh... house plans."

Ouch.

She frowned, turning to look at him, her blue eyes making contact with his own without any sense of discomfort. "That's not a house. That's a military fortress, a home for someone who considers himself a general or a king." She arched an eyebrow. "Do *you* see yourself as a king or a general?"

He stared at her. "That's... that's exactly the problem I've been trying to articulate." He shook his head. "These plans... they make it look like I'm about to launch an attack on the city. That's not what I want. I just want to feel safe. To feel like it's a place where a family could live without fear."

She nodded, chewing her bottom lip, an act that he found mesmerizing. "If you want it to be a place where a family could live, you might try getting more houses inside those... what are they, fences or something? If you keep *everyone* out, you'll do nothing but feel isolated and lonely."

He nodded, thoughtful. "That's a great point. The walls are there to keep those who'd try to hurt me or my family away. Not everyone will try to do that, though, and I don't want to keep away those who might like living there." He tapped the page. "This house as drawn is ridiculously large, as if I'm some kind of monarch trying to impress people. I'd rather have something simpler, smaller, something that gives more people room to join me inside."

She was watching him with deep interest as he spoke, and her look was suggestive of one who'd known him for years... a thought which both unnerved and excited him. "You said that with great sincerity, and I think you've found the problem. Those plans represent someone else's view of what you are, and what you want. But they've clearly misunderstood. I think if you're able to articulate what you just said to me, your architect will be able to draw up something that truly reflects who you are, and you'll be able to live somewhere that's a home, rather than a prison." She put her hand on his arm once more, and he felt those same sparks energizing him. "Do you think you can do that?"

"Come with me," Will blurted out. Then he cringed. *Smooth, Will. Real smooth.*

She sat up straight, bright blue eyes wide, subtly backing away from him. "I... what do you mean?"

He straightened as well. "Sorry, that was very... spontaneous of me. You don't know me at all, other than through the little speech you encouraged me to give just now. I think I might struggle to articulate that vision, those concepts, when I visit my architect.

Unless *you're* there to help me. But…" He paused, smiling weakly. "It was quite presumptuous of me to ask you to do something like that. I'm sorry."

She nodded, seeming to relax. "I don't think you mean me any harm."

I will kill anyone who tries to harm you, he thought. His eyes widened. Where had *that* come from?

She paused a moment. "It's just that…"

Will frowned, sensing that something awful was coming, and he was instantly on alert, ready to track down whoever might have threatened or actually harmed this young woman he'd just met. Even if it meant he himself was hurt in the process. "What's wrong?"

"It's just that…" She paused, and then smiled. "You haven't even told me your name."

He laughed, relief flooding over him. "I haven't, have I?" He held out his hand. "I'm Will Stark."

To his great relief, she didn't react to his name at all. She accepted his hand and shook it, and he once more felt that electricity that so captivated him. "I'm Hope. Hope Young."

"Such a wonderful name," he said. "I *hope* you might consider having dinner with me tomorrow." He cringed again. It sounded so much better in his head. Why could he control conversations with the rich and powerful, know just the right thing to say and when to say it… yet he couldn't avoid saying the stupidest things to this woman?

Because you don't care what they *think of you.*

She rolled her eyes. "That's a pretty awful joke." She paused, and then smiled again. "But yes, I will have dinner with you. I have to warn you, though… I'm not a cheap date."

He almost choked. "I… I hope we can pick just the right spot, then." *I just did it again! What is wrong with me?*

She stood up at that moment and walked away, leaving Will thinking that she'd perhaps wondered what she was getting into, and that she'd walked away to give herself a chance to reconsider. But she returned a moment later with a plate bearing his cheeseburger and fries, which she sat before him next to the milkshake. "I added something extra," Hope whispered to him, winking. She walked away, checking on her other customers.

Will caught her slipping the occasional glance his way as he nibbled at the cheeseburger. That warmed him far more than the hot food on this cold, rainy evening.

When he lifted the plate, he found a card with her name, phone number, address, a time to pick her up, and the name of the restaurant she'd chosen for their date. Will recognized the name: a high end steakhouse where a meal for two might cost more than she made in a month. He had vast mountains of money and no one he wanted to spend it on.

Until now.

Will cast a quick glance at the young woman with the platinum blond hair and captivating blue eyes, a woman who'd helped him articulate who he really was and what he was about. He had a feeling that he'd finally found someone with whom he wanted to share everything.

For all eternity.

●●●

Michael and Adam sat watching the events unfold on the viewscreen of the small, invisible aircraft hovering over The Diner. Michael, long the hardened warrior, wiped a tear from his eye. He shot a glance of warning at Adam, who was smirking.

"So that's how it all began," Michael mused. "He meets her, love at first sight, and he invites her to dinner."

Adam shook his head. "You don't understand what just happened here at all."

"Oh, really?"

"Yes. Really." Adam met Michael's challenging stare. "Will's life to this point has been about confusion, about betrayal, about a lack of acceptance. His parents emotionally abandoned him from the day he was born, taking from him any sense of self-worth. Throughout his adult and public life, people have been trying to take things of value from him, whether his money or his life. In other words, everyone he's ever met, everyone he's come in contact with… none of them ever gave anything of value back to him. Not the unconditional love he should have received from his parents. Not the acceptance that should have come from family, friends, and business associates. No, everyone has seen Will as someone to exploit, someone to use in an effort to feel better about themselves, often by trying to knock him down. And that's just what they've done."

"But the man's a *billionaire*," Michael protested. "You don't exploit people like him. He's gotten accolades and awards and...."

Adam shook his head. "Many of those awards are fake, and you know it... just like Will does. The awards he's gotten that never existed before? Please. Will's realized that those people only give in order to receive." His face clouded. "Given his life experiences, what Will's learned is that while some want nothing more than money—and they'll give him an award to get it—others want his life. Not long ago, one of those people included his chief of security, and Will doesn't even realize it yet. And maybe he never will."

Michael considered Adam's words, and then shrugged. "You may be overthinking this, Adam. He saw a beautiful woman. Like I said, it's simply a case of love at first sight."

"I don't think so," Adam replied. "You caught his thoughts. What made him happiest about that entire encounter? Her looks?"

"I thought it was the extra whipped cream on the milkshake."

"No. It's the fact that she accepted him instantly, for who he was, without showing any indication that she knew his identity. And even more critically... when she learned his name, *nothing changed*."

"She told him she wasn't a cheap date. He has to think she knew who he was with a comment like that."

"She saw plans of a mansion, and he told her he couldn't figure out how to tell his architect what was wrong with those plans. He told her, albeit indirectly, that he's wealthy. But she sat down to help him *before* that. She was interested in him when he looked like he might be the architect, or the construction foreman, or even a struggling college student working on a degree. She saw someone who was having a problem, and felt the compassion to try to help, and when she found out he was rich and could have walked away because, according to you, billionaires don't need help? She stayed. That's what was important to him. Immediate and total acceptance of whoever she thought he was... and no change in that acceptance with each new revelation, and each lame joke."

"You really think he processed all of that in those few seconds?" Michael arched an eyebrow, skeptical.

Adam matched Michael with an arched eyebrow of his own. "He told me all of that a few decades ago. So... yes, I do."

"And now, with that emotional backing he's never before

sensed… the sky's the limit for our Young Will."

Adam nodded, still deep in thought.

"Rather fortuitous that it all worked out so well, isn't it?" Michael asked.

Adam snorted. "Fortuitous? Hope had to use Energy to encourage the manager to put her on shift tonight. Aaron manipulated the limo driver to follow a specific route. Eva encouraged the head of security to say things that made Will angry, uncomfortable, and ultimately led him to choose to eat alone at the first restaurant he saw. There was nothing *fortuitous* about it."

Michael considered that. "It's ironic, then."

"How so?"

"A man like Will, such a proponent of the idea of living his life in his own way, making his own choices in complete freedom… yet something like this, so critical to his life and future, was orchestrated to happen. I find that incredibly ironic."

Adam shrugged. "We rarely have full control over the circumstances we find ourselves in throughout our lives, Michael. Others are always trying to push us in a direction they desire, and some push to a greater degree than others. Yet the choice of how to respond and react to those circumstances is the one freedom that can never be taken from us. Were events orchestrated by others so that Will was in position to enter that restaurant at that specific time? Yes. But nobody forced him to talk to Hope, to open up to her, and certainly not to ask her out to dinner. Given the circumstances, he made his decision about how to react… and *those* decisions are the ones that will lead him to be with Hope for the next thousand years."

Adam thought about how the next year would unfold for Young Will, about the whirlwind romance, the scandalous whispers from gossip columnists and tabloids and late night TV hosts savaging Will for dating someone so young. Hope would fare no better, mocked as a woman too young to be in such a serious relationship, a woman clearly old enough, though, to prey on the insecurities of the young, orphaned, billionaire bachelor, motivated only by money. As challenging as these times would be for Young Will, though, he suspected that had he known what was coming in the next year, he'd still make the same choice. And if he'd known the larger future and future history he'd live as a result of that choice, that he'd live a thousand years to ensure his wife survived to meet him this day?

He'd still make the same choice.
Every single time.

X
Construction

2021 A.D.

Hope sensed that Will was staring at her. That wasn't uncommon, but the expression of concern on his face was different. She turned her head slowly, pretending to try to read the expression on his face, before feigning a lack of success. "What's wrong?"

"Isn't it... bad luck for the bride and groom to see each other before the wedding?"

He looked so deeply concerned at the possibility that Hope couldn't help laughing. "That little myth is for the day of the wedding, silly, which isn't until tomorrow." Will grinned sheepishly. "In many cases, the families of the bride and groom have a final celebratory meal the day before the wedding, and the bride and groom are always there. So there's no concern about seeing each other today."

Will lowered his head, looking pensive. "And there's no family to hold a family dinner in any event." He let his expression soften in anticipation of what was yet to come this day.

Hope pointed up ahead, through the screen dividing the limousine's rear compartment from the driver, and smiled. "I personally think this is far more interesting than a meal."

Even from this distance, they were aware of the heavy

machinery. Gears squealed, pushing earth and mixing concrete. The scent of diesel fuel filled the air. As they moved closer, the vibrations of the equipment rattled the cabin of the limousine. The speed with which the heavily guarded estate community was materializing before their eyes was magical. It was "guarded" in only an indirect manner; Will's request for an exemption to allow his community guards to carry weapons had been denied.

The structure would have to be a sufficient deterrent on its own to those who might mean them harm.

The limousine came to a stop, and the driver opened the door a moment later. Will stepped out, nodded to his chief of security, Lance Maynard, and reached inside to help Hope step out of the vehicle. She emerged, blinking into the bright sunlight, and stared at the sight before her.

She shook her head in awe. "It's absolutely amazing."

Will nodded, his mood brightening. "Everything on the outside is built so that once we're *inside*, we have nothing to fear. We'll find peace, tranquility, and pleasant neighbors. Those who might want to do us harm have to first determine if they have the means and the will to get inside." He chuckled. "We're ensuring that they make the correct decision in that regard."

The community looked like an island, set off from the road and surrounding lands by a moat nearly one hundred feet deep. When they filled the moat with water, they'd have an intimidating initial physical barrier between the outside world and the community. A bridge over the moat provided the sole access point into the neighborhood.

Those of nefarious intent who somehow braved the swimming or sailing effort required to cross the moat in lieu of using the bridge would encounter the next barrier: massive walls that sloped outward, away from their base and toward the outside world. The walls were formed of a composite material designed to resist penetration by rappelling pitons. The surfaces were coated with a slick substance that made a suction-based approach to ascending the walls similarly impossible. Crews were testing the surface even now, and Hope winced as a man atop the wall leaned over to test the slickness… and lost his balance.

Thankfully, his safety rope was anchored on the other side of the wall. His efforts to try to climb back up were futile, his feet slipping and sliding against the slick surface, and he was forced to pull himself up by hand.

Will glanced at Hope. "I guess the slick coating works, doesn't it?"

She laughed, and then frowned. "What's to prevent someone from shooting a rope and piton over the wall into something *not* built of that material, and *not* covered with the slick stuff, and then pulling themselves up and over, just like that man is doing now?"

They walked over the bridge, hand in hand, imagining the sound of the water once the moat was filled. As they walked, Will pointed to where crews were using jackhammers to drill holes into the top of the wall. "See that? Those holes will be used to support a fence of barbed wire. This is a specialty grade of wire, incredibly sharp. A rope or cable shot high enough to do what you've described would be cut in half by the wire before a climber made it very far. They'd just fall into the moat. No threat."

"What if they use a cable?"

"We tested the barbed wire we're installing against a steel cable three inches thick. It cut through the cable in about three minutes with fifty pounds of pressure applied. Anyone attempting to climb the wall will weigh more than that; especially given the equipment they'd need to carry with them. And none of those climbers would be able to climb the wall fast enough to avoid having their cable sliced in half." A devilish look crossed his face. "And even if they did? They'd have to get over the wire when they reached the top. A wire with that much cutting ability isn't going to struggle with clothing." He paused. "Or skin."

Hope wrinkled her face. "That's barbaric."

"It's a deterrent. We'll very publicly announce some of the defenses this community possesses, and note that we've not told the public about all of them. Or the worst of them."

Will stopped them before they passed through the single gap in the walls. He pointed to his left. "We'll have two people on duty at all times here at the entrance controlling access. One person will sit in that building around the clock. The construction materials are resistant to flame and heavily reinforced, and the glass itself is bulletproof. If they confirm that the person looking to get in is a resident or an approved visitor, they'll open one of the gates, depending on whether the person is on foot or in a car. They'll be called guards, though they'd be powerless against anyone with a weapon who got inside. That's why we're making sure nobody gets that chance."

Hope nodded; she'd watched the videos of Will's memories of this complex so often that this construction tour was giving her a profound sense of deja vu. She glanced to her right. "What's that for?" She pointed to the tower rising forty feet off the ground. "I'm guessing it's not just for decoration."

Will smiled and nodded. "Another guard—" he wrinkled his nose "—will be stationed in the watch tower around the clock. That guard will scan the perimeter of the community, watching for anyone trying to breach the exterior defenses, and will notify the local police if he spots suspicious activity. The tower guard will also act as the backup to the guard in the ground level station to our left. If the station guard has to leave for any reason, they must wait until the tower guard relieves them. The primary job they have is making sure people who are authorized get in and out in an efficient manner; that's why the ground level station must be occupied at all times."

Hope thought about that, and nodded. It seemed logical, and would work—until the Hunters and Assassin arrived. This system hadn't been designed with men like that in mind.

The moved through the opening and into the community. "What type of gates are they going to install here? Wrought iron?"

Will grinned. "We just walked over the main gate."

Hope stopped and looked around, consciously avoiding looking at the ground. She'd professed no interest in the details of the access and security processes into the community, preferring instead to focus on the final design and furnishing of their future home. She'd thus have no way of knowing where to look for a gate that wasn't currently visible. "What? Where is it?"

Will pointed at the ground. "The gate is a steel and concrete slab that can be lowered into the ground and driven over. A car arrives at the gate and stops at a kiosk—like an automated teller machine—with biometric scanners used to identify them definitively to the guards."

"Bio… what? What are those?"

"They're machines that can scan parts of your body to guarantee that you are, in fact, you."

"What?" Hope asked, startled.

"Er… sorry, that sounded worse than I intended. In this case, one scanner will read your palm print and another will read your retina. If they match the prints stored in the computer and the guards have no reason to think anything's wrong, then the guard in the lower station will open the gate."

Hope chewed her bottom lip. "The visual inspection from the guard is in case someone… unfriendly is in the car?"

Will nodded. "Exactly."

Crews were clearing narrow strips of ground in paths leading off from the main drive into the community. The paths would serve as long driveways leading to the five individual home sites. Each site would be isolated; construction had been planned so as to leave the great majority of the large old trees in place, adding to the sense of seclusion that residents of this community would tend to prefer. Each homeowner would be responsible for overseeing the construction of their home, including coordinating the entry and egress of the crews performing the work once the security systems were installed and operational.

Will led Hope toward a handful of electric golf carts and the couple climbed aboard the first vehicle. Maynard stood on the back, ever mindful of potential threats to the couple in his charge. Will pressed the pedal, and the cart moved silently forward, crunching the gravel as it rolled. A construction crew worked on defining the boundaries for the gravel driveway that would lead to their future home, and Will swerved off the path. The cart switched from crunchy gravel to silent grass to the slurping sounds of the mud lining the well-worn path the remainder of the way to the home site.

The foundation had been poured for the full basement, a level they'd agreed to finish immediately as a prime area for entertaining in their home. The first floor would include an office for Hope, general living space, the dining room, a library, and the kitchen. The upper floor would include a master suite, an office for Will, and three additional bedrooms… rooms they hoped to fill with children in the coming years.

That plan for the upper floor filled Hope with sadness. She wanted to tell Will that the extra upstairs rooms were unnecessary, that the extensive planning to align the rooms with just the right layout for the expected foot traffic patterns, the attention to detail for the various accessories… all of that was just a waste of time. She wanted to tell him that in just a few years, the entire house be no more than a pile of ash.

In the end, though, she'd realized it was anything *but* a waste of time. The house represented their idealized view of the future, a future in which they'd have several children running around the house, laughing, full of joy, a future in which they'd have the opportunity to entertain friends in this house that was so very much their own. Did it matter that Hope knew the entire structure would be vaporized in less than a decade? Did it matter that she knew that only one of those children's rooms would ever be needed, that they'd spend far less time entertaining in the home than they'd ever expect at this point in their lives, or that their neighbors would be anti-social—at least on the surface? The dream of living the ideal their house represented, however fleeting, made it all worthwhile, and keeping alive the belief that everything would work out just fine, despite extensive video evidence to the contrary, was critical in playing her role in the entire production.

The work crews were beginning to frame the exterior of the upper levels, measuring and cutting the fresh timber, lining the pieces together, fastening the joists and the wooden ribs for the interior of the house together in a symphony of sounds and the faint odor of burning wood. Hope found the process mesmerizing, and stood, watching, as the crew wrestled the first skeleton of a wall atop the plywood flooring. Hammers and nail guns erupted into a cacophony of violence, fixing the wall in place.

Will was watching her when she finally turned to look at him. "What do you think?" he asked.

"It's amazing, far more than I ever expected growing up." Until Will had arrived in the North Village a thousand years earlier, the idea that she'd find true love and live a life of perfect health and incredible wealth would have seemed preposterous. And yet here she was, watching the construction of a home larger than all of the buildings in that original Village combined… all just for her and Will. The sheer massiveness of the project, though, paled in comparative importance to the emotion she sensed from the man next to her, emotion that told her that all that mattered was her happiness. That was the man who'd risk his life traversing into the unknown, who'd travel through time and live a thousand years, all to give those he loved a chance to live.

That was what this represented to him. And that was why it was so important to her.

Will watched the work crews in silence. "I've always been impressed by people who work with their hands," he remarked. "The ability to take raw materials, like a pile of wood, and use your hands to mold it and shape it into something like a house… it's such an amazing talent. It's a talent I wish I had."

"Really?" she asked, surprised. "You think you'd enjoy something like that?"

He nodded. "I wanted to take carpentry classes when I was growing up, but my parents refused. Didn't want me chopping off a finger, they said. So I picked up a wooden bat instead and played baseball." Will had a love affair with the game of baseball, and had played much of his life. The baseball diamond was a place where he felt he belonged, and it had been a place away from the emotional staleness inside his family's home during his childhood. He'd played through high school, even after his parents died, always using that wooden bat, until a freak collision had left tendons in his knee in shreds. By the time he'd recovered, the college scholarships dangled before him earlier had been withdrawn, and the orphan had moved on to the workforce.

It had all worked out for the best.

"You should put a batting cage in the back yard," Hope said. "Teach our children about the game you love."

A sheepish grin covered his face. "I, ah, already ordered one."

She smacked his arm. "Why didn't you tell me?"

"I just ordered it yesterday."

"Oh." She turned back to the house, watching as the framing crew hoisted the skeleton of the rear wall of the house into place and began attaching it to the plywood flooring. "This process impresses me, too. I wonder if the approach to building houses will ever change?"

"It changes all the time," Will replied. "The company we bought last month, though? Nanoscience? I think that what they do will give us the next evolutionary leap in construction."

"What do they do again?"

"The produce nanoparticles." At Hope's puzzled look, Will explained further. "They're basically little machines, smaller than our cells. Nanoscience has been perfecting a process to teach those particles how to join together in patterns. Because the nanoparticles are so small, it takes an unfathomably large number of them to produce something physical and tangible, like a wall. What they've found is that because those building blocks are so small, because there are so many connections holding the surfaces together, the building materials they can produce are both lighter and stronger than anything else out there today. That's a big leap forward in construction. But when they add more intelligence to those tiny machines, teach them to recognize gaps in programmed patterns? They can do repairs by adding batches of new nanoparticles to a surface, and gouges and holes will fill in, almost like magic." He thought for a moment. "They showed me a demonstration in their research lab when I went to visit before buying the company. The lead researcher, a man named David, asked me to look at and walk over a platform. I did; there was nothing on that platform. He had me push a button to start the demonstration. Nothing seemed to happen, but as I watched, I thought I saw bits of dust on the platform. The dust moved, all toward the middle of the platform. And then that dust piled on top of itself, and more of it came out of nowhere, and ten minutes later, there was a wall there, six inches thick, five feet wide, and five feet high. I touched it, and it was solid. I kicked it... and it hurt." He grimaced. "They told me that the approach they're creating will be the next step beyond 3D printing, because you don't need a printer. Size is no longer a limitation. With enough of the nanoparticles, and the right design program, you could literally create a house in a few hours." His face glowed with excitement. "*That* is the next evolution in construction."

His enthusiasm was contagious, and Hope couldn't help smiling. "And that's why you bought them?"

He nodded. "They were running low on capital, and I think it's a technology we need to explore. They're looking into medical uses as well, turning those tiny particles into robots that can go inside our bodies, find diseased cells, and either deliver medications directly into the sick cells... or, if they're cancerous, destroy them. Think about it, Hope. A cure for cancer that's far more reliable, less expensive, and less traumatic than anything available today. I *want* them to succeed. Humanity needs them to succeed. We have the cash to invest to keep their efforts going until they finish what they started. I've worked with Ashley Farmer before; she's a shrewd businesswoman, no frills, all focus. It was a no brainer."

"It sounds like it will provide a nice return on your investment," Hope remarked, watching as the crew lifted another wall into place.

"It might make us some money," Will agreed. "The health benefits of that technology are staggering. With enough time and research, they might be able to prevent a huge number of diseases by enhancing our natural immune systems with the devices. People will live healthier, longer lives. Can you imagine that, Hope?"

She could do far more than just imagine living a longer, healthier life. Not for the first time, Hope longed to tell "Young Will" the truth. "It's hard to comprehend all of it, but the potential uses sound nothing short of amazing."

"There are other possibilities for nanoparticle-based construction," Will remarked. The sounds of pneumatic hammers filled the air, as crews rushed to get the final first floor wall in place by nightfall. "Buildings could be of any shape. Roads could be repaired by simply driving over the surface and allowing new particles to replace those scraped away. There'd be no need to shut down highways for weeks or months on end. Buildings could even be programmed to change shape and color without expensive remodeling projects." He shook his head. "The ramifications of this are phenomenal. If these particles, these little machines, can be produced in bulk at low cost... just, wow."

Hope turned and looked at the city in the distance. "Think of what it could mean to a city like Pleasanton. A local company helps completely rebuild the entire city center in a manner that requires little ongoing expense for upkeep, modernizing the skyline and bringing in investment beyond even what the great Will Stark can provide on his own." Will looked horrified at being called great... until she winked at him. "And you could build something unique there, something that really puts the city on the map, that becomes the city's calling card, because you can build in any shape. St. Louis has the Arch; you can build something here that everyone will remember."

He nodded, thoughtful. "What would you do? What would *you* build there that's unique?"

She thought for a moment. "When I was younger, I remember seeing those little snow globes. Have you seen them? It's a small, clear plastic globe, with a wintry scene depicted inside. If you shake the globe, little flakes inside get stirred up and float back down to the bottom of the globe. It looks like it's snowing, like there's a dome covering the house or the little village depicted inside. It looks like the dome is making the snow."

"A dome-covered, weather-controlled city?" Will asked, arching an eyebrow. "That sounds impossible, Hope."

Hope grinned. "Impossible? That word has no meaning to me."

Will laughed. "Fine, then. If we ever get the chance, we'll build a domed city with weather control. Think that's possible?"

Hope thought of the Cavern, and smiled. "If you're involved, Will? Anything's possible."

●●●

Fewer than one hundred guests attended the wedding ceremony the next day. The guest list included Hope's friends and Will's business associates.

Neither the bride nor the groom had any family in attendance.

Social media and tabloid articles had proliferated leading up to the wedding. The story of an orphaned bachelor multi-billionaire marrying a woman who couldn't legally drink champagne at her own wedding provided all manner of fodder for gossip columnists and comedians. Hope was viewed as an opportunist, a gold-digger seeking to take advantage of a lonely man. Will was savaged for marrying one so young, for "robbing the cradle," a comment which never failed to amuse Hope.

Those who attended the wedding left with a far different opinion of the relationship of the newlyweds than what they would have expected after reading such articles and hearing such commentary. Will's associates were amazing by Hope's enchanting personality, describing her as possessing a maturity far beyond her limited years. Those who'd known Hope, who had felt genuine concern that she might be marrying too young, that she was perhaps too enthralled at the idea of the wealth and influence that would come with marrying the billionaire bachelor, left convinced that the pair was destined to be together.

Not a single attendee left doubting the genuine love the couple shared.

The reception was one of simple elegance, with quiet music performed by local musicians. The meal was prepared and served by a local caterer named Emily Adams. As enthralled as the guests were with the food, they were far more entranced by Emily's eleven-year-old daughter. Gena, a raven-haired, green-eyed beauty, flitted between tables, taking orders, refilling non-alcoholic drinks, and chatting up the guests. Her smile and laugh were infectious; there was never a doubt as to which table enjoyed Gena's presence at any given time.

"You'd think she was far older than eleven," one guest remarked.

"She's just an old soul," another commented.

Cain Freeman smiled at those words.

After Will Stark had purchased Nanoscience, he'd asked Cain Freeman to review the security at Stark's other enterprises. Cain had done just that, and in the process had given Will a set of core philosophies in designing security for any building or technical system. Those lessons had guided Will in the design of his new home and security for the surrounding neighborhood. Cain's work had earned him an invitation to the Starks' wedding and reception.

Cain glanced at Gena once more, relieved that she wouldn't be able to recognize him in his disguise, pleased that she'd grown into the healthy and happy young lady charming the crowds this night. He could only hope that she'd live a long and fulfilling life, and he'd do his best to ensure she did just that. The only thing he could conceive of that would prevent him from protecting her would be a conflict with his work with the Project 2030 team. The complete alteration of all of human history took priority even over his promise to Will Stark to protect the sister he'd never known existed.

Thankfully, there was no indication in any of their materials and guidance from the future that Gena Adams would be involved in those events in any way.

XI
Underground

2022 A.D.

Hope used her sleeve to mop the sweat from her brow. A stray bead trickled down her neck, and she swatted it away as if it were a fly crawling on her skin. The warmth in the underground cavern she'd excavated seemed more intense this day. She looked at the expanse, breathing deeply of the air pouring into her through the scuba equipment strapped to her back. There was limited air here, trickling in through several small tunnels she'd bored through the ground at angles designed to terminate in the woods, passages which brought the occasional small woodland creature along with the faint oxygen. The bunker was still thirty yards beneath the foundation of her house, though, and the air was pungent at best and inadequate at worst, and she took no chances.

The battery powered floodlights showed the rough edges of the rock she'd blasted away, using her hands and human excavation equipment. Though she'd routinely coated the ever-growing space with the scutarium-laced nanoparticles delivered by her Alliance peers, she was leery of using more Energy in this space than necessary. There was a risk of Energy leakage and detection with each teleportation hop back and forth between the bunker and the house. That Energy expenditure couldn't be avoided, though.

She swung the ax, and a chunk of stone and root and soil fell free from the patch of earth before her. Her Energy surrounded the debris, transporting it neatly into a burlap sack lying at her feet. Hope moved to the center of the cleared space, where a pair of measuring devices showed the dimensions of the artificial cavern. The nanokit sitting off to the side needed minimum clearances to unwrap itself into the room she'd live in for months just a few years into the future, and she wanted to ensure she'd cleared enough debris.

Based upon the readings, she'd achieved that goal.

With a smile of triumph upon her dirt-covered face, she seized the burlap sack and teleported back to the house, a common routine for her since the house became home. After seeing Will off to work, she'd spend time clearing space for the underground bunker. She had nowhere to stand for the first week, needing instead to extend her senses to the darkened space and teleport raw material into her home until she had the room needed to maneuver. She'd added the scuba gear after the first visit underground, and continued to wear it even after excavating the air tunnels. She'd brought the battery-powered floodlights with her as soon as she had room to stand in her underground lair. The lights freed her from using Energy to see where she needed to remove the dirt. The lights also revealed a great number of wriggly life forms she'd just as soon not see, and she'd taken to wearing thick layers of clothing to cover every inch of her body. The disgusted shivers didn't end, though, even now, when the creepers had learned to stay away.

Hope threw the sack over her shoulder and marched out her back door, veering to her right. She headed into the forest, moving about fifty yards in before she stopped. After spilling the contents of the sack on the ground, she dropped to her hands and knees and spread the below-ground dirt over the above-ground soil. She suspected the new soil was more nutrient-rich than that which she covered, and as such her transplantation efforts were beneficial to the surrounding ecosystems. Her absentminded Energy sharing with the surrounding flora and fauna, even at very low levels, would help as well.

With the new topsoil spread in the forest surrounding her home, Hope moved back inside the Energy-shielded walls and teleported back into the underground bunker. The measurements made it clear: she had the space to activate the nanokit, and she was eager to watch it operate.

The package she'd received was about the size of a large lunch box. She'd been quite skeptical about so small a box becoming such a large room, but her Alliance friends assured her the kit would indeed turn into a prefabricated bunker she'd be living in for two months in less than a decade. Hope located the trigger device from the top, which included a fingerprint scanner—paper thin—and a microphone used to give the verbal activation order to the kit. Hope slid her finger across the thin surface and spoke into the microphone.

"Activate."

The box disintegrated in her hands.

Hope jumped back, startled. Had she broken it? She sighed. If the kit was ruined, she wasn't sure if she'd be able to get another. Still, she'd excavated this space; she could bring building materials and tools down here in the same manner. What type of materials would work? Pressure treated lumber? Stone? Concrete? Would she need to hang drywall atop her base material, and if so, what would she do with the dust?

She was still thinking about building the bunker's interior by hand when she felt herself lift several inches off the ground. Frowning, she looked down at her feet... and gasped.

Her feet were no longer resting upon the dirt and rock, but upon a clean, manufactured surface. As Hope watched, the panel she stood upon stretched out, reaching for the moist, earthen walls of the excavated space. The nanoparticle surface crawled up the walls she'd cleared, hiding from view the dirt and rock and crawling insects and furry rodents she'd seen during her clearing efforts. The particles finished climbing up the walls, then raced across the "ceiling" until they met in the middle, above the spot where she now stood, leaving her in total darkness.

The entire process had taken less than ten minutes.

Hope glanced around. She'd been so mesmerized while watching the nanoparticle room form around her, she'd paid scant attention to the fact that her spotlights had been pushed along by the swarm and left outside the walls. A quick bit of clairvoyant work located both lights, and she teleported them back inside the room. The new lighting revealed a Spartan surface, clean and white, with a handful of markings on the walls, floor, and ceiling of the room. The markings proved to be notations identifying entry and egress points for ventilation, air filtration, electrical and telecommunication feeds, water and sewage pipes, and even a slot for a satellite or cable television feed. The team had recognized that this was a temporary solution; her longest stay here would occur only after the house above was destroyed, after she'd be presumed dead, and after all utility feeds would be shut down. Reports had reached her of an Alliance research project to use a remote control and a viewscreen to tunnel through underground deposits of dirt and rock. They'd be able to use the technology within the next few years to hook her bunker into a disguised Alliance couple's utility systems, ensuring the livability of the bunker when her need—and her son's need—was at its peak.

The specialized mobile phone she carried buzzed. That surprised her; typically, the phone didn't work this far underground. The phone was set to receive calls through Alliance satellite signals in addition to the standard human cell towers. Routing both signals to the same device meant she could take a call in public from someone in the Cavern without raising suspicion. Such calls would only ring, connect, and remain connected if Hope held the phone. They'd tied the activation of those features to her Energy signal, with sensors so powerful it took only a trickle of Energy—comparable to what she might leak even when Shielded—to activate the features.

The phone had a self-destruct feature as well. Efforts to access the call logs or reverse engineer the phone's design by opening the case would trigger a small amount of acid that would destroy the custom circuitry and render the phone, in the words of the engineers who'd designed the feature, "human." The phone would continue to send and receive calls and Internet signals using her public carrier, but she'd feel isolated nonetheless.

Hope read the text message from Michael. He'd be there in the next twenty minutes with additional equipment for the bunker. She'd need to let him into the house to ensure no alarms were set off, for he wanted to avoid teleporting inside unless absolutely necessary.

He didn't need help bypassing the neighborhood security, however.

Hope teleported back into the basement, and then, after a moment's hesitation, went into her bathroom to take a quick shower. Though she knew Michael wouldn't care, she didn't want a guest in her home while she was covered in dirt and grime, wearing filthy clothes, and undoubtedly emitting curious odors supplied by the underground terrain. She used Energy to instantly dry her hair and skin, donned a pair of jeans and a simple blouse, and then walked outside. She could feel the warmth of the single-person aircraft before Michael deactivated the invisibility feature, revealing a sleek sphere hovering a few feet above her lawn. An instant later, Michael stood before her.

Michael grinned. "Hello, Shadow."

Hope chuckled at his use of her Cavern pseudonym, one adopted to minimize the population who knew her current name. "It's good to see you, Michael." She leaned over to look at the craft behind him. "You mentioned you would come bearing gifts?"

Michael nodded. He moved to the craft and maneuvered his hands, and Hope watched as he detached invisibility-enabled tarps from the side of the craft. The tarps had been used to cover several pieces of equipment affixed to the walls with a bonding agent that released moments later. "These will keep the bunker livable for as long as you require, outside consumables. They won't produce food out of the ground surrounding you." He paused, and then grinned. "Well, not yet. We do have another seven years to work on that."

"Don't worry about it," Hope replied. "I'm happy to stock the bunker with supplies, furniture, …"

"Actually…" Michael paused. "There are a few self-assembling kits in the batch of equipment I've brought with me. Sofas, beds, chairs, tables, desks… They're all labeled, so you can generate the room layout you want."

Hope looked impressed. "Really?"

He nodded. "We're constantly setting up new safe houses around the world, and don't want to generate attention from something even as basic as buying a sofa and hauling it away from a store. It's best that we float in unseen with inconspicuous boxes that could fit in a coat pocket, and allow those boxes to become the furnishings we require."

Small enough to fit in a coat pocket? Of course, she'd just seen a room the size of an apartment generated from a box with the apparent mass of a lunch box. Furniture kits the size of a deck of cards suddenly seemed a perfectly reasonable concept. "Thanks, Michael."

He nodded his head once in acknowledgement.

It took them three trips to carry everything indoors. Once they finished, Michael gave her a quick fraternal hug, and then set off toward Pleasanton in his invisible flying craft, back to monitoring Young Will in a manner he'd never suspected in his human life.

The nanoparticle room now guaranteed complete Energy shielding, and Hope wasted no time transporting the supplies to the bunker. The machinery had small, robotic wheels attached to the bottom, and moved without any guidance to the correct spots in the floor and walls, leaving the majority of the living space unoccupied.

Over the upcoming months and years, she'd spend time reinforcing the center section, which would serve as an elevator to lift her and her yet-to-be-born son back out into the world following the fire that would destroy the building above her. There would be time to install the hydraulics that would generate the force needed to raise that portion of the bunker to the surface. She'd have time to excavate and reinforce the elevator tower between bunker and house; she wasn't certain they could push the concrete car through nearly one hundred feet of dirt and rock without a tunnel of some sort. She'd also have time to install the explosive device that would incinerate the future contents of the room and trigger the nanoparticles comprising the room's walls, floor, and ceiling to disassemble, erasing all evidence that this space ever existed. There would be time to spend connecting the machines Michael had delivered to the relevant utility services, and time to stock the supplies required to live in comfort during the time she and her son would spend here in the winter months of early 2030.

At the moment, though, she had to prepare for the board meeting for the charitable foundation she led.

Hope teleported back to her home and spent fifteen minutes ensuring there was no sign she'd been spending the morning engaged in hard labor. She fixed her hair, changed into a business suit, and finally settled into her private office on the first floor of the house. The office enabled her to participate in video conference calls with board members for the Stark Foundation, which she and Will had established to teach business and entrepreneurship skills in communities throughout the world. The board meeting was largely a formality. There weren't many critical decisions to make, save for which cities they'd visit next with their low-cost, high value workshops. Given the lead times for appropriate venues, they needed to give their event coordinators at least one year's notice to ensure facility availability, book advertising, and contract with vendors needed to provide support and produce supplies for the workshops. The calls served another purpose. One of the board members was Ashley Farmer, a woman forty years her senior, and the woman who had sold Nanoscience to Will several years earlier. Through their work with the Foundation, Hope and Ashley became friends in the eyes of the general public. When the Starks announced that they were taking applications from those who might be interested in purchasing one of the four available lots inside De Gray Estates, the relationship the two women developed ensured that the Farmers were among the first to apply for residence.

With the conference call completed, Hope terminated the connection, waited five minutes, and then activated the Alliance-supplied computer tablet used for the ongoing Project 2030 status calls. They'd all performed well in their human roles, and despite the visible aging and public crankiness, Hope saw the exhilaration in their faces during these brief conversations. They were truly enjoying the public work they were doing, not just playing their parts, but fully living them. In performing those roles, they'd built businesses in the human world that provided thousands of jobs, immeasurably improving the lives of those they employed.

Adam reported that he'd continued to build trust with Young Will, who'd proved to be an excellent pupil as well as a supportive employer. Will needed to be comfortable enough with Adam—or Cain, as Will knew him—to give Adam access to the family's Trust operations after the fire and their supposed deaths. With that access, Adam would be positioned to transfer the money into accounts that could be used by Hope personally and the Alliance collectively. Ashley, who provided day-to-day management of Nanoscience even after selling ownership control to Will, reported that her human researchers had made impressive strides in nanotechnology, surpassing the advances made by the Alliance researchers over a comparable time frame. Those discoveries had been shared with Alliance researchers, who had used the advances made by David Richardson and his team to produce the self-assembling kits Hope had seen in operation just hours earlier. Judith reported that she'd received a phone call from Hope Stark the day before, informing her that her application to move into De Gray Estates had been accepted. Everyone applauded, and Hope chuckled, joking that Will had needed to talk her into accepting "that crazy motivational speaker guy," a comment which drew loud laughter from Peter. As the laughter subsided, Judith added that that she and Peter would be meeting with an architect soon to develop house plans. They'd return to the Cavern first to refresh the mental images of their home as shown in Will's memories to ensure their estate matched the historical record.

"When we build, we'll include space in the basement for the cloning machines," Judith added. "The basement will serve as a safe house location for the Alliance as well."

"Good," Adam replied. "We're in agreement that we'll limit cloning to just the two guards. We have no way of knowing who or what family members the Hunters might target, but our suspicion is that they'll want to leave quickly in the face of what they'll see as evidence of an Alliance offensive and trap. That's their likely assessment once Will is rescued from their assault. We can't clone others because we simply won't have the time, and as I said, we have absolutely no evidence that anyone else was harmed during the day's events."

Eva nodded. "Aaron and I will submit our application for residence in the next week or two. Once our home is built, we will construct an office at the end of a hallway in our basement that Adam can use during his future interaction with Millard Howe."

The involvement of Millard Howe, the Starks' future estate lawyer, had been difficult to uncover. Hope would recommend that they store a copy of their will in one of their secure data centers. But Adam had scoffed at this statement in recent years; they'd never agree to use such a facility to store a personal document, or allow an outsider access to retrieve it. It had to be some type of misdirection. They decided to have Howe visit an Alliance safe house a moderate distance from Pleasanton, and Adam would meet Howe there. That led to concerns about an outsider actually entering an Alliance safe house, which could compromise the location. Eva had noted that they did not yet *have* a safe house in the proposed region of the country. They decided the new location would restrict Alliance activity to the basement and boast a dilapidated house aboveground as a cosmetic deterrent to the curious. Archie noted that such a setup offered an opportunity: Howe could enter the house and be teleported someplace else to conduct his business with Adam. Aaron and Eva had volunteered to build a conference room in their basement for just that purpose. A nanoparticle-based mist would be used to disorient Howe, preventing him from noticing the physical sense of displacement marking a teleportation hop. They'd need to be certain that the mist was in a scutarium-lined room so that Adam's Energy burst from the teleportation couldn't be detected.

With all status updates delivered, Hope terminated the connection and teleported the tablet down to the bunker for storage. There was no point in leaving it sitting around where Will might find it. He'd never seen her use it, and while they could certainly afford a new tablet, he might wonder why she'd never before mentioned its purchase.

Her phone rang, startling her. She glanced down at the screen, surprised to see that Will was calling. He'd been meeting with the Pleasanton city council today, and she suspected he wouldn't be in a good mood. The city, deeply in debt and running near-eternal deficits, had voted to raise certain types of taxes to unprecedented levels to help resolve the fiscal crisis. Though council members denied the accusations, the rate hikes had one thing in common: only the Starks, or Stark Enterprises, would be affected by the new rates. In essence, they were looking to force Will to balance their budget and even pay off the debt accumulated long before Will had arrived.

Hope answered the phone. "Hi, honey. I just finished my meeting with the board. How did your meeting go?"

"It was… strange," Will replied. She savored his voice; even knowing he wasn't yet the Will she'd met a thousand years ago, the voice, the compassion, the intelligence… those traits were present even now, without the life experiences to come in the next decade and future centuries in the past. "I noted that the taxes and fees were written so that they fell unilaterally upon our house and our businesses, and that the amounts of money in question would close not just the budget deficit but wipe out the city's entire debt load."

Hope let out a low whistle. "It's that much?"

"It is," Will replied. "I hadn't understood just how aggressive they'd been until my accountant ran all of the numbers this morning before our meeting. The body language when confronted with this fact told me all I needed to know. Though they might continue to deny it, the fact remains that they're looking to make us, and us alone, fix their budget problems."

"So what did you say?"

"I told them that in business, if you're providing so much money that you're paying off another company's debt obligations and eliminating their negative cash flow, it means you own that business. The check is written and control is transferred."

Hope gasped, and then laughed. "I can't imagine anyone liked *that* comment."

Will snorted. "One of them became rather belligerent. He asked me if I was suggesting that the city could be bought out like a company. And I told him I thought that was a great idea."

Hope forced herself to pause, to act like she'd never heard this idea before. "Wait... he asked if you were proposing to buy the *city*... and you said... yes?"

"I did."

"We should probably talk this over, you know..."

He chuckled lightly. "That's why I called. I wanted to run the idea by the person who suggested it in the first place."

When they'd moved in and learned about the city's dire financial situation, Hope had told Will that he just should buy the city and fire the incompetents who'd run it so poorly. "I was joking, you know."

"I know you were. But I'm asking if you're joking *now*, now that the idea's been raised by the council."

"I suspect they're joking as well."

"Perhaps not. After the initial righteous indignation, the group took thirty minutes to ask a simple question: what would such a deal mean for them?"

"Immunity from prosecution?"

"That's about the only thing I *wouldn't* agree to. I think we can actually make this work, Hope. Clear the debt, use our technological prowess to rebuild the city infrastructure and the decaying buildings, and turn it into a model of efficiency and sound planning. If we do that, I think we'll need to turn away businesses and people wanting to move in."

"Well, maybe. How can you do that if you have to follow all of their regulations, pay taxes to the state..."

"We agreed to write up the proposal as a ninety-nine year lease on the lands of the incorporated city of Pleasanton, which cedes all control and responsibility for executing and maintaining the laws, regulations, and tax policy of those lands to a city corporation. Naturally, said corporation will choose to *maintain* a lot of those laws out of existence."

"What's to stop them from taking the money and then ruling that we can't do what we're proposing?"

"The contract will state that no money changes hands until the council votes to approve, resigns en masse, *and* the state provides written guarantees that it will honor the terms."

"They can't like the idea of not getting tax revenue and still having to provide services like police and fire and schools and…"

Will chuckled. "Yeah, we agree with them on that. It's *not* fair. So the draft of the lease states that the corporation is responsible for providing a specific set of existing services. Not all of them, mind you, but definitely those you mentioned." He paused. "I think they're seriously considering it, Hope. And I think this is a chance to do something very powerful, something that can give the people in this country something positive to motivate and inspire them. We'd turn a crumbling, bankrupt city into a clean, modern, well-run and fiscally sound city quickly, make it a place where business and workers want to move and live." He paused once more. "What do you say?"

Hope paused. She knew what her answer would be, had known it since centuries before this version of the man she loved had ever been born. Yet the ramifications were enormous. Will was correct. People were used to seeing failure and excuses, whether from politicians, from business and union leaders, from students and teachers, from parents and children. But if they watched someone invest billions of dollars of their own money into a colossal project like this, and that effort succeeded? Their example might well be the inspiration that thousands or even millions needed to pursue their own big dreams. If this experiment worked, they'd enhance the Stark Foundation to provide grants and investments to the people they trained, and others, to build those dreams into a more prosperous life for themselves and others.

Pleasanton, Inc., might be their most ambitious means ever of being the change they wanted in the world. And that meant her answer was obvious.

"I say we go for it, Will. And that we don't just go for it, either. I say we succeed in so spectacular a manner that the whole world will take notice, and never be the same."

Even over the phone, she could feel his effusive smile.

XII
Life

2023 A.D.

The on-duty guard had called moments earlier, letting them know that the limousine had been granted entry to De Gray Estates. Will stood at the front window, waiting, looking at the remnants of a recent light snowfall dusting the lawn. The bitter cold hardened the glinting ice sheets on the massive trees that covered much of the acreage.

Hope watched Will, recognizing that he was looking without seeing. She could feel his powerful sense of anguish and guilt, feel it more deeply than he could possibly imagine at this moment.

The pain he felt was nothing compared to her own. She knew the awful truth, knew that she perpetuated the lie at the heart of the pain her husband suffered.

Both Will and Hope were eager to begin growing their family, and when results on that front failed to materialize at a pace commensurate with their impatience on the matter, they sought out specialists to understand why they weren't able to conceive. In the distant past, as he'd begun to share his memories of the future in words, Will had recalled this time, and even then she could sense the pain he'd felt when the doctors all reported the same thing. They didn't know about the ambrosia Hope had consumed since before the signing of the *Magna Carta*, and weren't permitted to recognize

138

that Will was perfectly capable of fathering a child at any time. Instead, every one of them told Will the lie he'd live with for decades: that Hope had no issues becoming pregnant. Their lack of success, the experts said, was entirely due to Will.

They delivered this message, not because their data showed it to be true, but because Hope, a master Energy user, forced each specialist they visited to report that conclusion.

She thus had to watch as the man she loved bore the burden privately, suffering in silence, believing he was a failure to the woman he loved so deeply. The only sign of his inner turmoil visible to the outside world was the gradual graying of his hair, something Old Will had told her would continue to progress until Josh's birth.

She could end his torment with a few simple words, merely by telling him the truth. She could do as he had done so long ago in telling her the truth of his origins, of this very moment in time. The trust he'd displayed in her so long ago, knowing that she'd not lose her cool or think he'd lost his mind as he told her what must seem impossible, was one the man before her would expect her to reciprocate.

But the man he would become, the man she'd come to know in the past, had told her, with a quiet reserve, that no matter the pain he might suffer in this era, she must allow it to happen. Nothing, not even his mental health, should derail her from ensuring that what had unfolded before in the future would happen once again.

Hope realized that too much knowledge of the future could be painful. It was something the Will before her now would learn in due time.

Will turned away from the window, finally noticing that she'd been watching him. His face was pained, and the glint of the sunlight off the snow provided all the illumination necessary to show the moisture on his cheek. Her heart wept in a silent grief she'd never let him see.

"I'm so, so sorry," he whispered.

She titled her head. "For what?"

"That I need to leave you for something like… this."

"The doctors could be wrong, you know." At least she could hint at the truth.

He shook his head. "All of them? I can't believe that. But I promise you, Hope, no matter how long I have to search for the answer to this… I will find it."

He'd tried to find the cure for ambrosia's sterility ailment for centuries, tried even though he knew that to test a possible cure meant risking that they'd actually succeed in becoming pregnant before their time. If they did, they might well end any chance of becoming pregnant in the future with Josh and Angel—and in the paradox of the time loop in which they lived, prevent themselves from ever meeting. "I know that, Will. Trust me, I do. And know this: I'd wait a thousand years, if necessary, to resolve this." She smiled with every bit of energy she could muster. "I feel quite positive about this option."

His face, still seared with pain, brightened slightly. "I'll be positive too, then." His head snapped around as the horn sounded out front, signifying the arrival of the limousine and driver, and he moved to her. They embraced for an eternal moment, and then Will stepped away, took a deep breath, and headed out to the waiting limousine with his small carry-on bag. The trip was expected to take only a day or two.

The limousine vanished from sight. Hope knew they'd pass by the reconstruction efforts underway in the city of Pleasanton on the way to the airport. They'd found a section of the city completely abandoned, and had begun the reconstruction process there, burrowing into the underground infrastructure for a desperately needed replacement of crumbling pipes and tunnels. Today, the first set of fresh new buildings was erupting onto the streets of the city. As store owners and office workers abandoned existing addresses to move to new real estate, they'd repeat the process, gradually razing and then replacing the entirety of the city's infrastructure and skyline. Construction was incredibly rapid, the buildings creative, and the enthusiasm within the city contagious. Their efforts used the nanoparticle-based panels built and continually improved upon by the Nanoscience team, panels which were prefabricated and shipped to each site. The particles now had sufficient intelligence to "lean" as necessary to square and level themselves, and to "stretch" to ensure panels all connected. Perfect cuts and sizing weren't necessary, and the technology would let the buildings sway in an unlikely earthquake or explosion before snapping back into place.

Will wouldn't notice the amazing transformation today. He'd leave it all behind to meet a doctor who wasn't a doctor for a cure he didn't need to atone to his wife for a failure he'd never committed. Hope had hacked his computer to direct his web searches to an Alliance-fronted think tank specializing in cases like theirs, touting an experimental drug cocktail found to have extraordinary levels of success in curing sterility. He'd be tended to by centuries-old Alliance members he didn't recognize, men and women who revered him and who would feed him a placebo of sugar water, food coloring, and zirple.

She allowed herself a chance to cry, saddened at what he'd go through due to his love for her, letting the tears flow for several minutes. Once the tears ended, she stood, smiled, and teleported to the bunker.

Today, she'd end ambrosia's curse upon their lives. Uncertain of the effects of long-term ambrosia withdrawal, she'd waited until the last possible moment to nudge Will to visit the miracle-working doctor. The date was chosen because it was the day she'd determined she needed her body ready to become pregnant.

Pregnant. She'd lived a thousand years, had seen countless generations of people born, live their lives, and die in every possible manner. She'd seen the world progress from a time when a small village possessing running water was an incredible advancement, from a time when buildings were constructed solely of lumber and stone, to a twenty-first century where electricity, the Internet, instant communication, and nanoparticle-based construction panels were appearing in the world. She'd nearly died on one occasion, and had suffered through more close calls than she cared to remember during her long life.

None of that terrified her like becoming a mother.

The physical aspect of pregnancy didn't frighten her. No, it was the responsibility she'd bear, often alone, that scared her. In less than seven years, she'd be raising two children, while her husband lived in another time. *Multiple* other times, actually. Could she raise her children successfully, helping them become the people who'd risk their lives to travel through time in an untested machine for the chance to save their very human father from certain death?

Would the elimination of ambrosia cause her to age more rapidly at some point? She wouldn't take another dose of the sweet berry until comfortably after Angel's birth. The idea that she might show her millennium-plus years of living, that her body might falter, that she might perish of old age—and that she wouldn't then be there for her children… all of those potentialities had started to generate nightmares. Nightmares in which her young children looked around, lost and frightened, crying out for her, wondering why she didn't appear, wondering what the big stone with Mommy's name carved in it meant.

She wouldn't allow that, not after all that Will and others had gone through to get her to this point. She'd survive and thrive, for her children, for Will, and for everyone in Will's future—her past—whose lives would be lost if she failed.

The safe in the bunker was purely cosmetic. No one who knew of the existence of the bunker would remove the contents, and others who might gain access via teleportation—like the Hunters—wouldn't know the significance. She dialed up the combination and opened the door, jumping slightly as the total silence was shattered with squeaking of the hinges. She removed four items and set them on the table before closing and locking the safe.

Two syringes. Two vials, one labeled "E," written in the hand of a man who'd died—unnecessarily—to save her life. The other, labeled "W," had been provided by the son of that same man. Within each was blood untainted by ambrosia, and the infusion she'd take would flush ambrosia's effects from her systems, ending her centuries-long sterility while reintroducing aging to her body. "E" stood for "Elizabeth," her birth name, the name by which the elder Adam had first known her, back when she was a mere child. How he'd gotten Arthur's blood, and how he'd cleared that blood of ambrosia's contamination… those were secrets the elder Adam had taken to the grave. The younger Adam, aware of Will's true date of birth, had made an appearance in the hospital on that day, and had extracted—with permission—the blood of Will's parents. Hope had no doubt that *Will's* vial would work, but would hers?

The elder Adam had experienced that reversal, and during that time sans ambrosia had fathered his only child, a son who bore his name and likeness. Eva had asked the elder Adam about the process and had interviewed Ambrose as well, and had confirmed that the initial effects would be felt once the injected blood had the chance to circulate through the body once. After four or five cycles, ambrosia would be flushed out of the circulatory system, rendering the person both mortal and fertile within minutes.

She wondered if the reversal would hurt. Eva hadn't asked, and Adam had not volunteered an answer.

There was only one way to find out.

Gingerly, she picked up her vial and tried to twist the top off. It was stuck. After thirty seconds of wrestling, she felt the top budge, and she spun it until it came off. She attached the hypodermic needle to the top and pulled the plunger back, drawing the blood into the syringe. After setting the syringe down on the table and putting the top back on the vial, she located the cord she'd stored on a bookshelf, and tied it around her upper left arm, cutting off the circulation and causing veins to stand out on her skin.

Hope picked up the syringe and stared at the red substance visible through the clear surface. She was about to inject herself with Arthur's blood, blood from a man who was the epitome of pure evil. Would that blood, cleansed of the effects of the ambrosia that had kept the man alive for centuries, taint her, corrupt her, and turn her into... him?

"No, I'm *Genevieve's* daughter," Hope whispered. *"That's* the blood that defines me. Not his. His blood is just the means to a wonderful end."

Without further hesitation, she jabbed the needle into a raised vein in her left arm and depressed the plunger, gasping at the sharp pain as the needle pierced her flesh. With the blood injected, she withdrew the needle and tossed the syringe into an empty trash can. She watched as the tiny piercing stitched closed before her eyes, an effect caused by her enhanced healing abilities and the internal nanos Will had transferred into her body over the centuries. She sat down and closed her eyes, hoping she'd done the right thing at the right time.

"I got your note."

She stood quickly. The voice was strange, the Energy sound buzzing near her unfamiliar. But there was only one man who could utter that sentence. She turned and looked at him.

"I look different. I know I do." He didn't move, but didn't take his eyes off her, unapologetically drinking in her image. "It's necessary for me to change everything that the world can see or sense about me in order to continue to do my work. To be the change I want in this world."

She watched as his image slowly morphed, the hair assuming

the familiar jet black color, the eyes sparkling the deep shade of green she knew so well. Moments later, he looked like himself, like the man she'd just sent off for an unnecessary infertility treatment.

"Will?" Her whisper still bore a hint of doubt.

"I figured out, finally, what the messages from the diary meant." It was *his* voice, not the voice who'd addressed her after teleporting into the bunker. "Why they always talked about there being no record of Will Stark. Why those messages always used the *name*, Will Stark, rather than just stating that it was *me* who'd vanished for all time. It was only when I was on the verge of leaving for the casino that I realized that it was the *name* that disappeared. I'd need to transform myself, to abandon the name of Will Stark to history and legend, and I'd need an event to convince as many Aliomenti and Alliance as possible that I'd died to accomplish that feat. But I also needed to do so with sufficient mystery. The Aliomenti would then wonder if I was gone, and they'd spend their time looking for the face and Energy signature they knew as Will Stark. They wouldn't look for what I might *become*."

Hope nodded. "No one believes you died, though," she told him. "Not now, not anymore. The Aliomenti… they're convinced it was some elaborate scheme meant to destroy them. The Alliance… to them, it's part of the legend, how Will Stark has the Aliomenti on the run chasing shadows after his alleged death at the hands of the Hunters. The core team is so convinced that you're alive that they keep telling me that you'll be the one to teleport me and Josh here to save us from the Assassin." Her tone on the last point was slightly bitter, reflecting her anger at the implication in the messages from the future that she'd be unable to teleport herself and her son a few yards.

Will nodded, and she noticed that the Energy sound emanating from him was changing, strengthening, the tone moving more and more toward the violin sound she knew so well. "I'll be here that day, no matter what, because it will give me a chance to see what truly happened for the first time. My eyes weren't working well at the end of it all the first time around." He smiled, and then frowned. "But I don't expect to be doing any teleportation for you and Josh that day, regardless of what any diary might say, or what our future friends told me directly. I think that wording was there to help me realize I needed to survive that day thirty years ago, to remind me that I have to be here when it all unfolds. But I don't take it literally."

Hope nodded. *He* believed in her, at least. And she couldn't deny him the right to be there that day, not given the historical importance of those events.

And if anything *did* go wrong… if she actually *did* fail to move them to safety… if she actually *did* need help? Well, Will would be there as her backup, ready to step in.

She switched topics. "Your Energy sounded… different. But it's changing."

He looked thoughtful. "I hid for a long time, probably not where you thought, but I did hide. And I spent time thinking, trying to figure out how I could live in hiding for so long without going crazy. My Shielding is good, but eventually I'll mess up and let it drop at the wrong time. With someone like Porthos, who can sense anything from anywhere, that's a risk I couldn't take. I didn't want you having to hide the truth about me in a Cavern full of people who'd want to know where I might be hiding out." He considered. "Changing my appearance? That was straightforward. But I realized I needed to do something with my Energy. I didn't know how to turn it off, and there were practical concerns with doing that anyway. So I began to wonder if I could change the Energy, make it sound different, so that whatever identification mechanism Porthos has no longer ties my Energy to the man he knows as Will Stark. Over the course of a couple of years, with nothing else to occupy my time, I learned to recalibrate my Energy so it gives off a different signal, and that's why it sounded different to you. It freed me to travel in public, to walk right by Porthos without him recognizing me. It was just like that trip we took to test scutarium all those years ago." He smiled at the memory. "Now I can go out into the world and help people, without worrying about being detected."

"You'll have to teach me that trick at some point."

"Of course." He paused. "It was you, wasn't it? That day, years ago, when my parents died? You were there, weren't you? Protecting me, making sure I survived something that should have killed me."

Hope nodded. It hadn't been long for her. But for Will, *this* Will, it would have happened centuries ago. "Nothing could prevent me from being there. You needed me that day. You've been there for me a few times in the past, and that was a chance for me to return the favor." She considered. "And you might do so again in the future."

His face showed doubt, but he nodded nevertheless. "Hope, why did you leave me that note? Why ask me to come here, on this date, at this time?" His smile was weak. "I'm not complaining about your company, of course; far from it. But that note was... different."

She didn't answer right away. Instead, she moved back to the table and began transferring the second vial's contents into a syringe.

"I went to the original *Nautilus* a few months after... the event," she said. "I went there as part of a trip I took to check in on the newborn you. It seemed like the place you'd go, and it fit with the information I had. Lots of Energy from the teleportation effort, a location that only you and I knew about, a place with scutarium plating so you could use Energy to heal up from whatever wounds you'd suffered. But I found... nothing. It was as if you'd never been there. Still, I suspected you'd go there eventually, assuming you still lived." She stared at him. "How did you survive? How is it that you're here? Did you make a sword splitter from those futuristic nanos you have?"

"That might have worked, and I thought about using that approach," he admitted. "The problem with that was that if the nano splitter failed... well, I really didn't want to get stabbed. I had far too much yet to do with my life to have it end that day." He shook his head. "I used a newer Alliance technology. The good news was that I was never *directly* at risk."

"But, how...?" Her eyes widened as understanding dawned. "It was a clone."

He nodded. "When I realized what I needed to do, I approached Aaron. He's been doing cloning tests for years, and he's constantly testing it out on different people to refine the technique, and always looking for volunteers. Those clones all die within a week or so of being born, though. But that was exactly what I needed. I asked him to make one of me, and to prioritize the effort, because I wanted to see the result before I left. I made sure my clone stayed asleep, told Aaron that it had died in a terrible accident, and got him aboard the craft surrounded with those futuristic nanos you mentioned so he was invisible. Adam never noticed. When we got to the casino, I teleported both of us out of the craft. After Adam flew off, I modified my own memories in the sleeping clone, enough to understand what needed to be done as far as that mission, but also to believe that I—my clone—still had the sword splitter on. I hid myself, with the rest of those futuristic nanos, staying close the whole time. When Porthos stabbed my clone… well, it was a fatal wound, and I think the clone's belief that I had the splitter on made the clone so shocked that he forgot to teleport away. So I teleported both of us to the submarine, just as you suspected, and allowed him to believe he'd done it on instinct, and gave him the time and the space he needed for the wound take its fatal toll. I did alleviate the pain somewhat. It's really tough to watch something that's basically you die a slow, painful death. When he passed on, I pulverized the body with Energy and allowed it to float out into the sea, cleaned up all traces of our presence, including the Energy, and left." He paused. "I thought you'd go there, realizing it was the only place I *could* go, notice that everything was gone, and recognize that it must mean I'd survived the attack. That I'd gone into hiding, as I've always known I must, even though it meant being away from you in this… maturity level." He gave a faint smile, a look replaced by a brooding face once more. "You found my clues, my message that I'd survived, and you maintained the illusion that you believed me dead all the time before going to the sub… and in all the time since. Yet when you reached the *Nautilus*, you left a note asking me to come here, to this exact spot, at this time, on this date. Why?"

She hesitated a moment before answering. "I watch your memories of the future quite a bit. I love watching the children, seeing them as adults. It was encouraging to see that I'd managed to raise two children to adulthood with some degree of success."

Will nodded, encouraging her to continue.

"But I watched the other memories of the future as well, especially the one where Adam explains what the different clothing colors meant. That… bothered me."

Will frowned. "Why?"

"Based upon his explanation, Josh and Angel's clothing should have been the same color. They have the same parents after all, right?" She paused. "But that wasn't the case. Josh's—Fil's— clothing was jet black. Angel's was a dark green. When I worked out the color coding, figured out the relative power levels, the difference was exponential in nature. Even with a seven year head start, Josh had no advantage over his sister that could have explained what I'd recognized. The difference was too great for two adults with the same parents."

Will cocked his head, thinking. "Perhaps Josh spent more time developing Energy than Angel did. He did have a few centuries to widen the gap from their respective births."

Hope shook her head. "Adam said that Josh's clothing color meant he was a special case. So much of what they told you in the future contained hidden messages. I think that was a message as well. There's something unique about Josh that explains why he was so much more powerful than his sister."

Will thought for a moment, and then his face clouded. "Are you suggesting...?"

Hope shook her head. "They have the same parents, Will." She paused. "But they were born at different *times*."

"Of course they were," Will said, confused. "What does that have to do with..."

He stopped, and a look of surprise covered his face.

Hope nodded. "The children of Energy users inherit a level of power that's a multiple or exponent of the power level of their parents. We know that my Energy levels, over the course of the six or seven years separating them in age, would remain nearly constant. That means that *your* Energy levels would have to explain that difference. Angel's clothing color is about what my coloring was when we tested out the arm bands. That means that your levels at her birth were essentially nothing. But for Josh? Your Energy levels were massive. As if you'd contributed a thousand years or more worth of Energy development to your son."

He stared at her, and then at the syringe. "Are you saying...?"

She nodded. "Adam was there the day you were born. He collected the blood of your parents, not certain why he did so. When we mapped the date I'd need to inject Arthur's blood, and the date Josh would be conceived, and the date of Young Will's trip to the infertility specialist... I knew *you* needed to be here this day to ensure your son becomes who he's meant to be. Not the young Will. The older Will, the man who's spent centuries fighting to keep his wife alive, to ensure his children are born. *You*, old Will, are Josh's father."

She handed Will the syringe.

He accepted it. And with a knowing smile, he jabbed the needle into his arm and depressed the plunger.

XIII
City

2026 A.D.

"Look, Josh!" Hope said. "See the big building where Daddy works?"

Josh Stark sat between his parents in the rear compartment of the limousine, his ice blue eyes devoid of all emotion and expression. Will often wondered just how much their son saw, heard, and understood of the world around him. Josh had met all physical developmental guidelines, but for reasons medical doctors could not explain, he'd never developed the ability to communicate verbally.

Hope could tell them exactly what was happening.

From the first instant she felt him moving inside her, she could sense the child's immense Energy capacity, burning like a raging fire within. Will could sense it as well; when he placed his hands on her protruding belly, the Energy within zapped him like a burst of static electricity. Josh was greeting his father in utero. Will thought they needed to get the house humidifier serviced.

Hope worried that, as a newborn, Josh's lack of control over a power that would soon easily eclipse her own would prove a danger, a beacon to Hunters looking for unexplained bursts of Energy throughout the globe. Hope's personal Shielding would mask her son until he emerged into the bright light of the world and

149

learned to control those bursts on his own. The effort required to maintain that Shield was immense.

Yet despite the great exertion, Hope found her pregnancy a joy. The telepathic bond she developed with her son enabled a depth to their relationship that most mothers and fathers couldn't fathom. She held conversations with her child in utero, teaching him about life, about the Energy he possessed, about the responsibility he'd need to develop for controlling that Energy, concepts he wouldn't really understand until he was older. She explained that other people in the world might be frightened of his ability, might seek to hurt him because of it, and that his mother would protect him and make sure those evil people didn't succeed.

That proved far easier said than done. Shielding Josh while she continued to carry him was one problem, but in practical terms it was the same thing as Shielding her own Energy, an act that had become automatic for her over the centuries. It simply took more effort.

Shielding him once he was born meant she needed to keep *two* Shields up at all times. The mental effort to *remember*, combined with the strength it took to restrain the nuclear levels of Energy the boy's body sought to throw off, drained her each day. Will thought the often haggard look on her face derived from anguish over Josh's inability to speak, but that wasn't the case. She conversed with Josh regularly, at a deeper level than Will would be able to comprehend right now. Her fatigue was exacerbated by her sense of remorse over leaving Will in the dark, as usual, about what was really happening with their son. Her husband suffered from guilt, borne of a belief that the treatment that had allowed him to give his son life had somehow rendered the child mute. The mental anguish for Hope far exceeded the suffering she'd endured as a child at the hands of Arthur.

And the fear that she'd lose focus, that she'd allow Josh's Energy—or hers—to leak led to near panic attacks every time the two of them ventured out in public. The closest thing to a fight she'd ever had with Will occurred when she'd insisted upon going with Will and Josh on a father-son outing, her comments leading Will to believe that she didn't trust him to care for his son. He didn't know, couldn't know, that he could never protect Josh from the greatest threats facing the boy.

Will heard her enthusiastic comment to Josh and sighed. *He* didn't hear Josh's excited mental chatter at taking in the completely rebuilt city of Pleasanton in person for the first time. Hope crushed Josh's external exhibition of excitement while encouraging the boy's internal enthusiasm, all while offering a sympathetic gaze to her husband.

She couldn't stand this duplicity. The next few years would seem to last a full century, and she *knew* what that was like. The only solace was knowing, in an unoffered commentary years earlier, that the older Will now knew why things had worked out as they had, and he bore her no ill will for keeping from him the secret of his son's true nature. He told her she must do exactly as she was doing, and, where possible, the older version of Will would provide his own aid in that effort.

The downtown area was surrounded by a decorative brick wall, punctured by a dozen openings for foot traffic into and out of the city. Even at this relatively early hour of the day, people swarmed through those openings, looks of anticipation and excitement on their faces. Shuttle buses parked near each entry, transporting people to and from the airport, distant shopping malls, and various residential areas of town. Digital advertising billboards announced all manner of excitement inside, ranging from tours of various businesses, to open air concerts by local bands *Untamed Thoroughbredz* and *Naked Prozac*, to food specialties available that day.

The limousine bypassed the pedestrian archways and approached one of four vehicular entries to the underground parking garage. The bright sunshine was replaced by muted ambient lighting, not quite so bright a light as the solar variety, but far more cheerful than the lighting in most garages Hope had visited in her long life. The bulbs were the product of a company she and Will had funded in its infancy, a business that had successfully produced a new variety of bulb that both reduced the cost and increased the brightness of the light produced.

That was the way they did things in Pleasanton now. New innovations to drive down costs and improve the standard of living provided to residents, visitors, patrons, and workers inside were announced almost weekly.

They came to a stop at the private entrance to Stark Enterprises International headquarters. The driver opened the armor-plated door of the limousine and the family stepped out. Lance Maynard and his team stepped forward, and Hope sighed. Humans wanted to kill her husband, the Aliomenti wanted to kill her husband—the older one, not this one—and the Alliance was trying to keep him alive for another three years so the boy whose hand she held, and his unborn sister, could retrieve him from the future and propel the man on an incredible journey through time.

Surely, that wasn't normal. Surely, understanding and living through these times entitled her to a few moments of well-earned fatigue and silent tears.

The entry system to the business was similar to that used at De Gray Estates, using locked doors to ensure individuals entering the building did so only if approved. Will used a palm print reader to allow his family and security contingent into a staging room, and the door locked behind him. Every person entering the staging room was photographed, and every person in the room had to be individually buzzed into the small "man trap" room that led into the headquarters building. In the event Will was kidnapped by a single person seeking access to the hidden parts of Stark Enterprises, the criminal would find themselves trapped inside this entry system. If those watching and verifying the entry process identified any sign of wrongdoing, they could flood either room with gases that would render those inside unconscious, and an easy arrest target for the security and police forces working above.

Hope had worried about another possibility. "What if someone *shoots* you? How does that room help?"

"They'll suffer through being trapped in a room with a dead body."

She smacked his arm. "That's not funny."

"No, but it's true. If I'm dead, they're stuck in a room and we have irrefutable video evidence of their crime. They'll be knocked unconscious and wake up in prison. Permanently."

"But you're still *dead*."

"We all die someday, Hope. It's what we do with the days we have that matters." He looked at her, saw her face lined with concern, and smiled. "There's no such thing as a life without risk, Hope. I won't take any that are unnecessary. I have no interest in turning you into the world's best looking widow." The smile turned into a devilish grin. "People thought Penelope had it rough when the world thought Odysseus dead. She's got *nothing* on you."

Hope smacked his arm again, but this time, her smile was tinted with a blush.

Today, there was no sign of an impending attack, whether human or Aliomenti in origin. Maynard went through the door into the single-person man trap after Will's palm print unlocked it. Once the door snapped shut behind Maynard, Will pressed his palm to the panel again, and Maynard was able to walk out into Stark Enterprises International headquarters. Hope followed, and then Josh moved robot-like through the process. The final two guards went, and Will followed. It was tedious, but their security policies, defined by a man named Cain Freeman, mandated that they separately screen and assess each person who entered the private side of the building.

The group entered an elevator that whisked them silently to the top floor of the tallest building in Pleasanton. Will generally avoided the penthouse office, preferring to walk around the building and the businesses populating the city. He believed he could make better decisions and develop better plans by seeing the people and process in operation, rather than sitting far from where the action occurred and speculating about decisions based on theories.

Today, though, Will made an exception. His wife and son would have the opportunity to take in the spectacular, panoramic view of the city and the environs available only here. In the distance, Hope could just make out the walls surrounding the De Gray Estates, easily identifiable by their size and the adjoining guard tower.

Below, a rejuvenated Pleasanton teemed with color and activity.

Moving sidewalks curved and meandered through a mix of green space and buildings. Visitors could go on a slow tour of the city aboard the built-in transportation system, giving them ample opportunity to view the wares on display in the colorful shops dotting the city. Larger corporate entities occupied the taller buildings, and the sidewalks acted like aboveground, outdoor subway systems, moving employees from garage or archway entry to office door in mere moments. Manufacturing facilities took advantage of the clean, cheap energy produced by the city's dual power plants, and the safety allowed by the unique construction methods of all the refurbished and rebuilt buildings allowed most businesses to provide tours to the curious.

Stark Enterprises International owned or held investment interests in nearly all of the businesses operating inside the corporate city, which amplified Will's interest in walking around the lively city.

"It's amazing to see it from this angle," Hope said. "I've been through on foot before, of course, but this view gives you a new appreciation of what's been done."

"There are a hundred thousand people working here every day, and we're getting more and more tourists coming through each month," Will told her. "We have a huge waiting list of companies that want to expand here. We've had to pay to move people to Pleasanton to fill all of the available jobs." He shook his head. "I get an average of three emails a day from government officials asking what legislation they can pass to mimic the Pleasanton miracle." He offered an amused nod toward a bookshelf, which held stacks of thin books titled *The Pleasanton Miracle*. "It's all right there. There's no secret as to what makes this work. We make it easy for people to get work done, we show the profound impact that work provides—for example, using products made here to enhance the whole city, like the parking garage lights—and seeing everything that happens inspires greater creativity, innovation, and success."

There was a knock at the door, and a smartly dressed woman stepped in, her nose buried in a folder as she shuffled papers. "Mr. Stark, I saw that you were here. I have the operational reports from yesterday and…" She looked up and broke off, realizing others were in the room. Her gaze fell upon Hope, and her face lit up. "Mrs. Stark! I didn't know you would be here today! It's such a pleasure to see you!" She dumped the folder in Will's hands and rushed forward to pump Hope's hand, beaming.

Her face clouded when she realized what she'd done. She turned to Will, her face turning a deep crimson. "Mr. Stark, I'm… I'm so sorry. I don't know what came over me."

Will laughed. "I completely understand. I have the same reaction when I see Hope. I just forget everyone else exists." He flipped open the folder. "Two package mix-ups yesterday? That's an improvement, but not good enough. Did we get the root cause identified?"

"Visual identification error. Clerk couldn't tell identical twins apart."

Will snorted. "Go figure." He paused. "How did that cause a

problem, though?"

"Delivery to the drop-off point and sorter was fine. It was the pickup that caused the problem. The print reader system isn't online there yet, so we're still doing visual identification to match and confirm packages and owners. The pictures work well, but the clerk matched up the wrong twin for the two bins."

Hope glanced to both of them. "Something new?"

Will nodded. "Rather than having people carry purchases around, we've built something akin to an airline luggage processing system. You buy your items, state that you want to pick it up when you leave, and that's it. The purchased items go onto underground conveyance systems and get stored in a climate controlled underground warehouse. When you leave, you go to pickup spots near the entrances and in the garages to get your purchases. We're looking for total automation; palm print to purchase, palm print to trigger the delivery of your packages to you at those final depots. But the palm reading systems aren't online just yet in the pickup areas. Our workers have to ask for a name, verify identity via a digital photo attached to bins holding purchases, and hand over purchases once payment is confirmed. That works well as a temporary system, but if you get people with the same last name who look exactly alike, mistakes can happen."

"Twins," Hope said, nodding. She paused for a moment. "The palm print purchasing system works, then?"

Will nodded, though he glanced at his assistant. "Any issues there, Sheryl?" He flipped through the papers in the folder she'd given him.

Sheryl shook her head. "Yesterday was a good day." She started for the door. "I can come back later, Mr. Stark. I suspect you'd like to spend time with your family."

Will nodded. "Thanks, Sheryl."

After she left, he turned back to Hope, who stood watching Josh. To Will, the boy was simply facing in the direction he'd been left after entering the room, but Hope knew he was amazed at his father's creation, marveling even at the age of three at the imagination and planning required to enable the organized chaos unfolding below. Will watched his son for a moment, and then nodded at Hope. "Let's go meet a few people, and then we can head outside and get something to eat."

She sensed wariness from him, invisible on the surface, a concern that venturing from this sanctuary might be dangerous for his wife and son. Inwardly, she smiled. If any threats materialized, it could be neutralized in an instant—and with it, the entire city—if she merely dropped the Shield from a frightened Josh. He need not worry about them.

But of course, she couldn't tell *him* that.

She glanced at Will as they moved. "How are you getting people to use the palm print payment system? And by the way, that's an *awful* tongue twister."

Will chuckled. "Everyone entering the city has to provide a palm print and have a three dimensional picture of their face taken," he replied. "We do that mostly as a deterrent to theft or other crimes; that information gets fully erased unless the person asks us to retain it for a future visit to the city. But we also realized that it gives a chance to offer something to those entering the city and thus raise operational funds. We can't tax anything, and we don't want to implement anything like a cover charge, which leaves us with transaction fees. Simply put, the more people buy here, the better the city's financial position. We provide a lot of conveniences for people who pay for things our way. We can't *require* it due to legal tender laws, and people can and do pay with cash or credit cards at the point of sale. But fewer and fewer are choosing to go that route, now."

The elevator opened, and the group of six moved inside. "When they do their scan prior to entry, each person is given the option of swiping their credit card or depositing cash into something like a debit account. We tie their palm print to the credit card or cash balance. When they go to make a purchase, they can use a palm reader and it automatically treats that palm print like their credit card or cash. No need to get out a card, fumble with cash and coins, sign receipts, and so on. At the end of the day, when they leave, they get receipts for all purchases at once. We charge a transaction fee and a merchant fee for vendors who use the system. Given the volumes that we work through, though, and the way we work with the credit card companies, our combined fees are less than what the individual merchants would pay on their own, and they can charge people less than if they paid with cash or a credit card at the point of sale. It's a win for the businesses in the city and for the people who buy goods and services here. But it's also a win for us, because those fees and the rent we charge building occupants provide enough revenue to operate this city. We ran at a loss the first six months in operation when we just collected rent, even though the waiting list of businesses looking to move in meant we could have raised the rents. We wanted to keep those costs down, however, so that our businesses could offer better prices here than people get outside. Once we added the payment fees, we started to break even and even earn a bit, despite adding more services in the city."

She looked intrigued. "You'd talked about that, but it still surprised me that it works. Don't you need to collect huge amounts of money?"

"No, not really, because we have no debt, and all of our expenses are current," he replied. "The Pleasanton city council before reached the point where they paid for everything with credit, and then had to start borrowing to pay interest, and so on. That's why they'd gotten so desperate; they were reaching a point where they couldn't collect enough in taxes to pay even the interest fees, let along new and current expenses like payroll. If we don't have cash, we don't buy anything new or hire anyone else for our city operations. Our expenses are tightly monitored and if we see an area creeping out of control, we devote the time needed to fix it. Innovations like the payment system are one-time efforts we fund from a special projects account we established with our fixed rental income. It's more than paid for itself."

They elevator doors slid open on the second floor, and Will led the way to a door marked Security. "You have to fund police, fire, schools, and all of the other services of government with that money, though," Hope said. "How can you do that without taxing everyone? It seems like those expenses would take more than you could obtain from rents and transaction fees."

"We handle things differently," Will said. "One of the challenges we saw in looking at how things worked before was that expenditures were handled in a manner that was actually least beneficial to all involved. Firefighters would sign longer term contracts but that meant the city had to offer lower wages because they didn't know what the future would hold. Teachers might seek a healthier retirement package, but because the total amount of money the city could pay in total was finite—salary and benefits couldn't go over a certain total—we saw they'd get paid less in current dollars as more and more needed to go to fund pensions or something... and if the projections on returns didn't pan out, they'd be in huge trouble down the road. Or the city would bankrupt itself trying to refill funds.

"We made a decision up front: pay top current dollar for top talent but keep those expenses current. If we could afford to budget, say, one hundred dollars per firefighter, for example, it used to be that fifty dollars would be current salary and benefits, and fifty dollars would go to fund future benefits. The firefighters would look at their salaries and wonder why they only made fifty dollars. We agreed. Now, if we can afford to pay one hundred dollars in total to each firefighter, then we get to put eighty or ninety dollars to current salary and benefits, and the remaining can go, at the employees direction, to a private personal pension, a retirement investment account, college savings funds for their children, or just additional salary. Suddenly, they're making ninety dollars instead of fifty and can decide how to handle their future individually. And we have a sustainable expense model. Win-win.

"We use the same approach to deciding about new tools or technology for our public servants. If there's a new type of fire extinguishing material, or a piece of technology that helps police track down criminals more quickly, or a new teaching tool shown to be effective in educating students, we make every effort to get them, if we have the cash available and if we can make a one-time purchase. We have to prioritize and let each group decide which expenses of those types are best—they do the work, right, so they know—based upon the funds available."

"I wish more cities would follow that example," Hope mused.

Will shrugged. "It may not work everywhere. The nice thing is that we've had the chance to try new things here, and thus far, those experiments have worked well. Maybe the whole model won't work elsewhere, but people can pick out pieces and test them in their localities."

They walked to an open office occupied by a dark-haired man who looked up as Will knocked. "Mr. Stark?"

"Hello, Cain. I've brought a few people to meet you."

Cain stood up from his desk and walked around to greet them. "This must be your wife and son." He held out his hand to Hope. "I'm Cain Freeman, in charge of the security of the physical buildings and data processed throughout Pleasanton and the rest of the Stark Enterprises businesses."

Hope shook his hand, and felt a tiny trickle of Energy from the man. *Adam.* "Pleased to meet you, Mr. Freeman. My husband speaks of you all the time, and your work seems to be the spark of energy this city needs to operate." She smiled. "Sorry. With all the talking he does about you, I just feel like I've known you for an eternity."

Cain smiled. "Thank you for the very kind words, Mrs. Stark. The pleasure is all mine. Your husband seems to bring out the best in all of us. And please, call me Cain." He turned to the little boy, who stood staring ahead into space. "This must be Josh, who looks just like his father." He tousled the boy's hair. Hope caught the look of shock when the contact was made. Adam had felt the massive Energy stores she was suppressing inside her son, and the look on his face, though brief, showed an awe and understanding of the effort it took to keep the boy hidden from the Aliomenti.

"That's my son, all right," Will agreed. "Be nice to him, Cain; he'll be running the place one day." Will's voice pitched higher as he spoke, doubting his own words.

Cain smiled. "I'm sure he'll be just as innovative as his father."

"Nothing terribly innovative about me," Will said. "I just hire very smart people and give them the tools they need to succeed to their greatest potential."

"That *is* innovative, Mr. Stark," Cain replied. "Many leaders try to suppress their strongest talent because they think it makes them look less impressive by comparison."

Will shrugged. "Glad to hear you're happy working here, Cain. Is the palm system close to going online for the pickup system? Sheryl told me we had near perfect success doing matching at the pickup depots, except…"

"The twins, right," Cain said, sighing. "Yes, the systems people tell me that the expanded computing capacity is online, and they just need to finish up the final bit of fiber wiring to the pickup depots. We'll go online with them one at a time to test the systems over the next few days."

Will nodded. "Excellent work as always, Cain. I'm going outside with Hope and Josh for a bit, but I'll swing by later."

"Of course," Cain said. "But be careful; it's raining outside. We've got the air temperature control systems to keep the outdoor temperature comfortable for pedestrians, but we can't do anything about precipitation." He glanced at Josh. "Perhaps that will be Josh's innovation when he takes over."

Will groaned, peeking out the window and spotting the drizzle falling outside.

Hope laughed. "Just put a lid over this place, and then you *can* control the precipitation."

Will and Cain stared at her, and she felt a moment of discomfort. "Sorry," Hope said, her face turning the same shade of crimson as her original hair color. "Did I say something wrong?"

"No, not at all, Mrs. Stark," Cain told her. "In fact, I think it's a brilliant idea. Our lead nanoparticle researcher told me a couple of days ago that the technique they're working on now, to build geodesic domes for use as tents by military personnel, could actually be expanded to build something of a similar design of nearly any size. Your comment about putting a lid over the city made me wonder…"

Will nodded. "I had the same thought, Cain. I'll stop and talk to David later about his progress and about Hope's idea." He smiled at his wife. "The snow globe again, isn't it? That might be the next big project for the city."

Cain nodded as the Stark family exited his office. "Enjoy your stay, Mrs. Stark and Josh. I hope the rain isn't too uncomfortable for you. Or you, Mr. Stark."

"It won't be," Will said. "Once we put that lid over the city, we won't have to worry about rain at all. Won't it be fantastic? It will be like our own little underground city."

Both Cain and Hope laughed, loud and nervous.

"Yes," Cain said. "That would definitely be fantastic. But also a fantasy. I think an underground city is impossible."

"Impossible?" Will snorted. "Nothing is impossible."

Hope smiled. "If you're involved, Will, nothing is."

XIV
Seeds

2027 A.D.

They found the property they sought, one parcel for sale inside a larger abandoned tract of land several miles from the nearest interstate highway. Only one building stood on the property, a ramshackle shed badly in need of repairs. Timbers forming the exterior walls were warped and allowed outside air, precipitation, and vermin inside. What little furniture remained was beyond repair and unusable.

Peter and Judith didn't care about that. The critical factors, for them, were the size of the property—several thousand acres of non-tenable land—and the isolated location a few hours' drive from Pleasanton. It didn't take long to hold the wordless conversation and agree to go after the entire tract of land, not just the parcel offered for sale.

Theirs was a task of curious origin.

Old Will had made it clear that he thought it best if the fortune he and Hope amassed was retained by them after their supposed deaths. They'd recognized that they couldn't simply will the money to an Alliance member posing under an alias, nor could they leave the money to a charity managed by the Alliance. Both approaches would result in significant attention from the Aliomenti who would—rightly—find the acts suspicious and move to investigate the beneficiaries. They decided that the best way to move the money would be through a massive series of automated transfers of small amounts of money into hundreds of accounts, all secret, all interconnected in ways impossible to trace, and then maneuver the money around until all of it arrived in a bank controlled in secret by the Alliance.

In short, they'd steal it.

But the Starks couldn't avoid setting up an estate plan as if such a "theft" wouldn't occur. From Young Will's perspective, the money must live on after his death, put to use to continue helping the overall economy survive and thrive. They'd devise processes that their Trustee could following to give and invest the money as they did while living. Such investment activity was fine, for a time, but they needed to get the money away from the Trust as quickly as possible after the Starks' "deaths."

Adam's technical expertise, combined with Ashley's, made devising the coding to perform the transfers relatively simple. There was only one problem: they couldn't find the account information in any of Will's memories. Somehow, they'd need to get that information. The timing suggested that they'd only get final account information set up in the days before the attacks, and they couldn't guarantee Hope would get the information in time to pass it along, or have the opportunity to do so.

Hope would, they decided, ensure that she built a mechanism into the estate plan to allow Adam into the inner circle of the Trustee, gaining access the account information he needed. That meant Adam would need to gain the trust of both the Trustee, a man named Michael Baker, and Millard Howe, the estate lawyer. And they needed to do it in a way that seemed in line with Will's character in particular, as Will would be the Stark both Howe and Baker knew best.

They found an odd snippet of conversation Hope and Will held after a meeting with Howe. Hope talked about the wisdom of storing an extra copy of their plan somewhere nobody could find it, and thus allow Howe to ensure nobody had modified the document without their knowledge. Hope had opined that the decision to use one of Stark Enterprises "secure data centers" to store that safe copy was brilliant, because "the site could be anywhere, even right under our feet."

It was another clue.

It meant Howe would need to travel to a location called a "secure data center" that could, indeed, be anywhere. Or, at least, the place he'd find the will could be anywhere. After much discussion, they'd realized he'd travel to some far-off place, only to be whisked unawares back to Pleasanton somewhere underground. That spot would be an office in Eva and Aaron's basement, reached via teleportation from the location Howe thought he was visiting. They could use nanos to confuse the man, and create a mist that dulled sensory perception so he didn't notice the feeling of displacement from teleportation.

The only problem? They didn't own land in a spot that fit with the available clues. Peter, who'd offered the idea of buying property for a new safe house and using it as the beginning and ending point for Howe's journey, found that his plan was well-received by the others, who volunteered him to locate and purchase the property.

That was how Peter and Judith came to be looking at a small house that should be condemned, on a piece of property that most in the area had long forgotten, and found the property to be perfect for their needs. They frowned, pointed out flaws (they'd need to raze the house and rebuild, the only water on the property came from a well, there were no feeds for electricity), and drove the price down during the rapid, indirect negotiations with the distant owner, who in practical terms just wanted the property out of his hands. When the final price was defined, they offered a higher price for the entire tract of land, and the owner, ecstatic at this good bit of fortune—and the small monetary fortune that would soon arrive in his bank account—agreed to their revised offer.

Three days later, funds were paid, documents signed, property liens were confirmed nonexistent, and the couple owned the property, free and clear, with deed in hand. Peter sent word of their success to the Project 2030 team via a brief, coded text message.

Hope's combination mobile phone twitched. It wasn't the standard buzz or tone her "human" number would produce upon receipt of the text, because she didn't want to draw attention to the fact that she'd received a secret message. She was completing her final bits of makeup before she and Will would depart to meet with an estate lawyer named Millard Howe, and she was reflecting upon what she needed to accomplish at the meeting, meshing her current human interests with the key items to further the goals of Project 2030.

On a human level, today was unusual for another reason: it was the first time she would leave Josh's side, trusting his care to someone else for a few hours. As a human mother highly protective of her son, leaving him alone with anyone else made her nervous. As a centuries-old member of the Alliance, knowing that four-year-old Josh would be cared for in her absence by Eva left her mind far more at ease.

She finished her final makeup work and risked a quick glance down at the phone, read the coded message from Peter, and tapped the screen, releasing a tiny trickle of Energy into the device. As programmed, the phone thoroughly erased all traces of the message she'd just read.

After a final glance in the mirror, she reached for her phone and knocked it on the floor. She stared at the phone, terrified she'd damaged the device... and then burst into tears. Shocked at her reaction, she composed herself, fixed her makeup, and carried phone and purse separately as she headed downstairs, still baffled at her reaction.

Will was already downstairs chatting with Eva. The woman looked nearly seventy years of age, and she'd ensconced herself in a chair. Her eyes tracked Josh, watching as the boy sat on the floor, his blank stare failing to follow the playful black Labrador retriever puppy bounding around the room. Hope caught the emotional delight from Josh as he watched the dog's antics, as did Eva. The women shared a sober glance, one that communicated the private glee at the happiness the boy felt, along with the public sorrow that his father couldn't know of that joy.

"We aren't sure how long this will take," Will told Eva.

"Take your time," Eva replied. Her voice as a human had taken on a southern drawl. "I have no other plans for today. The puppy... she is very entertaining and full of spirit."

As if on cue, Smokey barked.

Hope chuckled. "Smart girl, isn't she? Eva, I'll give you a call when we're heading home."

Eva nodded. With Hope gone, the task of Shielding Josh's

Energy would fall upon Eva. The house was so thoroughly encased in scutarium that she could drop the Shield for a time and allow Josh to be himself. Hope's call would alert her to the need to snap the Shield back on the boy, meeting the cruel need of hiding from Will his son's development. Eva would be exhausted by the effort, as Hope often was. With Josh being so docile, only a spirited puppy could generate the level of fatigue Will would see in Eva when they returned. The comment about Smokey was meant to plant that idea in Will's mind.

The couple climbed into the back seat of the armor-plated limousine, joined as always by Lance Maynard, who sat apart from them, giving the couple moderate privacy. The drive lasted only twenty minutes, and they pulled up in front of a modest, one story office building. Hope gave the building an appraising look, and then glanced at Will. "I have no idea how successful this man is, but I appreciate that he's not trying to sell us on his skill with a large, plush office."

Will nodded. "The people who sent me the reference say he's worked loads of high profile cases over the last twenty years or so. I did some research. He's high character and has enough money from his previous work that he doesn't need to continue to practice, which is why he moved here a few months ago from New York. He wanted to get away from the fast-paced lifestyle and constant influx of new and demanding clients. He's very good, and very selective. We're pretty lucky to get an appointment."

Hope gave him a wry grin. "Do you know who you are, by the way? Will Stark, architect of the American Recovery, richest man in the world, budding philanthropist and impromptu angel investor? I dare say this Millard Howe is antsy at the thought of meeting *you*, and is hyperventilating in his joy at the prospect of having you as a client."

Will smiled faintly. "He'll just be excited to be working with you."

Hope snorted. "Whatever."

A handful of paralegals huddled around a desk set off to the side, conversing quietly over documents spread across the surface. They didn't look up when the bell rang, announcing the opening of the door. A moment later, an older man stepped out of an office and walked toward them, his face a confused mix of exhilaration and sheer terror. Hope elbowed Will in the side. "Told you," she whispered.

"Mr. and Mrs. Stark? I'm Millard Howe." He held out his hand, which both Will and Hope shook in turn.

The activity in the office ground to a halt as Howe spoke their names, and everyone turned to stare.

Will, about to say something to Howe, became aware of the gazes upon him. He glanced nervously around the office, and then waved gingerly. "Um… hi, everyone."

Five minutes later, after the Starks had autographed dozens of papers and accepted gushing outpourings of thanks for the transformation of the city and the employment their businesses had provided for loved ones, Hope and Will were finally seated in Howe's office. As the lawyer shut the door, Hope looked at Will. "Know who you are, now, mister?" she whispered.

"I still say they're reacting to the gorgeous blonde," he whispered back.

"Thank you for coming, and I apologize for the… groupie behavior you've had to endure from my employees," Howe said, moving to sit behind his desk. "I assure you, a reprimand will be delivered."

"Quite all right, Mr. Howe," Hope said. She glanced at Will. "My husband does need the occasional reminder of the impact he's made. I'd prefer you offer them my personal thanks, rather than a reprimand."

Howe considered her request, and then nodded.

The lawyer pulled out a folder and slid it across the desk. "I took the liberty of drafting some initial paperwork we can use as a baseline." He stood, walked around the office, and launched into a complex sequence of legal terms that neither Will nor Hope were familiar with, referring in rapid succession to pages and paragraphs and sections in the document from memory.

Howe looked up and found two blank faces staring at him. Hope blinked several times, as did Will. Neither had opened the folder.

Howe's face softened. "I'm sorry, I'm moving too quickly. Most of my clients have been older, people who believe death from old age is imminent, and who have been considering this for some time. It must be difficult for you to consider. We can walk through it step by step, section by section, to familiarize you with the basic structure of the document, and then talk about how we should customize it for your situation and wishes."

Will sat staring straight ahead. Hope watched Will, before turning to face Howe. "Mr. Howe, before we do that, I have a question. I've heard stories of couples in our... circumstances having people break into their homes, access safes or locked drawers, and altering legal documents like wills to benefit the intruders. Have any of your clients experienced that? And do you have any suggestions for preventing it?"

Howe nodded. "It's not happened to any of my clients, but I suspect that it's only a matter of time. You're right to be concerned. My practice would be to compare my copy of the document to one bought to me by the person named as a beneficiary. If they match, there are no issues. If they don't... well, then we'd have to go through a process to prove which version is correct."

Hope nodded, and then, as if in a burst of inspiration, asked a question. "Why not make a third copy?"

Howe considered that. "A third copy?"

Will finally snapped out of his trance, looked at Hope, and grinned. "Love it!" He motioned for her to continue.

"You complete the documents," Hope explained. "You keep a copy. We keep a copy. And we hide a third copy in a separate location, one that no one else knows about. That copy is the true master copy, the one that's the true record. It wouldn't, and couldn't, be altered. If issues are found with the other copies, we'd know, because the copies the two of us hold won't match the third."

Howe nodded. "Intriguing. I... take it you have a place in mind?"

"Yes," Will and Hope both said. They glanced at each other, looks of surprise on their faces. Hope gave Will's mind a gentle touch, and a look of understanding covered his face.

Howe didn't seem to notice. "We will make sure that you have a third copy in your possession at signing, then, and I'll remain ignorant of your secret location until such time, as any, that I need to know. Now, there are various mechanical steps involved in transferring your assets over to the Trust. Alternatively, you can opt to transfer everything in the event of your deaths to designated charities or other beneficiaries, which can then expend the money toward their stated aims in perpetuity."

Will shook his head. "No. Things change too quickly. Even if there's a charity, or several charities, that we like today, they may completely change in a few years. No, we need a way to ensure that the money that survives us—" he paused, gulping "—continues to work in ways we'd find satisfying."

Hope nodded. "We figured we'd set up a trust, as you're suggesting, and give the Trustee the ability to spend the money over time in line with our beliefs, just as we would have done if we'd still been alive. We'd write everything down, of course, explain how to decide if an opportunity matches the goals we have."

"That's a rather large amount of responsibility, especially given the amount of money in question," Howe noted, stroking his chin. "Perhaps you should look to appoint a team of people to provide assistance to the Trustee, or even a team of Trustees?"

Hope sensed that Will was about to disagree, and used Energy to silence him. *Forgive me*, she thought. *But this is critical.* "That makes sense, Mr. Howe. In fact..." She drummed her fingers on the desk. "The approach used to store copies of the documents? Why not do the same thing for our team? Three people. One would be a member of the family or our designated appointee, who would handle the primary bits of decision making. That person would be our Trustee. One, frankly, should be *you*, or the person you designate to work this case. You'll know us very well by the time it might actually matter, and can ensure that everything happens as we'd like."

Howe paled. "I.... fear that may look suspicious. If I'm crafting the documents, and the documents say that I'll have control over the money..."

"You won't have final say on anything," Hope said. "You could just act as an advisor to the Trustee, who would make the final decisions. In practice, might you help a lot? Yes. Officially, will you have control? No." She looked thoughtful. "But you raise a good point. What if there's suspicion that the Trustee or you—sorry, the advisor—is having a... problem?"

"Problem?" He caught on quickly. "Like... an attempt at extortion?"

"Exactly," Hope said. "If there's an effective extortion attempt, there needs to be a way to shut everything down. That would have to be someone else, a third person, who could stop it.

Nobody would know who that person was, other than the Trustee and you—sorry, the advisor. That third person would be a… a… hidden advisor."

"Who would that be?"

"You mentioned concerns about suspicions raised about you having too much control over the process already, Mr. Howe," Hope said. "Let's just say that this secret person will reveal themselves to the Trustee in a manner that eliminates all doubt about our wish to have them participate."

Will looked puzzled at this, but Howe nodded, thoughtful. "Very intriguing idea. We'll have to work through it in more detail."

They spent the next several hours wrangling over the details and language, covering a variety of topics, including the approach Howe would use to retrieve the hidden copy of the will for verification. With promises to meet again in two weeks, the Starks left the office. Hope called Eva to let her know they were on their way, and soon afterwards they were waiting for the great concrete gate to lower into the ground and allow them entry to the neighborhood.

Eva looked tired and haggard, and it was clear that Smokey had been having a great deal of fun in their absence. Hope stared at the overturned plants, the chairs lying on their sides, and the muddy paw prints throughout the house.

Hope scowled at the dog, and then glanced at the clock and at Will. "Don't you have a meeting with Michael Baker?"

Will, who'd started scooping excess potting soil back into overturned planters, looked up. "You're right. But the house is a mess…"

Hope waved him off. "I'll take care of it. The maid is coming tomorrow anyway. Go meet with Michael Baker, and have a good time."

Will looked doubtful, but finally left for the garage. He climbed into the modest sedan featuring the same bullet-proof glass and armored sides as his limousine, and drove off. He enjoyed the occasional excursion without a heavy security presence.

Hope grinned as he pulled away. She turned back and laughed at Smokey, who stood panting, wagging her tail, as if expecting a reward for her hard work.

Instead, Hope suddenly collapsed to the ground and burst

into tears. No amount of comforting by a shocked Eva or Josh, or wet doggy kisses, could console her. She cried until the tears were exhausted. Hope then wiped her eyes dry, stood up, and looked around.

"Well, let's get started on this mess."

Eva and Josh looked at each other. Neither understood what they'd just witnessed.

While they cleaned, Will made his way to the meeting with Michael Baker. The Pleasanton Athletic Complex had been completed years earlier, not long after Will had purchased the land that would become the De Gray Estates. The complex featured a large building capable of handling a half dozen basketball games or volleyball matches simultaneously, along with outdoor tennis courts, a swimming pool, a driving range, and four baseball diamonds. Will and Hope donated funds to handle all of the operating expenses for the facility, and also covered the costs for officials, supplies, and uniforms. It wasn't cheap, but it was an expense they barely noticed, and one which provided a great deal of happiness to the residents of Pleasanton.

Especially the children.

Will parked the car, stopped the engine, and climbed out. He'd made the journey without noticing the presence of the invisible man who'd ridden along with him.

Adam exited the car as well, following Will. The Trust was partially formed. The Trustee would be the man Will was about to meet. Adam needed to make sure that Michael Baker knew something that no one else did.

Baker was directing a collection of four-year-old boys, including his son, in a series of drills on one of the baseball diamonds. He saw Will and walked over, and the two men shook hands. He glanced at the youngsters with a wry grin. "They aren't putting pressure on any major leaguers just yet, but they're having fun."

Will laughed. "That's the important part, right?"

"Exactly." They watched as one of the boys tried repeatedly to pick up a ground ball with his glove, finding the mitt empty each time he looked inside. Baker chuckled, and then nodded at the man who moved to show the youngster the proper technique. "John there is going to take over as head coach of team six. Jason was transferred out of town, as you know, so we're happy to have someone willing to handle the vacancy."

"Volunteers are difficult to find," Will agreed. "So, how are the finances?"

"So far, so good. We only had to replace one base and one tee from last year, so our equipment budget is in good shape."

"Good," Will said.

Now, Adam thought. He nudged his way into Will's mind, and directed the conversation from there.

"Michael, do you ever think about what the next great technological breakthroughs might be?"

The police officer frowned. "Excuse me?"

"Technology made all of that—" Will waved in the direction of downtown Pleasanton "—possible. But what's the *next* great innovation?"

"Wouldn't you be the one to know that? Not to sound rude, Will, but what does this have to do with baseball?"

"I'm researching things, privately, that would make your head spin, Michael." Will paused, grimacing. "Things that would change the social order in this world on a degree not seen since... well, ever. And I've heard of people who want to stop me from doing that. They're far too comfortable with the status quo to allow me to succeed."

Michael frowned. "Will, you seem a little... off. Are you feeling okay?"

"They want to silence me, Michael. But these changes? They're important, they need to happen, and I won't let them stop me. These changes are what I want to see, what I dedicate my life to achieving. *Exsisto change vos volo obvius universitas.* Do you know what that means?"

"It sounds like Spanish."

"It's Latin, actually. It means *be the change you want in the world.* Don't be afraid to do something difficult, Michael. The greatest challenges we face help us to influence events around us, and in doing that, we make the world a better place through our efforts. Don't let fear of what others think, or what others might do, deter you. Don't forget that phrase. Ever."

Baker's face did little to hide his confusion. "O...kay, Will. I'll remember. But... can we talk about baseball now?"

Adam removed the mental lock on Will, who seemed instantly back in control. "Absolutely, Michael. So, the real reason I called you out here today is that I was thinking of hiring a pitching coach for the older kids. What do you think about that?"

Adam, still invisible to the two men, walked away.

Everything was on schedule and on plan. It was time to move on to the next phase of their operation.

XV
Test

2028 A.D.

"Do you really think this is wise?"

Will sat behind the wheel of the jet black, antique, 1995 convertible sports car, revving the engine, his face lit up like a child's on Christmas morning. He looked at Hope as the engine purred and rattled the ground around them, and offered her a weak smile. "I'll leave the top up so no one sees me. I swear."

Hope rolled her eyes. "Why can't you just admit you want to drive the car?"

"It's not fair to send other people to do my work for me," Will replied with mock innocence. "I should handle these things myself. Besides, we really don't want anyone seeing the car with Millard."

Hope shivered internally. His words were a near match to those he'd offered in explaining his decision to face the Hunters in 1994, the encounter that most believed ended with him dead. He was extremely consistent in his philosophy in that regard. "Well, if you put it that way," she said slowly, "then I guess I should move out of the way and let you go. But please, be careful. I don't want Lance coming back to tell me you drove the car off a bridge or something."

Will winced, sucking in his breath, and Hope, eyes wide,

stammered out an apology. "I'm so sorry, Will, I…"

"No, no, it's okay," Will replied, his face flushed and his eyes wide. "It's just… I don't really want to think about… that."

Hope nodded. The car crash had been the formative event of his young life, a day he remembered with absolute clarity even ten centuries later. Today, it was the realization that he'd been so near death that affected him. But after living so many centuries, what stayed with him was a powerful sensation that *someone* was watching over him, protecting him, ensuring that he lived when physics stated he should have joined his parents in being zipped into a body bag that day. He'd asked her during his visit to the bunker several years earlier if she'd been there, having deduced that the presence he'd felt so many years earlier had been that of his wife.

Will revved the engine once more and smiled again, though with less enthusiasm than before. Hope returned his smile, gave him a kiss on the cheek, and stepped aside. Will moved slowly down the driveway toward the entrance to the De Gray Estates, and from there he'd meet up with his security team convoy. The convertible, filled with the supplies Millard Howe would need to carry out the terms of their will, would be the means of conveyance for the lawyer to reach the site of the "secure data center" where the documents were stored without risk of alteration. Will didn't know that "secure data center" was a euphemism for a little used Alliance safe house, a site that would be used only as transfer point for the location of the actual document handover.

Hope headed back into the house. She'd been unusually tired lately, and wondered if the mental fatigue of masking her son's massive ability had something to do with it. Josh had more than enough power to break through her defenses even now, and that power grew by the day. Yet he never tried to do so. Even at the age of four, Hope was communicating with him telepathically, behind the outward veil of silence that shut him out from his father and the rest of the world. She used those conversations to impress upon him his uniqueness and the responsibility that came with such power. He needed to practice keeping himself under control. He did well, but she reminded herself that Josh, despite his intelligence, was still a young child, not yet at an age where self-control and self-discipline were well-developed and practiced. It would take only slight lapses in her concentration, or his, to cause trouble. Will had been surprised one day to find that a massive tree had fallen in the woods behind their home. He suspected that the trunk had rotted away, and was thankful nobody had been hurt as the tree fell to the ground. In reality, Josh had watched Smokey's comical, futile efforts to catch a rabbit, and as Hope momentarily startled at the dog's frantic barking, she dropped the Shield. When Josh laughed heartily at the scene, the release of Energy toppled the centuries-old tree.

They used it as a teaching moment, an example of what Josh could do if he lost control. She was frightened to think of what her son might do, without any malicious intent, if he lost control when got older and his power was more developed. That fear scared her to tears on a regular basis, immobilizing her with panic.

Whatever the cause of her fatigue, she had work to do. With the telepathic bond she held with her son, Hope could travel freely about her house, and she carried the equivalent of a baby monitor app on her phone to allow her to keep a remote "eye" on Josh if she needed to visit her Alliance neighbors. She'd swing by to visit Judith and Peter in a bit for the first tests of the newly installed cloning machine. Timing during that day, drawing ominously close, was critical. They needed to know without question the minimum amount of time required to create clones from living people.

Hope had her role to play in testing that process today.

She donned a running outfit, brushed out her golden blond hair, and wrapped it in a ponytail before heading downstairs. She watched Josh for a moment, marveling as the boy coordinated obstacles for Smokey to traverse in search of a prized tennis ball. Her joy was muted because Young Will could see nothing of this. His memories made clear that Josh had made no sound and showed no signs—in Will's presence—of connecting to anyone before Will left for his journey through time. He'd be ecstatic to see Josh like this, though, running around, laughing, and chasing the barking dog through the house. But it wasn't meant to be.

She took a deep breath, a wave of guilt and fatigue sweeping over her, but she managed to quell the strong urge to break down in tears once more. It was the fatigue of protecting her son, she reasoned. That was one of the many reasons she dropped the Shield on Josh when Will left each day; any break from the strain of Shielding her powerhouse child was a welcomed relief.

She planted a kiss atop Josh's sandy brown head, exited the

house, made certain the door was securely closed, and trotted down the driveway. She focused on inhaling the fresh air, feeling the gravel crunch beneath her feet, enjoying the light breeze that scattered her hair behind her. By the time she reached the front of the neighborhood, a glistening sheen of sweat covered her.

Hope walked to the door leading into the guard station and knocked. As soon as she saw the door handle turn, she started to dance awkwardly on her feet.

The door opened, and the on-duty guard stood there, staring at her. "Mrs. Stark? Is there… something I can do for you?"

He was young, only twenty or twenty-one, she remembered. He'd moved here only a year or two ago, and they'd hired him to be part of their security crew. His work ethic was exemplary, and Will had taken a strong liking to him. Hope had held periodic conversations with him as well, and agreed with Will's assessment that Mark Arnold was an exceptional young man.

She tried not to think about the manner in which he'd die in less than two years' time.

"Could I get the key to the bathroom?" She accelerated the urgency of the dance to match her rapidly delivered plea.

Mark nodded, and after disappearing into the guard station, he returned with the key.

She jabbed her hand at the key, in an apparent desperate need to reach the locked facility, and in her haste to take it from him jabbed the key forward in a slashing motion. The point dug into his skin, and a small crimson trickle flowed from the wound. Mark cursed, dropped the key, and seized his wrist with his uninjured hand before holding the wound to his mouth.

"I am *so* sorry!" Hope gasped. She bent to seize the key. "I'll be very quick and then help you stitch that up."

"Ish naw big dil," Mark said, slurring the words over his bloodied hand. He pulled his hand away from his mouth and repeated, more clearly, "It's no big deal."

Hope nodded briskly and darted out of the station to the free standing restroom. It had been built primarily for the guards, but separate from their stations to remind those on duty that even calls of nature required them to ensure proper backup. It also provided residents a place to refresh themselves if they opted to tour the community on foot. As most of the residents were—to Mark's eyes, anyway—quite elderly, the outdoor facility got little use from those paying for its upkeep.

Hope unlocked the door, went inside, and locked herself in.

She took a deep breath, hoping it had been enough.

The small pouch attached at her waist carried supplies one might expect for one out for a lengthy jog: a spare pair of socks, a bottle of water, and packets of a powder she could mix with the water to help replace nutrients lost during her workout. It was the contents in the secret compartment of the pouch she needed now, though.

The materials were straight from a crime scene investigators kit, and within moments Hope had removed the faint traces of Mark's skin and blood from the point of the key. She'd sent a tiny blast of Energy at the key before reaching for it, ensuring that there were no other skin cells lining the device, and she'd "caught" the key with a small Energy field before it hit the ground. She hoped it was enough to ensure a pure sample. The small vial, now holding Mark's tissue sample, was returned to her pouch, stopper firmly in place, before Hope washed her hands and walked back to the station door to return the key.

Mark opened the door, flexing the injured hand. He gave a weak smile and held out his uninjured hand. Hope dropped the key into his palm, but pushed her way into the station before he could shut the door.

"Where's the first aid kit?"

"Really, Mrs. Stark, I'm fine. There's no need to—"

"We're not taking chances, Mark, and that gash is my fault. Where's the first aid kit?"

With a sigh, he pointed. Hope retrieved the kit, pulled out the supplies she needed, and motioned him into a chair. "Sit."

He saluted with his uninjured hand. "Yes, ma'am. People don't tell you no often, do they, Mrs. Stark?"

"You got that from my husband, didn't you?"

He smiled. "Possibly."

Mark hissed as she flushed out the wound, and then watched with obvious admiration as she expertly affixed the large bandage with medical tape. Mark flexed his hand experimentally and nodded. "Very professional. Thank you."

"I have some experience in helping injured people," Hope

told him. And she did. Centuries of experience, in fact.

"Ah, yes, with your charitable work," Mark said, nodding. "That makes sense."

Hope noticed the picture of the young woman on his desk. She had shoulder-length hair, jet black, and dazzling green eyes highlighting a face that seemed capable of lighting up a room. "Friend of yours?" Hope asked, nodding at the picture.

"My girlfriend," Mark said, and the grin that formed on his face was that of a young man very much in love. "Gena and I have been together for about six months now."

"She's beautiful," Hope said. She frowned at the picture. "She looks very familiar, but I can't place her."

"Her mother owned a catering business for years before her health deteriorated. She worked at your wedding, and Gena helped. She thought you were a princess out of a storybook."

Hope smiled as the memory of the event returned. "I remember her now. You've chosen well, Mark." After a moment, she frowned again. "Is her mother ill? You mentioned deteriorating health."

"Dead, unfortunately," Mark said, and his expression clouded. "It was very traumatic for her. Gena never knew her birth parents, and had the great fortune to be placed with the Adamses. It was a horrible experience, losing her mother like that."

"What happened to her father?"

"Cancer. They say some of the new treatments coming out now probably would have saved him."

Hope patted his arm. "I'm so sorry. Give Gena my best."

"I will, Mrs. Stark, and thank you."

Hope stood. "I should probably get back to my jog before I accidentally stab you again."

Mark laughed. "It would take a bigger blade than that key to scare me."

Hope left the station, pulling the door shut behind her, and set off at a jog toward Peter and Judith's home. Once she was out of sight of the guard tower, she increased her pace to a sprint, moving at a speed that was impossible for humans. In mere seconds, she'd reached Judith's home, just as the owner opened the door.

Judith had aged well in her human guise, but still looked like a woman in her seventies. "Come in, Hope."

Hope moved by in a blur before slowing to a stop inside and taking a deep breath. Judith shut the door behind her, and then took the time to change her appearance from the elderly matron the human world knew, to the ageless early-thirties appearance that Hope had known for centuries.

As Judith completed the transformation, Hope finished catching her breath, then dug into her pouch to produce the vial. "I got the sample. Is the machine ready?"

Judith nodded, and led the way to the basement. "Aaron stopped by yesterday. He and Peter upgraded the power in the house so that the machine can operate at maximum capacity. They're hoping we're at six hours now."

Hope grimaced. "That's better than before, but we need to get under four hours. There's too much uncertainty in the timeline to trust a six hour cloning cycle."

Judith nodded. "I know. But you know those two; they'll tinker with that machine as long as they can, and they'll get it to work. And Archie will help as well. And then they'll need to test it all again once the second machine is installed."

They reached the bottom of the steps of the finished lower level, and Judith led the way toward a floor-to-ceiling painting of her and Peter. The faces of the couple in the painting could only be described as smug. "I hate that painting," Judith muttered, glaring at her elderly image. She glanced at Hope. "Phase out."

Both women used Energy to turn their bodies permeable, and in that phased-out state they walked through the wall supporting the painting. Hope found herself in a small room with nothing but a stairwell. The women phase back to corporeality and descended the stairs. "We liked the bunker idea, so Peter insisted that we build the cloning machine inside our *own* secret lair." She chuckled. "The man's three centuries old and is playing the part of a mad scientist. Do you suppose he'll grow up one day?"

"Not a chance," Hope replied, and the women laughed.

A horizontal platform roughly four feet off the ground was covered by a sealed glass top pumped full of highly oxygenated air, providing the growing clone with an optimal environment for development. The computer system responsible for turning raw cellular material into a fully functioning clone of a living human being was housed beneath the platform. Testing showed that clones had an expected lifespan of between a half million and a million heartbeats, a matter of days, before their hearts and vital organs would shut down. Until that time, they had the same cognitive and physical abilities, and the same memories, as their sources. Clones could safely be released into the public within that short window of time without concern of exposure; they just needed to be retrieved before they ran the risk of dropping dead in public.

On January 7th, 2030, they would collect tissue samples from the two on-duty guards after Will Stark and Myra VanderPoole left for the day. They needed the clones' memories to be as current as possible, but couldn't risk being seen abducting the men off the street or out of their homes over the weekend. Each guard would receive a high speed education about the Aliomenti, the Alliance, and the fact that they'd be brutally murdered within hours. They would be told that their murders were an act the Alliance would not prevent, as it would disrupt history in an unpredictable manner, possibly resulting in the deaths of millions, including the men and their loved ones. Each man would be given the option of having a clone sent back to face the Assassin's wrath, an option they fully expected both men to accept. If they declined the cloning offer, their memories of the encounter, and knowledge of what was to come, would be erased.

Given the lack of time available that day to perform cloning efforts, they'd elected to clone only the two guards. After the nature of Will's escape, the Hunters would suspect an Alliance trap and leave town quickly to regroup, unlikely to stay in Pleasanton long enough to execute family members and loved ones of the two guards in an effort to close any possible loose ends. The greatest risk to the success of the plan was that they'd be unable to clone the guards in time to get them back in their places before the Hunters and Assassin arrived.

Today's cloning test would illustrate how far they needed to progress in the next fourteen months. Four hours, from insertion of genetic material to completion of the clone, would provide them the flexibility they needed to execute the plan. Each additional minute or hour put the plan at risk.

Peter lifted his head up, and he grinned as Hope walked in. "Welcome to my secret mad scientist lair, Mrs. Stark," he said, offering a maniacal laugh to complete the greeting. Peter looked the part of the mad scientist. His face was covered with smudges of grease, and his hair was frizzed as if he'd had a losing encounter with an electrical outlet. "Have you brought your offering to sacrifice on the altar of science?"

Hope rolled her eyes, but couldn't help laughing. "I have."

Peter rubbed his hands together with glee and walked over to her, and as he approached his demeanor turned serious. "What steps did you take to ensure the sample is free of impurities and other human DNA?"

"I blasted the, ah, extraction tool with Energy to clear it of any contamination immediately before impact. I also used Energy to prevent touching the tool until I was able to collect the sample and put it into the vial."

Peter nodded in appreciation. "That should be sufficient. I'll run a DNA check first, though, just to be certain." He deposited the entire vial into a slot in the cloning machine. "It's wonderful that they've been able to engineer vials out of those nanoparticles, like they did with the nanoparticle plates and such back in the Cavern years ago. The transport device—the vial—dissolves and we're left with nothing but the full sample." He tapped several buttons, read the readouts that appeared over the next few minutes, and then nodded. "Good. There's a single unique DNA strand here, which means we can proceed."

He moved to a second set of controls, and his face morphed into one of absolute concentration as he activated the cloning machine with the parameters needed to create a full clone. He scowled at the readouts. "It's still estimating just over five hours until completion." He sighed and shook his head. "I'll have to touch base with Archie and Aaron to see what else we can do to reduce the time. That's still too long."

Judith patted him on the arm. "You still have time, you know."

"Not really," Peter admitted. "We have just over a year to go." He grimaced. "Do you ever think about what life will be like when we *aren't* focused on this? What will life be like after January 7th, 2030?"

Hope scowled. "Well, in my case, I'll be a widow with a son and a baby girl on the way, forced to move far away from home with a new identity." She trembled, fighting back the tears that strained to explode from her eyes, but even with her effort a fine mist began to cover her cheeks.

Judith gave her a hug. "He didn't really mean it that way, Hope. None of us will abandon you. That's the advantage of our human personas nearing the end of their natural lives; we can all 'die' and do something new, which in my case will be focusing on you and the children." She smiled. "It will be wonderful to watch them grow up."

Hope wiped her cheeks dry with her sleeve. "Thanks, Judith. I know I won't be abandoned; we're a big family now, right? But it's tough to think that that day will be the last time I know I'll see Will." Her eyes widened as she spoke the words, and then she dissolved into tears.

Judith held her for several moments, and Peter watched, shifting his weight uncomfortably, before he walked over and patted Hope on the head. "Don't worry, Hope. I'm sure that the old Will is out there somewhere. You'll see *him* at some point, right?"

Hope looked up, and again wiped away the tears on her face. "You believe that, Peter?"

Peter nodded. "There's no chance those nimrods actually killed Will Stark. He's out there, like some guardian angel, watching out for all of us, but mostly for you and for Josh. You may not see him, but he'll be there when you need him."

Hope's eyes brightened as they hadn't in ages. She reached up and grasped Peter's hand, squeezing. "Thank you." And then she leaned over and kissed him on the cheek.

Peter blinked. "What did I say?"

Judith laughed. "You're right, Hope. He'll *never* grow up." She motioned with her hand. "Shall we head upstairs while we wait for the results?"

They teleported to the living room directly above, and Hope left for a few moments to take an Energy "shower," blasting away the perspiration from her body and clothing. When she finished, there was no way to tell she'd just been out for a two mile jog and sprint. She joined Judith and Peter on the sofa, and Peter offered her a glass of lemonade.

"How is the estate plan coming along?" Judith asked, sipping on her own drink.

"We finally signed it last week," Hope replied, enjoying a sip of the sweet beverage. "It's a rather intricate document, because we had to provide a mechanism that will allow Adam to appear anonymously. He'll be able to do that, in a role we defined, and get the account numbers for all of our money so he can steal it and give it back to us in our apparent afterlife." She giggled at the statement, surprising herself. "See, we have to make it look like all the money was stolen, or the Aliomenti will think any person or group we specifically gave it to will be Alliance and they'll hunt them down. And if we just leave the money, they'll probably use their banking connections to take the money for their own purposes, which is the last thing we want. We made a map for the lawyer to the safe house property you bought, and Will bought him a car to drive there because…"

"Blah, blah, blah," Peter said with a sigh. "Nobody likes hearing complicated stuff like that."

Hope chuckled. "Sorry about that. Although I must say that Adam did a fine job manipulating young Will into providing the Alliance motto to our identified human Trustee. In Latin, no less. Now Adam can recite that phrase so the human man recognizes Adam as someone we trust. That was a rather clever move on Adam's part."

Peter looked intrigued, opened his mouth to ask a question, and then threw up his hands. "No, no, I don't want to know about all of that. I'll leave it to Adam."

The alarm in Hope's running pouch beeped. "Will's at the entrance gate," she told her hosts and she stood. "Let me know how it goes with the cloning. At the moment, though, I have to go repress my son's childhood to prevent his father from hearing the child speak." She gave a fake smile, and then vanished from their sight.

Josh glanced up as Hope appeared in the living room of the house, a baseball in his hand. "Hi, Mommy! Smokey won't catch the ball in her mouth." He frowned, and tossed the ball in the air, watching as his beloved furry friend skittered out of the way, letting the ball bounce twice before she snatched it out of the air.

"She'd lose her teeth if she tried to catch it, sweetie. The ball is very hard. Roll it for her, or bounce it, and she'll have much more fun."

Josh considered this, and then nodded. "Okay."

Hope sat on the sofa, picked up a children's picture book, and patted her lap. "It's story time. And… Daddy's coming home."

Josh's face clouded. "I don't like doing this. Do we have to do this? Why can't we just let Daddy hear me talk?"

Hope sighed. "We need to help Daddy prepare for what he needs to do, and the greatest motivation he'll have, for a very long time, is hearing your voice. I don't like it either, sweetie. But sometimes, we have to do our part, no matter how painful it is, or how sad it makes us."

Josh's look told her that it was difficult for a young child to understand the concepts of duty and personal sacrifice. But he handed Hope the slobbery baseball, climbed into her lap, and leaned back against her. "Can you tell me the stories about Daddy again? I like those stories."

Hope smiled. "Of course I will, sweetie." The Energy shield surrounded her son and condensed inside him, and she watched as her son's ice blue eyes, so full of fire and Energy, faded into dullness. She took a deep breath to hold back the tears, opened the story book, but said nothing aloud until she heard the front door open.

Until then, she met her son's request. She told him of Will's heroism in saving her from all the people who tried to hurt her over the years, showed him her memories of his protectiveness in ensuring those people didn't know she still existed, his willingness to sacrifice everything to protect the people he loved. *And none of those people were his son, Josh. Imagine the sacrifices he'd be willing to make for you. He loves you more than anything.*

I know, Mommy. I can hear it in his thoughts. I wish I could tell him the same thing.

I'll tell him for you.

When the door opened, Hope automatically began reading the children's book in front of her, the story of a small blue train climbing a hill. Will walked in and saw her there, and smiled as he recognized the story she read aloud. "I love that story," he said.

Hope smiled, rolling the baseball along the floor for Smokey. The dog retrieved the ball and dropped it in Josh's lap, thumping her tail expectantly. Will's face twitched, and he watched, hoping his beloved son would pick up the ball, would notice the furry friend waiting near him.

But Josh didn't move.

"I love this story, too," Hope replied. "One day, Will, our son will climb his own hill. And it won't be a hill. It will be a mountain.

And he'll climb it to honor the father he loves."

Will sighed, forcing a brave smile. "I hope I'm there to see it."

Hope smiled. "You will be. Trust me."

XVI
Farewell

January 4, 2030

"Three more days," Hope said, smiling. "How does it feel to be an old man?"

Will rolled his eyes. "I'm not thirty-five *yet,* young lady. And just because I've got a few years on you doesn't make me old."

"Age is but a number," Hope intoned. "It's how old you *feel* that matters, right?"

"Indeed it is," Will agreed. "And if you want to feel young, marry someone much younger than you. I highly recommend doing so if you get the chance."

Hope nodded, stifling a strong urge to laugh. "I'll keep that in mind." She paused for a moment. "Seriously, though, what do you want for your birthday? You haven't told me."

Will sighed. "It's pretty stupid, actually."

"Not *telling* me is pretty stupid. I can't get you what you want if I don't know what it is. I'm not a mind reader, you know." Hope could only imagine the laughter this conversation would generate for an audience of her Alliance friends. She, of course, knew *exactly* what he wanted, and knew that giving him exactly that would play into the plans they'd made for that fateful day on Monday.

"The truth is... I'd like to be normal, for just one day," Will

186

said, his tone almost apologetic. "I don't want a driver, or a group of bodyguards following me everywhere. I want to drive myself to work, sit at a desk, and just do work. And then I want to come home to my wife and son and go out to a nice dinner with them. Nothing like that is possible now. And I don't like it." He sighed. "It's like I've forgotten who I am. I just want to be the real me for one day."

Hope had known about his fear of losing his true identity to that of the business tycoon the world knew for some time. And she knew how desperately he longed for greater simplicity in his life.

It wasn't just the demands on his time. Will had developed a reputation for spontaneously funding new businesses, and his unprecedented record of success in doing so had accelerated his wealth accumulation. He couldn't spend, invest, or give money away faster than it came in. Such success didn't go unnoticed, and many were willing to threaten Will directly to get that lucky charm of a Stark investment into their own lives and businesses. While the frustration of another avenue of threats upon his life weighed upon him, the true pressure he felt was the pressure he put upon himself. Each publicized success seemed to spur the economy forward just a bit more, and now, with the country officially out of both depression and recession, Will had no interest in making a mistake that would destroy the psychology of confidence in the country. Some might view that as arrogance. For Will, though, the amount of influence he possessed in national and international economic matters was a burden and a curse, one he'd happily transfer to anyone else with the proper ability and motivation.

Will didn't see himself as an influential global leader. In many ways, he was still the boy who wanted nothing more than to be accepted by, and loved by, his parents, a child who wanted to fit in more than stand out. Fate had a different role in mind for him, one that pushed him into a spotlight he hated, but one he accepted as his duty.

For a man like that, anything simulating normalcy was a gift of inestimable value.

"I understand what you mean, but you've forgotten nothing. The world is a better place for you being in it, and the enthusiasm it shows for what you say and do… I think of it as positive feedback for someone who's earned and deserves it. Don't be afraid of who you are, Will, and don't be afraid to do what's right." She grinned.

"And on your birthday, what's right is whatever you decide you want to do."

He smiled. "Then let's be normal people on Monday. We'll finish the day as a family going out to dinner at a nice restaurant." He looked wistfully over to where Josh sat, emotionless as ever in his father's presence. "And maybe… maybe he'll talk to me. That's the greatest birthday present possible."

Hope smiled. She'd taken the pregnancy test yesterday, confirming what she'd known for the past few days. Will had another wonderful gift waiting for him, but it was one that he'd not learn about until their adult daughter revealed her identity nearly two centuries into the future. Will's focus was on the present, though. "Maybe he will," she replied. "Where do you want to go for dinner?" Her eyes twinkled. "I think I know this answer, even without being able to read your mind."

He smiled. "You know me too well. But yes, I would definitely like a steak dinner."

"I'll call and make reservations, then. I assume you'll tell Lance to take the day off on Monday, then?"

Will nodded. "And I'll have to put up with hours of his stories about what horrors await and what tragedy will destroy me without his constant attention." He shrugged. "I can take care of myself."

Not yet, Hope thought. "He cares about you, Will. But tell him. And don't forget, *you're* the boss, not Lance. If he doesn't like it, fire him."

"Maybe I'll take the gun with me," Will muttered. "He'll know I'm serious then, won't he?"

"I think it's probably best that you not go around showing off your illegal weapon, or the incredible accuracy you possess for someone who's never legally *fired* that weapon."

"I'll take that counsel under advisement," Will replied, chuckling. He paused, as if remembering something. "Do you have the vouchers?"

She nodded, and retrieved an envelope on her desk. "I'm really happy for the two of them. It's nice to help out such a young couple just as they're starting their lives together, isn't it?"

"You do realize that she's older than you were when we got married, right?"

"Really? There's someone in the world who married at a more advanced age than me? I haven't heard that in... well, not in the last day or two."

Will laughed and accepted the envelope. "And on that note, I'm off to make Mark's day and ruin Lance's. I'll see you later." He gave her a quick kiss, and then headed out the front door, where the armor-plated limousine with bulletproof glass and security contingent waited for him.

Hope waited until the vehicle rounded the bend, and then teleported to the bunker, where she typically did her work related to the Project 2030 efforts. She initiated a video call using the secured Alliance communication channels on her tablet computer.

Adam, in his Cain Freeman disguise, sat in his data center office located in downtown Pleasanton, and nodded as he accepted her call. "Morning, Hope. I've gotten approval for my two weeks of vacation. They were only waiting to make sure the project we completed before the end of the year didn't have any unexpected problems, and it didn't." He paused, noticing her look. "Something's bothering you, isn't it?"

"Outside the fact that I have only three days left with my husband?" She sighed, and then choked back a sob, drawing a raised eyebrow from Adam. "Yes, something else *is* bothering me. Will came home from work yesterday quite excited. That young couple I've mentioned? It seems they got engaged on New Year's Eve. It was very romantic, I'm sure." She paused. "I don't know, Adam. That just... something about the timing bothers me. He's one of the guards who will have an unpleasant encounter with the Assassin."

Adam blinked several times, and Hope felt sorry for him. He'd spent decades worrying about everything that needed to be done to ensure Will survived the attack on Monday without alerting the Aliomenti to an actual Alliance presence. Their information from the future—through the diary, through Will's memories—said nothing about a newsworthy event like an engagement involving one of the expected victims of the attack.

Adam finally spoke. "You think this changes the plan for Monday, then? That the news of the engagement is something that the Hunters will uncover, and that it will change their plans before or after they... visit?"

She nodded at the screen. "Possibly. Yes. I'm having these

visions of things going very poorly for the newly engaged young woman on Monday. But it's more than just a plan being altered, Adam. I'm really fond of that girl. And all of this has me worried that we made a mistake in choosing not to clone her or the MacLeans, even though, with the information we had until now, it made complete sense." She paused. "*Have* we made a mistake, Adam?"

Adam wondered if they'd made a mistake as well. Gena was engaged to a man set to die a brutal death in mere days. Might that change in relationship status mean the Hunters would be more likely to target her for elimination? It would certainly be their style... they frowned upon committed relationships. And he, like Hope, suddenly had a premonition of Gena coming face-to-face with the Assassin or one of the Hunters, and not living to tell the tale.

He needed to maintain his cool, both to avoid suspicion as to his motives in protecting Gena, and as the man coordinating their efforts for Monday. When he spoke again, he ensured he did so in a confident tone. "I'll follow her for the next day or so, and see if anything looks suspicious. The Hunters should be here no later than tomorrow, prepping for the attack. I'll walk around as Cain because the Hunters... sort of know my real face."

Hope nodded. Adam's father, also called Adam, was a founding member of the Aliomenti like Will, and his betrayal of the Elites on behalf of the Alliance had only been discovered and confirmed as the man lay dying ninety years earlier. If the Hunters saw Adam, a man known to be dead, they'd be extremely suspicious. "That's a good idea," she replied. "Nothing's changed with Deron's family; still married, still one young child. I don't have that same sense of foreboding. But... if you find anything, we have to move quickly to protect the families."

"I'll watch her, Hope. I promise."

"Thanks, Adam."

"Any updates on the timing?"

"I talked to Archie yesterday. They found a way to bypass a step that's supposed to cut about twenty percent off the total time for the cloning. Said he can't believe they didn't find it before. So... that should put us at around three hours, forty-five minutes now."

Adam whistled. "They got under the four hour barrier? Nice. Is Graham ready?"

"Yes. He knows Myra needs to get out of the neighborhood

as early as possible Monday morning to give *us* as much time as possible to replace the guards with their clones. Graham said he told her there's some construction on the way to one of her favorite shops, and they need to leave early to avoid it. I hope that story works."

"Got it. That's good. Based on the lighting in the memory videos, he should get her back to De Gray Estates around five o'clock."

"He knows, Adam. Michael's going to be hovering above everything and will be in constant contact with Graham to make sure Myra's back on time."

"Sorry, I'm just... really nervous. It's almost here."

"I'm well aware of that." Hope's expression turned icy. "Early Monday evening, I'll be staring down an Energy-wielding Assassin with blood-red eyes, while trying at the same time to hide the existence of my immensely powerful son."

"Right," Adam said, feeling awkward. Hope watched him glance away from the screen briefly, and then focus back on her with a look of deepest concern and sympathy. "Looks like Will's here, Hope. I should get going."

"Okay," Hope said. "Talk to you later."

She ended the connection, stunned at the thought that Adam had accidentally projected at her when they'd been discussing Mark and Gena. Was it possible? It couldn't be true, could it? She shook her head. It certainly explained a lot, though. But she had no time at present to decide what to do about his revelation; at the moment, it changed nothing about the next few days. She put the thought from her mind and went to check on Josh.

Adam sat in his office, feeling the cold air of the chillers inside the data center. The machines were meant to keep the high cost machinery in the room from overheating, but at the moment, he was certain he needed it more than the computers. Gena had gotten engaged. Hope had had some sort of vision, or premonition, that something bad was going to happen. She'd even suggested that they'd need to alter their plans, somehow clone the families of the guards. He took several steadying gulps of air. After everything he'd done to make sure Gena lived, would this one act seal her death, especially since he'd argued strongly against cloning significant others and family members due to their low perceived risk of suffering an attack?

He'd need to follow her. He had to make sure that she didn't somehow run into the Hunters, draw their attention, and make herself a target for their human cleanup efforts after the failed attack on the Stark house.

And he'd thought everything was going so well.

Once he'd finally managed to compose himself, Adam, as Cain, rose from his chair and moved out of his office inside the data center. They'd offered to warm his office, but he'd insisted that the room be kept at the same temperature as the outside floor space so that he could work on a machine at his desk if needed. The cacophonous blast of computers and fans, the thrum of the vast amounts of electricity required to power it all, the vigorous, fresh blast of cold air as he walked from the room, all jarred him back into his role as Cain Freeman.

He left the data center, letting the door close behind him with an audible click as the electronic lock system engaged. He was one of few people allowed physical access inside the room, where the company housed its most sensitive and confidential data. He chuckled. Millard Howe had no way of knowing that the data center he thought he'd be traveling to in a few weeks was actually located in Pleasanton itself.

Cain saw David Richardson, his former classmate and longtime work colleague, walking down the hallway. The man's freckles, which covered his youthful face, were scrunched together, reflecting the somber, pensive look David bore. David often walked around, seeing nothing, trying to resolve some complex production issue with the nanos. Like Cain, David had made a name for himself at Stark Enterprises. It was David who'd figured out how to get the nanoparticles to bind to each other in programmable patterns that had allowed them to build the Dome two years earlier. If David had something in mind, it was undoubtedly brilliant. Cain moved to the side of the hallway to ensure the freckle-faced man could pass.

David seemed to realize he was being watched and looked up, as if surprised anyone else was in the building. "Oh. Hey, Cain." He seemed to lose his train of thought for a moment before realizing more communication was necessary. "How... how are you?"

"I'm okay, I guess," Cain replied. "I just have a lot of things on my mind."

"Work related?"

"No. Just… worried about a friend. You? You look a bit… distracted."

"Yeah, I am," David said, exhaling a deep sigh. "Remember how I mentioned that my cousin was having some health issues? She's taken a turn for the worse. Her parents—my aunt and uncle— are having to take time off work to be with her, and it sounds like my uncle just lost his job. They've always been there for me, Cain, and I think I need to go there now to help them out."

"Will they be okay?" Cain asked, frowning in concern.

"I… I think so," David replied. "But I won't know for sure until I go check on them." He glanced up. "Anyway, I hope your friend's issues get resolved."

"I hope your cousin regains her health, and your uncle gets his job back," Cain replied, acknowledging David's concern with a nod. Cain offered his hand, the two men shook, and both continued on their way.

Cain walked through the maze of hallways and took an elevator to the seventh floor, where Will kept his day-to-day office. The penthouse suite was rarely used; Will felt uncomfortable with the ostentatious layout and furnishings, and so they reserved the penthouse for large corporate meetings. Cain heard loud voices inside Will's office as he approached the door, slightly ajar, and paused.

"…must strongly argue against the idea, Mr. Stark." The voice belonged to Lance Maynard, Will's chief of security. "While I appreciate the sentimentality, it is my job to keep you safe so that you can continue to have such foolish sentiments again tomorrow."

"I appreciate your concern for my well-being, Lance, but that's my final decision. One day. That's all."

"I do *not* want to hear that I'll have another day off on Tuesday because some crazed lunatics realized what you were doing and were successful in an abduction or assassination attempt, Mr. Stark."

"I'll leave word with my public relations team, Lance. Should anything of the sort happen, they're to make it clear in press releases that my actions Monday were against your advice and that you and your team were not on duty at the time of the mishap."

There was a pause. "You do realize that we'll continue this conversation on the way home this evening."

"It's why you're the best, Lance. You stubbornly refuse to listen to me."

A moment later, Lance Maynard squeezed himself through the door. He seemed startled to find Cain Freeman standing there, and glared at the smaller man. "Freeman. Perhaps you'll be able to talk sense into the man. I certainly haven't had any success on that front today." And he stormed off.

Cain watched him, puzzled. That was the appropriate reaction for one who didn't know that Will's "sentimentality" for Monday was essential to the history of the world. Then he shrugged, as Maynard disappeared from sight, and knocked on Will's door. "Come in, Cain," Will called.

Cain Freeman entered the main office of Will Stark. The founder of Stark Enterprises International, a man with a net worth estimated at a half trillion dollars, a man whose philanthropic budget dwarfed those of most nations, a man whose shrewd investments and advice over the past decade were viewed as singularly responsible for pulling his country from the abyss of an economic depression… that man sat with his shoeless feet propped up on his desk, lounging back in his chair, fingers laced behind his head, with his eyes closed.

Cain shut the door. "Sir… are you okay?"

Will's jade green eyes snapped open, and there seemed to be an unusual intensity to them. "Never better. Why do you ask?"

"I… well, Mr. Maynard seemed upset, and…"

"Lance? He's a worrywart, but that's his job, and he does his job well. I'd be far more worried if he *didn't* consider my idea to be one of sheer lunacy." He smiled. "I take it you've come to discuss the status of the system upgrade?"

"Yes, sir. The team performed sensational work. Flawless, in fact. A week in and we're seeing a tripling of performance, which is *better* than we'd projected. To say that I'm pleased would be a significant understatement."

"And to your area of expertise…?"

Cain chuckled. "Ironic I'm following Mr. Maynard in to talk with you, isn't it? We reran our data security and integrity tests, and the information is still as inaccessible as ever. Unless someone points a gun at me or you, they aren't getting anything without going through our formal processes."

"Don't let Lance hear you say that," Will muttered. "Storage concerns?"

"None. The new compression system reduced raw storage requirements, and we're now consuming storage at early 2028 levels. We have room to grow for a year or more without bringing in new equipment."

"At some point you're going to demand a raise from me, Mr. Freeman, and I'll be forced to comply."

Cain chuckled. "The stock option valuation and vesting schedule are quite generous, Mr. Stark, and I truly enjoy what I do. But I won't complain if you decide to increase your generosity on my behalf."

Will slipped his feet off the desk, donned his shoes, stood up, and walked over to Cain. "I'll talk to payroll next week. You're taking some time off, if I recall. I suspect everything should be processed by the time you return."

He held out his hand, and Cain shook it. "Thank you, sir."

"Go home, Cain, and get an early start on your vacation. Beat the traffic out of town. That's an order."

"Thank you, sir. Again."

Cain spun on his heel and walked out of Will's office. His departure, though ordered, was meant to hide the emotion on his face. Given that his boss had just commended him and offered to give him a raise without being asked, one might suspect Cain would be overjoyed, dancing out of the office for a well-earned vacation and the promise of greater compensation when he returned.

But Cain had to hide his face because he looked anything *but* happy. Instead, he was distraught.

What no one else in the office realized was that the handshake he'd just shared with Will, the conversation they'd held, would be the last contact he'd have with the man for nearly two centuries. The farewell he'd shared with Will, before he began his drive to the safe house in West Virginia to await Millard Howe's eventual arrival, felt like saying goodbye to a loved one with a terminal illness, waiting for death to finish its claim.

But in this case, Adam couldn't even grieve his impending loss.

There was work to be done. A young woman needed to be protected from potential supernatural harm. Two fully grown clones needed creating. And they needed to steel themselves with the discipline to avoid interfering while they watched their worst enemies unleash their wrath on a man they'd known for centuries, knowing he could do nothing to defend himself.

Starting Tuesday, he'd have one hundred eighty-nine years to grieve.

XVII
Choices

January 4, 2030

He floated over the gated community, invisible to human eye and electronic sensor alike, looking for his landing spot. The layout and terrain came back to him in an instant, though he'd last spent significant time here centuries ago. Upon locating his target spot, he drifted down to the ground, his feet settling gently onto the frozen earth. The invisible skeleton formed of quadrillions of subatomic, intelligent particles dissolved around him. His appearance would be unfamiliar to any who saw him, as would his Energy signal, for both had been modified decades earlier. Much of his disguise would be discarded this day, and to ensure he wasn't discovered prematurely, he'd settled down into a thick grove of trees.

Trees, of all sizes and shapes and leaf patterns, had been a key to his successes over the centuries. It was only fitting that he was among them today, the day when he would trigger everything that was to come, and everything that had already happened.

The man looked around. No one was nearby, which was to be expected. The residents of the community, many of whom were united by a bond far deeper than mere household proximity, were even now working to preserve the life of a friend.

His life.

And he was here to ensure that those preparations were necessary.

Since his presumed death at the hands of the Hunters, Will had found himself with plenty of time to think, to do research, to push the bounds of everything he'd ever tried before. He'd figured out how to "recode" his Energy so that it produced a different signal. Someone like Porthos could still sense Energy emanating from him—if he didn't Shield that Energy—but would be unable to tie that Energy to Will Stark. He could walk among them without recognition.

He'd taken the nanos he'd been given a thousand years earlier and had enhanced them, tinkering and tweaking everything about the devices until he could adjust their capabilities and programming as needed. The Alliance would one day acquire the ability to produce the nanos he'd once been gifted, once a man called the Mechanic, among others, joined the organization. Until that happened, and until Will could avail himself of those advances and production capabilities, he needed to develop the expertise on his own. His efforts over the past decades enabled him to produce more nanos, and those he produced were more powerful, with greater computing and problem solving capability, than those he'd owned for centuries. Those enhanced nanos served him well, both in maintaining his stealth existence and caring for those he loved.

He wasn't here to reminisce. His task, after centuries of contemplation, was clear. And so Will Stark went through the process of changing his Energy signal back to the one he'd called his own since the beginning.

Something had attracted the Hunters to Pleasanton on his thirty-fifth birthday, like insects homing in on a bright light. Something had triggered Porthos' enhanced senses, had led the Tracker and his cohorts to this city. Something had helped them realize that Young Will lived here and was married. They would reach the conclusion that, by rules of the Aliomenti—rules Will had never agreed to follow—Will Stark was due for a very long prison term. Something had forced them to summon the Assassin as well. The quartet would formulate a plan that would bring about a fire that would leave his younger self believing for months that Hope and Josh had died, a plan that would leave him beaten and close to death in his own back yard, a death he desperately wanted as a man believing he was, once more, all alone in the world.

The Hunters had not located Young Will through anything as simple as an Internet search. They'd never think to look for him in the human world, not even Porthos, a man who relished his forays into human haunts. There was only one possible trigger to the events. Porthos had told him the answer, had said that the Energy burst he'd detected was unequivocally Will's, that the burst was too powerful to belong to anyone else. In one of the more morbid conversations the Project 2030 team had held prior to Will's indefinite departure, they'd hypothesized that they might need to build a machine that could mimic Will's Energy and set it off in the Stark's yard a few days before the attack if Will didn't return from his journey to the casino.

Yet they'd never tried to build that machine, not even when most thought Will was lost forever. They would trust that fate would bring the Hunters to Pleasanton.

He'd wondered for a time—years, in fact—if Josh's Energy signal was so similar to his own that Porthos would be fooled if the child's very immense Energy gift was briefly unleashed. Perhaps Josh, in becoming Fil, had altered his Energy signal as well as his name, forever hiding its similarity to his father's. When Will had gotten close enough to Josh during one of Hope's rare Shield outages, though, he'd realized that wasn't the case. Josh's signal was unique, nothing like Will's at all.

If Porthos had detected Energy from Will Stark, it was because Will Stark had produced that Energy. Since Will Stark's Energy signal had been transformed years earlier and was now silent to the entire world, he had to face the cold reality.

Everything he'd experienced, everything those around him had gone through, every bit of the pain and suffering… all of it had come about because he'd chosen to make it happen.

He couldn't give off that much Energy by dropping his Shield due to a lack of concentration. He couldn't give off Will Stark Energy at all… unless he *chose* to change his Energy back to the signal of his birth.

Would he make that choice, though?

It *was* an option. He could choose to stay in hiding, keep his Energy signal in its new, altered state, and let this time go by while doing nothing.

Porthos wouldn't detect a Will Stark Energy burst.

The Hunters would have no reason to come to Pleasanton.

Hope and Josh would never come face-to-face with The Assassin.

And he'd never suffer the brutal, painful, near-death experience here in his back yard.

What would happen with the future, though? Would Adam and his children build their time machine, travel here... and find no one to take forward in time with them? Would they take a healthy Will forcibly, despite the fact that there was no compelling reason— no inferno consuming his home, no presumed deaths of his wife and son, no near-fatal injuries—to do so? What would happen to Hope and Josh and Angel then?

Every time he considered that option, every time he felt the temptation to spare all of them the pain they'd experience in three days, he always came back to the same sobering conclusion.

They were going to find him at some point. It was inevitable.

His fame in the human world had reached such astonishing heights that no amount of effort could hide his existence from the Hunters forever. Porthos spent enough time skulking about in human communities and entertainment venues that he'd eventually hear someone mention Will's name. Aliomenti banking interests would eventually be involved in some massive business buyout or stock offering, and the Aliomenti would recognize the name. The Aliomenti might try to recruit one of his employees and in performing scans of memories and Energy potential locate his name.

The events he remembered were going to happen.

The only choice afforded to him, then, was the timing of when those events would happen. He could choose only to delay the inevitable.

He wouldn't do that. No, he'd force the events to happen at the time and place of their choosing. He'd force everything to happen here and now, giving them the optimal chance to ensure the outcome they needed, and to minimize the damage and injury and death that would inevitably come from the efforts to seize him. Delay meant introducing variables into the events that they couldn't predict or control. The only true chance to avoid these events had passed long ago, when they could have prevented Will from entering into his business career... or forced him to legally change his name. None of that had happened.

Was this act a choice when all options beyond timing had been denied him, long before he'd understood that those options existed?

In the end, it didn't matter. In spite of everything that had happened, everything he and others had endured and would endure as a result of this action, he knew that the choice was the correct one. There were far too many positives that traced their origin to this single event in history, advances that had meant better lives for untold millions.

It was what he'd spent his entire life striving for, with or without Energy.

Will looked at the tree directly in front of him, reaching out a tendril of Energy, feeling the tree reciprocate the connection. He moved along to the next, and the next, until the entire grove was ablaze in Energy, feeding him, growing his Energy stores far beyond their usual massive capacity. He could feel the thrum of Energy buzzing around him, vibrating the ground ever so slightly. At this point, he suspected that the Alliance residents of De Gray Estates had noticed the uptick in Energy, and if they hadn't yet... well, what was coming would leave no doubt in their minds that Will Stark had indeed survived that fateful journey to the casino decades earlier.

He allowed the feedback effect to continue, uninterrupted. He'd rarely had the chance to stay in one place more than twenty or thirty minutes, yet today the connection continued, building upon itself, for over an hour. His Energy levels soared, replenishing faster than he could possibly expend them.

At last, he reached the point where he could hold no more.

With a silent plea for forgiveness to his younger self and all those who would be affected, Will pushed every bit of Energy out of his body at once, willing it to seek out Porthos wherever the Hunter might be.

●●●

Eva raised her eyes from the lunch plate before her and looked at Aaron. "Do you feel that?"

Aaron, who was chewing his food, looked at her, puzzled. As he swallowed, though, his eyes widened.

The table began to shake, rattling the dishes.

"Is that an… earthquake?" Aaron asked. "In *Ohio*?"

"No," Eva said. She rolled up her sleeve, and observed the tiny hairs on her arm standing on end. "That is *not* an earthquake. *That* is an explosion of Energy."

"I've never felt *anything* like that," Aaron said, his voice full of awe. The hairs on top of his head spiked as if struck by static electricity. "Who could possibly…?"

Aaron's eyes widened. Eva dropped her fork, which clanged noisily against the fine china plate. Neither noticed the noise. Lunch was forgotten.

They knew who had generated that Energy explosion.

Seizing their coats, they raced from their home, allowing their aged human forms to dissolve into their youthful Alliance personas as they moved. They ran at their enhanced Energy-fueled speed, dodging trees, heading for the Starks' house.

The Energy hung in the air, thick like a dense fog, and the vibrations drove their own Energy stores skyward. The trail to the source of the Energy was so dense with the powerful surge that they felt as though they were swimming. As the moved along, they were joined on the trail by Archie and Ashley, and then Judith and Peter, each entering the clearing from the direction of their own home. No words needed to be exchanged, aloud or telepathically. They all knew what they sought.

Will Stark was alive. And he was *here*.

Two minutes after their trails converged, they found him.

Will was lying on the floor of the forest, seemingly oblivious to the cold, his eyes closed, his jet black hair a sharp contrast to the grays and browns and frosty whites of the terrain around him. The gentle rise and fall of his chest indicated that he was very much alive; whether he was unconscious, resting, or asleep, they did not know.

They knew only that he was here.

Eva stepped forward to kneel beside Will, laying a hand upon his chest, as if still suffering disbelief at the idea that he was alive, needing the confirmation of his beating heart to eliminate all doubt.

She looked up, and her radiant face provided the confirmation and encouragement they needed to move to surround his sleeping form.

Ashley looked in the direction of the house. "Shouldn't we tell Hope that he's here?"

Peter shook his head. "She knows, Ash. She felt it, no doubt. Maybe she already suspected he was alive. Because if not? She would have been the first person out here."

"She can't come running out here, though," Ashley protested. "She's Shielding Josh so he can't be detected by the Hunters."

Peter snorted. "The amount of Energy Will just unleashed means that Shielding Josh is no longer necessary, not until this Energy fades away." Peter paused. "What he's done will bring the Hunters here, without question. Porthos will notice this, regardless of where he is in the world at this moment."

Eva's head snapped around. "You are correct, Peter. We must therefore remove Will from this place and hide him."

"Why? He can sleep it off and then, when they get here…" Peter slammed a fist into his hand, eyes glinting. "Pow. We can rid the world of the Hunters for good."

"No," Eva said, and her voice was firm, startling all of them. "They would find *two* Will Starks, Peter. That cannot be allowed to happen. We must remove *this* Will from this place, masking his presence in this time, until he recovers. We can then determine, with *this* Will, what his and our next actions should be."

They picked him up, three on each side, and moved at tremendous speed until they reached Eva and Aaron's home, the closest to the Starks' house. Will remained immobile during the entire journey. They carried him inside, setting him on a bed in a guest room. Eva removed the boots he was wearing, and they covered him with blankets to keep him warm, suspecting it was the appropriate thing to do.

"Is there anything else we can do for him?" Ashley asked. "He just released so much Energy that I can't believe it didn't kill him." She wrinkled her nose. "Again."

Eva shook her head. "He will recover, but he needs rest. He has done something similar to a maximum teleportation effort, expending all of his Energy stores in an instant." She glanced at Judith, who nodded, acknowledging her own experience in performing such an act. "He needs rest to allow his Energy to replenish and to reduce his fatigue. The best thing we can do for him is to provide him the space he needs to do so."

They all left the room, and Eva shut the door behind the sleeping Will.

Archie glanced back at the room as he walked away. "Should we… tell someone? Will's *alive*."

"Who would we tell?" Aaron asked. "And what would we tell them? That Energy burst was felt by any Energy user within a hundred miles. Or more. Word will spread."

"I'm wondering if we should actually *tell* our people that we've seen him and he's alive. Call the Cavern, send emails to the ports, make sure people know it's true, rather than just hearsay."

"That would be inadvisable at the moment," Eva replied. "We have a very precise schedule for the next seventy-two hours. If throngs of Alliance come to see Will here, it would significantly impede our progress against that schedule, far more than the Hunters." She shook her head. "There will be time enough for Will to reunite with everyone when everything here has finished, and we can tell others our stories of what we have witnessed as well."

Judith glanced at Eva. "I still think we should tell Hope."

"I rather suspect Hope sensed that Energy burst," Eva replied, a trace of irony in her voice. Her eyes narrowed. "And I further suspect she did not need an Energy burst of that sort to know that Old Will has been alive all this time."

●●●

Adam retained his Cain Freeman appearance after his meeting with Will. He wanted to be very noticeable in leaving town, so that no one would wonder where he was when he failed to return after several days, and he'd allow word of his sudden resignation from Stark Enterprises after Will's death to explain Cain's permanent departure from Pleasanton. He'd drive to the safe house in West Virginia, where he'd meet Millard Howe in a few weeks. He could teleport back and forth as needed, including for quick forays around the city over the next few days to check in on Gena's safety. The drive began to become monotonous, as flat fields of grass gave way to other flat fields of grass, with only minor bends in the road giving any relief from the boredom of driving the route.

The tsunami of Energy coursed through him, a wave of power that eliminated the need for the artificial heater in his car. Yet that warming Energy still chilled him to the bone, far more than any air conditioning system or cryogenic chamber ever could.

He knew it had come from Will. There was no other explanation, and certainly no other Energy user who could generate something like what he'd just experienced.

He'd watched as the Hunter stabbed Will decades earlier, had watched the man collapse, near death, before teleporting far away. His initial assumption as the sole eyewitness to the event had been that Will must have died from the injuries. Over time, though, he'd begun to doubt what he'd seen, and the lack of tangible proof of death, along with the intelligence suggesting that the Hunters themselves doubted he'd perished, had swung him to the camp that believed Will had survived, and had been in hiding ever since.

There was no doubt now. Will had made an appearance, and a dramatic one at that.

His first thought was of Hope, who'd lived as a widow for decades before marrying Young Will. Had she sensed the Energy burst? And where had it originated from, in any event? It was bound to draw the attention of Porthos; bursts far smaller would bring the Hunter scurrying forth from beneath whatever rock he called home. It was strange timing on Will's part, because if the Hunters went to investigate this Energy burst, then…

Adam's eyes widened. He pulled to the side of the road, allowing his breathing to stabilize.

Will had done it on purpose. He'd known he would need to do what he'd done. Yet somehow, he'd never seen fit to tell Adam, the man responsible for coordinating all of this activity, the organizer of the plan meant to keep the young, very human Will, alive.

Adam felt a surge of anger that shocked him.

It vanished quickly.

None of the clues contained in the diary entries had mentioned what, exactly, had prompted the Hunters and Assassin to visit Pleasanton that specific day. The human Will Stark had long been a very public figure, and the fact that he'd not come to the attention of the Aliomenti before now was, frankly, stunning. All of the future communication suggested Will might well be dead, but the wording was oddly ambiguous. And nothing in those communications suggested that Will would not only live, but perform the equivalent of setting off an Energy bomb to lure the Hunters to Pleasanton. The team had never discussed what might trigger the Hunters' journey, outside a vague idea of creating a machine that would generate a synthetic burst of Energy coded to match Will Stark. Peter had suggested sending an anonymous email to the Aliomenti, noting that Will Stark, leader of the Alliance, was flaunting his massive wealth among the humans and lived in Pleasanton with his wife, but that idea was shot down. The Aliomenti had made mistakes in the past, but they'd never be so foolish as to chase an obvious attempt to draw them to a specific spot on a specific day, encouraged by an anonymous source who knew of their special interest in the man. His idea, though, had put the idea in Adam's head that some type of Internet search or TV news story about Will, likely initiated by Porthos, would be the trigger to get the Hunters to Pleasanton.

And foolishly, they'd never discussed that triggering event again.

Adam cursed his own stupidity. That had been a tragic flaw, an unspoken assumption that the trigger had been a natural occurrence beyond their control, and that the Hunters had stumbled upon Will through happenstance at just this precise moment in time. They'd allowed nothing else during this entire cycle of history to happen by chance, whether ensuring Will survived the car crash that claimed the lives of his parents, to nudging his people to say certain things and drive down specific roads so that Will had to visit the Diner the night his future wife was on duty and had an open table.

That turned Adam's thoughts back to Hope.

Had she known that Will had survived? And if so, how long had she known?

He wouldn't suggest that some secrets in life weren't meant to remain between husband and wife, and that had been their relationship status for centuries, even if it hadn't been confirmed in a traditional ceremony. But he struggled with the idea that Will and Hope had privately agreed upon the need for Will to bait the Hunters to Pleasanton. It was far too critical a decision not to share, and Will had never in the past left people in the dark about information they needed to do their jobs. It could only mean that Will had realized what he'd needed to do *after* his apparent death at the hands of the Hunters.

Nor did he think Hope knew that Will would do this; she'd no more leave Adam guessing about critical information of that sort than Will would. But Will was pretending to be dead, and Adam couldn't help but wonder once more if Hope had known he was alive before the events of this day, and had elected not to share that information.

To be sure, the diary entries had made repeated references to Will saving Hope and Josh from the Assassin, a point which raised Hope's ire every time it came up. They'd all assumed it was there to keep Will's spirits up as the end approached. After his disappearance, they'd speculated that his saving Hope was metaphorical, that it was the continued efforts to live to Will's example, working to better the world, which would save Hope from any unforeseen calamity. Hope seemed to appreciate that idea, noting time and again that she could teleport two people a hundred feet without any help.

But none of them believed their own words.

None of them wanted to be the one to say aloud that time during this cycle might have changed, that Will was never meant to die in 1994. What if Hope *did* need help? Who would save Hope and Josh on that fateful day?

But now? It seemed the words from the future might be literal. Will was alive. He *could* save Hope and Josh from the Assassin, if it proved to be necessary

Perhaps that was why Hope had been so angry for so long at the idea of Will saving her life. She'd known Will was very much alive and, therefore, in a position to come to her rescue. Since the words from the future were therefore literal, not metaphorical, they suggested some type of weakness or failure on her part. Adam didn't think it was weakness at all, but recognized he wouldn't win that argument with her.

He thought back, starting with the immediate aftermath of the Hunters' casino attack and his return to report on what he'd seen. While she's seemed to show genuine grief at the news Adam delivered, she'd stabilized quickly, and at some point over the next several months her good humor had returned. Her face showed some level of pain when she overheard stories about Will, but she'd seemed to adjust remarkably well for someone who'd lost a spouse she'd been with for centuries. When he'd thought about it, Adam had reasoned that she'd known the day was coming almost since she'd met him, and thus had plenty of time to adjust her mindset to accept that fate.

Now, though, he wondered if she'd known he hadn't died the

whole time, and knew they'd be reunited again in mere decades. And not just through her meeting and marrying the younger Will.

Adam pulled back onto the road. He'd have to talk with Hope later. Find out what she'd known, when she'd known it… and why she'd seen fit to hide that knowledge from the people putting their lives on hold to protect hers.

●●●

Hope had felt the surge of Energy, just as the others had, and it was like an alarm shattering a deep, restful sleep, catapulting her from a relaxed calm to a state of panic.

It was really happening.

Josh was reading a mystery novel and glanced up at her. "What was *that*, Mommy?"

Hope's weak smile didn't quite reach her eyes. "It was something that means things are about to get very interesting."

The little boy gave her puzzled look. He was laying on his stomach, propped up on his elbows, holding his face in his hands, his inquisitive, Energy-rich ice blue eyes absorbing the expression on her face. He didn't like what he saw, his mother's face lined with worry and concern, and his brow furrowed. He stood up, padded across the thick carpet in his socked feet, and stared out the back window.

And he watched.

And he waited.

He watched as people with the faces of strangers but the Energy signals of friends moved into the trees. He watched as they milled about, searching for something he couldn't identify in the thoughts that seeped in through the scutarium-lined infrastructure of his home. Then they moved with haste toward a single spot, and a moment later, he watched as they carried the inert form of a man through the trees.

"Mommy! Look!" He pointed.

She didn't dare move, didn't want to see what her son saw. Yet some maternal instinct forced her to her feet, and she moved across the carpet slowly.

Josh opened the window, just a crack, and gust of frigid air burst into the house.

Something more than air rushed in as well… and more

important, something rushed *out*.

She raced forward to close the window.

●●●

Will could sense everyone around him as he rested on the bed in Eva and Aaron's home. To them, he appeared a man worn to exhaustion by a massive release of Energy earlier that day, a man who was sleeping or unconscious as a result.

In reality, he'd never felt more energized and alive. The feedback effect, an Energy replenishment and growth technique he'd discovered centuries earlier, had worked wonders. Perhaps he'd imagined it, but the effect had seemed stronger than ever before, possibly because he'd not practiced the technique in centuries. Regardless, the approach had been effective. He felt more Energized now than he had before he'd issued his summons to the Hunters.

Energy responded to emotion and direction. He felt no malice, no destructive impulses, just a desire to communicate in his own fashion with the men who sought to deliver death to his home. His Energy release was felt as a small tremble in the ground nearby, detected by more powerful Energy users in the vicinity, and would make its presence felt with the Hunters soon, if it hadn't already. But the emotion behind the release, one of passive intent to communicate, meant no harm had been done, no destruction rendered. Had he been angry or vengeful, De Gray Estates and the city of Pleasanton would, in all likelihood, be nothing but rubble now.

The powerful effects of Energy feedback weren't what left him feeling so strong at this moment, though.

As they'd carried him away, he'd felt something, an Energy so pure and powerful that it overwhelmed even the thick vibration of his own massive Energy storm. His mind matched the pattern to one in his ancient memories, one from a man who'd made him feel unwelcome against his will, in order to ensure he felt motivated to leave the future to travel back in time to fulfill his destiny, an Energy signal that mapped to one he'd learned to recognize again in the present.

It was Josh.

They must have opened a door or a window with Josh out of

the restraints of Hope's Shield, a combination that allowed Josh's Energy to make its first public appearance in the world. It wouldn't last long; Hope would close whatever opening Josh had found for his own protection, as she should.

He wouldn't get another chance, and he'd fired off a telepathic message of love to his only son. It wasn't words, it wasn't something he could sign and put his name to, it was just a powerful Empathic push of love and pride of who his son was and would become, and an understanding that no matter how bleak times might seem, no matter how distant he might seem, his father was out there protecting him. And he loved him more than anything in the world.

The reply was instantaneous, but brief. Like many children, Josh didn't recognize the signs of a deeply emotional message from others, and with his "young" father still with him all the time, the message might not have the same power it would hold in future years. And thus Josh took the opportunity, not to respond to the message of love and the imparting of strength for the boy's future trials, but to pass along a message to his father. And it wasn't a message of love.

It was a warning, and a plea for help.

Something's wrong with Mom. Help her.

XVIII
Altered

January 5, 2030

Adam completed his drive to the West Virginia safe house. He parked the car in an underground garage they'd built, its entry disguised with dirt and underbrush. He waited until after sunset before teleporting back to his home in Pleasanton.

That had been a mistake. He'd spent weeks talking about his trip and made a point to be seen leaving in the car the previous day. Now, he was back in Pleasanton… without the car. He covered it up as best he could, using the garage opener to partially raise and then lower the door several times so that his neighbors would hear the sound and assume he'd returned for some reason in the middle of the night. That would lessen the surprise of seeing him walking around the city when he was supposed to be hours away on vacation. There was the option of using his natural appearance, one unknown by the human population in this town, but he was far more concerned about the Hunters mistaking him for his long-deceased father. He didn't have time to invent a new image, either. Best to invent an excuse for his temporary return that would interest no one than make a mistake on the more critical project. He checked the mirror to ensure he still bore Cain's face, and then slept.

He wasn't sure when he'd next get a chance to do so.

Cain left the house very early in the morning. He saw a couple of his neighbors and explained that he'd realized he'd left a few items behind that he needed for his trip and couldn't replace on the road, and as such he'd turned around and come back home, arriving in the darkest hours of the night. No one seemed interested in his story. With his breathing misting the cool air that kept him awake, he set off toward De Gray Estates, the spot he suspected would draw the Hunters upon their arrival in Pleasanton as the men surveyed the landscape and decided the best way to go about capturing their prey.

Today, he needed to find out what the Hunters were up to, and what, if anything, they knew about Gena. He must ensure she was safe from their attacks… and, by extension, ensure the safety of Deron MacLean's family as well.

He could run the five miles faster than he could legally drive his car in the city. But that would garner attention he wanted to avoid. Teleportation in a city about to play host to the Hunter Porthos was a similarly bad idea. He alternated a brisk walk with a jog at human-level speeds, and managed to make the trip in around ninety minutes.

Cain walked along the sidewalk toward the sole entrance to the De Gray Estates. He could feel the Energy here; even a day later, it hung heavily in the air, generating a crackling noise any Energy user could detect. He suspected that humans would experience some unexplainable sensation as they moved by this place, and wondered how—and if—the human news might explain the phenomenon. He walked slowly along the sidewalk, entertained by the formation of water vapor as he exhaled each breath, until he neared the guard station at the formal entrance to the community.

And then he froze.

Porthos was there.

The man was dressed in a business suit, his long brown hair pulled back and hidden beneath the heavy overcoat he wore to protect himself against the chill in the air. He made no effort to hide his Energy, which didn't surprise Cain. The Aliomenti never bothered to mask their own Energy; they only restrained the Energy of people they wanted to punish. Making up his mind, Cain moved slowly forward, making a point to put two fingers on his wrist as if checking his pulse. His enhanced hearing picked up the conversation.

"—thought he was supposed to be working here today and wanted to come by and say hello," Porthos told the guard through the speaker.

"He's not here today," the on-duty guard replied. "Perhaps you misunderstood him?"

"No doubt, no doubt," Porthos said. His eyes focused on something inside the guard station. "Who's that in the picture?"

The guard frowned at Porthos. "You don't recognize a picture of your friend's fiancée?"

Cain felt his stomach turn. Porthos had identified Gena.

"Sorry, my eyes are a little fuzzy right now. Long, late night on the town, you know. He's probably spending time with her, then."

"I don't think he spends his off days at The Diner," the guard said, laughing. "I mean, yes, he loves Gena quite a bit, but you can only stand sitting in that place for so long, right?"

"Yeah, bad for business, too," Porthos said, returning the laugh. "Tough to get new people in if he's taking up a table all by himself all day. I'll swing by The Diner for lunch, though, and figure out why my pal gave me his work schedule when I was inebriated and couldn't remember it correctly."

"Tell Mark I said hi," the guard said, as Porthos moved away.

"Oh, I will," Porthos replied. He hopped into a black sports car and sped away.

Cain jogged up to the window. "Hi. I don't suppose you know if there's a bus station nearby?"

The guard chuckled, noticing Cain's sweats. "Ran a bit farther than you should have, huh? I do that, too."

Cain grinned sheepishly. "Brisk air, you think it will cool you down enough to run farther, but I guess I overestimated how far I could make it."

The guard nodded in sympathy. "It's about a mile down the street that way," he replied, jabbing a finger to Cain's left. "Not too many buses run on Saturday mornings, though. Hope you aren't waiting too long."

"I'll make do," Cain replied. "Thanks for the info."

He walked with a fake limp until he was out of direct sight of the guard, and then began to jog. Porthos had a head start on him, but Porthos was trying to be judicious in his use of Energy as well, as evidenced by his use of the car. He didn't want to alert Will Stark to his presence, any more than the Alliance wanted Porthos alerted to theirs. If Cain could teleport to The Diner, and get there a few minutes after Porthos, the man might not notice that a jogger had made similar time to the restaurant that Porthos had made in the car. Cain was also aided by the fact that Porthos wouldn't know the best routes to the restaurant from his current location.

Once clear of the guards, once he'd confirmed there were no human eyes on him, and once he'd looked for the tell-tale sign of the in-wall security cameras of De Gray Estates that he'd long since uncovered, Cain phased into invisibility and flew over the wall into the neighborhood. He flew straight through the hurricane of Energy Will had generated into Eva and Aaron's house. He phased back to his solid state and immediately teleported from within their scutarium-lined walls back to his own house, conveniently within walking distance of The Diner. Seconds later, he'd walked out his front door once again.

The same neighbor watched him with interest. "I didn't see you come back."

"I turned my walk into a jog and came in the back entry to grab a drink. Now I'm hungry, of course, and since I got rid of my food before leaving on my trip, I'm heading to The Diner for lunch. See you later."

"Okay," the neighbor replied, shrugging.

Cain walked at a brisk pace to The Diner and arrived there five minutes later. He spotted Porthos' car—easily visible amidst the aging minivans and sedans filling the rest of the spaces in the lot—and walked inside.

The warm air hit him, as did the smells of meat and grease that always dominated the small restaurant. It was their prime lunch hour, and many seats were taken. He did a quick scan of the restaurant as if looking for open seats and spotted Porthos off to the right.

"Hey, Cain!" Gena walked by, scribbling a few notes on an order ticket. "Your usual seat's available. I'll be right with you."

Cain grinned. "Thanks, Gena. I'm going to hit the restroom first, though."

His usual seat was to the left, but he veered to the right, toward the restrooms and toward the booth Porthos occupied. He'd dumped the overcoat for the cloak he normally favored, which surprised Cain. The Hunters usually made a concerted effort to avoid attention in human environs, and in this restaurant his tailored suit was noticeable. The cloak, with its oversized hood hanging down his back, made him an even greater curiosity.

Cain didn't like that. Porthos was being either overly confident or extremely sloppy. Either could mean danger to those he encountered—and those who remembered that encounter.

Cain walked by casually flexing his fingers as if warming himself from the chill. As he passed Porthos' booth, the flexion changed just enough for the microscopic microphone to slide from his hand and under the table. Cain continued along, washed his hands in the restroom, and walked back past Porthos to his usual table. Gena was chatting with the cook in the back as he walked by, and she caught his eye. "Usual order, Cain? I can just put it in now since I'm standing here."

"Perfect," Cain replied.

He sat in his usual spot, a booth by the windows that provided a panoramic view of the great Dome covering Pleasanton, and pulled out his headphones and a book while he waited for his order. He often sat here during lunch, reading and listening to music… or so it appeared. In reality, he was spying on Gena, trying to find out what was happening in her life. The headphones picked up audio signals from the microscopic microphones he dropped around the restaurant on each visit. That allowed him to listen in on conversations with and about Gena, allowing him to make sure she was safe.

Now, he'd use that same method to find out what Porthos was planning to do.

Cain focused his attention on the earphones, waiting for the conversation to start to filter in. It was unusually quiet; typically, he'd hear multiple conversations at the same time, often overhearing the same person more than once as the microphones picked up the loudest talkers. He'd then have to try to isolate on what Gena was saying and what was being said to and about her. There was little to worry about; she was well-loved and, outside a few men suggesting they'd be okay if something happened to Mark so she'd be available again, nothing that could be construed as threatening was ever uttered about her.

Now, though, he was expecting a subtle threat to her very

existence to come from a man he knew could execute her on the spot without a hint of effort.

"You're new here, aren't you?" Gena said.

Porthos' oily voice came through clearly over the microphone. "That's right. I'm here to do some research for my television show."

"Oh?" Gena sounded intrigued. "What show is that?"

"We're scouting out a few artifacts for a new reality TV show that's starting up. We identify those artifacts, lost objects from the past said to hold some special value—financial, historical, sacred, even magical—and try to figure out if they ever actually existed, and if so, what happened to them."

"Sounds interesting," Gena said. Cain almost choked. Even from this distance, he could detect the mild boredom in her voice.

Porthos chuckled. "Yeah, really dry stuff, I know. But, in the event we find something, there's quite a bit of history that can be made. Plus, we get to introduce our television viewers to residents of the towns and cities where we find these artifacts, and ask them—on camera, of course—about how the items in question might have altered the history of their area."

"Really?" Now Gena sounded interested, and Cain silently cursed. Gena had long wanted to move into a career in film or television; part of the reason she worked in a popular local restaurant was to increase the chances she'd meet someone who could "discover" her. Unfortunately, this wasn't the type of discovery she needed. It could prove fatal.

"Right. That's why I'm here, actually. We traced this old amulet across from France and into the States, and it seems the last record of it places it right here, in Pleasanton. Which is interesting, in a boring, yawn-inducing way."

Gena laughed.

"Unless…" Porthos paused.

"Unless… what?"

"Unless the legend is true. If it's true… well, it's such a nice little city. I'd hate for… well, I won't bother you with the details."

"No, please, tell me." Gena sounded concerned. Cain sighed. Porthos had centuries of practice at extracting information from humans through a type of long con. Gena wasn't the first to fall for his verbal spells.

"The story goes that this amulet has a true owner. If it's in that owner's possession, it brings about peace and prosperity. If it gets separated from that owner, though, it starts to build up a type of energy inside. Negative, *explosive* energy. If enough time passes before that amulet returns to the possession of its true owner, it will... blow up." Porthos made a sound like an explosion, and from the far side of the restaurant, Cain could see his hands move apart.

He could almost see Gena's eyes widen in terror. He chewed his bite of cheeseburger very carefully as he continued to pretend to read the book in front of him. Absentmindedly, he turned the page with a greasy finger. He liked paper books, but the old vellum scrolls were better. Especially the pictures.

"How explosive would it be?"

"It would probably be enough to decimate an area roughly the size of a modern city block. And it's been missing from its true owner for a long time. Centuries, in fact."

Gena gasped. "That would be awful! And you say it would happen here? Soon?"

"Very soon. The records indicate that the amulet can only store so much of this negative energy, and due to a few... errors in the past, we've calculated that it's due to explode again in just under a week. The clues we collected helped us to identify the coordinates where it was last buried, deep under the ground. We'd hoped the amulet would be in an open field so that we could dig it up without any trouble—or risk of major damage or injury—but... " He shook his head sadly. "No such luck."

"Where... where is it?"

"It's under the wall surrounding a big housing community here. I think it's called... the De Gray Estates?"

Gena gasped again, her hand going to her mouth. "But... my fiancée... he *works* there."

"He does?" Porthos said, and if Cain didn't know any better, he'd swear the man hadn't been aware of that detail. "Look, I really don't think there's anything to worry about..." He let his voice trail off.

"We can't really take that chance though, right?" Gena had fallen completely under his spell, and Cain couldn't tell from here if any subtle use of Energy had helped in that effort. "If there's any possibility... we just have to make sure we get that amulet back to its owner. The people who live there…. well, most of them aren't very nice, but the Starks are pleasant, very good to me and my fiancée."

"The… *Starks*, you say?" Porthos' voice was strained, higher pitched. *He realizes Will's not alone now,* Cain thought. *She's just told him something critically important. I hope she doesn't mention Josh…*

Gena nodded. "Mr. and Mrs. Stark employ my fiancée as a security guard there," she explained. "And they take very good care of him; they gave us first class airfare for our honeymoon. I… I really don't want to take the chance that something bad might happen to them, either."

Porthos took a long time to respond. "Right, nothing… bad. To the *Starks*."

"Are you okay?"

"Fine, fine. I just… I hadn't realized Will Stark lived here. With his *wife*. That's… yes, we should definitely warn them. I'll call his office and try to talk to him… see if they'll let us in… Good for the show." Cain heard a rustling noise, and risked a glance in their direction. Porthos was standing up, straightening out his cloak. "Thank you. For *everything*." He passed a piece of green paper to Gena, and Cain could hear her gasp. Cain suspected Porthos had just given her a *very* generous tip.

Porthos walked out the door, throwing the hood of the cloak over his head. And Cain could hear him thinking. *Will Stark is married. Will Stark is married. We can use his wife to get to him. I have to get back to the others. And after it's done, I need to take care of that waitress. She'd be able to identify me.*

Cain felt a chill that had nothing to do with the air Porthos' departure had allowed into the restaurant.

Gena stopped by a moment later. "Everything okay here?"

Cain nodded. "I'm not that hungry," he admitted. "Could you bring me a box?"

Gena nodded, and within moments Cain was moving at a rapid pace back to his house.

He pulled out the special phone that all members of the Project 2030 team carried, and sent a group text. *Need to have an emergency meeting. Just learned of critical information that will alter our plans for tomorrow.*

Twenty minutes later, they were all there, watching him over the secure video link that tied them all together.

"Hope raised the point yesterday that the security guard named Mark Arnold became engaged just a few days ago," he began. "By itself, that's not critical to our efforts, but the news generated several premonitions that our belief about a lack of harm to the guards' loved ones might be incorrect. I followed Gena Adams, the young woman recently engaged to Mark Arnold, this morning. I wanted to see if there were any encounters with the Hunters that might provide evidence that she, or the MacLeans, are in greater danger than we suspected." He paused. "Unfortunately, my eavesdropping efforts today suggest that is the case. Porthos, through clever dialogue, extracted from Gena the news that Will is married. The Hunters will now be required to call upon the Assassin to execute Hope. Porthos' thoughts also betrayed the fact that he will definitely go after Gena now, as she provided him that information, and their conversation was extensive enough that she'd be able to identify him."

Eva spoke first. "Until now, we had not known *how* they got the information about Will's marriage, only that they were aware as they brought the Assassin along specifically to target Hope. We now know how they obtained that information. His thought specific to executing Gena Adams in the aftermath must be addressed in the context of our larger plan."

"The expectation has been that the families would remain unharmed, because the Hunters wouldn't want to stick around long enough to target them," Aaron noted. "Does this new information really change that? Sure, Porthos *thinks* he needs to eliminate the girl after everything's done, but he's thinking that in his current context of the situation. In his mind, their arrival is a surprise to Will, there's no reason to believe there's a huge Alliance presence waiting to ambush him, and so on. He'll find out, and will likely *still* decide going after her isn't worth the risk of facing *us*. So… how does this change anything?"

"Don't you *get it*?" Adam shouted. "He's going to *execute* her!"

The faces on the screen looked back at him, bewildered at his emotional outburst. Only Eva's face showed a hint of compassion, borne of the fact that she alone understood Adam's deeper connection with Gena Adams. "The Assassin plans to execute Hope," Peter pointed out. "You don't seem quite as worked up about that."

"Of course I'm worked up about that," Adam snapped. "But Hope knows what's coming, and she can handle herself against the Assassin and all of the Hunters—simultaneously, if needed. And she wouldn't break a sweat while doing so. Gena is a human with no knowledge of what is to come, and no ability to defend herself against a Hunter even if she did." His eyes blazed.

"So, what are you suggesting?" Ashley asked. "Are you saying we need to focus our efforts over the next thirty-six hours on locating Gena, along with the wife and son of the other guard, and cloning them because their lives are now at risk?"

"That's *exactly* what I'm saying. And I'd use a stronger term than just *suggesting*, too. We have direct proof now that at least one of the other humans has a direct target on her head; do we want to take the chance that the Hunters double back and execute *all* of them while we're finishing up in the aftermath of the fire?"

"We don't know that they'll go after *any* of them," Archie muttered.

"We could split a few people out to guard the families," Judith offered, cutting off Adam's rebuke toward Archie.

"We can't do that," Adam snapped. "The records show that only two people leave the Estates on Monday: Will and Myra VanderPoole. If any of you leave, or are witnessed outside without going through the gate, we've altered history and possibly raised questions in the human and Aliomenti worlds we don't want asked."

"What about you, then?" Archie asked. "You could guard the families in your Cain disguise. You're pretty well-known around here. And to that point… why couldn't some of the rest of us discard our human disguises and handle it that way?"

"I suspect that there's a memory somewhere of Porthos remembering slaughtering Gena, or a police record of her death," Adam replied. "We can't prevent that execution from happening if that's what history records as happening. We can only save her—and all of them—if we clone them over the next thirty-six hours, just as we're doing for the guards."

"I think Adam's solution is the correct one, given the number of variables we cannot account for at the moment," Eva said. "This change of evidence as to what the Hunters will do on Monday and beyond is something we have not allowed for in our planning. Cloning is the most expeditious means of ensuring that the humans survive the next few days—and I will remind everyone that the survival of the humans was a core requirement we set forth from the beginning of this effort. We must determine what we will do with them in the aftermath of the cloning, however."

Peter spoke up. "They have to come to our house to go through the cloning process. We have unused space in the basement, and I have a few bedroom nano kits in a closet upstairs. We can build rooms for them in the basement and let them stay with us." On the screen, Judith nodded.

"Are we agreed, then?" Adam asked.

Heads nodded.

Their plans had changed.

They could only hope that the final outcome wouldn't change as well.

XIX
Contingency

January 6, 2030

He hid in the shadows, watching, as the young woman left The Diner after her shift ended.

He'd learned that the young couple had chosen to be frugal with their money, limiting themselves to a single car to share. Mass transit, via the city-wide bus system, brought her close to both home and work, and thus her fiancée used the couple's only car.

Gena waved goodbye to the owner of The Diner from the doorway. As usual, the man had shooed her out before the final bits of closing-related cleanup were completed. He'd long since stopped offering to drive her home after these late night shifts, allowing her instead to leave a few minutes before he did so that she could catch the bus, the final one each night that would get her within walking distance of the couple's small apartment.

Porthos was aware of her thoughts, his thoughts, and drank the information in, plotting the best way to silence her. He wouldn't do anything now; Will Stark would certainly notice mysterious deaths and disappearances of close family to those working to protect his home.

While Porthos watched Gena, someone else watched *him*.

Adam was there to bring Gena in for her cloning, a task best performed while Mark worked his overnight shift. They didn't want him coming home to find her gone, and the time between the end of her work shift and the end of Mark's provided them with the window they needed to complete the process. The appearance of Porthos didn't help matters, and Adam gritted his teeth. Porthos was trying to determine when he should get to her apartment Monday evening so that he found her home for her permanent silencing.

The Hunter watched the young woman step aboard a bus, made note of the time, and vanished into the night.

Adam sighed. That was close.

He'd brought the invisible flying craft with him this time. It would enable him to transport her quickly to and from the cloning station without an Energy trail. Now that she'd boarded the bus, he needed to find her again. He flew overhead, following the vehicle as it weaved through the city streets, watching as she stepped off at a stop a modest walk from her apartment. Street lighting was moderate, but not perfect. Adam scowled. He'd like to have a talk with Mark about leaving Gena without the car that would ensure her safe commute. How could he stand the idea of her walking the streets alone at night?

Perhaps it no longer mattered. In a few days, the couple would leaving Pleasanton in favor of the Cavern, where there was nothing to fear from a walk alone in the dark.

Gena wrapped her coat around her more tightly as a gust of wind howled in the night. She shifted her weight, wincing, as her feet groaned after the strain of standing for a fourteen hour shift. And then she started walking.

Adam lowered the craft until it was just over her, the engines silent, the craft invisible to the human eye.

And he watched as Gena paused, turned... and looked straight up at him.

He didn't waste any time, teleporting her into the craft while simultaneously activating the sleep centers of her brain.

Her last thought, before she drifted into unconsciousness, was that she recognized his *sound*.

●●●

Dana MacLean tucked Dash into his bed and kissed her son on his forehead. She hated the nights when Deron worked an overnight shift, but there was nothing to be done about it. The work was good, the official benefits generous, and the unofficial benefits were definitely something she'd never want to lose. She and Dash had adapted to Deron's odd hours over time; she allowed her young son stay up late with her on weekends while Deron worked. They'd watch movies and eat snacks until Dash fell asleep. She'd carry the young boy up to his bed and retire to her own room, wondering how Deron was doing, and hoping against hope than nothing at all interesting happened while he worked.

To either of them.

She glanced at the clock. It was well past midnight already. In a few hours, Deron would be home, and she'd be up, putting together a large breakfast feast. It had become a tradition in their home, and it was one she truly enjoyed. They'd sit around the table, laughing, telling stories, while Deron ate large amounts of food. The massive calorie intake also made him drowsy, and within an hour he'd be catching up on the sleep he so desperately needed. She needed to get some rest herself in order to be ready for the alarm that would sound all too soon.

Dana walked to the window overlooking the road below. Streetlights offered just enough illumination to show the frost covering the grass, the frost heavy enough to give the appearance of snow. She closed the curtain so that the room would be completely dark once she turned off the light.

She felt a slight brushing sensation against her skin, and the terror rose inside her as she whirled and screamed at the sight of the two people standing in her room.

They looked young, perhaps in their early thirties, and quite fit and healthy. Neither seemed concerned that Dana was screaming. The woman was fiddling with something that looked like a vial, while the man watched Dana with a deep curiosity. He continued to watch her while he held out a small box and depressed a button on the top. The box dissolved in his hand. She ignored the box as she screamed, watching him, waiting for the attack she was certain would come.

But there was no malice in his eyes; rather, he looked upon her a calm sympathy.

Too calm, given that she was screaming so loudly.

The man finally spoke. "We apologize for startling you. I assure you that you are in no danger from us, but it is reasonable for you to doubt me. If screaming helps you, please continue to do so. But we have little time, and much to discuss with you and Dash."

Her scream caught in her throat at the words, and her protective instincts engaged. They could do what they wanted with her, but she'd not let them hurt Dash.

"Dash is in no danger, either," the man said, as if reading her mind. "We need to discuss an urgent matter relating to the future for both of you. Would you like to get him? If not, I can bring him here."

"I won't let you hurt him!" Dana screamed. She charged the man, throwing herself at him, meaning to tackle him and hit and scratch and claw at the stranger who threatened her only child.

She froze in midair.

As her eyes widened in shock, she floated to rest gently upon her bed, too stunned at what she was experiencing to scream any more.

The woman spoke. "Mrs. MacLean, I'll get Dash. We need to talk with both of you."

The woman never moved, never left the room. But Dash was *there* before Dana could open her mouth to protest, suddenly sleeping next to her, his head propped on her leg as if it were a pillow.

How in the world...?

"Mrs. MacLean, I realize this will be difficult to understand, and difficult to accept. But it's important that you wake Dash up. We need to take a short trip, and both of you will need to make an important decision. Fate hasn't been kind to you, or your son, or your husband. Our mission is to reverse that fate and make things better."

Dana blinked. "Fate? What does my husband have to do with this? And how did my son get in here? Neither of you left to get him."

Dash stirred at her side, and she forgot her own terror for a moment, offering soothing tones as the boy woke. Dash blinked a few times, sat up, and stared at the two people in his mother's room. "Who are they, Mom?"

The woman glanced at the man. "Let's go."

Before Dana or Dash could ask where they might be going— or could protest the decision to leave—they were overcome by a strange sense of physical displacement. Everything flashed... and they were suddenly in someone else's home.

Another couple sat there, chatting with a young woman with dark hair who, from the frazzled expression on her face, looked to have come here under similar suspicious circumstances. A tall man with thinning brown hair and intense brown eyes looked up, unsurprised that four people had materialized in front of him, and nodded at Dana. "Welcome, Mrs. MacLean. I apologize for the abruptness of our get-together, but there's little time."

"Abruptness?" Dana snapped. "You do mean *abduction*, right?"

"You're free to leave at any time," the man replied. "But I really encourage you to listen to what we have to say. It's literally a case of life and death."

"We're leaving," Dana said. "Let's go, Dash."

"How did you do that?" the little boy asked. He was speaking with the man who'd invaded their home and… moved them.

"I can teach you," he replied. "But first, we need to talk to you and your mom about something that's going to happen on Monday."

Dana felt a chill of apprehension. "What's going to happen on Monday?"

The brown-haired man leveled her with his gaze. "People able to do what you've just seen us do are going to murder your husband."

●●●

The three people present in the room against their will sat on a comfortable sofa in front of a large television. Dana and Gena sat on either side of Dash, as if reaching an unspoken agreement to protect the child from the strangers holding them captive.

With the way they could move, though… Dana wasn't sure what she could do if her captors proved malicious.

"I'll be blunt and to the point," the brown-haired man said. "As you've gathered, we're not normal. There's a large group of people in the world able to do what you've each experienced tonight, including moving instantly from place to place. The group with the majority of such people in its ranks is comprised of men and women willing to kill to keep the secrets of those skills from becoming public knowledge. We, in the minority, are of the opinion that we should share that knowledge with all of humanity, gradually, along with other advances we've made. The larger group has learned that our leader and founder lives here, in Pleasanton, and they're going to come and attempt to capture him. They'll kill if necessary to achieve that goal."

"You said that they're going to… murder my husband," Dana said slowly.

"And my fiancée," Gena added, looking pale.

"That's correct."

"Why, though? Why would they do that?"

"Because the men you love guard the man they seek. He lives in another house in De Gray Estates."

"We're inside De Gray Estates?" Dana said, shocked.

"Will Stark," Gena whispered.

The woman who'd transported the MacLeans looked at Gena with interest. "How did you know?"

Gena shrugged. "I just… I don't know. I just knew."

"Wait a minute," Dana said. "There are men coming here to kill *Will Stark*, and they're going to kill my husband, and they're going to kill her fiancée… and you know this and aren't going to stop them?"

"We can't," the brown-haired man said. "It would be catastrophic."

"Catastrophic would be my son growing up without his father!" Dana shouted. "You act like this is no big deal. Why tell us?"

"While we won't prevent the murders… we *can* prevent the men from dying. Both men will, on Monday morning, be escorted here to have a conversation like the one we're having now. And they'll be offered the same chance we're about to offer the three of you."

"So you admit that you *could* stop the murders and you *won't*?" Dana replied. Her tone was one of exasperation. "You're no better than them!"

"If these men do not proceed with these murders, and believe their efforts successful, it is no exaggeration to say that the history of the last millennium will be completely altered, and all of us will cease to exist. With those stakes, with the lives of millions—billions, even—altered, we will not stop them from *believing* themselves successful." He paused, holding up his hand before Dana could explode again. "We have developed cloning capabilities that would enable us to send *copies* of your loved ones to work on Monday. It will be the *copy*, not the men you know and love, who will suffer that horrible fate, leaving their original bodies and minds intact." He paused once more. "If they choose to do so."

Gena looked puzzled. "Why wouldn't they take that deal?"

"And again, why not just stop the killers to begin with?" Dana snapped. But her tone was slightly less acerbic.

"We don't know," the man replied, addressing Gena's question. "We believe in giving people information and letting them make their own choices. Deron and Mark will have the chance to decide if they want to sit in this room while their clones—perfect copies of them in every way, save for their built-in shorter life spans—suffer what fate has dealt them. Might they choose to believe that it is truly their time to die? They might. But it won't be something forced upon them. And if we wanted to force the decision, we could."

"That's not the specific reason we brought the three of you here today, though." It was the man who'd abducted Dana and Dash speaking now. "We've gotten new information that suggests that after finishing their work here, the men seeking Will Stark will go after the three of you next." He looked at Gena. "They have specifically named *you* a target."

Gena gasped, and Dana wrapped her arms around her son, who was drifting off to sleep due to the late hour.

"With that in mind," the brown-haired man continued, "the same offer is open to the three of you. We can create perfect replicas of each of you that will be put back exactly where you were when we retrieved the samples necessary to create them, with no recollection of this conversation, while you wait here in safety until everything is finished."

"You've already retrieved… *samples?*" Dana said. "How…?" But she remembered the strange brushing sensation she'd felt just before finding two strangers in her bedroom. And she changed her question. "Why?"

"Whichever version of you returns to your home must have no memory of this conversation. Your very cells retain memories. We had to get samples with no memory of meeting us, because it's critical that all of you live the next few days normally."

"What if I choose not to be cloned?" Gena asked.

The brown-haired man grimaced, and his eye twitched. "Your memory of this encounter will be erased and you'll be transported safely home. The material taken from you would then be destroyed."

"What happens next?" Dash asked, stirring.

"What do you mean?" asked the brown-haired man.

"You said… the bad men would…" The boy paused, unable to say the words. "But if that's a copy of Daddy… where would he— my *real* Daddy—go? I want to go with him."

Dana stared at her son, surprised at the depth of understanding he showed.

The brown-haired man nodded. "You are correct, Dash. Because dead bodies will be found, anyone cloned whose clone dies cannot return to their previous way of life. Your Daddy—and you and your Mom, if that is your wish—would have to come live with us, in our special home." The man smiled. "It's pretty far away, but you'd really enjoy it. And you'd learn how to do this." Suddenly, the man was standing behind them, having vanished and reappeared in an instant.

"That's what I want to do," the boy replied, eyes gleaming. He turned to his mother. "We can't leave Daddy, Mom. Please?"

Dana was uncomfortable. "What if… what if Deron chooses not to be cloned? What if he…?"

"You and your son will still be able to come with us. We'll… arrange things here to explain your disappearance, assuming that we're incorrect and these men choose to limit their killing efforts to Mark and Deron… their clones, that is."

Dana took a deep breath, looked at Dash's eager face, and tried to imagine a world without her son. The world deserved a brave, kind boy like Dash. He needed to live. She glanced at the strange, powerful people gathered around her, and then she nodded her consent.

Gena looked at the people in the room with her, with a particular focus on the man with the brown hair. "I want to spend the rest of my life with Mark. If this is the only way… then so be it."

The strangers exchanged glances. "Very well, then." The brown-haired man nodded. "We'll get everything started and set you up with rooms here. In a few days, we'll start transferring your most prized possessions here as well. We can't do that right away, because your clones would notice things missing."

The boy looked saddened.

The woman who'd brought Dash here looked at him. "I think we can reproduce your teddy bear. Would that help?"

The boy stared at her. "You can do that?"

She smiled back. "You'll find that there's very little we *can't* do."

Dana sniffed. "Except prevent murders you know are coming."

●●●

Gena glanced down at the strange clothing now covering her body. Adam, the brown-haired man, had told her it was made of tiny machines, that it would show her progress in learning the new skills they'd teach her. She was happy to see that her clothes had streaks of pink in them. Pink was her favorite color. Dana and Dash seemed pleased that their pure white clothes were missing that same pink streak.

Under ideal circumstances, they'd collect the tissue samples just at the start of a sleeping cycle and return the clones to their beds, eliminating the need to modify memories to explain missing gaps of waking time from the clone's memory. That would be the case with Dash, who'd been asleep until after the tissue sample was taken. For Dana and Gena, though, they'd need to take special precautions. Dana had been looking out her bedroom window to the moonlit view of the front yard below, while Gena had been walking home in the dark. Given the time required to complete the process, the clones for both women wouldn't be available until the early morning hours. Both women consented to have their clones' memories modified. Dana would remember lying down and falling asleep instantly. Gena would remember completing her walk in a mental haze, changing into her standard sleepwear and falling asleep instantly as well. The clones would receive a potion that would accelerate their sleep, allowing them to wake at a normal hour with an appropriate level of physical refreshment.

All three clones would need to wear—or, in Gena's case, possess in a hamper—the clothes they'd worn during the collection process. Waking with different clothing could lead to a profound sense of displacement that might cause severe mental instability. Gena's memory modification was the most critical; they'd need to install a memory of her changing clothing. Lacking other options, they crafted a perfect replica of her nightclothes with the tiny machines. With only Ashley in the room, Gena then went through the physical process of removing her work clothes and donning her sleeping attire in the cloning room; Ashley watched and transferred the mental images into the memory of the clone to ensure the most realistic memory possible. Neither woman relished the task, but both agreed it was necessary for the mental health of the clone growing nearby.

All three humans wanted to watch as their clones were placed into their beds, sound asleep. Archie and Ashley injected the sleeping potions directly into the bloodstream of the three clones, and expertly dressed the clones in the clothing worn during the collection process. They then split up to return the clones to their homes. Adam took the Genas, and Archie and Ashley took the MacLeans.

Dana and Dash were directly teleported to their home, and the sleeping clones were placed in their beds. After a few minutes watching the clones sleeping soundly in the beds they'd never again use, the quartet teleported back to the house owned by Judith and Peter. The humans needed sleep as well. Though her trust of the strange men and women was still developing, Dana accepted a vial of the same sleeping potion her clone had taken. Dash needed no such help; he fell asleep the instant his head hit the new pillow.

Adam and Gena had a more difficult challenge in placing the clone inside the apartment.

"When we teleport, our bodies emit something called Energy," Adam explained. "If too much Energy escapes, the people here to find Will Stark will be able to find us as well, and we don't want that to happen. Archie and Ashley were able to plant a device in the MacLeans home that established something of a force field inside, a force field that prevents Energy from escaping. They can teleport between the MacLeans house and one of ours without issue. We got lucky with the two of them, at least to a degree. They weren't home when Archie and Ashley first arrived, and they were able to plant the force field device ahead of time. They'd hoped the two would get to sleep at a reasonable hour, but they stayed up late." He shrugged. "Archie activated another device that eats Energy, basically. Once that force field goes away—and it's only a temporary device—the Energy that was inside the house would slip out. That Energy eating machine takes care of that problem."

"I'm guessing you couldn't plant anything like that in my apartment," Gena surmised, glancing around the cabin of the flying craft they'd entered. She tapped at the window. "Won't *this* get a lot of attention?"

"It's invisible."

"Really?" She thought for a moment, and then nodded. "You followed me in this, before, didn't you?"

Adam nodded. "We'll float close to your apartment in this, and then I'll send the force field device into the bedroom of your apartment. Once it goes off, we'll take your clone in, put her in bed, make sure nothing else needs doing, and then leave. The machines we'll leave behind will ensure that none of the Hunters, the men out to get Will Stark and possibly you, will know someone like me was ever there." He sighed. "I wish I'd been able to plant the machines ahead of time, especially since neither you nor Mark were home. We just didn't realize that Mark's address and yours were the same."

Gena shrugged, and then gave him a stern look. "I want you to know that I'm not accustomed to allowing strange men into my bedroom." Her face softened, and took on a more thoughtful look. "But I can't shake the feeling that you're no stranger, that I've known you for a very long time."

Adam stiffened slightly. "I just have one of those faces that everyone thinks looks familiar."

"Perhaps," Gena said. But her tone said she didn't believe his explanation.

Adam pulled a small box, roughly the size of a book of matches, from his pocket. "I need you to visualize your bedroom for me."

"Why?"

"I'll feed the image into this box, and it will crawl along the walls until it finds the room. Once the force field is set up, I can use that same image to teleport us inside."

Gena looked intrigued. She closed her eyes, and Adam was easily able to see her mental picture of the room and its simple furnishings. He floated the hovercraft directly over the roof of the apartment building, just above the unit where Gena and Mark lived, and tossed the box into the air. It passed directly through the permeable clear membrane that served as the top of the hovercraft, and then disappeared through the roof of the building below.

"How… how did that just happen?"

"We've made a lot of progress in the last few decades with what are being called nanoparticles or nanomachines, the same materials used to create the clothing you're wearing," Adam explained. "They now have enough intelligence to allow specific items to slide through as if the solid surfaces were permeable membranes. In this case, the box is allowed to pass through without breaking the airtight seal forming the clear top of this flying craft." At Gena's look of confusion, he shrugged. "It works like some kind of magic. That's all I know."

To his relief, she chuckled.

Ten minutes later, a light flashed on the control panel of the craft. "The shield is up and we're ready to go," Adam announced. He took Gena's hand, and then the hand of her sleeping clone, and teleported them into her bedroom.

Adam helped Gena move her clone into the bed and under the covers. Once satisfied everything looked normal, Gena put the work clothes she'd worn earlier into her hamper and collected the originals of her sleeping clothes; they didn't want the clone wondering why she suddenly had two pairs of the same set of pajamas. They also ensured that her personal items—keys, purse, mobile phone—were on the kitchen table and nightstand where she normally kept them. With everything in order, Adam teleported both of them back to the hovercraft. He pressed a few buttons to tell the "force field" device to deactivate and the "Energy eating" device to activate, and sent the craft flying invisibly and noiselessly back to De Gray Estates.

"Won't my clone find that box?" Gena asked.

Adam nodded. "She might. We can always go back and pick it up on Monday when your clone goes to work and the apartment's empty."

"I won't have a key to get in."

Adam chuckled. "We can handle that."

"What's that place like?"

"Which one?"

"The place you said we'll all go after everything happens."

"It's amazing," Adam told her. "All of it. The journey to get there, the history of the place, the people who live there… every aspect of the place is beyond words. We'll talk more about it over the next few days, because I'm sure Dana and Dash both want to know about it as well. For now, though, you should sleep."

They returned to Peter and Judith's home, where a small bedroom that hadn't existed an hour earlier had been prepared for Gena. She was exhausted, having never slept after her long shift at The Diner and the emotional shocks of the past eight hours. Adam offered her a sleeping potion, but she waved it off. "I won't need any help falling asleep."

He nodded and left.

Adam wasn't able to sleep, still too emotional from the events of the past twenty-four hours. He'd ensured that Gena would survive what he now suspected was an inevitable attack by the Hunters in the aftermath of the events coming on Monday evening, now less than thirty-six hours away. That had also had the benefit of ensuring the long-term survival of Deron's family; he admired the protectiveness Dana had showed for Dash, and the very reasonable skepticism she'd displayed toward them and their admittedly unconventional introduction.

The most important part, though, was that Gena was safe, and would be with them for a very long time.

His mind wandered to her, able to watch and sense her dreams now that there was no risk of Energy detection by the Hunters. To his shock, she dreamed of life inside a glass dome, of the decade she'd spent just trying to survive while Adam worked to rebuild the body that kept failing, until she became viable.

And she remembered *him*.

Even as she slept, she remembered him. And his "sound." His Energy sound.

It shouldn't be possible. She couldn't have Energy, not yet, and thus she shouldn't be able to sense it, let alone identify it. She'd not undergone any type of training, no zirple or morange treatments. But his eyes widened as he remembered the pink streaks in her clothing.

And they widened further as her thoughts floated to him from her dream.

I remember you, now. You're the one who saved my life.

XX
Fate

January 7, 2030

Gena Adams woke and stretched, feeling her limbs lengthen and muscles loosen, before rolling her head to the side to look at Mark. But Mark wasn't there. The bed she rested upon wasn't her bed, nor was it large enough to hold both of them. A momentary bout of panic set in, until she remembered why she was sleeping here, a strange bed in a stranger room in a stranger's home.

Alone.

The understanding that memory brought did nothing to dispel her panic. It merely altered the reason for it.

She'd slept fitfully until late Sunday afternoon, and spent the remainder of the day getting a very preliminary introduction to a group called the Alliance. The members of that group would become her new family, her new world, as she'd given up any chance of returning to her previous way of life when she'd agreed to the cloning arrangement. She'd never called them abductors, as Dana MacLean had. She had a lifetime of living ahead of her with this group, and holding a grudge would make the time spent with them unpleasant.

Eva explained that their group, and a larger original group called the Aliomenti, had discovered how to unlock the innate human ability to manipulate something they called Energy, which sounded like either magic or quantum physics to her. It was something Adam had alluded to as they'd returned her clone to the apartment. As Gena unlocked that ability and grew the amount of Energy her body could produce and store at a given time, she'd gain new abilities. They could move objects with their minds, read minds, and move instantly from place to place. The Energy expended began to accumulate in the air, because she could hear and feel it buzzing around her. Perhaps it was just her growing excitement at the idea she'd be able to do the same things soon. Dana and Dash, the wife and son of the man Mark would work with today, didn't seem to notice the sizzle in the air. They looked terrified every time Adam or Ashley or Archie or the others did something... unusual.

Archie told them that most of the people living inside the De Gray Estates were in disguise, living a public life as aging business and media tycoons, while they privately worked to ensure Will Stark's life proceeded exactly as they intended, minimizing "collateral damage" to others in the process through efforts like the cloning they'd just done with Gena and the MacLeans. She wasn't a prisoner; they'd wanted to be certain she didn't die in the crossfire of the war between the Aliomenti and the Alliance, and with her clone in place she could leave at any time she chose.

Gena turned around and walked out the front door, waiting for someone to stop her, to chase her, to do that disappear-and-reappear thing they did. None of them had given chase. She truly was free to leave if she so chose.

She'd gone back into the house, to the education session, in part because she was cold, in part because she didn't know where her clone was, in part because she was genuinely curious about Energy and the Alliance and the secret base Adam had hinted at the night before. She also worried that Mark would see her and wonder how she'd gotten through the supposedly impenetrable security system... and why she'd done so and jeopardized his job as a security guard for the community.

After reflecting on the previous day, Gena stretched again and rose from the bed. She'd developed a basic understanding of the layout of the house over the past day or so, and could always follow the humming Energy sounds that hung in the air. The trail of sounds now led her to the large, modern kitchen. The room was a hive of activity, full of anxious members of the Alliance, each waiting for the day to play out according to a plan they'd apparently had in place for some absurdly long period of time.

Peter offered her breakfast, and she accepted a beverage that looked like slop but tasted like heaven. The drink left her feeling alert and energized. If this was her future, she was feeling happy about the decision to join them. So far.

Ashley, who had started several high tech companies, including one recently bought by Will Stark, glanced over at Gena. "I'm going shopping today, and need to know your clothing size and style preferences."

Gena looked interested. "Can I go with you?"

Ashley considered her response before answering. "Your clone is living life on the outside. If you go went with me, how would you explain to people the fact that you were in two places at once? What would happen if you encountered your clone?"

Gena scowled. So much for being free to leave. But she realized Ashley hadn't told her no, just reminded her of one of the challenges she'd face if she left the house. In effect, she'd made her choice to stay in this house when she'd agreed to undergo the cloning. Her scowl turned to a puzzled frown as a new thought entered her mind. "Ashley, what happens if my clone *isn't* killed?"

"The clone will die in the next few days, whether she is killed or not."

Gena winced. "But during the next few days, she'll have experiences. A funny story from a friend, a meal shared with Mark, things like that. Things that she—I—should know. What if the clone isn't murdered and I elect to go back to being the old me? How do I get those memories into my head?"

Ashley turned and fixed Gena with a stern look. "I believe you said you were planning to come with us after all of this was over, didn't you? Why are you worried about that?"

Gena folded her arms and returned the glare. "The memories she's experiencing and living are mine. They belong in my head, regardless of where I'm living a week from now."

Ashley looked taken aback and blinked several times. Clearly, the idea that Gena—or the MacLeans—were being deprived the memories their clones would experience was something she'd not considered. She opened her mouth several times as if to respond, but struggled to formulate an answer.

At long last, she gave Gena a reply. "I honestly don't know what to tell you. I'll ask the others what we can do."

Gena nodded. "Thank you." It was all she wanted, the knowledge that an effort would be made to determine if those memories could be salvaged. Ashley was correct on the other point, though. She'd truly made her choice to leave her current life when she'd agreed to the cloning; reneging now wouldn't be wise.

Eva and Aaron walked into the kitchen, and Eva glanced sharply at Ashley, fully aware that she'd been involved in an intense conversation. That didn't surprise Gena; they'd told her that Energy sensitivity enabled a person to project and sense thoughts and emotions. Eva's glance fell upon Gena, and the expression suggested that the "old" woman of the group was unsurprised as to the source of Ashley's discomfort.

Eva's gaze returned to Ashley as Archie joined them. "We are moving to our positions. Graham has checked in; he is working to expedite Myra VanderPoole's departure."

Gena glanced at each of them in turn. "Who is Graham?"

Dana entered the kitchen as Aaron answered Gena's question. "Graham is one of us. He drives Myra VanderPoole around town so the woman can shop and eat, and helps her carry her purchases to and from the car. Outside Will, Myra's the only human here—meaning, she doesn't know about or use Energy. We need as much time to work with Deron and Mark today as possible, but we can't start until Will and Myra leave the community. Graham's doing everything he can to get her out the door and the gate as soon as possible, and we expect Will is leaving even now. One they've left, Eva and I will handle bringing both Deron and Mark here for the cloning conversation."

Dana nodded. She'd mellowed somewhat over the past day, less because she agreed with the approach of the people who called themselves the Alliance, and more because she'd come to believe that these people truly did know the future. She'd come to accept the fact that they were acting to preserve the lives of her husband, Mark Arnold, Will Stark, and others. "I'm looking forward to talking with Deron."

Eva shook her head. "That will not be possible. Like you, Deron must make his decision on his own, without the input of others."

"But I *didn't* make my decision on my own!" Dana snapped, her anger returning in an instant. "Dash, Gena, and I were all here, together, and—"

"You made the decision for Dash, and Gena's decision would have no impact on your own." Eva's words were like ice. "Nor would your decision impact Gena's. Both of you attempted to divine what your loved one would choose to do, and made your choice accordingly. Both men will have that same chance. If Deron would normally choose not to be cloned, but knew you *had* made that choice, he would feel a sense of obligation to make the same choice. If he had preferred to live through our cloning option, but found that you had elected to decline our offer, would he still choose to live, or alter his decision and choose death rather than live without you and Dash?"

Dana glared at Eva, but said nothing.

"No, both men will have their options presented to them, just as we presented them to you. If they opt to choose cloning, they will join you here and we will return the clones to the station or tower. If either opts against cloning, they will lose their memories of our meeting and will return to work, none the wiser, to face their fate."

"And you'll just let them die," Dana added, her tone bitter.

"Our group operates under the belief that information must be shared, but that each person must take on the responsibility of making their own decisions using that information. It would be counter to everything we stand for to force them to choose cloning... or to deny them that option if we are able to make it available."

"If Mark chooses not to be cloned?" Gena's voice was soft, barely above a whisper, and the noise in the kitchen seemed to vanish as each of them waited to hear her next words. "Then... I would prefer to reverse my choice. I made my decision because it gave me the only chance to know Mark's final decision, and to adapt accordingly."

"We will not end your life," Archie said, gently.

"But your very credo means you won't prevent me from doing so on my own," Gena replied.

Adam, who'd entered the kitchen, froze. "I see no reason to speculate on this," he said, his voice shaky. "We have yet to present the information about current circumstances to either Mark or

Deron. I suspect both men will, at a minimum, make the practical choice as you have, electing to undergo cloning to have the ability to learn what you've chosen."

Gena sighed. "I don't know if he will, though. Mark… he's always been one willing to make any sacrifice for others, for as long as I've known him. But he hates the idea of asking others to do something for him. He might think it… I don't know, noble or something. Allowing fate to take its course. Choosing to face that killer head on, even though he'll not know it's coming. Thinking that sending a clone to face the killer is somehow asking someone else to accept the fate meant for him." She gritted her teeth. "I don't know if it's a given that he'll choose cloning."

Adam's cheek twitched. "Only time will tell." He glanced at Eva and Aaron. "When are the two of you heading out?"

"Now," Aaron said. "Graham's indicated that Mrs. VanderPoole is being a bit, uh, intransigent this morning."

Ashley snorted. "Surprise, surprise, right?"

Aaron's mouth twitched briefly into a smile. "Surprise or not, the longer she takes, the less time we have to act. We'll be in position to move as soon as she's gone. Judith and Peter are already off warming up the cloning machines to perform their double duty today. We'll be back as soon as we can."

Gena nodded at them. "Good luck."

•••

De Gray Estates provided a fleet of covered electric golf carts for use by residents. Since the homes inside were often a mile or more apart, they were intended to enable visits between neighbors as well. They were rarely used for that purpose, however. Myra VanderPoole had no interest in interacting with the others, and the remaining residents had no need for carts to traverse the space between residences.

The carts, though, were also used to travel to and from the entry without the accompanying need to park their own expensive automobiles outside in the elements. The wealthy residents used limousines to travel around the city when they emerged from the fortress, and didn't want to spend the time signing their drivers up for community access. Nor did they wish to wait for the concrete gate to lower into the ground so they could exit or enter the community. There were more carts available than residents so that visitors could use the carts as well… and because residents who drove carts home wouldn't return them until they needed to leave the neighborhood again

Eva and Aaron would take full advantage of those facts today. The golf cart they'd borrowed to make the drive home from the front gate had been modified, with new features that would come into play once they'd successfully removed the guards from the buildings near the entry.

The cart crunched over the gravel driveway leading from Peter and Judith's home to the central roundabout near the entrance. As they neared the entry and came within visibility range of the tower, Eva drove the cart into the trees near the entrance.

And then they waited.

A moment later, a limousine moved into the roundabout and pulled up to the gate. The window on the driver's side rolled down, and the face of an elderly man known as Frank appeared. "Good morning," he said, speaking into a microphone mounted in the kiosk near the exit. "This is Frank, the driver for Myra VanderPoole. I am asking that the vehicle gate be lowered so we can leave."

"Good morning, Frank. Out for a drive today?"

"Yes, sir," Frank replied. "Mrs. VanderPoole has decided that some retail therapy is in order. I suspect we'll be gone much of the day."

"I have you marked down, Frank. I'll start the gate now."

A rumbling noise started, and the ten foot high gate slowly began its descent.

Once it went back up, it would be time for Eva and Aaron to act.

Frank's head pulled back inside, and even from their vantage point, Eva and Aaron could hear the sounds of Myra VanderPoole speaking, and Frank's exasperated replies. The driver leaned his head out the window once more, and, with an exaggerated sigh, spoke into the console. "Hold the gate, Mark. Mrs. VanderPoole needs to… powder her nose before we leave."

"Um…I'm not sure I can stop the gate once it's started lowering. Let me check on that. Can you come to the door to get the restroom key?"

"Of course," Frank replied. He exited the car and walked

241

briskly around the vehicle, exhaling deeply into frigid air. He cast a brief, worried look in the direction of Eva and Aaron.

"This is *not* good," Eva muttered. "We do *not* have time for something like this."

"There *is* some interesting irony in play here, though," Aaron said. Eva smacked his arm, and he shrugged.

Frank knocked on the door, and Mark Arnold appeared a moment later, shortly after the gate's descent halted. Mark, one of the men they'd come to collect, chatted briefly with Frank before handing over the key to the bathroom. They'd stopped the gate's descent, but it would take nearly fifteen minutes after Myra reclaimed her seat in the car before the gate would allow the limousine outside. And Eva and Aaron couldn't make their move until the gate was fully raised.

Aaron glared at the limousine. "I never did like that woman."

There was nothing they could do but wait.

"We need to alter our plan," Eva said.

"I know," Aaron replied, raising his wrist to his mouth and tapping on the screen of the watch there to activate the communicator. "Peter, we have a delay at the entry. See if you can pull in extra electricity from our house to speed things up. We're going to lose at least another twenty minutes before we can get started here."

Peter offered a muffled curse of frustration. "I'm not a miracle worker, Aaron."

"That's not what Judith tells me."

"Is that what she says about me? I'm sure it's quite true, then."

"Please, work on it, Peter. We'll try to salvage as much time on this end as we can."

"On it, boss. See you soon." Peter disconnected.

"We can only hope," Aaron muttered.

●●●

Thirty minutes later, the gate finally began rising above the ground. Mrs. VanderPoole suffered from arthritic pain in her legs, and the walk to and from the facility was an exercise in frustration for Eva and Aaron, who blew excess air from their lungs each time the elderly woman paused to rest.

"We need to begin immediately," Eva said.

"But the gate—"

"I am fully aware of the gate, as it is directly in front of me. The fact remains that we cannot wait until it has completed its ascent to begin our work. Move out."

Aaron nodded and hopped off the cart, followed by Eva, and the two marched toward the guard station. Aaron glanced at the restroom, amused at the key role the simple building would play in saving the lives of two good men.

As they walked, Eva and Aaron let loose tiny robots toward the guard station and tower, robots programmed to seek out Mark Arnold and Deron MacLean. Each robot contained a specially formulated serum which would be secreted into the bodies of the two guards. They expected that the serum's contents would drive both men out of their seats and out of the buildings... and out of the range of the cameras recording their every movement.

"How long should it take?" Eva asked.

"Should only take a few minutes. The robots move quickly, and the serum, I'm told, has an almost instant impact on the, ah, target."

Three minutes later, as the "elderly" couple shuffled close by, Mark Arnold burst from the guard station, looking decidedly uncomfortable. He spotted them, and looked apologetic. "I called Deron, and I'm pretty sure he's coming, but I couldn't wait, I..."

Mark sprinted for the bathroom door, fumbled with the key, and managed to get inside, slamming the door behind him.

Aaron glanced at Eva. "The dosage may have been a bit strong."

"Regularity is a good thing."

"There's such a thing as too much of a good thing, you know."

Eva snorted.

A minute later, Deron MacLean burst from the inner door of the tower, trying to run for the bathroom, rather than the guard station. He barely noticed Eva and Aaron, so desperate was his need, and he sprang upon the door, seized the handle, and shook it with vigor. "Mark! Let me in!"

Mark's muffled voice couldn't be heard, but it was clear that whatever afflicted him hadn't quite cleared up. Deron, desperate, darted into the trees a mere twenty feet from the golf cart, and the noises made it clear he'd failed to resist the effects of their serum long enough.

Eva glanced at Aaron. "I'll let you work with Deron."

Aaron rolled his eyes. "Thanks a lot."

He walked into the forest, ensuring he covered the ground at a slow, noisy pace to alert Deron to his approach. "Deron? Are you okay?"

Deron's voice was weak. "I could use some help."

Aaron nodded. He wrinkled his nose at the smell as he approached the stricken man, and moved to help the guard stand in his fouled clothing. As he did so, he scraped a sample of skin off the back of Deron's neck and directly into a sealed vial. With the cloning sample collected, he injected a small burst of Energy into the sleep centers of the man's brain, and Deron collapsed, instantly asleep. He floated the man's body to the back seat of the golf cart and propped him into a seated position. Eva arrived a moment later, hauling Mark's unconscious form with ease, as if the man was a slip of paper, and dropped him next to Deron. She wrinkled her nose. "What is that *smell?*"

Aaron smiled and handed her the tissue sample from Deron. "Like I said, the dose was too strong. Now it's your turn to deal with it."

Eva smacked his arm, climbed into the driver's seat, and drove away.

Aaron pulled a photograph of Mark Arnold from his pocket and concentrated. Five minutes later, he emerged from the woods, looking exactly like the unconscious guard in the back of the golf cart racing to Project 2030 headquarters. He moved to the door of the guard station, opened it, and stepped inside.

Mark Arnold was back on duty.

To the outside world, it would look like business as usual at the entry to De Gray Estates.

●●●

Eva flipped the first special switch on the dashboard of the golf cart, and the open sides were instantly encased. The modification was intended to keep the two unconscious men from falling out of the cart, but she now had to deal with the unintended and unexpected consequences of the morning as well. They'd distilled some of the internal cleansing effects of morange to trigger an urge that the guards couldn't ignore, the only non-Energy method they could conceive of to get both men to leave their camera-riddled work environments at the same time. The dosage had worked far better— or, perhaps, worse—than expected. Neither man had been successful in his efforts to respond to the effects of the serum before soiling his clothing.

The enclosed cabin gave Eva an opportunity to test just how long she could hold her breath.

Eva forced herself to focus and hit the second switch. The engine power was amplified by an order of magnitude, and the golf cart shot forward down the gravel driveway toward Peter and Judith's home at nearly one hundred miles per hour. It wasn't as fast as teleporting, but in seconds she arrived at a door to Peter and Judith's home, an opening just large enough for the vehicle. She entered without slowing down, and Ashley slammed the door shut behind her. With the scutarium shield fully operational, Eva teleported the entire cart to the cloning room in the sub-basement while simultaneously stopping the engine and halting the rotation of the four tires. The teleportation eliminated the inertial effects on driver and passengers, and her instant halt resulted in nary a movement from the unconscious men in the back seat.

Ashley joined her in the sub-basement level an instant later.

The noses in the room all wrinkled in unison as the cabin panels on the golf cart disappeared. Peter, whose eyes were watering, frowned. "I take it the dosage was a smidge too strong?"

"Yes," Eva replied. She inhaled gulps of the relatively fresh air.

Peter and Adam nodded, and quickly stripped the guards down before using Energy bursts to clear the excrement from their bodies. They put fresh clothing on the two men while their original clothes were cleaned. They'd erase memories related to the serum's aftereffects before returning clone or original to the respective work environments. Focus gradually returned as the air purifiers cleared the stench, and fresh air once more filled the room.

Eva handed the two tissue samples to Peter. "I think you

need to start the process immediately, even before we have had the chance to talk to them. Time is too critical at this point. If they choose not to be cloned, we can interrupt the process or allow the clones to meet their natural end if they've already finished growing when we learn of the decisions."

Peter nodded, and moved to the machines to initiate the cloning procedures. Within minutes, the tissue samples were examined by the cloning machines, and the cloning process was underway.

They awakened the guards in the same room where Gena, Dawn, and Dash had learned of the Aliomenti, the Alliance, Energy, and the impending events of this day only hours earlier. Both men were staggered at the news.

Deron looked disturbed. "I'm really not sure what to do, though."

Adam nodded at him. "It's not a fair position to be in, and I don't envy you. I'd recommend talking out loud as you think things over, and don't hesitate to ask questions. The only question we won't answer is whether your loved ones chose the cloning process when given the option."

"It's not quite the same thing, though," Mark noted. "In their case, it might be a moot point. If I've understood the story correctly, there's no proof that they'll actually die. Sure, there's a greater chance now, especially for Gena." He paused. "But in our case, you've confirmed it. It *will* happen. And you won't stop it from happening, because of the greater good."

Adam could only nod at the summation.

Deron sighed. "I feel like I'm cheating death, and I'm not sure if that's wise. Yet if I have a chance to continue to live with my family, even though the world I've known thinks me dead, even if it means I must leave life as I've known it behind forever… I think I need to go through with the cloning process." He looked at his hands, and then at the floor. "Maybe I'm just a coward, too afraid to accept my own mortality."

"You aren't a coward, Deron," Adam replied. "It's our nature to try to survive, to fight death to the very end." He motioned to the door of the room. "Step outside and let them know your decision. They'll take you to another room to wait out the events of the next day or two. When your clone is finished growing, we'll return him to the tower."

Deron left the room.

Mark watched him go, and turned to Adam. "Deron's words and thoughts... well, they reflect mine as well. I've made my choice."

Adam nodded. "Then you'll need to step through the door as well."

"No," Mark said, shaking his head. "I don't want to be cloned. I'm going back to my station."

Adam froze.

"If it's my time to die, Adam, then it's my time to die. I won't remember this, I know, and I won't know what's coming. But I've had the chance to meet Gena, to know love, and now I have the chance to play my part in something far bigger than me. That's a good life, isn't it?"

Pain scarred Adam's face. "Are you sure? You don't want to go through the cloning process, if only to find out what option Gena chose?"

"I already know what she chose to do, Adam. And she knew what I'd choose to do as well when she made her decision, even if she hoped I'd do otherwise. If I allow my clone to die in my stead, then, in my mind, I've basically asked another to suffer on my behalf. And I won't do that. And who knows?" He smiled weakly. "Maybe I'll land a good punch and knock that Assassin out cold."

Adam looked at the ground as he fought to compose himself.

Mark walked over and clapped him on the shoulder. "I don't blame you for any of this, and she won't either. Just... tell her I love her, okay?"

Adam looked up, his face moist, and nodded once.

Mark took a deep breath. "Then let's get going. I think you need to give me a ride back to the station and erase some memories." He paused. "Just... don't erase anything about Gena, okay?"

Adam stimulated the sleep centers of Mark's brain, and as the man slumped toward the ground Adam's Energy caught him, letting him stretch out in a deep sleep on a sofa in the meeting room.

Four hours later, they piled the unconscious forms of the two men—one of them a clone—into the back seat of the golf cart, and Adam climbed into the driver's seat to take the men back to their stations.

By then, word of Mark's decision had spread to the rest of

the house.

Gena watched them drive away from an upper window of the house.

Her screams of agony and grief, and the pained emotions she projected, so overwhelmed Adam that he could barely keep the cart on the gravel road.

XXI
Forgettable

January 7, 2030

"Happy birthday, Will."

Will smiled and stretched out on their bed, feeling his limbs lengthening and his muscles loosening. He relished the sound that woke him, the sound of the most beautiful voice in the world. Her beauty and goodness expressed themselves to every sense he possessed. He'd noticed that just being in her presence lately seemed to generate a flute-like sound, a tone of purity that was beyond anything he'd heard from even the greatest master musicians of the day.

He rolled over and sat up, smiling, drinking in her image. "Thanks."

She held up a card. "I made sure to find your driver's license, Mister I'm-Going-To-Drive-Myself-To-Work. Oh, and I made you some breakfast as well." She pulled a small plate from behind her back, laden with a small cake and a single lit candle protruding from the top. "Shall I sing?"

He leaned forward and blew out the candle; she knew what he'd wished for without asking. "Too late for that, I'm afraid." He sat back up and accepted the plate from her. "How long have you been up, anyway?"

"Approximately five minutes. My compliments to the person who invented microwave ovens."

"I thought you hated microwaving food?"

"Well, you only turn thirty-five once, right? Live a little."

"I'll keep that in mind for when you hit thirty."

She winced a bit, but managed a smile. "Fair enough."

Will finished eating the cake before showering. As he did each morning before leaving, he slipped into Josh's room to whisper a farewell, and to utter a silent wish that the boy would greet him upon his return later in the day. Josh slept soundly, an expressionless look upon his cherubic face. The sandy blond hair was, in Will's mind, a perfect blend of Hope's platinum blond and his own jet black. Will imagined the icy blue eyes hidden behind the closed lids, eyes which to him seemed to show an unusual intelligence for one so young, and wondered, not for the first time, what wrong he'd done that caused his son to be rendered mute, the symptoms of an ailment that the best doctors on the planet couldn't identify.

"Maybe today, Josh," he whispered. "There would be no greater gift on any day." He reached out and tousled his son's hair, letting his hand linger a bit longer than usual. Smokey, Josh's pet and constant companion, looked up from where she'd nestled against the boy's side. Will smiled, and patted the animal on the head. "Take care of him, Smokey. I know you will." Smokey thumped her tail in response, though Will could only wonder whether she did so in appreciation of the attention or in agreement with the words Will uttered.

It was another part of what he wanted to be normal about this day. He wanted to drive himself to and from work, to go out to dinner with his family, and to hear his son speak and laugh. Those weren't wishes that required billions of dollars, though he'd happily trade his billions for the experience. Today, perhaps, he'd see that wish come true.

He wandered downstairs, where Hope sat at the table in the kitchen, near the sliding glass door to the backyard. She looked unusually tired today, a trend he'd noticed over the past several years. She still had far more zest than he did, but instead of the usual consistency, she was prone to bouts of adrenaline and fatigue. "Are you okay?"

She glanced up, almost startled at his presence. "I'm fine. A little sleepy still, I guess. How's Josh?"

"Still asleep." He gave a thin smile. "And still quiet."

"You'll hear him talk, Will. I promise."

"Today?"

"I predict that the odds are in your favor."

He gave her a thumbs up. "That's the spirit." He walked over to give her a kiss goodbye. "Thanks for breakfast. And everything else."

She held his hand tight. "Thank you, as well. For everything you do, and for everything you *will* do."

He smiled, and then headed out to his car.

Hope moved to the large window at the front of the house, watching him drive away. As soon as he was out of sight, she ran upstairs, threw herself on her bed, and sobbed uncontrollably.

To the best of her knowledge, it was the last time she'd ever see her husband.

●●●

Once she'd cried until no tears were left, once she felt drained of any emotion, Hope worked to pull herself together. Much as she hated what was happening, she realized she had to play her part and ensure everything went as planned today. If not, the lives of Josh of Angel were very much at risk. She put on jeans and a sweatshirt and pulled her hair back in a ponytail.

She released the Energy Shield on Josh as she walked downstairs, and moments later her son bounded down the steps with Smokey nipping at his heels. "What's wrong, Mommy?"

Hope sighed. Nothing could be hidden from her son. "There's a lot going on today, sweetie, and it makes me tired just thinking about it."

"Can I help?"

She thought about that, trying to anticipate how the day's events would unfold. "Yes. Go put all of your stuffed animals in a big pile in your closet."

The little boy nodded and ran off to his room. Smokey, thinking it was a game, raced after him, and the little boy laughed in delight.

Hope ran through the list of things to do, trying to ensure

that she could act as normal as possible when the Assassin arrived. She checked the safe to make sure that the gun was there, along with the two clips of ammunition. She took one clip with her and locked everything back in the safe for later. Will's spare set of glasses were in the bathroom. She moved downstairs with both the clip and the glasses, and placed both on the counter in the kitchen. Her grown son would retrieve both items later.

She choked up a bit. It was difficult to imagine the little boy giggling in his room upstairs as a grown man. She let her senses drift to him, and watched as Josh carried out her orders. The boy tossed stuffed animals into the closet, and laughed as Smokey would rush to retrieve the projectiles and return them. She smiled.

Hope found a couple of baseball gloves and stowed them near the bat rack at the rear of the house, and made sure several bats were there. They were all made of wood. Will preferred to take his practice with the wooden bats because he enjoyed the feel of wood connecting with a baseball far more than metal, and preferred the sounds produced by wood as well. She glanced into the backyard, to the automated batting cage he'd built there years ago. He'd hoped to watch his son take an independent turn in the cage, but Josh had never been able to do so.

At least, not in Will's presence.

The unfairness of it all dragged on her once again, exaggerating—or exaggerated by—her fatigue. Why would she agree to a plan like this, one that demanded she hide her son's soul, intelligence, personality, and voice from the wonderful man he called Daddy? Why would she deny the boy the relationship he needed and deserved with the man he rightly considered the world's greatest hero?

And why would she agree to say goodbye as if she didn't know she'd never see him again?

Get it together, Hope. The future and the past depend upon it.

Josh trotted back down the steps, with his dog in tow. "All done, Mommy. Smokey thought we were playing fetch, though."

Hope smiled at her son. "Very good, Josh." She glanced at the clock. Where had the time gone? "It looks like it's lunchtime. Let's have something to eat and then do some quiet reading before our naps, okay? We're going out to dinner for Daddy's birthday later, so we need to be wide awake when Daddy gets home."

Josh looked at her. "Mommy, you always tell me not to lie."

Hope took a deep breath. "We're going to *pretend* that we're getting ready to go out to dinner for Daddy's birthday."

The boy studied her face, reading the half-truth there. But he nodded. "Okay, Mommy. We can do that. But I wish you weren't so sad all the time, or so tired."

"So do I, Josh," Hope said with a sigh. "So do I."

They enjoyed a simple lunch. She and Will had made the conscious choice to keep the house to a modest size—relatively, anyway—because neither wanted to live in a home so large that they'd require live-in servants just to maintain it. Thus, lunch was a private affair, just her and Josh, with no one else milling about. It was a wonderful time for them to bond. She'd refrained from explaining to Josh too much about his abilities, that he was unique in the history of the world, as she didn't want the Assassin to figure out exactly what the boy was through the child's own thoughts. If he gave that information away, the Assassin might well leave them and try to locate the Hunters for assistance. They couldn't allow that to happen. Josh knew he had special abilities that needed to be hidden, and so he made no effort to use or restrain them, pretending they were an imaginary skill. That would change after today as well. They'd spend their time in the bunker training him, especially in Shielding.

Josh yawned after lunch, and walked to his room, unbidden, for a nap. She knew the instant he was asleep, and she collapsed into a chair to rest. Why was she so tired all the time? It wasn't the pregnancy. She was aware of her pregnancy, knew it would impact her, knew it would be a somewhat different experience since she was carrying a girl this time. But it couldn't be *this* different. And she'd been sensing the growing fatigue before her second pregnancy began.

What was the cause?

So deep was her focus on that question that she didn't notice the man who'd entered the room until he spoke.

"Hello, Hope."

She screamed.

●●●

"Hope, are you okay?" Adam asked, frowning. "It's just me."

She calmed herself, grateful that Josh hadn't woken up.

"Sorry. It's just… it's been a long day."

"It's been a long few centuries," Adam agreed. "But yes, the last few have been the worst."

"I'm so tired all the time, and I'm constantly focused on what's going to happen to Will," Hope admitted. "It's been like this for a while, and I don't know why."

Adam frowned. "Do you think it's just stress and worry about what's to come today?"

Hope shook her head. "No. I mean, yes, I'm worried about today. But it's more than that. I've known this day would come for centuries. I've had every opportunity to prepare myself for it. And even a decade ago, an amount of time that seems like nothing to me… even then, nothing was wrong. But lately? That worry and despair are destroying me."

"You're afraid you won't see Will again, aren't you?" Adam surmised.

She nodded, stunning herself by not breaking down at his words. "But I've *always* known that was a possibility. I knew when I watched him leave to go meet the Hunters that he might not come back, that I might not ever see him again. But I dealt with that without much drama. Maybe I just suspected from what I knew that he would survive, and therefore it was just a temporary separation. We've been apart for a century before, Adam. Maybe we'll be apart for another century, or two centuries. Yet I have this fear that he's going to be gone for good." Her face crumbled. "Or maybe I will."

"You just saw him a few days ago. He summoned the Hunters here."

She gave a faint nod. "But I didn't really see him, or talk to him. And now he's gone again."

Adam sighed. "He wasn't gone until earlier today. We hid him at the house to give him a chance to recover, so that we could all reunite and plan what to do next after today's events finish. But when Eva went to check on him this morning he was gone. No trace of him."

She threw up her hands. "See? I could have seen him once more. But now? Now, he's truly gone."

"Our notes from the future say he'll be here today."

"Yeah, to save me." She fumed. "I do *not* need to be saved. I can take care of myself and Josh. It's the *Assassin*, for crying out loud.

He's an Energy lightweight."

"We all know that, Hope," Adam said. His voice was calm, gentle, full of compassion. "All of us have been asked to do things we'd rather not do, you more than most. Events and circumstances may come up later today that we haven't known about before now, and maybe given those new circumstances we'll all decide it would be *best* if Will *does* take care of things. We just don't know. All I ask is that you allow yourself to adapt to circumstances and do what is best for you and for Josh."

Hope scowled. "That would mean taking my son and leaving the house now. Would that be so bad?"

Adam sighed. "If you do that, the Assassin will wait for you to come home, for however long that takes. And we'll arrive from the future wondering why nothing's happening."

"You're here *now*, though. You could adapt future plans based on that new approach."

He shook his head. "No, Hope. Too many things may change as a result of that alteration, and a mere rescheduling of our arrival may not fix everything." He paused. "I came here to talk to you for a different reason."

She recognized the attempt to change the subject and elected not to fight it. "What reason would that be?"

"I'm trying to reconcile what we know with what our future notes tell us. Specifically, I've been wondering, like you, why Will needs to move you away from the Assassin when you can do so without issue on your own."

"Thank you. My current emotional state notwithstanding, right?"

"That's… part of it, too," he admitted.

Her eyes flashed.

He held up a hand. "Hear me out, okay? My general belief is that the clues we've been given from the future are important, and that there's hidden guidance to be found within them. As strange as that advice might seem, we have to ask why it might be correct, and why it was provided to us. Make sense so far?"

She shrugged.

"So I asked the question: why the obvious and repeated references to Will coming to the rescue today? At first, given circumstances, I wondered why because it seemed he'd died at the hands of the Hunters several years ago. Clearly, our future guidance was a mistake, right? Maybe it was metaphorical. Not only were you capable of handling things on your own, but Will didn't look like he'd be around to be able to do anything."

This time, she nodded. "Go on."

"I saw him, though. So did the others. You surely sensed his Energy blast. He's alive. And therefore, I had to reopen that line of thinking once more, but I made a subtle change in the question. I asked why you *wouldn't* handle things, rather than why you *couldn't*. Just knowing Will was coming in wouldn't be enough. He spent years doing everything he could to keep your existence a secret from the Aliomenti; at a minimum, you'd handle things here just to keep his survival a secret from them now."

Hope blinked a few times, and then nodded. "I hadn't thought of that, actually. I'd been so… offended at the idea that I needed to be protected and helped that I hadn't considered the possibility of how my handling the teleportation effort could protect *him*."

"So let's ask the question: if you want to handle it because you can, and because it could protect Will… why would history still tell us you don't? There *must* be a reason. Because on the surface, you handling things makes far more sense."

She studied him. "And you know that reason, don't you?"

He nodded. "I think so. And if you think about it, so do you. We've already mentioned everything."

She considered it all, their conversation, the events of the past few days, and tried to reconcile that with what history said would happen.

And then she knew.

"He summoned them here," she whispered. "They already *know* he's alive, don't they?"

"It's reasonable to assume that," Adam agreed. "True, they may think we invented a machine to simulate Will's Energy, but they'll probably consider that unlikely. And with good reason. We talked about that machine idea years ago, remember, but nobody could figure out how to build it. So they know that Energy burst came from Will. And they know he's alive."

"If I expend Energy to teleport us, the Hunters will learn something they didn't know. They'll learn that Will Stark didn't marry a human woman."

Adam nodded. "And that's why I think you'd *let* him handle things. Not because *you can't* handle things, but because it keeps new information from getting to the Aliomenti. If we've kept your existence a secret this long, I see no reason to volunteer information about your existence and power to our... friends."

Hope watched him. "There's something more that you're not telling me."

He sighed. "You're right. That's because it's the part of my thinking that you'll hate."

"Try me."

He considered for a moment. "We've speculated what the Assassin might do if he arrived here later and learned that you're a powerful Energy user. We think he'd probably try to flee and let the Hunters know about your true nature. We don't want that to happen. That speculation is based on your *use* of Energy, of you letting your Shield drop. It seems unlikely that you'd do that, though. At least, not on purpose."

She let that slide. "How else would he know?"

"You'd *think* about it," Adam replied, his voice quiet. "If you're planning to teleport the two of you to the bunker, you must first *think* about doing so. You're likely going to think about it because you must pick the right time to do so. Too soon, or too late, and something we don't like might happen. Your thoughts would provide to the Assassin—and by extension, in some fashion, the Hunters—exactly what we don't want him to learn."

"But how could I *not* think about it?" Hope asked, frustrated.

"There's only one way," Adam said. "And that's if you don't *know* that you can."

She stared at him, the truth dawning. "You want to wipe out my memory. Just like you did with all those people you cloned."

He shook his head. "Not wipe out. *Block*. We don't want those memories gone, just repressed until today's events are complete. I think it would be best to try to put a trigger of some kind in place, something that we know should happen that indicates it's safe for you to know and reveal your ability to him, when it's too late for him to do anything about it."

Hope looked at her hands, clenched together. "You're asking me to forget who I am. To forget *what* I am. And that could put my son's life at risk."

"Who you are won't change, Hope. You're a mother who's going to protect her son to the best of her ability. You just won't know how powerful those abilities are."

"How do we ensure that the Assassin isn't successful, then? You talk of something triggering my memories to return. What if that doesn't work? What if my memories don't return in time for me to protect my son? What if—?"

"Your *what if* has a name, Hope. I think that's where Will comes in."

"You *think*?" Hope shook her head. "That's not good enough, Adam. I'll not agree to a strategy that relies upon guesses of who might be available to help out. Guesses might mean my son dies."

"Then I'll stay in the house, and if I see anything go wrong, I'll take care of things myself."

Hope watched him. "You'd stay in a house that's supposed to explode and burn to ash?"

Adam nodded. "All I'm supposed to do today is watch everything with the cloned originals. There are others who will be there, though. I can do more good here."

Hope stood up and walked around, pacing across the plush carpeting in the room, thinking. She finally looked up. "There are very few people I'd trust when my son's life is at risk, Adam. You're asking me to put my faith in two of them. And for that reason, and that reason only, I'll agree."

Adam nodded. "Close your eyes."

She did.

He moved Energy into her mind, finding those aspects of her memories that dealt with her Energy skills. He blocked memories of Will before she'd met him in Pleasanton, blocked knowledge of the Aliomenti and the Alliance, and blocked memories of those she'd known for centuries. When he was done, she truly believed that she was a twenty-eight year old human woman with a husband and son she adored, and her accessible memories reinforced that image.

She'd fallen into a deep sleep as a result of the extensive intrusion into her mind. He picked her up and carried her to her room, took off her shoes, and tucked her under the covers. She'd wake up in time for the events later in the day; he'd make sure of that.

As he left to let the others know of the change in plans relating to his location, he thought about the memory of *him* that he'd found in her mind. He had no idea how she'd found out, or figured it out, but it wasn't something he could have her repeating to others. One day? Maybe. But today wasn't that day.

That memory was blocked as deeply as he could bury it. There was only one other person who knew, and he'd keep it that way as long as possible.

One day, Hope would know what he'd hidden from her.

He wondered if she'd forgive him for keeping it secret.

XXII
Direction

January 7, 2030

Peter and Judith had transformed a large media room into their headquarters for the day. The Alliance team on the grounds for the attack had to both remain hidden and be on the alert for anything that might go wrong. Hope had scattered invisible cameras and microphones throughout the house, and Aaron had spent his time doing the same earlier that day while posing as Mark in the guard station. They hadn't considered how to get into the tower without leaving a video record of their presence. They'd finally decided to plant nanobot cameras on Deron's clone before Adam drove him back to the tower. Once Deron was back in the tower, they were able to remotely drive those cameras into prime viewing position.

Mark's cloning process had progressed too far to stop, and they'd elected to allow the procedure to continue, keeping the clone sedated and asleep through the day. Deron had been advised to stay away as well; watching your clone die a violent death might have unexpected and traumatic consequences. Deron opted to sleep as well, concerned that if he stayed awake to spend time with Dash, he'd feel too strong a temptation to come watch everything unfold.

They'd warned the humans of what was to come, and invited Dana, Dash, and Gena to join them or remain outside the room as they preferred. The Assassin was a brutally efficient killer, and the deaths on the screens would be graphic. Dana, knowing she'd still have her husband with her at the end of the day, had elected to stay, though she'd sent Dash into another room with video game consoles and satellite television.

Gena had fled the room in tears.

She wouldn't be watching a copy of Mark die a violent death. For her, his death was real and permanent.

Adam excused himself and went in search of her.

She'd believed Mark might not choose the cloning option, and he'd done just that. She'd sobbed, not only because of his choice, but because he'd not made any suggestion or move to say a final farewell. Aaron suggested that he might have believed a clean separation would be less painful for her; if they'd talked, and she'd tried to talk him out of it and failed, she might forever blame herself for his death. She'd gone silent after that, which worried Adam.

Because Gena had said before that if Mark chose death, she'd take her own life as a result.

And they'd agreed that they wouldn't stop her.

He hadn't, though. He wouldn't accept her choice of suicide. She was far too special, far too important, and had overcome too much already to simply end it all now. No, he'd go talk to her, make her see things more clearly.

He wouldn't let her go without a fight.

Adam trotted down the basement stairs, walking past the hidden doorway leading to the cloning room, moved past the room where the original Deron lay sleeping, and finally came to Gena's temporary bedroom. The door was slightly ajar, and the light was out. No sound came from inside the room.

His breath caught in his throat. Was he already too late?

Tentatively, he knocked on the door. "Gena?"

There was no response.

He raised his hand to knock again when her voice came to him. "I'm here." There was no emotion in her voice. Her voice was that of one who'd lost her reason to live, even though she still drew breath. It evoked a powerful despair in him, an emotion that triggered his empathic senses in an overwhelming manner. He took a moment to steady himself, and then entered her room.

Gena sat on the bed, pressed up against the backboard, with

her knees near her chin and her arms wrapped around her legs. It was a posture he'd seen Will adopt on many occasions, a pose that indicated he was engaging in deep thinking.

She didn't look up as he entered. "When I was younger, there was a big tree in our back yard. Whenever something would go wrong, I'd go outside and sit next to it. I don't know why, but it always made me feel better." She turned her head slightly to look at the headboard. "Maybe if this was real wood it would work." She gave a faint smile, barely noticeable in the dim light of the room.

Adam smiled back at her, but the expression was hollow, and reflected the pain he felt on her behalf. "I just wanted to tell you that I'm sorry for everything you've been through."

She gave a faint chuckle. "A few days ago, I was poor, happy, engaged to be married to a wonderful man, and had no idea that I would probably be dead within the week. I'm not sure which of those were good or bad. But none of them are true anymore."

He caught the hidden meaning. "Perhaps some good will come from this."

She snorted derisively. "Really? I'm alive, but my reasons for living no longer exist. I'm alive, but for what purpose? Why am I still alive?" She shook her head. "I told myself it wasn't worth living without Mark, that I'd take my own life if he chose not to save his. And yet… I can't do it." She rested her chin on her knees. "Maybe I'm just a coward."

"You're no coward, Gena," Adam said. "Facing the unknown, an unknown that's taken on an entirely new meaning after Mark's decision, and involving things you never before knew existed? All of the changes in your entire world you've gone through in the past few days? That's not cowardice. That's courage."

She sighed. "Perhaps. Something inside tells me that I have something more to do with my life, something important, something worth living for. And part of me thinks that taking my life would be an insult to Mark. I know him well enough to know that he believes that him sacrificing his life means I'll keep mine, that somehow if he'd opted for cloning, I'd truly die. I don't want to dishonor his memory." She looked up at Adam in the darkened room. "Does that make any sense?"

He nodded. "It's what our overall Alliance membership does. We find that greater good, something to sacrifice our time and energy and skill to achieve, and put everything into it. You work with others to accomplish something, and you can't let them down, so you work at it no matter what happens. I've gone on two missions as part of a group, and on one of them the Hunters tracked us down and hauled one of our team members away. We were devastated because we'd lost a family member, but we had to finish what we started to honor her. And our work, even without run-ins with the Hunters, can take us away from loved ones for a very long time. You may finish up your mission, head home, and find those loved ones gone on their own journeys. But you respect what they're doing, just as they respected what you were doing, even if it means experiencing those long separations. You know that one day you'll be reunited again, and that makes the wait and the separation bearable."

Gena sat in silence for a time. Adam said nothing, giving her time to process everything that had happened.

She finally looked up at him. "Can I ask you a question?"

"Of course."

There was a hesitation before she spoke again. "Why is it that you seem so familiar to me?"

Ouch. Of all the questions she could ask… she had to ask the one he didn't want to answer. "I've been told I have a very familiar-looking face."

She shook her head. "You've told me that before, but it's not how you look that makes you seem familiar. When I met you the other night, it was…" She paused. "This will sound strange, but… there are some people who seem to have a special sound to them, like the people in this house, other than the MacLeans. But *your* sound? It's something I remember from long ago, like a memory from a dream. It's like I've known you from before I was born."

"That's… that's an interesting story," he said slowly. He opted for redirection. "What do you mean, people have sounds?"

She hesitated. "It's hard to explain. But when I'm near someone like Ashley or Peter, there's a sound I hear in my head. It's like a ringing in my ears, but it's more internal than that, and it's not annoying or painful. Each person like them, like *you*, has a different tone, a different pitch. It's gotten to the point that I know people are coming into the room around here before I can see or hear them. I knew you were coming to my room before you ever got here."

He nodded. "That's not so strange. Well, it's not strange that it can be done, but it is strange that you're able to do that right now." He paused. "We touched a bit on what it is that makes our group unique, and you've seen enough to know that we're not… normal."

"I've seen enough to know that's not a personality assessment, except perhaps for Peter."

Adam laughed. He was pleased to see that she was able to engage in humor. "He's unique, that's for sure. We talked yesterday about how we're able to sense and manipulate something called Energy. Over time, we're able to increase the amount we can produce and absorb and store. With enough Energy, there's almost no limit to what we can do."

"Yes, so I've heard," she said with a wry smile. "I get to live the rest of my days with a bunch of witches."

"We aren't witches, though admittedly there's a fine line between teleportation and witchcraft," Adam replied. "Of course, we don't turn people into toads or ride broomsticks, so we've got that going for us." He paused. "The Energy we use has some type of signature to it, something that makes it unique to each person who uses it. While any of us can sense the Energy coming from another, we can't detect it at a distance… and we certainly can't tell *whose* Energy we're sensing. Well, *most* of us can't. A limited number can detect that unique Energy signal and use that gift to identify who produces the Energy they're sensing. One of the men coming for Will Stark today has that gift, and to a far greater degree than anyone else. He's able to detect Energy usage from hundreds of miles away and identify who generated that Energy without error. That's how they can track our people down. That's how they knew where Will was and how it is that they'll be here in a few hours. It's not unprecedented, then, that someone can… feel and interpret Energy from others." He frowned.

"But I shouldn't be able to do so." Gena replied.

"No, you shouldn't."

"And the reason I can is the same reason you seem familiar, isn't it?"

That startled him. "I'm not sure why you can do this, but I have no reason to think it has anything to do with why you recognize me."

"Ah, so you *do* know why I recognize you!" Gena exclaimed, her face brightening. She leaned forward. "Well?"

Adam shook his head. She'd baited him into admitting that he knew. No amount of denying it would save him now.

She didn't need to know *everything*, though.

"How much do you remember of your parents? Your birth parents, that is?"

She frowned. "I don't remember them at all. But I shouldn't, should I? My parents took me to the orphanage when I was a baby, a newborn."

Adam shook his head. "No, they didn't. A... friend of mine took you to the orphanage. Your birth parents didn't know you were alive."

Gena shook her head. "No, you've got that wrong. My birth parents took me to the orphanage... when I..." She paused. "Wait a minute. That's why I know you, isn't it? You were involved in getting me there." Then she frowned. "You're not using 'friend' as a euphemism for yourself, are you?"

"No," Adam said. "I didn't take you there. And I ask that you not try to find out the identity of the friend who did. Perhaps one day, the identity of that person will be revealed to you. For now, let's just leave it at that."

Gena shrugged. "Okay, but I don't understand the secrecy. Why shouldn't I know? Why shouldn't everyone?"

"I'll tell you why, but you must promise not to tell anyone else."

She snorted, which on some level pleased him. If she had enough mental energy and spunk to do that, she was recovering well. "Again, why the secrecy?"

"Promise, or I'll walk out the door."

She sighed. "Very well. I promise. What's the story?"

"Years ago, I worked in a hospital. A couple came in to have their baby, a baby girl. They were very excited. But sadly, the little girl was stillborn. The parents were distraught. They said their farewells to the child, and it was left to me dispose of the remains. Except... I found out that the baby girl *wasn't* dead at all. She was alive, but barely, in a tiny body that couldn't function well enough to remain viable. Her mind was alive, and above all else she wanted to live and survive. It was too late to take her back to the doctors and her parents. They wouldn't have been able to save her, even if I'd returned with her then. And so I used my... abilities, left, and took that little girl home."

Gena's eyes widened. "That… was that… *me?*"

Adam nodded. "Of course it was you. By every record of this world, you died the day you were born. Perhaps your name wasn't recorded. I don't know, because I didn't stay long enough to find out if they did, or if your parents even named you. I was sad to be carrying a tiny baby in my hands, especially one that had died before ever having a chance to live. To find out that you still lived, still had a tremendous desire to stay alive? Well, we say our mission is to be the change we want in the world. And the change I wanted was for you to live.

"I took you to my home. Your body failed. Constantly. I used an earlier version of the cloning machine we have here to try to rebuild everything from scratch. Day after day, month after month, I kept re-growing everything, but every time I did it would fail again. Nothing worked. Nothing. Every organ failed, every limb stopped functioning. I could only consistently keep your brain and your mind alive."

"How… how long… did it take?" she asked, staring at him.

"It took… longer than I could ever have imagined. But I finally figured out how to keep your body from dying. Finally, after all that time, you had a body and looked like a baby girl. I talked with my friend, and we agreed that, as difficult as it was, you were best served growing up with a normal family. I… made sure that you were placed with good people, who would love you as their own. And I've made sure that nothing bad ever happened to you ever since."

"Wait… you mean you've been *spying* on me?" Gena said, incredulous. "But… why?"

He thought for a moment. "I'm not sure, exactly, but I think I was overcome with just how strongly you wanted to live, and having finally seen you achieve that goal, I didn't want your life to be anything but a happy experience. I wanted to protect you in whatever way I could. When we figured out that Mark would be a target today, and that you'd gotten engaged, I followed you more closely, worried that the news would reach the Hunters and you'd be at risk." He shook his head. "When you talked to one of *them*, I realized they'd come after you to clean up all the loose ends after this was over. And that's why we brought you here."

"What do you mean I *talked* to one of them?" She thought

for a moment before her eyes widened, and he could feel her shock through the darkness in the room. "It was him, wasn't it? The man who said he was putting together a TV show." She slammed a fist against the headboard, startling Adam. "How could I have been so *stupid?*"

"You aren't stupid, Gena. You were manipulated."

Her head snapped to him. "Manipulated?"

He nodded. "We can influence people's thoughts and actions. *Can*, not *do*. We'll teach you how it's done, so that you can ensure that as your skill grows you avoid doing it… and avoid having it done to you. Our friends in the Aliomenti perform those manipulations on a regular basis. The man you met would consider anything fair game to find out more about Will Stark. He knew many things, but wondered if there was something you knew, due to your association with Mark, that might be critical to their having a successful mission. Nudging you to trust him, to talk freely? That was an easy decision for him."

"I told him something important, didn't I?" Her head slumped back down.

"Relax, Gena. We *want* them to succeed. What you told him was important, but…"

"Why do you want them to succeed?"

He sighed. "Will is the key to everything. He doesn't know that yet, though. The events that will happen later today are the trigger that will help him achieve his destiny. Anything that helps that to happen is a good thing."

"Even if it means I lose Mark forever," Gena said, her tone laced with heavy sarcasm.

"We knew that would happen, knew it wasn't fair, and that's why we gave both men a choice to escape a permanent fate. That's why we gave you and Dana and Dash a choice as well. You're not to blame for what is to come, and though we couldn't move everyone out of the way, we *could* offer all of you the chance to escape permanent death."

"You *know* what's coming, and won't stop it? How do you know? Why don't you stop it? And you still haven't explained how I'm able to hear… that stuff."

Adam nodded. "I know." He held up his hand, and let a small amount of Energy escape, coalescing into a sphere floating above his palm. The sphere gave off a light that brightened the darkened room. Gena watched, fascinated, as the sphere moved toward her, the sound from the vibrating Energy reverberating like a welcome memory in her very soul.

"Energy is an amazing thing. It can illuminate a darkened room, allow the transference of thought and emotion, transport people and things from place to place… and it can heal." The sphere plunged toward Gena and surrounded her in a protective cocoon. "You know that sound like most children remember a loved one's voice or a special blanket, because for you, it served as both while you healed. You spent months surrounded by a field of Energy, just like you are now. That's why you recognize it, in your own special fashion."

Gena gazed in wonder at the light surrounding her, poking at it with her finger as if unsure it was real. She looked at Adam. "I shouldn't be able to feel this though, should I? Not until I start to learn how to… use this stuff?"

Adam sighed. Her intuition was spot on. It was no wonder she was frustrated at being deceived by Porthos. "In theory, yes. Some people seem to take to it more naturally, though. We aren't quite sure why. You appear to be a natural."

She frowned. "You said you basically had me surrounded in this stuff for a long period of time, right?"

Adam nodded, remembering just how long it had actually been. But she didn't need to know. It was a clue, however tenuous, to her parentage, and he didn't want her to find out about *that*.

"Well… maybe that's the explanation. If you're exposed to Energy, even if you haven't gone through whatever process is supposed to enable you to use it, you're just naturally better at it. If you had me living inside an Energy cocoon for a long time… well, that would explain a lot."

Adam considered it. Could it be that simple? "I'd never thought of that, but it makes a lot of sense. We've never really pursued an understanding of why some people seem more predisposed to Energy development, but perhaps we should. I wish there was a way to test out your theory."

Gena shrugged. "The best way to test it would be to separate identical twins at birth, expose one to this Energy and keep the other one away from it, and see what happens. But that would take a long time to evaluate, wouldn't it?"

Adam was startled. Could she be the answer to her own question? Could they figure out the impact by checking…

But no, that wouldn't work. *He'd* been exposed to a lot as well. It did suggest his future pupil would have a strong knack for Energy work when the time came to train him.

"Gena, I think your theory merits testing. And don't ever let your ideas be limited by something like time. As you and the MacLeans will soon find out… time is something we have in ample supply."

It was just a matter of using that time in the best manner possible.

He wondered what Gena would do with the unlimited amount of time life now afforded her.

XXIII
Spectator

January 7, 2030

The media room was full when Adam returned from his conversation with Gena. Aaron and Peter were tinkering with a device positioned in the back of the room that would control audio and video feeds coming in from their army of cameras, projecting selected streams to the largest screen in the room. Smaller screens enabled them to follow activity in other parts of the neighborhood throughout the day. At the moment, the screens were blank. Adam positioned himself in one of the chairs as Gena entered the room, blinking rapidly to adjust her eyes to the bright screens and lighting. She located Adam and settled into the chair next to him.

Food and drinks were set out on a table at the back of the room near the door, and close to where the controller was positioned. Their record of events suggested that the action would start in the late afternoon and continue for several hours, and they couldn't pause the live video feeds to eat. Today, they'd serve as eyewitnesses to the upcoming events for past, present, and future members of the Alliance, and record those events for posterity. Perhaps, just perhaps, they'd find something in the video or audio on this journey through the time stream that would improve everything for everyone during the next cycle.

The screens sprang to life. Several of the displays showed views of the interior and exterior of the ground level guard station and the elevated tower, as well as the area between the two buildings. Others provided views inside the Starks' home and around the perimeter. They'd be able to record sound from each location, but only one audio feed would play in the room at any point in time.

"Any chance we're forgetting anything?" Judith asked.

"No," Eva said. "We have done our parts. We must now allow events to unfold, as painful as those events would be." All eyes flicked in Gena's direction, and she drew in a deep breath. Dana, who had taken the seat next to her opposite Adam, squeezed Gena's hand. "I must remind each of you, especially those trained in the use of Energy, that we may intervene only in the case of an obvious failure in the objective, not in the case of injury or... worse."

Gena winced again, and her face burned red and her breathing became shallow. But she said nothing. She located Mark on one of the screens and watched him, barely daring to blink. The man was working through checklists, watching different screens, occasionally turning on the communication link with the tower to talk with Deron, his friend and coworker. It was an eerie scene to watch, knowing, as they all did, that Deron was a clone and both would soon be dead.

And in Mark's case, he'd be dead permanently.

Adam glanced at the Stark house video feed and glanced at Eva. "I promised Hope that I'd hide out in her house, just in case something goes wrong."

"I am not certain that is wise, Adam," Eva replied. "We are watching video feeds to ensure we can move into position as needed. Your presence in the house is not necessary."

"Probably not," he agreed. "But I gave my word."

Eva gave a pointed glance at Gena, who didn't notice, who saw nothing but Mark's every move on the screen consuming her vision, and then cast a worried glance back at Adam. Adam sighed. *She's fine now, Eva. This is her chance to grieve. She's no threat to hurt herself anymore.*

"Hey, no whispering!" Peter said, his own voice a stage whisper.

Adam gave Peter a withering glare. "Stop snooping, Peter. I gave my word, and I intend to keep it."

"Won't it get a bit, um… toasty over there?" Peter asked, his voice filled with concern.

Adam shrugged. "By the time that happens, I expect to be gone. I can take care of myself."

Peter shrugged. "Your funeral." His eyes fell on Gena, who didn't seem to have heard him. "Sorry," he whispered.

Adam rolled his eyes, headed for the door, and walked outside. He shivered as the cold wind struck him, and then took off at a run for the Starks' house. He arrived a few minutes later. The back door heading into the laundry room at the rear of the house was unlocked, and after entering he flipped the lock closed. He walked through the kitchen and dining nook areas and the sliding glass doors there, and through the first floor living areas of the house, but found no sign of Hope. Was she still sleeping? It shouldn't take that long for her to recover from the memory blocks he'd set up. He hoped he didn't need to forcibly wake her.

Adam removed the mobile phone in his pocket and activated one of the hidden apps. The app allowed him to receive and display the signals from the miniature cameras the Alliance had installed throughout the primary venues for the action yet to come this day. With the app, he could keep an eye on the events unfolding throughout the neighborhood, including those taking place inside the Starks' house.

He silently climbed the stairs, opened the door to Will's office, slid inside, and shut the door quietly behind him. The room was expected to remain unused throughout the day and would make a perfect place for him to hide out without using Energy. He sat at Will's desk and used the holographic projection capability of the phone to display the images from the cameras, and muted the sound. As interesting as the dialogue might prove, he couldn't risk Hope or Josh hearing him or the phone.

He flicked through the images from each camera to get a quick status check. Hope slept. Josh slept, with Smokey nestled by his side. The house was silent and otherwise empty.

For now.

●●●

"What's he looking at?" Gena asked.

Heads turned to the smaller screen showing the scene inside the ground level guard station. Mark's attention had shifted from his checklists to something outside.

Eva looked at the clock hanging on the wall in the room. "I suspect he has spotted the Hunters. The time of day is in line with their expected arrival." She exhaled deeply as the tension in the room became palpable to human and Energy user alike, and glanced around, her face taut with the weight of the moment. "It has begun."

On the screen, Mark stood and walked slowly toward the window and the external communication system, appearing to talk to himself. His face registered concern.

"Where's the Assassin?" Peter asked.

Dana gasped. "He's in the tower!" she shrieked.

A man with a hideously scarred face had suddenly appeared inside the upper room. Deron, who had been looking out the window on the opposite side of the tower's interior as he watched the Hunters approach, didn't see the killer.

"Run!" Dana screamed.

Deron turned slowly toward the killer. He opened his mouth as if to speak, but no sound ever emerged. The Assassin's blade was a blur, moving from scabbard to hand and carving a vicious arc across the screen in an infinitesimal fraction of a second. Deron's throat vanished in a shower of blood and gore.

He fell to the ground, eyes wide, unable to make a sound, hands grasping at his throat in a futile effort to seal the fatal wound in his neck. Dana's screams more than made up for his silence.

●●●

Adam sat watching the video feeds from the cameras. The Assassin had appeared and claimed his first victim. Hope still wasn't awake, and it was getting late. Should he wake her up? He was hesitant to do so, as the memory blocks would make him a stranger, and she'd spend time worrying about his presence rather than preparing for the man who'd soon be on his way to kill her. Then he wondered about yet another loose end in their plan, one they'd not needed to worry about until he'd performed those memory blocks.

How would Hope know to prepare herself for a man like the Assassin? It wasn't as if one of the neighbors would call and alert her.

He was still wondering what he'd do to wake Hope when a powerful wave of emotional Energy coursed through him, heavy with feelings of fear and hopelessness. It was the Energy mark and calling card of the Assassin.

On his screen, Hope bolted upright in her bed, eyes wide, jarred from her deep sleep.

He flipped his screen to the camera in Josh's room, watching as the boy woke as well.

Adam breathed a silent sign of relief. The Assassin had taken care of the problem of waking the Starks for him.

●●●

"Run, Mark," Gena begged, her voice strained with emotion. Her teeth were clenched with such force that it was a wonder they didn't crack. "Please. You have to leave. You have to get out. You have to run before he comes after you." She gripped the arms of the chair, her nails tearing into the fabric. Her face, moistened by sweat and tears, tightened, and the pulsing vein in her forehead was clearly visible.

Her plea went unanswered. Gena and the others watched on the video screens as the Assassin hurled Clone Deron's lifeless body through the bulletproof glass and through the roof of the guard tower below.

"He *had* to use Energy to do that," Archie muttered. "Bulletproof glass doesn't shatter that easily, and the body should have fallen to the ground below after slowing down when it went through the glass, not made it to the roof across the driveway." He caught Ashley's withering glare. "What?"

Dana, who had rushed to the corner of the room and vomited at the sight of Deron's injuries, returned in time to see his body impaled and lifeless on the floor of the guard station. She spun around and moved back to the same spot, overcome with dry heaves. Judith went to put a comforting hand on her back.

"Get out *now*, Mark!" Gena screamed. "Run!"

On the screen, Mark turned as the Assassin leaped from the gaping hole in the tower, landed on the station roof, and dropped to the floor inside.

"Nimble for a five hundred year old guy, isn't he?" Peter

remarked.

Ashley, Judith, and Eva all shot him withering glares. Peter held up his hands.

On another screen, Josh, still trembling after waking from his nap, found a baseball and tossed it against the wall. Smokey chased after the ball, retrieved it for Josh, and barked at him.

Hope, who had just retrieved a loaded gun from the safe in her room in response to the horrific sense of fear that had jolted her awake, snapped her head toward the sound of the baseball. Her face made it clear: she thought the noise indicated that Josh was in danger, and that Smokey was barking at an intruder.

Hope flipped off the safety of the gun and ran toward her son's room.

"She's… she's not going to shoot *Josh*, is she?" Judith asked the screen. "Doesn't she realize it's her son making that noise?"

Nobody responded, and none of them dared to breathe.

On the screen, Josh paused, and his expression went blank for a moment, as if he'd heard something inside his head. After a moment, he nodded, and then tossed the ball against the wall again.

Smokey barked with glee as Hope, eyes wide, burst into the room with the gun in her hand.

In the media room, someone screamed.

●●●

Mark sat by the telephone in the guard station, trapped there by an Energy-wielding maniac with red eyes pointing a sword at his throat. Gena's eyes were riveted on the screen, her terror so great that her body nearly forgot to breathe. They'd stopped playing audio in the media room. They'd given up trying to switch the sound around, and everyone had moved forward to watch the myriad of screens. Every bit of video and audio was being recorded, and they'd be able to go back to watch and listen as needed.

Gena watched Mark, and would watch the events only once.

The others were focused on the scenes in the Starks' home. Hope, thankfully, had not shot her son. Rather, she'd put the safety on and put the gun down before smothering the little boy with her hugs. She made a call, tears streaming down her face, before chatting with the boy and showing an ever-growing level of concern on her face.

Gena could wait no more. She leaped from the chair and raced out of the media room, but not before slamming her hip into the table holding the barely-touched food. She bounded toward the stairs, needing to get to him, wondering if the miraculous Energy development she'd shown would help her get there in time. Her breathing came in rasping gulps of air, and she'd nearly ceased blinking.

As she reached the front door, a hand grabbed her from behind.

Gena whirled on Ashley, slapping the woman's hand off and pushing her with more force than she'd intended. Gena then spun back to the door.

The cocoon was nothing like the one Adam had demonstrated earlier. The sound was different, and she was well aware that Ashley wasn't doing this to save her from her own genetic deficiencies.

"Let me go!" Gena screamed, her eyes full of a malice that would leave even the Assassin withering. "I have to help him! I have to go to him!"

"You cannot help him, Gena," Ashley told her. Her voice was calm, but full of genuine sympathy. "Even if you reached the station in time, what would you do? You cannot best the Assassin. If you go now, you'll do nothing but sign your own death warrant."

"You told me I wasn't a prisoner here," Gena seethed. "Is lying a required skill to join this group?"

"No, not *this* one," Ashley replied. "Gena, you aren't a prisoner, and I'm not doing this to trap you. I'm doing this so you think through what you're considering before you do it. Tell me what you'll do if you get there and Mark's still alive, still held hostage by the Assassin."

Gena glared at her, but said nothing.

"Do you think Mark would want you to come for him now, knowing that doing so would mean you'd die as well?"

Gena had no answer for that.

"I'm going to let you go, Gena. If you leave, you leave, but understand that what's started can't be stopped. I encourage you, as your friend, to come sit with the rest of us. Stay here, where it's safe. Don't throw your life away out of some strange sense of nobility."

The cocoon of Energy released her, and true to her word, Ashley turned around and walked back toward the media room.

After a moment, Gena followed her, hugging her arms to herself as if trying to reproduce a cocoon on her own, one that would protect her from the horrors yet to come.

When she entered the room once more, her eyes instantly went to Mark's screen. He was talking on the phone, his face tense with concentration, and his gaze continually flicked in the direction of the red-eyed killer near him.

On the other screen, Hope's face registered first embarrassment. Then confusion. Then horror. And as her call with Mark ended, her face registered determination.

"Look away," Eva told Gena.

She didn't. She watched as the man she loved charged the supernatural killer, watched as he did what he thought he could to protect Hope, to protect Gena, to protect unnamed others from the madman in the room with him. She watched as flame burst from the evil man and consumed the flesh of the man she loved, watched as the killer's sword flashed again, watched as Mark fell to the ground in horrific agony.

She watched as the last light of life left his eyes, as those eyes stared at her through the screen without seeing, his cold face still etched in the agony of the throes of his death.

She didn't cry; the tears were long since gone. She didn't scream; it would no longer do Mark, or anyone else, any good to waste her breath on screams. Her face was a steely mask of controlled anger and determination. There was a fiery light in her eyes, the light of a woman who knew her new purpose in life, the reason she would live on even with Mark gone for good.

When she spoke, her voice held a hint of ice and fire, and the hairs on the arms of those in the room stood in response to her tone. And her promise.

"If it's the last thing I ever do… I'm going to kill that man."

●●●

Adam's hiding spot enabled him to hear Hope's phone conversations, first with Will, then with Mark, and he was encouraged. Her words and emotional impulses betrayed no hint that she knew any of this was coming, or that she knew she had the power to stop it at any time she wished. Her thoughts wouldn't betray her to the Assassin, reveal her true identity, and in so doing alter the course of history.

His memory blocks were working perfectly.

He heard her coming up the steps, and made certain his Energy Shield was up. She might not remember her skills, but she'd feel something if someone as powerful as Adam was sitting unshielded in a nearby room. She'd just realized that the powerful dream she'd experienced—a dream that was, in fact, a shared clairvoyant experience of a powerful Energy user—was real. She was now determined to protect her only child from the killer or killers on the way to her house. He watched on his screen as she entered Josh's room and spoke to him. He turned up the volume and listened in through his earpiece as she explained that a bad man was coming to their house, and that it was very important that he remain in his room until either Mommy or Daddy came for him.

Josh nodded, but looked confused. Why would his mother be worried about something like that? Why did she think he needed to hide, when she could easily vanquish anyone who walked—or teleported—into their house?

Josh was starting to understand that something *else* was now wrong with his mother.

Adam winced. He'd not considered how the memory blocks and the resulting behavioral changes in Hope would impact Josh. Apologies would need to come later, but his brow creased with concern.

What else had he missed?

●●●

"Hope's acting very strangely," Archie noted, frowning at the screen. They watched as their friend, a confident and powerful woman they'd known for centuries, worked in a frenzied manner to bury her son in a pile of stuffed animals. She shooed the dog inside the large walk-in closet with the boy, gave him a clear word of warning, and then shut the door. She paused a moment, and then barricaded the door shut with a heavy chair.

"I get hiding Josh in the closet, because they don't want the

Assassin finding out Will has a son, but she doesn't need to act scared yet," Judith added.

"She's acting almost… human." Aaron spoke slowly, as if not trusting his assessment. But when he looked around, he saw looks of agreement among the Alliance members present.

"Human?" Dana asked. "Of course she's human. Why would that be a surprise?"

"*Human* is the term we use to describe anyone not yet trained in our special skills," Eva explained. "In those terms, Hope is as non-human as one could be. But she is *acting* as if she is *very* human."

"What's strange about how she's acting?" Dana was puzzled. "I'd be hiding my son if I was her as well."

"Hope has more than enough power to protect herself and Josh," Eva explained. "She knows this. She has no reason to be afraid. I understand that she must act in a convincing manner for the Assassin, to prove that she is no threat. But…" Eva paused, thinking, and then a look of realization crossed her face. "Adam." She shook her head.

"What?" Peter asked. "What's Adam got to do with Hope acting strangely?"

"She is not acting, Peter," Eva replied. "Adam has blocked her memories of who and what she is. It is something we ought to have thought of before and planned out, and it is a good thing he has thought to do so even so late in the timeline. She can betray nothing, even by accident, if she does not know there is something she must hide." She nodded. "That is why he went to her. If she does not realize her power, she cannot betray her identity, but she will also be unable to save herself, or Josh. Adam must be there to restore her memory—and, therefore, her power—at the last moment… or save them himself."

"Bloody brilliant," Aaron breathed, nodding. "I wonder when he figured that out and decided to act?"

"I do not know," Eva admitted. "But I am glad that he did. I had just started to wonder how Hope would be able to conceal her thoughts of what she must do from the Assassin, given the intensity of the events to come. Now we know."

She turned to glance back at the screen. "I hope Adam doesn't come to regret his decision."

● ● ●

He could hear Hope moving once more, and her undisciplined mental control led her to project out her intent to check for intruders in Will's office. Adam ended the holographic projection of his phone screen, grabbed the device, and slid off the chair to hide beneath Will's desk. He'd barely stopped moving when the door opened and Hope entered the room.

Adam glanced at his screen and flicked the image over to the video feed in the room, using the phone to watch as Hope scanned the space. Her eyes seemed to settle on Will's chair, which had spun ever so slightly after Adam slid off the seat and under the desk. He watched her on the screen, his muscles tensing, trying to figure out what he'd do, what lie he'd tell, if she moved further into the room and discovered him hiding there. He couldn't risk a teleportation hop now.

After what seemed an eternity, Hope shook her head, muttering to herself. "I'm really losing it now, totally imagining things that aren't there." She left the room, closing the door behind her.

Adam waited a moment, just as he had years earlier when he'd nearly been discovered in the offices of the orphanage where Gena had lived. But Hope had lost interest, and didn't double back to see if she could catch him crawling out from his hiding space, convinced that her idea that someone was already in the house was without merit.

He flipped through the camera feeds and tracked her movements. Hope headed back to Josh's room for the gun, and then returned to her bedroom and the wall safe for an extra clip of ammunition. She frowned as she had to dig around among the special papers inside, wondering if they actually *had* a spare clip. She finally snapped her fingers, and her thoughts once again betrayed her, proclaiming her realization that she'd left the spare clip downstairs on the kitchen counter. She sighed and shut the safe.

Hope marched downstairs, gun in hand, and waited for the arrival of the men who were coming to kill her.

● ● ●

"There's Will!" Ashley announced.

With the action inside the house ended for the time being, they'd switched their collective attention back to the entry to the community. Graham, in his disguise as Frank the driver, had pulled up with Myra VanderPoole, and the elderly woman had fainted after viewing the carnage inside the guard station. A police officer named Michael Baker had arrived in response to Graham's call for an ambulance. While they waited for the paramedics, Baker began a cursory examination of the site, making observations and listening as Frank recounted what had happened. Will stepped out of his car and walked toward both men.

Gena finally took her eyes off Mark's body to turn her focus to the action. She frowned. "Why is a billionaire driving himself around? Doesn't he have a limo?"

"Will does not especially care for the trappings of wealth," Eva replied. "Today is his birthday, and it was his fondest wish to live his life in a more normal fashion."

"Today is Will's birthday?" Gena asked. Her voice had lost the icy edge it had earlier, and now registered nothing more than a sad fatigue. "It's mine as well."

"Happy birthday," Eva said. The others offered Gena similar good wishes. Gena didn't smile.

On the screen, Will had pointed to the roof of the guard station, a look of concern and horror on his face. Michael Baker paced toward the window and gazed upon the interior before moving away and vomiting onto the side of the building.

"I know the feeling," Dana said, her voice full of sympathy.

They watched as Will Stark first tried to scale the ten foot high concrete gate, and then as he used a downspout to pull himself to the roof of the guard station.

Moments later, he dropped to the ground inside the neighborhood, landing awkwardly and twisting his ankle in the process. After discovering that the intruders had set fire to the motorized carts normally waiting for his use, he ran as fast as he could toward his home, in a futile effort to save his wife and son from a supernatural Assassin.

Gena felt an odd sense of deja vu as she watched.

●●●

Adam watched on his screen as the Assassin unlocked the back door. He rolled his eyes at his earlier protective, if futile, gesture. If the Assassin had been thinking, he would wonder why his victim, who lived inside an immensely secure community with few neighbors, would feel the need to lock her doors at all. She'd only do that if she knew someone was coming after her.

The Assassin, though, had only one thing on his mind. Blood. Hope Stark's blood.

His Energy skills were minimal, especially for one so old. They were more than sufficient to rapidly disarm a "human" woman like Hope Stark, though, and Hope's weapon was soon devoid of useful ammunition. The Assassin pulled out an aerosol can that contained his latest fire accelerant and used it to cover the interior walls of the house. The fire would serve its purpose: shocking Will Stark, crushing his spirit, and ruining his concentration. In such a state, the Hunters would be able to subdue him and load him into a secured transport with relative ease. It was a brilliant plan, but Will wouldn't be captured when he arrived here in the next few minutes. Nor would he be killed.

Adam would arrive from the future with Will's grown children, likely in the next few minutes. Together, they'd protect Will in ways the Hunters couldn't understand, couldn't trace, and couldn't defeat. By the time the Hunters would realize what was happening, they'd be gone, taking Will with them as they returned to their point of origin nearly two centuries into the future. There, they'd teach neophyte Will the basics of Energy and send him to the past in a time machine the Alliance had yet to invent.

He watched as Hope hurled a knife at the Assassin, planting the blade in the killer's shoulder. Even from this distance, he could sense her terror, but also her shock. She didn't know what had possessed her to hide the knife, nor did she understand how she'd managed to hurl it with such accuracy. Adam knew, though. Hope had trained in armed combat for centuries, and those skills weren't something he could hide by blocking memories of her past. Her body worked on instincts honed by her decades of training.

Adam heard a rumbling next door. Josh had sensed his mother's fear, and used an Energy he didn't quite understand to blast open the door of the closet where he'd been hidden. Josh ordered Smokey to stay, grabbed the baseball he'd used during their earlier playtime, and crept silently down the stairs.

So intense was Josh's concentration on keeping quiet that he didn't notice his faithful companion padding along just a few steps behind him.

●●●

Everyone's attention was riveted to the screen showing the Assassin and Hope. They watched as the killer's mangled face contorted in rage and agony while he pulled the large knife from his shoulder, and then he advanced on Hope, one menacing step at a time. He shouted something at her.

"What was *that*?" Dash asked. He'd been allowed in the room once they'd turned off the screen showing the bodies of Mark and Deron.

On the screen, the Assassin jerked backward and fell to his knees on the floor. He dropped the knife and held that hand to his face, where a welt had appeared. They all noticed the baseball rolling on the ground nearby. Josh entered the screen and shouted at the killer.

"Strike three," Peter muttered. "Hope that batter's out… cold."

But the Assassin was only temporarily disoriented. He stood, ready to silence the new threat… and then stopped, his jaw agape at the sight of the boy in front of him.

"What's… why did he stop?" Gena asked. "Is he… actually *afraid* of Josh?"

"He *should* be," Eva muttered.

"The Aliomenti swear an oath not to reproduce, and undergo various processes that ensure it," Aaron explained. "It's one of their more… arcane policies. We give people access to those same techniques, but they're optional. The Aliomenti require it. Their rules are simple: if a member dares to have a child, everyone involved is executed."

"I can't believe that," Dana said, glancing protectively at Dash.

"It's true, though," Ashley replied.

"And nobody's ever *reversed* the process," Aaron added. "It's supposed to be impossible, oath or no oath."

"That is why the Assassin is stunned at the sight of Josh," Eva said. "The Will that they know went through those processes. Which means…"

"Which means that not only did he do something impossible in having a son… he's now subject to death by their rules," Gena said. "Lovely group of people."

"That is why we left them," Eva said.

"Or, in our case, never joined," Judith added.

The Assassin had finally regained his composure and started moving at them again.

This time, Smokey emerged from the shadows, charged the killer, and sank her fangs into the killer's leg. The room erupted in cheers… until the Assassin's blade flashed.

Blood flowed from Smokey's side.

"No!" Dash wailed. "Not the dog!"

"She'll be fine," Aaron told him.

"This is it, then," Eva said. "Hope must teleport them out of danger."

"But she clearly doesn't know *how*," Gena reminded her. "Adam made her forget, right? She's not remembering!"

Eva's eyes widened. "Then we must rely on Adam to save them."

Peter glanced at the screen. "Adam… or Will."

Gena pointed at a screen showing a scene outside the Starks' front window. "He's almost there!" Will was limping around the final bend of the long driveway, clearly winded and in severe pain.

"*That* man isn't capable of saving them," Ashley told her. "He doesn't know how."

"Then why do you keep talking about Will saving them?" Gena shouted.

On the screen, Hope pushed Josh behind her, and stared defiantly at the red-eyed killer advancing on her. Her face told the story, though, and if they'd doubted her humanness before, there was no doubt about it now.

Hope knew they were about to die.

XXIV
Eyewitness

With death approaching in the form of red-eyed madman, Hope's maternal instincts took over. She must protect Josh, regardless of what happened to her. The attempts to hide him had failed. She could only hope to slow the man's progress long enough for Will and the police to arrive, to give them a chance to apprehend or kill this man before Josh's life was snuffed out.

She pushed the boy behind her as the scar-faced killer advanced, feeling his heavy boots as they thumped on the floor. He was enjoying this, savoring each step as he moved toward his prey.

Why wasn't she afraid? Was it adrenaline? Was her mind simply accepting the fact that death was imminent, and therefore the emotion of fear was one she no longer needed to experience?

The only thing she felt was a strange tickling sensation. Was that how the body felt when it accepted death? Was she in the process of dying of a fear so deep she wasn't consciously aware of its presence?

And then, to her shock, the Assassin stopped moving forward. Confusion covered his scarred face. Anger flashed in his blood-red eyes.

●●●

"Come *on,* Adam!" Gena shouted at the screen, watching as the man who'd so ruthlessly butchered Mark moved toward the now-helpless Hope. "Why aren't you helping them? If you aren't going to help them, why are you there?"

"He will help them," Eva replied. "But only if they need that help." Her tone allowed for no debate.

Or so she thought. "It looks to me like they need that help!" Dana snapped, her eyes wide with fear. She clutched Dash's hand. The boy seemed unfazed, for he'd not seen his father and Mark die at the hands of the Assassin earlier. For him, what unfolded on the screens was a mere television show, with no basis in reality. He found the action exciting rather than terrifying.

And then, on the screen, Hope and Josh vanished.

The camera focused on the Assassin's face, a face that was so contorted in rage it looked as though he might explode.

Eva's eyes widened, and her phone was in her hand instantly, dialing the first number on her list.

●●●

Adam had been watching the holographic video feed from his phone, feeling more anxious as the fractional seconds ticked by. History said Will, not Adam, would protect Hope and Josh, and yet they'd never know until it was too late if history had changed. How long could he wait to reveal his presence to the Assassin with the powerful burst of Energy required to transport mother and child to safety? Where was Will?

On the screen, Hope and Josh vanished from sight.

Adam blinked and looked again. Why didn't he see Will? Why didn't he *sense* Will?

His phone rang, and the ring tone identified the caller. Why was Eva calling at a time like this? He activated the connection.

"Leave!" Eva shouted.

Adam recognized that tone of voice. She'd used it infrequently over the centuries, but each occurrence stood out in his mind. It was a tone that meant she'd figured something out, something critical, and she'd succinctly summarized what needed done in that instant. It was best to do as commanded and get the explanation later.

With Hope and Josh clearly safe, with his promise to ensure their safety fulfilled, Adam's purpose for being in the Starks' house had ended. He detonated one of the Energy eating devices he'd described to Gena a day before and teleported away.

An instant later, the Assassin threw back his head and let loose a massive burst of uncontrolled flame, and the fire hit the accelerant coating the walls.

It was a unique substance, one the Assassin had developed over the preceding decades. The foam coated the walls, rather than being absorbed, and the flames would do a slow, bright, hot burn through the coating before reaching the original surfaces. With the foam, the Assassin could keep a building aflame far longer than should be possible. The Hunters had coated much of the exterior before he'd arrived, which should have enable the Assassin to use a small bit of flame to light the entire structure, generating the visual effect that would incapacitate Will Stark. Thus disabled, the traitor would be an easy target for the Hunters, and only then would the flames eliminate the foaming, specialized accelerant and consume the building.

He'd tested the substance several times, and in each case he'd needed only a small bit of flame to set the test surfaces on fire.

He'd never tested the formula against an inferno-like blast like the one he'd just unleashed.

The effect was the equivalent of setting off a bomb inside the house. The flame set the entire interior and exterior of the house ablaze in an instant, but the wall he faced—which bore the brunt of the blast—had no chance to withstand the force he'd unleashed. The rear wall and the section of the house directly above him, the part of the house he'd been looking at as his head went backward, exploded out into the backyard.

The room directly above him, relocated to the frozen surface outside, had been Will's office. It had been the room Adam had occupied until just seconds earlier.

●●●

Hope felt nothing more than a wisp of wind as the flame erupted from the red-eyed man, and passed by her and Josh without any sensation of heat. They suffered no burns, and weren't even knocked from their feet. She heard the sound behind her, impossibly loud, as the flame that had left them unscathed contacted the rear wall of the house and knocked it, and the space directly above them, into the backyard.

The killer froze, eyes widening, and his hands went to his throat. The sounds he made were those of a man choking.

Hope frowned. It didn't make sense. He was behaving as though he couldn't breathe, yet she and Josh had no such trouble. Smokey's sides still rose and fell, though unsteadily. She had no idea why only the killer was so afflicted, but the man's bloodied sword fell from his hand and he went to his knees. His eyes rolled back in his head as he lost consciousness and his body crashed to the floor.

Something was tickling at her mind, a hint of a memory. She'd seen the killer before today. She *did* know about the group he'd mentioned. The impossible acts he'd performed today were skills she'd seen demonstrated before, by people she knew and trusted and loved.

Aliomenti. Alliance. Will, the Oaths, and the Hunters coming after him.

The memories knitted themselves together slowly, rebuilding in a patchwork manner. The challenges they'd undergone to bring the special little boy before her into the world. The fact that she'd suppressed her son's gifts to protect him from exposure to and attacks by the very men who'd arrived here this day.

She remembered that she could do things that, until seconds ago, she'd considered the realm of fantasy and magic, the myths and lies of fairy tales. As she remembered her skill, she felt the warmth, the electric current coursing through her body, and her eyes lit up as the very familiarity of the sensation triggered instinctive memories of the usage of the power inside her.

Hope frowned. If she was able to do all of this, why hadn't she realized it in time to fight off the killer now lying unconscious just a few feet away?

And why hadn't she ever shared with Will the truth of her identity and ability?

He learned the truth when he needed to know. At one time in my life, I was ignorant of my own future and abilities, as much as I had once been ignorant of yours. That time in our lives has now ended. The need for secrecy has passed.

Her eyes widened in shock. *Will?*

She and Josh began to sink through the floor.

●●●

"Something's wrong," Adam said, frowning. He'd appeared inside the room a fractional second after Eva's command to leave the house, and was re-acclimating himself to the media room, watching events unfold on the larger screens. He was also adjusting to the fact that the room he'd just occupied had been permanently relocated.

Eva glanced at him. "You appear to be unharmed."

He shook his head. "No, it's not that. *I'm* fine. I watched along, as you did. I watched them vanish, as you did, before I departed. But before I left, after they'd vanished... I never sensed any Energy usage in the house."

Peter frowned. "Did we put scutarium between floors?"

Adam shook his head. "The Energy would still reach me through the open hallways and doorways. Whether Hope's memories restored in time and she teleported them away to safety, or Will arrived and teleported them to safety from a distance, the Energy burst from the effort should have hit me quite hard from only twenty or so feet away. I'd suspect you'd be able to detect it as well, Eva." He paused. "Except that the house was sealed shut with a scutarium barrier. I forgot about that."

"But the Assassin left the door open when he went in," Archie noted. "I thought it was strange that he'd do that, thinking that most killers would shut a door to keep a victim from escaping, or from the *sound* of their victims escaping and alerting neighbors. But if he thought he was going to attack a human woman in a house a mile from the nearest neighbor, he probably didn't worry about that." He glanced at Adam. "By the way, we figured out that you'd blocked her memories so she couldn't expose her abilities or her plans. Wish I'd thought of that earlier."

"I thought of it about three hours before the Hunters were expected to arrive, and just took care of it," Adam admitted. "Sorry for not bringing the rest of you in on it."

Ashley waved her hand. "No worries about that. Let's get back to the current issue. You're saying there was no Energy used to help Hope and Josh escape?"

He shook his head. "None. I didn't do anything. I honestly don't know if her memory restored fast enough, based on the emotional vibrations she was emitting right up until the time she and Josh vanished. Which means that either the person who saved them can mask their Energy even when they use it…"

"Or they did not use Energy," Eva finished. "There is only person who could be responsible."

Heads nodded. If something was done they couldn't explain, it meant Will Stark was involved.

He hadn't traveled far when he'd left Eva and Aaron's house earlier in the day.

●●●

"Hope! Josh!"

The sound barely reached her ears above the roaring flames. Will was outside the house, had seen the fire, and was screaming out their names. Whether he'd taken one of the golf carts or run from the entrance, he'd made the effort to try to help them, even when it seemed hopeless. His plaintive tone, detectable even in his faint screams of agony, made his assessment clear. To him, she and Josh were dead.

And she couldn't call out to him because her head had just moved inside the floor on its way to join the rest of her body in the basement. Her heart ached for Will, for what he must be suffering right now. He'd wanted nothing more than their happiness, had built this home and this neighborhood to ensure it, and would see in this burning house proof that he'd failed them, a guilt he'd carry with him for a very long time.

More memories came to her, prompted by the voice in her head more than the one calling out her name. The man watching the house burn from the outside would, this very day, travel through time, into the future, and there learn his true destiny. The man outside would then go back in time, into the distant past, and live an impossibly long time. His only goal was to make sure that she survived, that she lived through this attack, and that their children were born.

Children?

Her hand went to her belly, and she remembered. The child growing there would join Josh in escorting their father to the future, and would then send him forth on his epic quest into the distant past. Her children, her fully grown children from the future, would travel back through time to this date, to this time, to this location.

But that meant…

Hope and Josh settled on the floor of the basement, into a moderate darkness near the stairs leading to the first floor and the inferno that raged above. As they stopped moving, still surrounded by the covering that had protected them from the Assassin's flame, she saw it.

The vehicle shimmered into existence before them, appearing without a sound in the middle of the floor in the basement, seeming to glow in the modest lighting provided by the fading bits of sunlight streaming in from the outside. Somewhere out there, even now, her young husband was being beaten by Hunters who thought him more than capable of fighting back.

Josh had no idea that was happening, and was staring at the time machine. "Cool!" he exclaimed. "How did that car just show up in the basement, Mommy?"

She patted him on the head. "You'll figure it out one day."

The top dissolved, revealing three occupants.

A young man with jet black hair leaped from the time machine, holding a backpack in one hand while affixing a mask to his face with the other. He whisked silently up the steps, and as he ran by, they could see that his eyes were covered by sunglasses that seemed glued to his face, hiding any hint of his eyes.

Hope's hand went to her mouth. *Josh.*

The young woman leaped from the vehicle as well and moved to the back of the house, her bright red hair streaming behind her. Hope was overcome with emotion, fighting back the tears of joy that threatened to moisten her face, knowing she was watching the woman the child inside her would become.

Angel motioned toward the wall as if throwing something, and a huge hole appeared. Dirt and rock and debris poured into the basement, pushed to either side to allow ever more material inside. She turned and trotted back to the third man, who had climbed out to look at the time travel machine.

"Everything look okay?" Angel asked.

The man looked up. "I don't see any damage."

Josh tugged on Hope's arm. "Mommy, what is Mr. Adam doing with those people and the neat car?"

Hope frowned. "Who?"

"Mr. Adam. You know him, Mommy. He's like us. He comes and visits us and you talk about fires and Energy and Hunters and Assassins."

She shook her head. "I don't recognize him."

Josh giggled. "Mommy, you're being silly. Mr. Adam is one of our best friends!"

She sensed he was telling the truth, that the stranger traveling with her grown children was someone she should know. But there was nothing there, no memory that said she'd ever met him before. "I... I'm sorry, Josh. Mommy's memory is a little... off right now."

The elder Josh thundered down the steps. He carried the backpack over one shoulder, and over the other shoulder...

"Mommy, why is he carrying the mean man?"

"I'm... not sure, sweetie."

"I wish he wouldn't help the bad man."

"Never hesitate to help others, Josh, even if they don't deserve it."

The elder Josh sprinted across the floor, moving at a speed that suggested the Assassin's weight was no more a burden than a sack of feathers. He kicked the back end of the time machine, and a panel flipped open, revealing a trunk. He hurled the Assassin inside, making no effort to keep the man's head from slamming against the side.

Hope winced. Young Josh giggled. Hope shot him a withering glare.

Josh looked confused. "Mommy, that man wanted to kill us, didn't he? I'm not sad if he gets a headache."

Hope sighed. Teaching children not to relish the pain of others was difficult in cases like this. Especially since she'd done an inside cheer at the cranial contact herself.

They didn't hear the conversation of the three time travelers, but became aware that all three had gone silent and turned to look at the back wall.

Will Stark emerged from the hole that had formed there, barely conscious. Hope gasped. Her husband's skin was raw and red, burned from the intense heat of the fire raging above. There were bruises covering his face, and his left leg dangled at an angle suggesting a complete fracture. She remembered more, even as the tears came.

Josh had recognized the man floating through the air into the time machine as his father, and burst into tears. "Daddy!" he screamed. He tried to run to Will, but the cocoon that had protected them from the fire and moved them to this spot held him back. Josh turned instead to Hope and wrapped his arms around her waist, the side of his moist face pressed against her. She wrapped her arms around him.

"He'll be okay, Josh," Hope said, struggling to keep her voice steady. "Your father loves you, more than anything. He could have prevented himself the pain you're seeing right now, very easily. But he knew that doing so meant risking the worst possible thing he could imagine. Do you know what that is?"

"Dying?" Josh said, his voice weak through the thick tears.

"No. He knew it meant you might never be born. He let himself be hurt, rather than risk anything happening to you. If you ever find yourself wondering if your father loves you, Josh... remember what he looks like right now."

Young Josh said nothing, and his eyes never left the injured man. Hope watched her young son for a moment, wondering how the experience would affect him. She turned back toward the time machine... and found her grown son standing in front of her.

"I can't see either of you, and I don't have much time, but I know you're there. Mom, don't be discouraged, and please... don't be afraid to ask for help for what's happening to you. You'll get the help you need if you ask. Just don't wait too long. Once she's born, take action." Hope stared at her grown son, longing to reach out, to hold him, but he turned to face his younger self. "Josh, take care of your Mom, and *demand* that she take care of herself, no matter how much she might fight you. I know exactly how you'll feel about your Dad in the coming years, and as natural as those feelings will be, as justified as they'll seem... you can't let those feelings consume you. Oh... and take care of your sister."

Young Josh looked puzzled.

The older Josh nodded at both of them. "I need to go take care of an old friend." And he was gone, racing back up the steps.

Angel stood in front of them. The daughter she'd not yet held, the child growing inside her, was standing in front of her now, and Hope wanted to scream at the injustice of it all. Why could she not be freed of whatever it was that the older Will used to keep them here?

"Mom, I'll keep this brief. You've spent lifetimes taking care of others. Now, you need to take care of yourself. Don't let it get too bad before you ask for help. And don't fight those who are trying to provide that help. They're the ones who love you the most. *Let them* help you. Please. Do it for me, do it for Josh, and do it for Dad."

She turned to the young boy she couldn't see, and even in her confusion at the words just spoken, Hope was amused that the young woman with the fiery red hair and violet eyes was looking a foot over where Josh's head was located. "Josh, that—" she pointed at the hole in the wall, and at the dirt and rock flowing back into the tunnel that had been created "—is something your sister needs to return to take care of. She needs to come back here and claim what's rightfully hers. You won't understand this, not yet. But remember my words, and when you *do* understand them, pass them along to her. Remember to take care of your mom. Oh, yes… and be nice to your sister."

Angel winked at both of them before she turned and moved back to the time machine, sliding into the backseat with her father, who was barely conscious. Adam affixed a small device high on the wall nearest the time machine, and then turned toward the invisible mother and child. "It will go off five minutes after we leave. You should be certain you've left this place before the timer hits zero." He climbed into the front seat.

The elder Josh moved down the stairs once more, with no less speed but with far greater care than before. He cradled Smokey in his arms. She felt the tears rising again, and whispered to both versions of the son she loved. "Thank you."

The younger Josh didn't seem to notice the gesture. He tugged on Hope's sleeve once more. "Mommy! Smokey said she's getting better!"

Hope watched Smokey as the elder Josh climbed into the time machine. The dog didn't seem to be breathing. But if Josh said the dog had *told* him she was getting better… well, who was she to argue? "Those people will take good care of her, sweetie."

She hoped that was true.

The top of the time machine started to materialize, but they were able to hear a brief snippet of conversation.

"You... you saved Smokey," Will said. His voice was barely a whisper, but they could hear him clearly. "Thank you. My wife, my son... were you able to save them as well?"

The older Josh turned around to face the man in the seat behind him, but Hope could feel his eyes on his younger self, for the words were meant for the invisible boy, not the beaten man who'd asked the question. Or perhaps they were meant for his father, hidden from all of them. "They were already gone when I got there."

The lid snapped opaque, cutting off the view of the people in the cabin of the time machine. Seconds later, the craft vanished.

"Will they bring Smokey back?" Josh asked.

"If they're able to," Hope said. "They have to help her get better. But you'll see her again. I'm sure of it."

"What about Daddy?"

She sighed. "Daddy will have to hide a lot, to get the men who did this to stay away from us."

On cue, Porthos bounded down the stairs, followed seconds later by Athos and Aramis. The Hunters stared at the sight of the dirt and rock flowing back into the hole in the basement wall.

"Who are they?" Josh asked Hope. "I... I don't like them."

"I don't, either," Hope replied, as memories of the trio worked their way back into her consciousness. "Those men... they're the one who hurt Daddy, and their... friend is the one who tried to hurt us. The men you see are called the Hunters. Their job is to find Daddy and our friends, to Hunt them, and to capture them. Tonight was the closest they've gotten to succeeding."

"Their friend, the bad man with the ugly face... he was supposed to kill us, wasn't he?"

She was amazed at his perceptiveness at six years of age... but realized he'd been born with Energy potential she could barely fathom. Hiding anything from him, including the fact that there were people in the world who wanted him dead, would be impossible. "You're right, sweetie. He was supposed to kill us. But he didn't succeed. That's what Daddy is going to focus on now. The men here, the Hunters—" she gestured at the three in the basement "—they'll assume the Assassin was successful, and that we're dead. They'll continue to try to find Daddy, though. If they find him with us, they'll know we survived and will try to find us again and try again to kill us. To give us a chance to live, to give you a chance to grow up without being chased like that, to live without having to move around all the time… Daddy will stay in hiding, making sure they don't know where we are, or even that we're alive at all. It will be difficult for all of us, Josh. But the time will come when we'll all be together again."

She said those last words with far more conviction than she actually felt. And she hoped that Josh believed her words.

One of the Hunters had noticed the countdown timer on the device Adam had planted earlier. The three men exchanged worried glances.

Go now, Hope. Go to the bunker. You know how to do it. And I know you can do it.

She remembered her skill and the location at his prompting. Her Energy was fully awakened once more, and she surrounded herself and her son within its warmth, picturing in her mind the two of them being inside the bunker dozens of feet underground. It was the place she'd spent years building, knowing they'd need it for just this point in time.

An instant later, they were there.

Hope was exhausted. The emotional toll of the past twenty minutes—seeing Will's injuries, seeing her grown children, the strange warnings to take care of herself issued to both her and the younger Josh—overwhelmed her. She moved to one of the beds and climbed under the covers. Josh climbed in with her, snuggled up next to her, and was soon asleep.

As she dozed off, Hope felt a sense of triumph that she couldn't quite define. The memories would return with time. But she knew that the fact that she was sleeping in this bunker with her son meant they'd succeeded in completing something that had been in the works for a very long time.

Lifetimes, in fact.

It was no wonder she was so tired.

XXV
Chances

January 10, 2030

Gena woke, unaware of what day it was, where she was, or even *who* she was. The entirety of the events she'd gone through since Adam had abducted her—there was no other way to describe it—was overwhelming, and her mind and body demanded sleep as the only way to allow her to process and internalize everything.

She'd known she was adopted, abandoned at the orphanage in Pleasanton when she was only a few months old. There were no clues to the identity of her birth parents. She'd long since given up wondering about them. They'd made the decision they'd felt was right, and without knowing their circumstances, she had no way to judge if their choice had been best for her. It wasn't as if she'd suffered from their decision. The Adamses had been stellar parents, and never once had she doubted that they loved her as their own. Any mention that she *wasn't* their flesh and blood brought looks of such sadness to them that she'd stopped mentioning it, even during her teen years when she'd sometimes *wanted* to hurt them. Some blows were too cruel, even when delivered in anger.

And in time, she'd stopped wondering about the people who'd given her life and started being thankful for those who'd given her life meaning. *They* were her parents. *They* wanted *her* to be their daughter, and they'd filled out massive volumes of forms and endured countless interviews and waiting to get her. They were, in a word, heroes. And she got to call her heroes Mom and Dad.

Now, though, everything she'd thought she'd known—or, more to the point, *not* known—about her past had been resurrected by the man who'd abducted her.

Her birth parents hadn't abandoned her.

They'd thought her dead, listened to the medical professionals who'd said their daughter was stillborn. The couple had accepted those proclamations as fact, had grieved, and in some fashion had moved on to the rest of their lives. They'd never known that their daughter lived.

Adam had been there, had realized after the proclamations of death that she lived, and realized that she'd never survive with the medical technology available to those he called "humans." With his skills, with his technology, though, she had a chance, and he'd spent months—perhaps years—working to fix what ailed her.

She owed him her life. She had complete confidence that what he'd told her of her birth—and her rebirth—were completely true. But she also knew that he wasn't telling her everything.

He hadn't mentioned why he'd never gone back to her birth parents and told them she'd lived. Why? Why had he and his "friend" elected to place her in an orphanage when they knew who her birth parents were? Was it possible it had taken so long that he'd figured that her parents wouldn't have recognized her, would not have been able to accept the infant as their own child? Were her birth parents even alive by the time she was restored to health?

He hadn't mentioned if she had any siblings. If he'd met the family in the delivery room, surely he'd know if she had any older brothers or sisters. That, she decided, was the worst part of the whole thing. She'd grown up thinking of herself as an only child; the Adamses had turned to adoption, and to her, when they found themselves unable to have children of their own. The new information about her origin shared by Adam brought that old question back to her mind, one she'd stopped thinking about years earlier. What if her birth parents *did* have other children? Were *they* still alive? Would those potential siblings want to know about her, want to get to know her? Would they welcome her as family, or treat her as a stranger?

Adam knew the answers to those questions; of that, she was quite certain. But she was also certain that, for reasons she couldn't fathom, he wouldn't tell her the answers.

He'd also been evasive when she'd asked him how it was he'd been in that specific hospital on the day she was born. He'd told her that he'd been interested in medicine, and as it turned out, he was on duty at the time. But that hardly explained things. One didn't simply walk into a hospital, don medical scrubs, and participate in the delivery of a baby. Well, someone like Adam probably could, because she'd no doubt he could convince anyone that he belonged there. But why would he bother?

How was he old enough to do this? He looked to be around forty. She'd just turned twenty. How would a twenty-year-old have enough interest in medicine, and enough skill with this Energy stuff, to decide to walk into a hospital delivery room? She had the feeling he was older than he looked, but the math still didn't work well.

And why had he asked her not to tell anyone about the circumstances of her birth, and of his involvement? She'd given her word, but now wished she hadn't. The others didn't act like there was anything unusual about her, but she wondered what they'd say if she related the story Adam had given her. He'd alluded to one other person knowing the truth. Perhaps that person, if identified, might tell her what secret Adam was hiding from her and the others.

Perhaps the secrets he kept might explain why she was able to "hear" this stuff he called Energy, and do so in a far more convincing manner than her own theory about the effects of living an extended period of time inside an Energy cocoon. It was something she'd be able to study in more depth after the journey she was about to take, another means to understand her own origin and to take her mind off Mark and the burning anger she felt toward the man who'd murdered her love.

She'd be leaving on a journey to their primary facility to begin her initiation process, which sounded ominous. She wasn't sure she had reason to doubt them. In her time here, they'd never hurt her. Outside the original abduction, she'd never been restricted in her movements, except during her brief attempt to run to Mark's aid three days earlier. And even then, Ashley had only slowed her down, given her something to think about, and then set her free to make her own decision about what to do next. She'd asked about leaving yesterday, told them that she'd like to return to her apartment, but they'd showed her the stories of her murder on the local news. The note someone had left behind—probably one of the evil Aliomenti they spoke about—said she'd killed herself after learning of Mark's violent death.

It had nearly been the truth. But she'd been given a choice, had made her decision, and now she'd make the most of her remaining time on this planet.

She didn't like the idea that her friends would think she'd taken her own life, though they'd know that nothing short of Mark's death would ever push her to such a decision. But the only way to tell them it wasn't true was to show that she was still alive. The Alliance—Adam, Judith, Aaron, Peter, Eva, Ashley, and Archie— asked her what would happen if she *did* reveal, even to a single best friend, that she'd lived. She considered and realized the awful truth, the reality of the world she now lived in. *They* would find out. *They* would come looking for her. And she had no idea if the Alliance people would be able to defend her. They'd considered Mark and Deron expendable—in fairness, they'd given both men a chance to live, but refused to prevent the public murders from occurring—so she held out little hope she'd get much protection from them after revealing she'd survived having her throat slashed. The Alliance had no interest in any type of exposure; it was the one thing they seemed to have in common with their Aliomenti foes.

Leaving the old life behind was as practical as it was therapeutic. It gave her the chance to make a clean break from her past and from Mark, letting the dead sleep in peace. And he'd want her to move along, to take advantage of the opportunity she now had.

Gena left her room and went to locate the others. The kitchen upstairs was empty, which was unusual. Typically, she'd find them there, congregating, planning their days—both their public, elderly, and wealthy human lives, and their secret, younger, Alliance lives—and she'd be able to develop a deeper understanding of each of them and their culture just by listening to the conversation. They never asked her to leave the room, which helped her feel more at home and welcome.

She vaguely remembered conversations from the previous day, about what each of them would be doing. Adam was going to settle in a house several hours away, waiting for Will Stark's lawyer to arrive. They had apparently set in motion a plan to recover the Starks' fortune for use by Hope and Josh without giving any hint of their whereabouts to the Aliomenti, who had a deep presence in matters of international banking. The process would start when the lawyer met Adam. Eva and Aaron—back in their elderly human disguises—were off to take a trip to Oregon to check on a rental property they'd purchased a few months earlier. Archie and Ashley were pretending to leave on an extended trip out of the country; in reality, they'd be escorting Gena and the MacLeans to the Alliance headquarters.

That accounted for most of them, but she couldn't remember what the homeowners, Peter and Judith, were planning to do today. Were they still sleeping?

She walked back down to the deserted basement. The door to the media room was open. Gena tentatively moved inside and glanced around. The video screens they'd positioned three days earlier were gone; only the single large projection screen remained. The screen was powered down, the audio was silent, and there were no signs that, only days earlier, she'd witnessed things she'd like to forget, and others she hoped she'd one day understand.

Gena walked back to the main congregating area in the lower level, her footfalls silent in the thick carpeting on the floor. She saw the life-sized images of Peter and Judith on the wall and she walked forward, frowning. She'd watched as they'd walked through that painting to get into a secret section of the house, and she suspected that's where she'd find the homeowners. She moved closer to the portrait, suspecting that it was a mirage and she'd go through into the secret rooms.

She slammed into the wall and bounced back, and her hand moved to rub the pain out of nose. Why wasn't she able to get in?

An odd thought came to her. Adam had spoken broadly of Energy, the substance they used to perform their miraculous feats, the force of nature she could hear in her mind. He'd vaguely described it, in one of their conversations, as a warmth or tingling sensation. Was it possible that the wall could only be penetrated by someone who wielded that power?

Could *she* do that?

With no guidance, she focused on trying to sense the warmth or tingling in her body. After several minutes of effort, she still felt nothing. That angered her, because if she was right, they could use that lack of ability, that *humanness*, against her, to keep her out of the more important rooms in the house here and elsewhere. She concentrated, achieving a level of focus deeper than she'd ever achieved before.

In those depths of focus and concentration, she found the spark.

It was tiny, faint, and something she'd probably missed in her life until now. But it was there, a feeling of warmth that seemed alive, a sensation that moved through and around her body as she focused on it. Enthralled, she focused more on that spark, spreading that tingling sensation throughout her body, feeling lighter and more alive than she'd ever felt before.

She hadn't realized her eyes were closed until that moment, and when she opened them once more she saw the wall with the portrait in front of her. Feeling emboldened by the sensations she now experienced, Gena moved to the wall once more, with caution, her body tingling with Energy.

This time, she fell through into the room behind the wall.

The tumble took her to the ground, and she quickly stood. She descended the circular staircase before her to the hidden sub-basement. The fall had also ended her deep focus, jarring her concentration and ending the euphoria brought on by the tingling sensation. It didn't worry her; she knew she could find that spark again, and she would. The experience provided an incredible rush, and if the people she'd been working with for the past few days had tapped into this ability…

"Gena?"

She turned toward the voice, saw the speaker, and screamed, falling to the ground.

"Gena? Are you okay?" Mark's voice was tinged with concern. He moved to her and held out his hand to her, offering to help her stand. "It seems like it's been forever since I've seen you."

But Gena couldn't speak. Her eyes were wide, and her face was as pale as the ghost she felt she was seeing.

Alerted by the scream, Peter raced out of a room toward both of them, taking in the situation in mere seconds. "Mark, can you give me a quick moment with Gena?"

Mark looked as if leaving Gena was the last thing he wanted

to do, especially with her in such an obvious state of distress. But he finally relented, rose to his feet, and walked slowly back into the room Peter had just exited. He glanced back at Gena, concern etched on his face, before shutting the door behind him.

Peter helped Gena to her feet. "How did you get in here?"

Gena recognized the tone; Peter knew the answer to his question, but either he didn't want to believe that answer, or he wanted *her* to believe it. There was no anger or threat in his tone; he was curious, and she felt comfortable in his presence. Was that another effect of wielding the Energy?

She took a few gasps of air to steady her voice. It didn't work. "How... how is he... I saw him... you saw... that man..."

Peter held up his hand. "We had to start the cloning process before we were able to talk to Mark and Deron, Gena. The process takes hours to complete, and we had a deadline we couldn't exceed to get them back in place. By the time Mark made his choice, the process was too far along to stop. Clones live only a few days. He's enjoying himself, keeping busy, learning a lot about who we are and what we do, before..."

Gena's horror mounted. "You're going to let him die *again*?"

Peter sighed. "I'm not going to *let* him do anything, Gena. Mark was given the information needed to make a decision. The lifespan of our clones is well-known. It's inevitable. We've never figured out how to expand that lifespan." He paused, watching her mounting ire. "I'm respecting his choice, Gena."

"It's not a choice!" she hissed, gesturing at the room. "You can describe what this new life would be like with words, but words can't do it justice. He might well have believed you were bluffing before, because the story you offered was too far-fetched to believe, even with the little magic show. Now, though? He needs to know what his reality is."

Peter shook his head. "Why would you want to do that to him? So we show him the reality, show him the video of his death, show him what we—and you, apparently—can do. To what end, Gena? What happens if he *does* change his mind? We just told him of the great life he could live... but because his original chose against living that life, he's going to die in the next seventy-two hours, at most. Nothing can save him. Why make his final hours anything but a true joy?"

Gena glared at him. "I'm talking to him. And then… we're going to save him."

Peter sighed. "I really don't think that's a good idea, Gena. You're only going to hurt him… and yourself."

Gena ignored him as she walked into the room. Peter made no effort to stop her.

Mark was watching the cloning machine at work, watching as the machine took a small sample from his skin and rebuilt a living hand from the tiny cells. He looked up as Gena entered the room, smiling. "Hope I didn't scare you before. I tried calling you, but the signal was too weak. Did you get my message?"

She shook her head. "I need to talk with you."

He spread his hands. "I'm right here."

"What day is it?"

He frowned at her. "It's Monday, of course. Peter asked me to help him plan a birthday celebration for Will Stark. I told him it's your birthday as well, and we should be sure to include you in the party. Are you here early?"

She shook her head, tears of exasperation filling her eyes. "It's not Monday, Mark. It's Thursday. The people who live here… they're not normal. At all."

He laughed. "Gena, now you're being silly. Of course they're not normal; they're obscenely *rich*. I'm not sure why you think that makes it Thursday, though."

"Look at your phone, Mark."

He pulled his phone from his pocket. "OK. What am I looking it?"

"Look at the date, Mark."

He glanced at it, and then frowned. "I don't get the joke, Gena. It's—"

She pointed at the phone. "Open your news app, please. Read the top story."

He frowned, but did as she'd asked. His eyes widened. "How can the Starks' house have burned down? I would have seen it, would have needed to let the fire engines in. And Peter wouldn't have asked me to help him out if something like that was going on."

"Read the article, Mark. There's far more."

Mark tapped the phone, sliding down through the article on the screen.

She knew he'd found the key details when he dropped the phone. It fell to the titled surface with a loud clatter, and the screen shattered.

"This isn't like you, Gena. Why would you do this? Why would you play a joke like this on me?"

"How could I get an article like that on a major news site, Mark?" she snapped. Why was he blaming her for telling him the truth? "I know it's hard to believe. But I know it's true, because I watched it happen, and even though I experienced it happening directly, even *I* don't believe it. But the reality is what's in the article, Mark. Three days ago, you died, as did Deron, in an assault that led to criminals entering this neighborhood and burning down the Starks' house, with Mrs. Stark and Josh still inside. You haven't read far enough yet, Mark, but later that night, they came to our apartment and killed me, because I'd unknowingly given them information that helped them succeed in their attack, and they didn't want me around and able to identify them."

Mark shook his head. "This is insane, Gena. If we're both dead, then how are we still talking to each other?"

"The people in this neighborhood? They're… different. Not because they're rich, but because they can do things I'd call magic. I don't know if it's magic, but it seems like it. And they can make *clones* of people, Mark." He snorted derisively at this, but she ignored him. "They brought me here because they knew this would happen, and told me they could make a clone of me to live through the time when the evil people came for me. They asked you the same question, if you wanted a clone made to die in the attacks, and we'd live on in secret afterward, with their powerful organization of people just like them. It was the same thing they'd asked me. I said yes." She paused, unable to continue.

He recognized the implication immediately. "And I said no?"
She nodded.

"Then why am I still here talking to you?"

"The timing was such that they had to start the cloning process before they had your answer. When you declined… they couldn't turn the process off."

His eyes widened. "So… I'm… a *clone*. Of myself?"
She nodded.

He studied her face. And then he started laughing,

uncontrollably laughing. "Okay, okay, I get it. I give up. You got me, Gena. You totally had me going there. For a minute, I actually started to believe this was real."

Gena said nothing for a moment. He watched her face, and she could feel his fear growing, fear that she was telling the truth. She knew her sensation was no mere hunch, either; she knew his sense of fear with a certainty like nothing she'd ever known before. "They told me... clones, they don't live long after they're... created."

His eyes widened. "But...then..." He took a deep breath. "I guess you aren't joking, are you?"

She shook her head.

"How long do I have?"

"How long do you *want* to have?"

"You said clones don't live long."

"They don't live long *yet*. I think they have the chance to live a very, very long time. So, knowing what you know now, that these people offer an opportunity unlike any other, that I've chosen to take advantage of it... would you still make the same choice? Would you still choose to let your life end?"

Mark turned away and began to pace around the room, thinking.

At last, he turned back to face her. "I know that before I would have chosen to ignore the cloning offer. But now? I'd choose to live. I don't know what I was thinking when they asked me the first time; maybe I thought it was a joke, maybe I thought that, knowing what was coming, I'd be able to escape. But I was wrong." His eyes moistened. "I'd prefer to live, Gena. To be with you."

She nodded, and the tears streamed down her face. "Then I'll help you."

He smiled, moving forward, and they embraced.

Then he sagged toward the ground, a gulping, gagging sound emerging from the back of his throat.

She pulled away far enough to see his face, to see the sheer terror in his eyes. It was the terror of a man who knew, in that instant, that he was dying.

"No!" she screamed. "You *can't leave me again!*" In that instant, she knew the man who could save him, knew the name of the man who had performed this same miracle once before. As Peter rushed into the room, as Judith appeared there an instant later, materializing out of nowhere at the sound her distress, Gena screamed for Adam's help.

He was there in an instant, assessing the situation even as he materialized near Gena. Her grief was overwhelming, even more powerful than earlier in the week, for this time, Gena knew that this end *wasn't* what Mark wanted, or at least accepted. Adam knew why she'd called out to him, blasting out an emotional plea that he could feel from so far away. Perhaps there was an attachment that had been formed over the years he'd worked to save her life. Whatever the reason, he was here now.

And he knew it was already too late.

Death had come too quickly for Mark. Where she'd wrongly been proclaimed dead by human medicine, Mark was truly gone. There was no spark of life left to salvage, no matter how much he wanted to save him for her, to give her that ultimate gift of happiness.

He did the only thing he could do. He held her in his arms, warming her with the familiar cocoon of security and warmth, allowing her to drain her eyes of tears against his shoulder as Mark crashed headlong into his true final oblivion.

XXVI
Transition

February 7, 2030

Adam checked his appearance in the mirror. His hair was mostly gray, with just a few flecks of his natural brown showing through. The aging simulator had recommended he lose some hair as well, but Adam had elected to ignore the simulator's recommendation, even if it was just a cosmetic change.

He walked out of the bathroom and climbed into the taxi waiting for him.

The month since the fire had been hectic, but things were starting to stabilize. News crews had provided near round-the-clock footage of the powdery remains of the Starks' house. Their neighbors stated in interviews that they knew of no one who might want to hurt the Starks; after all, few had done more to improve the quality of life of everyone than the young couple. Three of the four remaining estate owners had put their homes on the market within a week of the attack, citing a fear that the community was cursed, and the risk of further attacks were risks they'd rather leave to others.

With a sales pitch like that, they'd gotten no showings and received no offers.

The Alliance members didn't mind, for they had no interest in selling. The houses gave them a public base of operations in the human world, and the community would receive far less attention now than when the Starks had lived there. Those were exactly the sort of conditions the privacy-conscious members of the Alliance preferred.

Eventually, the news crews and cameras went away.

Three days earlier, Myra VanderPoole had been found dead in her home by her driver, Frank. There were no signs of foul play. She'd died of old age, and the stress of recent events had likely hastened her demise. The surviving residents would be attending her funeral today, and had invited an "old friend" named Adam Trask to join them.

Adam's taxi pulled up to the cemetery. Those attending the funeral service would arrive shortly, part of the caravan trailing the hearse. Adam paid the cab driver, added a bit extra so that the man would wait around for a bit, and then walked to Myra's grave site at a leisurely pace. He sat on a bench nearby and pulled out his mobile phone.

They'd put in place an elaborate scheme to get the funds amassed by the Starks into Alliance possession. A direct transfer of everything to an unknown person, or an obscure charity, would raise too much suspicion among the Aliomenti. They'd settled upon "stealing" the money, setting up the lawyer and the Trustee to take the blame. That plan had seemed brilliant until he'd met the two men whose names would be forever tarnished for their apparent theft—and loss—of the Starks' fortune. Both Millard Howe and Michael Baker were good, honest men who deserved better. Adam had used actual and lightly modified private email communications to provide evidence that others were guilty of the destruction of the Starks' estate after their deaths, and would show Howe and Baker as innocent victims caught in the wrong place at the wrong time. Both Howe and Baker, along with Baker's wife and son, would be offered the chance to disappear from the human world and join the Alliance after the conspiracy was revealed.

He activated the secret functionality in his phone and ran the app tracking the high speed micro transfers of funds. Ashley, Archie, and Judith had helped set up the massive network of interconnected bank accounts and shell companies needed to execute the entire scheme. The apps would trigger monetary transfers from the primary account of the Starks' Trust into hundreds of different shadow accounts, each of which were "swept" daily into dozens of other accounts. The web of transfers would take decades to unravel, if someone had the means and patience to do so, and by then they'd have the entire amount elsewhere and the majority of the accounts shut down. According to the app, it would take just under four days before the Trust funds ran out and the media descended upon the "embezzling" lawyer and Trustee. He'd need to be back in town before that happened to work with the men and protect them from the public anger and outcry that would follow.

Adam deactivated the app and the hid the special Alliance features before pocketing the phone. There'd be more time for that later.

The funeral caravan rolled into view, led by the hearse carrying Myra's coffin. Cars followed the hearse to the grave site, and mourners emerged from the vehicles. Few of those in attendance were crying. Perhaps it was due to the lack of family in attendance; Myra had outlived her husband and siblings, and had no children. The few nieces and nephews in her family tree had never been close to the cantankerous woman, and Adam wondered if any of them were present. It was a marked contrast to the public mourning after the deaths of the Starks. Of course, Myra had never been the charitable sort; she took as much as she could and never looked for or took opportunities to raise others up. The Starks, in contrast, looked for every possible chance to get money in the hands of people they judged able to multiply it, create opportunities for many others in the process, and change the world for the better.

You got what you gave, Adam decided.

Eva and Aaron, back in their disguises as elderly business magnates, emerged from one of the final cars in the procession, and Adam wandered over to Eva. She glanced at him, feigning surprise to see him. "Mr. Trask? It's been ages." She gave him a polite hug, then stepped back to look at him. "You look well. How's the family?"

He shook his head. "Not well, I fear. My son..." He looked away, allowing the fake tears to come and the crying to shake his body.

Aaron stepped over as well. "Adam Trask? What are you doing here? What's wrong?"

"My son... there was a house fire... he was trapped, never had a chance to get out... asphyxiation..."

Eva's hand went to her mouth. "I'm so, so sorry, Adam. I don't know what to say. Is there... is there anything we can do for you?"

He wiped a sleeve against his face, clearing the tears, and nodded. "He had a wife, a young son... the house is a total loss, and they really want a fresh start, away from the memories of their loss. I... I know you do some real estate investing, have some rental houses available. Do you have anything available for rent? They have money coming from a life insurance policy on my son, but I'd rather stay away from anything too extravagant."

Eva considered. "I believe we just added something out west, a smaller house that we've renovated with three or four bedrooms. Nice, quiet neighborhood, good schools... how old is your grandson?"

Adam had to pause, before realizing she was speaking about Josh. "He's six."

She nodded. "The school there should be a good fit. Let me send you the address for the house and my property manager out west. I take it they'll want to move in soon?"

"They will. *We* will. I'm going to move in with my daughter-in-law and grandson. I have no real ties to my home anymore, and my son's family... well, they could use my help, and I think it would be good for me as well. My daughter-in-law, Phoebe, needs a few more weeks to put my son's affairs in order back home, so I'll go arrange everything if the house and neighborhood look like a good fit."

Eva typed on her mobile phone. "I just emailed you the particulars."

Aaron tapped Eva's arm. "We'll need to head to the grave site to pay our final respects to Myra." He held out his hand to Adam. "It was good seeing you again, Mr. Trask. I wish it was under better circumstances, though."

Adam shook Aaron's hand, nodding. "Agreed, Aaron. I need to get going as well. Please offer my respects and condolences to those gathered here."

The couple nodded, and moved toward the grave site.

Adam turned and walked away.

He didn't need the address Eva had sent; he'd traveled to the small community two weeks earlier, posing as an assistant to Eva, and was familiar with the renovation work that had been done. But now, the man known as Adam Trask had been seen in public talking to the wealthy couple, who'd acted as if they were old friends, and he'd have a record of an email communication from them with a recommendation of a house for rent. With those tracks covered, he could now head to the airport for his flight out to Oregon.

The trip was uneventful, and Adam slept most of the way, uninterested in conversing with the salesman in the middle seat next to him. When the plane touched down, he maneuvered his way through the gate and to the rental car agency where he'd made his reservation. If anyone was paying close attention, they might find it strange that he'd been ready to board the flight and had a previous rental car reservation before talking to his old friends. They might also find it odd that he'd made the trip and would never make arrangements for lodging.

He doubted anyone would notice or care, however. The Aliomenti wouldn't know to look for him, and after the debacle at the Starks' house a month earlier, they were likely to spend every resource looking for Will. They'd not notice something as obscure as odd coincidences surrounding the travel habits of a single elderly man traveling to a remote community in the northwestern United States.

He drove the nondescript rented sedan to the neighborhood and pulled the car into the driveway. There were no people outside, but he did spot a For Rent sign in the yard, confirming he'd found the correct place. The house had undergone significant renovations, including new sod in the front yard and a fresh coat of paint on the exterior. The house was, generously, a quarter the size of the house the Starks had lived in before, but they weren't billionaires now, just a widow, her father-in-law, her son, and, eventually, her newborn daughter. The house would be perfect for their needs. Josh would need to adjust to having neighbors living so close to his house, just as he'd have to adjust to going to school. But his enhanced senses, intelligence, and maturity left him well-equipped to handle those adjustments. And he'd have his mother and Adam there to help.

He glanced around, tried the front door, and found, to his surprise, that it was unlocked. He walked inside. "Hello?"

A woman popped her head out of the kitchen area. "Oh! Hello, there!" She had a bubbly personality, one his enhanced senses judged to be genuine, and he took an instant liking to her. "Did you have an appointment?"

"I didn't, no," Adam admitted. "But I talked to the woman who owns the house and told her I was looking for a rental here in this area. She recommended I check this unit out. I'm really here for my daughter-in-law; she recently lost her husband—my son—and she and my grandson are looking for a fresh start."

Her hand went to her mouth and her eyes widened, and she seemed on the verge of tears. "I'm so, so sorry!" Adam's empathy sense suggested that, while the emotion was genuine, she was exaggerating the effect with the tears in an effort to build rapport with him.

"Thank you," he said. "It's been difficult but I'm ready to move on."

She nodded. "Would you like me to show you around the house?"

He nodded. "That would be great."

He spent the next thirty minutes touring the house with her. The entire interior had been redone, the woman explained, as the previous owners had lost their jobs years earlier and hadn't maintained the home well. Eva's renovation company had made the space livable, and they were charging a bargain rate on the rent. He asked about the neighbors ("quiet for the most part, but they do have block parties during the summer that run somewhat late") and the schools in the area ("very highly rated and within walking distance") before he asked about terms. He showed her the power of attorney that "Phoebe" didn't know she'd signed, and put a deposit down to rent the house on a two year lease. Move-in date was set for roughly a month later, which, according to the owners, would give the renovation team and cleaning crew time to finish their work. Adam smiled and nodded. The human renovation team would finish the structural and cosmetic repairs, and would be followed by a "cleaning" crew from the Alliance that would coat the inside of the house with a variety of scutarium-laced substances.

He walked away with the signed lease, climbed into the rental car, and drove away.

They now had a place to live. He'd next need to start purchasing supplies and furnishings for their new home. He rented a large storage unit, which he lined with scutarium when the owners weren't watching and after he'd temporarily disabled the security cameras. It gave him a place to store his purchases as well as a teleportation base until the house was prepared. He drove around town in his rental car and found a used minivan in good condition and paid for it in cash, with the title in the name of his daughter-in-law. He returned the rental car and took a taxi back to the minivan. With the additional transport space, he visited a secondhand thrift shop and purchased two chairs and a dresser, and then called it a day. He'd return to the city several times over the next few weeks, more easily now that he could teleport safely, and finish purchasing the remaining furnishings and supplies they'd need to set up their household.

After unloading his purchases into the storage unit, he made his last stop for the day, a local credit union. There, he set up a checking account, savings account, and obtained both credit and debit cards they could use for purchases and cash withdrawals. He presented a cashier's check to fund the accounts, explaining that it was the partial proceeds from the life insurance policy on his son. The community would be well aware of the back story for the Trask family by the time they moved in.

Adam walked out with the checkbook and cards an hour after entering, around closing time, and drove the minivan to a long-term parking facility. He then hailed a taxi that he used to return to the storage facility. Once there, he phased invisible—a task that required far less Energy than teleportation—and moved inside his scutarium-lined rental unit. With his chance of detection finally eliminated, Adam teleported back to the safety of the basement room within Judith and Peter's house.

Peter was working with the cloning machine, but glanced up as he sensed the Energy burst announcing the arrival of a long-range teleporter. "Hey, Adam," he said. "I think I've figured out a few techniques we can use to extend the lives of clones. I wish we'd had this a month ago, but, still, having clones live longer than a few days may prove handy in the future."

Adam nodded. "Sounds promising, Peter." He held out a folder containing the personal documents for the newly created personas of Phoebe and Fil Trask. "Can I ask you to hang on to these? We'll turn them over to Hope and Josh when they emerge from the bunker in the next few weeks."

Peter nodded. "I've got a safe we can use." He accepted the folder from Adam before asking his next question. "Where are you off to next?"

"Ashley and Archie's house. They're running the servers handling the account transfers. I want to recheck the sequencing of the sweeps from account to account, and it'll be handled best directly at the source."

"Give them my best," Peter replied.

Adam nodded, and teleported to Ashley and Archie's house.

Ashley walked into the basement area and nodded a greeting at him. "Hey, Adam. How'd everything go in Oregon?"

"Perfectly. Peter's got the paperwork and will be storing it in his safe. Any news on Myra's house?"

Ashley nodded, and a smile emerged. They'd wondered what the childless, heirless widow would do with her home upon her death. "Ironic, in a way. She didn't have any children or any relatives she cared for. She left the house and a large portion of her estate to Frank, her driver. Said she appreciated all he'd done for her while she was alive."

Adam chuckled. "So the entire neighborhood is full of the Alliance now? That's pretty impressive."

"I know," Ashley agreed. "All we need to do to finish this effort is get Hope and Josh to the Cavern to make sure they're fully recovered from last month before they move on to Oregon." She paused. "Do you think Hope will still have issues with her memory?"

"She probably does," Adam admitted. "I'm not terribly skilled at memory blocks, so I'll have to check all of them and remove any that haven't cleared yet. I suspect I was a bit too aggressive when I set them."

"That's not surprising," Ashley said. "It was something of an impromptu decision. Judith's actually really good at those, by the way, if you're ever in need of really good memory blocks in the future."

"I'll keep that in mind." Adam started to move away.

"Gena said hello, by the way," Ashley said. "I talked to her earlier today, and it sounds like she's adapting and learning at a very high rate of speed. She wants to come back and be here when Hope and Josh emerge from the bunker."

"I think that's a great idea," Adam replied, nodding. "She was a big part of the events that drove them underground. It would be wonderful if she's there to see the end result."

"Any idea when Hope and Josh will leave the bunker?"

"We suspect it will be during the first week of March, though we don't have an exact date. It won't be long now."

"I'll let Gena know."

Adam nodded. Getting Hope and Josh out of the bunker would finish this era of his life. It had been an exhilarating time, full of twists he hadn't seen, even with the advantage of the hindsight of future history. And despite the many sleepless nights, he wouldn't trade his role for anything. He'd done a good thing—no, a *great* thing—and had helped out the people considered family through one of the most trying times in their lives.

But he was eager to move on to the next phase of his life with Hope, Josh, and eventually Angel. They'd start standing in wait for them each evening, watching the abandoned home site for any sign of activity. And soon, Gena would join them.

The thought made him smile.

XXVII
Emergence

March 7, 2030

The moon was a slender crescent in the sky, providing scant light to those gathered in the forest of the De Gray Estates. They had gathered here each evening for the past week, waiting. Tonight, perhaps, their wait would be rewarded, and Hope and Josh would emerge from the bunker.

They'd spent the previous evenings opining as to why they'd needed to use the bunker in the first place. Why, they asked, not simply teleport Hope and Josh directly to Peter and Judith's house? Why the elaborate construction project, the creation of the elevator hydraulics, and the two month hiatus before mother and son emerged to breathe fresh air once more?

They'd realized the answer the night before.

"Will didn't use Energy," Judith noted.

"Well, right," Adam said. "He didn't want to alert... *oh.*"

"You're kidding," Archie said. "We had to build a bunker and go through all of that elaborate scheming because the Assassin forgot to shut the door to the house?"

Eva shook her head in amazement. "Much of the scheming was employed to deny the Assassin the opportunity to understand Hope's nature and thus alert the Hunters and destroy the timeline for

317

the day. But it does appear that the reason Hope moved to the bunker was for no reason other than the fact that teleportation was unsafe."

"But why is she still there?" Peter asked. "I'm still not sure how Will got her to the bunker without anyone detecting any Energy, but I'm willing to chalk that up to a Will Stark innovation. But why does she need to stay there so long?"

"I think that's my fault," Adam said, frowning. "Those memory blocks? I don't know if I did an optimal job with them, and I don't know which of them, if any, are still in place. She might be in that bunker still because she doesn't remember how to get out. Or she might not know who to contact to determine if it's safe. And she may have no idea where to go."

"Or her memory might be fine," Aaron said. "The historical record says she stays in the bunker for two months and then uses the elevator she built to get out. Whatever the state of her memories, then, we're likely to see similar timing on their emergence."

"She wants to avoid using Energy to get out of the bunker at this point because she doesn't want to take the chance she'll have a welcoming committee of Hunters when she leaves," Ashley had noted.

Hope would have a welcoming committee. But it would be composed solely of friends.

Adam yawned, watching his warm breath turn to vapor in the cool air. "Think our neophytes are doing well?"

Ashley nodded. "I talked to the MacLeans yesterday. They've gotten settled into their home in the Cavern and are going through the initial zirple treatments." They'd found that taking large quantities of zirple before the morange purge lessened the most brutal effects of the berry. "They're also talking to people there about ambrosia and the implications. Obviously, they have plenty of time to think about it—especially Dash—but the MacLeans have already provided blood samples for Dash's future use."

Adam nodded. New recruits were advised to give blood samples over time, up until they opted to take ambrosia, so that any children would have ample supplies of the cure available to them in the future. They'd had two cases where a newer recruit accidentally drank ambrosia before they were ready, and thus they encouraged everyone to give blood immediately as a precautionary measure.

"Good to know. What about the Bakers and Millard Howe?"

"In transit to South Beach at the moment," Peter replied. "Michael—our Michael, that is—is flying them down at the moment. With Project 2030 coming to a close, he's looking forward to some down time in the Cavern."

"He's earned it, that's for sure," Adam said. The Bakers and Howe had been offered the chance to join the Alliance, an offer all had accepted. Like the MacLeans, they'd "died" in freak accidents that would leave no identifiable traces of them behind, giving them clean breaks from their lives in Pleasanton.

"I suspect they will run into Gena, then," Eva remarked. "She remains at South Beach."

"Really?" Adam raised an eyebrow. "She still hasn't gone to the Cavern?"

"She has not," Eva replied. "She felt at home at South Beach, and took up a role operating the teleportation desk. Her resulting schedule prevented her from being here today. Gena displayed Energy in the pink range before she departed, and we told her there was no need to rush to the Cavern with the remaining new recruits."

Adam nodded, thoughtful. "That makes sense. I wonder if she'd be able to do morange without taking the zirple dosage first?"

"She does not need zirple or morange, Adam," Eva told him. "What good would it do her? Most leave the Purge with less Energy sensitivity and capacity than she had when she left us two months ago. She will develop into a powerful Energy user, and need not suffer the Purge to do so."

"Really?" Peter said. "That's amazing. I wonder why that is? I wouldn't mind losing the memory of that Purge experience." He shivered.

"Indeed," Eva replied. She didn't look his way, but Adam knew that she had a strong suspicion as to why Gena's Energy development had progressed at such an unusual pace.

"Think this is the night?" Archie asked, nodding toward the clear gray concrete that stood as the only reminder of the house that once occupied these grounds.

"Not sure," Adam admitted. "The messages we have received said only that they would emerge in March, during the hours just after midnight. It makes sense; media interest has vanished, and we have no humans within the grounds any longer."

Graham chuckled. "Have to admit, that was a huge shock to me." Graham had served as Myra VanderPoole's driver, dinner guest, porter of shopping bags—and, to everyone's shock, as her sole heir. He'd been stunned to receive the call, but had recovered and settled into his new home inside De Gray Estates. He'd suffered through a week of unwanted fame; few could resist the allure of the story of the chauffeur inheriting millions. Interest had died down quickly, though, for "Frank" had proved to be unlikeable and a nightmarish interview on camera.

"All part of the plan," Graham had told his Alliance friends after each interview made him less popular with the public. Soon enough, the requests for interviews stopped coming, the cameras left, and the group—and the neighborhood—were left alone once more.

Each night for the past week, they'd all left those unmonitored homes and traveled to stand in the trees surrounding the remains of the Starks' home. They'd wait there until the sun's appearance announced the arrival of the dawn, and then return home to resume their normal lives.

Graham's head tilted to the side. "Anyone else hear that?"

Ashley put her hand on Archie's shoulder. "I don't just hear it… I *feel* it, too."

Adam nodded, as a rising thrill of excitement overcame the gathering. "Tonight's the night, then. Remember: Hope's memory may still be a bit fuzzy, and it's possible she won't recognize any of us. I'll approach her alone at first, and look for any memory blocks that haven't self-destructed since the day of the fire. Once that happens, once she remembers everything, the rest of you can come out."

Peter saluted him. "Yes, sir!"

Adam checked the folder in his hands, making sure that the identification papers were all there, and then moved closer to the house.

The sound and vibrations came from the hydraulic lift deep under the ground, which even now worked to push the platform within the bunker up to the level of the former basement. The engines driving the lift encountered strong resistance as the platform elevator car reached the solid concrete of the foundation floor. Adam watched as Hope's concrete-cutting laser sliced through the material, and a line formed around the perimeter of the area of the elevator car. There was an audible crack as the engine burst through the last resisting bit of concrete, and the elevator car resumed its ascent. Dust and a few leaves blew off the rising slab in the cool, overnight March breeze. As the slab rose above the foundation floor, Hope's golden hair became visible, and moments later she and Josh stood inside what had once been their basement, breathing in fresh outdoor air for the first time in two months. Mother and son walked to the concrete foundation walls, and Hope, after a cautious glance around, levitated both of them out of the basement and onto the grass.

Adam made his way closer to the foundation, listening to mother and son talk about the need to go into hiding, to assume new identities. "You'll need money and a place to live," he called out.

Hope spun toward him, her face anxious. That meant she still didn't recognize him. After stepping out from the trees, Adam held up a hand, generating an Energy-based glowing orb. "I'm one of you, and I'm on your side." Josh's clear sense of recognition of Adam seemed to ease Hope's concerns around their discovery.

While Hope spoke about their time in the bunker, Adam focused his efforts on finding and removing the memory blocks still in place. She knew about Energy, and remembered a great deal of what she and Will had been through together before Josh was born. She remembered a few members of the Alliance, but she didn't know who Adam was.

But she did think he looked familiar.

He worked on her mind, vaporizing the blocks he encountered, smoothing over the rough patches, while she discussed her memories of the night of the fire. "It was so difficult not to blast the Assassin; he really is too awful to let live," she said. That was a memory based upon what she'd *expected* to do, to let the Assassin get to the point where her death seemed imminent before teleporting the two of them to the safety of the bunker. She didn't remember their conversation, their decision to block her memories so her human-like behavior was no act.

He found that memory block and removed it. "Have you been talking to Josh about everything?"

She nodded. "We've discussed Energy, and why it's important for us to keep our Shields up at all times."

"I don't envy you your part in all of this, especially given the side effects. Josh does know what happened, right?"

Hope nodded, and Adam felt the wave of sadness at her memories of what the Shielding of Josh had meant to her personally. Her efforts to keep her son's existence secret from the Hunters meant she'd also hidden from Young Will the personality, intelligence, and skill of his son, how she'd suffered doubly at Will's every moment of sadness and guilt over Josh's condition. Hope wondered if Old Will had forgiven her for denying him that time together with Josh. Adam also detected a sense of understanding from Josh; the boy knew at a far deeper level now why she'd felt the need to protect him as she had, regardless of the consequences.

Hope confessed—after a prompting by Josh—that she was pregnant, and he reached out to Angel with Energy-based words of greeting. The warmth and affection from the girl were startling in their power and potency. Angel's mother might not fully remember Adam just yet, but her daughter did.

He asked both of them questions about Shielding, stressing the importance, as he found and removed the final memory blocks he'd set, including those blocking her lifetimes of memories of him. As he did so, he found the memory she had from the fire, of the events after the video feeds had been lost. He was able to immerse himself in her memories, and, in an instant, those memories became his. He realized that she'd seen *him* climb out of the time machine that day. *That* was why she thought he looked familiar, and was able to understand he was a friend even if she didn't truly know him. She'd seen him with her grown children, coming through time to rescue her husband.

A final sweep of her mind revealed that all of the memory blocks were eliminated, save for the single block he hoped he'd *never* need to remove. Adam handed over the identification papers that he'd produced, and helped the newly minted Phoebe and Fil Trask transform their appearances with Energy. Moments later, mother and son were sporting jet black hair just like Will's, with narrower facial structures than before. The difference those simple changes made to their appearances was startling, and even Adam, who knew they were the same people, struggled to convince himself that they were Hope and Josh.

Hope, now known as Phoebe Trask, gave Adam a curious look. "You seem very familiar to me. I know we worked together recently; you were a major part in creating our will and getting all of the money out of the Trust and back in our hands. But I have this strange feeling I know you from somewhere else."

Adam smiled. Her memories were slowly working their way back into her consciousness, but it would take time for the recall to become instantaneous. She *was* just over a millennium in age; there were a lot of memories to reconnect. "It's not the *where* that's important, Phoebe. It's the *when*."

She caught the hint, the emphasis on the timing of their first meeting, and her mind sought out ancient memories relating to the man standing before her. Her smile gradually broadened in understanding. "I met you centuries ago, when you and Eva first came to the Cavern. We've planned so much, put so much effort into making all of this happen, all to ensure that Josh—Fil—was born." She glanced at the little boy, who looked so different now, so much like his father, and so alive with the gargantuan Energy stores buzzing inside him. "Thank you."

Adam nodded. "It's truly been my pleasure, Phoebe. But I'm not the only one who was involved. There are others here eager to see both of you again."

They stepped out, one at a time, allowing Phoebe the chance to let her memories reconnect. She called to each of them by name, slowly at first, and then with greater confidence as each face meshed with centuries' worth of memories, and her sense of being among her extended family grew.

"So, in the end, it *was* Will who saved you," Graham noted.

Phoebe bristled. "I did *not* need saving." Her eyes burned, threatening and angry.

Graham held up his hands, surprised. "We all know that, Phoebe. You were playing your part in all of this, including allowing Adam to block any memories that would alert the Assassin to the fact that you were no mere human woman. That's the only reason the Assassin's not part of the dust on the floor there." He gestured toward the foundation, and the few dusty remnants of the structure and possessions once inside.

Phoebe relaxed a bit. "I know. I'm sorry. It's just... it's just..."

She burst into tears.

Graham looked around. "I'm... sorry. I didn't know that she'd..."

Eva patted Graham on the shoulder. "She has been through a great deal lately, Graham. It will take time to process everything."

"She's been puking, too," young Fil told them, trying to be helpful.

Adam nodded. "She's pregnant with Angel. We knew that." He paused. "Do you suppose the mood swings are…?"

"Possibly," Ashley said, frowning. "But it seems that her fatigue and sadness started before her pregnancy. And she didn't have the same symptoms with Josh."

"You know, I *am* right here!" Phoebe snapped. "Stop talking about me!"

Eva fixed Phoebe with a steady gaze. "You have been sad, and tired, and tearful to a degree I have not seen in all the centuries I have known you. I am concerned, Phoebe. This is not normal behavior for you. All of us are concerned, and we wish to understand the cause of these symptoms, and to help you overcome what ails you."

Fil nodded sagely, his young face lighting up. "Mommy! The people from the fancy car… remember what they said?"

Phoebe seemed not to notice her son's words. "The *cause?*" She laughed without humor. "My home was destroyed, and I watched as my husband, young and naive, was set up to be attacked by men able to destroy him. I've watched as the time we'd have together rapidly dwindled, from centuries, to decades, to years, to months, to days, and then hours. And now that time is gone. *He's* gone. You don't spend that much time with someone, knowing for a fact that it would one day come to an end, and watch as that day finally comes, without suffering an emotional breakdown. And while I appreciate your concern, I'd like you to at least consider the possibility that my reaction to all this means that there's nothing *wrong* with me, other than reacting as anyone watching a loved one disappear forever would react."

There was silence in the clearing as they absorbed this, uncertain if she was scolding them, pointing out the obvious. Could it be so simple?

Fil tugged on Phoebe's arm, his icy blue eyes filled with fear and the beginnings of tears. "Mommy? What do you mean Daddy's disappearing forever? I thought you said…"

Phoebe's eyes widened as she realized the trap she'd set for herself with her own words. "I'm sorry, sweetie. Mommy just doesn't know where Daddy is or where he will be now, and it's very... frustrating."

"Oh." Fil's tone suggested he was no more convinced by Phoebe's explanation to his question than the rest of them were by her comments about the cause of her recent mental and emotional state.

Adam clapped his hands together in an effort to get everyone's attention and change the subject. "Anyway. Phoebe, Fil... as I mentioned a short while ago, we've got a house rented for you, in your new names, quite a distance away. We can leave at any time, to get ourselves settled into our new roles and lives."

Phoebe looked as if she was ready to protest, to argue that those preparations were tasks she could have handled herself... but remembered that she'd picked out the general location herself several years earlier. "Let's go, then." She hesitated, and then looked back at each of them, her taut face relaxing as she smiled. "Thank you, all of you, for everything you've done for me, for my son, and for Will. If it weren't for all you, none of us would be here, and we would never have been able to save Will's life and start him on the journey all of you have spent centuries witnessing."

There were murmurs of appreciation at her comments.

Hugs were exchanged while Adam summoned the invisible flying craft to the interior of the De Gray Estates. As he waited, Adam allowed his appearance to transform back to that of Adam Trask, using the printout before him to ensure his appearance matched that of the man who'd made purchases, signed leases, and opened bank accounts in Oregon. As the craft landed, the elderly Adam Trask phased out and walked through the walls into the cabin, followed soon thereafter by his daughter-in-law, Phoebe, and his grandson, Fil. Adam tapped the controls on the screen, and the craft slowly rose into the air, silent and unseen by those on the ground. It continued its ascent until it was well above the levels of commercial and military aircraft, and then accelerated to the west, into the darkened sky.

Phoebe and Fil each sat in one of the comfortable chairs in the cabin. Fil had fallen asleep, but Phoebe stared out of the walls of the aircraft, which were transparent for those on the inside. "I wish I knew where he was."

"I saw your memory of that day, Phoebe, when I was in removing the memory blocks that hadn't already fallen." She didn't seem surprised. "I saw what happened. I know you didn't need help, and you really didn't get help, not in the way the words seemed to suggest, anyway. What you got was far more important and far more valuable. You got confirmation that he's still alive, and you saw your children, fully grown. What he gave you wasn't the aid to teleport a few feet, but the new memories you'd need to go on without him directly in your sight all the time."

She nodded without looking his way. "I know." She watched the lights far below for a few more minutes before turning back to face him. "What do you think, Adam? *Is* there something wrong with me? Or is it just what I said earlier?"

Adam considered. "When Will appeared dead at the hands of the Hunters, you reacted far differently. But I have to remind myself that you probably knew, or at least suspected, he was alive, and that you'd be seeing that version of him again. Roughly seven years ago, if my guess is correct." His eyes flicked in Fil's direction, and the briefest trace of a smile touched Phoebe's face. "Now, though? You have more of a sense that he's out there, somewhere, but don't know the circumstances under which you'd see him again. I think anyone would be upset." He took a deep breath. "But I do think there's more to it than that. You're the strongest person I know. You've spent centuries apart before. There's no reason to believe you won't be reunited again one day, because you *know for a fact* that he's very much alive. But it's like Eva said… you have been more fatigued, more prone to emotional outbursts and tears, than at any time I've ever known you. I think there's something else exaggerating the emotional effects of your current circumstances. The question for me, then, is what, beyond your admittedly stressful life experiences, made the past few years different?"

He let his head settle back against the headrest and he closed his eyes. "If we can figure that out, Phoebe, we can answer your question with confidence, once and for all. And more importantly… we can do something about it."

XXVIII
Angel

September 1, 2030

After sitting at the hospital for the past fourteen hours, Adam Trask was left with the realization that the depiction of labor and delivery found in television shows and movies was inaccurate at best and an outright lie at worst.

They'd left home the previous day, departing from the small house they'd lived in for the past six months. It was time for the very pregnant Phoebe to place herself into the hands of human medical professionals to deliver her daughter. They'd slipped through Saturday evening traffic comprised of people trying to get to the nearby college football game. Phoebe—he'd finally gotten used to calling her that, overcoming centuries of habit in the process—had sat in the passenger seat, hands upon her abdomen, breathing as she'd practiced. Her face, to Adam's surprise, was one of blissful calm.

He wanted to be nervous, to panic, and to drive at speeds twice the posted limit. He thought he'd pull up to the hospital, and she'd be whisked away in a wheelchair, screaming in pain. He thought that he'd park the car and race to her room, to find her holding Angel in her arms.

Life was never quite as planned, though, and any plans or expectations of a dramatic and rapid delivery were vetoed.

The children were doing the vetoing.

"I need to be there when Angel is born," Fil had declared as they were preparing to leave.

"I'm sorry, sweetie," Phoebe Trask told her son. "But the hospital requires you to be at least ten years old before you're allowed to be in the room when a baby is born."

"That's silly," Fil declared. "Besides, I'm very mature for my age."

And while that was true, his age wasn't in dispute, and that was the rule.

"Angel said she's not coming until I'm there," Fil announced.

It's true, Angel projected. *How can my big brother not be there when I'm born?*

They did their best to convince Angel not to cause trouble. The girl went silent. That worried Adam. She could cause trouble at the hospital; of that, he had no doubt. But at least now they'd be able to get out of the house.

Aunt Eva and Uncle Aaron had arrived, cramming themselves and their luggage into Fil's bedroom while the boy "camped out" in the living room. Fil had the sense not to ask why they couldn't use a nanokit to build a spare bedroom in the basement for their guests. He took the time to build blanket forts instead, just as any boy approaching seven years of age might do, tucking blankets into cushions even as he protested the fact that he'd be left behind.

"I promise I'll take good care of her, Fil," Adam said. "I'll take good care of both of them."

Realizing there was nothing else he could do, Fil grumbled, but went back to playing in his fort. Eva and Aaron watched Adam and Phoebe drive away.

Check-in, to his surprise, was no less dull. He'd dropped her off at the hospital entry, but she'd walked in under her own power to the check-in desk. She was still filling out the last few forms when he returned. She grimaced at him, and he couldn't help but smile. Will's company had drastically cut the costs of health care, but the industry still demanded the sacrifice of several trees prior to providing services.

He wheeled her upstairs to the tenth floor, and the medical staff there began fussing over her. She was eventually wheeled into room 1018, a number which made her chuckle.

And then… nothing happened. Angel was apparently throwing a temper tantrum.

They waited, and waited, and waited. With an epidural in place, the mild contractions gave Phoebe little discomfort, and she fell asleep a few hours later. Adam amused himself by chatting with Angel telepathically. It made him think of the decade he'd spent talking to Gena in a similar manner, with one major difference: Angel was in no danger of dying.

Why are you waiting? Your mother is eager to see you. And I know you'd like Fil to be here, but there are rules in place that we must follow. You'll be able to see him with your eyes soon enough. There's no need to wait.

Silly, I know that! I'm not waiting for Fil anymore. I'm waiting for Daddy.

He'd learned that the Stark—no, the *Trask*—children were rarely wrong in their intuitive proclamations. Fil had offered insights about people and situations throughout the summer that astounded him. He supposed that was to be expected. Fil, and his sister, would be born with the kind of ability, awareness, and confidence that would make them unique in the world.

But Angel was now waiting for *Will* to arrive before she'd permit herself to be born. Could she be right? Would Will make an appearance?

Angel, I'm glad you want to wait for your Dad. But I'm not sure where he is. How long will you wait?

He'll be here in a few minutes. I can feel him. Can't you?

Adam looked around, startled. Will was on his way here *now*? Perhaps he was taking Adam's approach, disguising himself as a member of the hospital staff so as to enter the delivery room without suspicion.

Okay, Mr. Adam. Daddy is here now. Wake Mommy up so I can be born. And Mr. Adam?

Yes, Angel? He was trying to avoid sounding shocked at the news that Will was in the room… because Adam couldn't see or sense the man at all.

Something is wrong with Mommy. Her body is changing for some reason, like it is missing something. Please help her get better.

Adam frowned. Phoebe's body was changing because it was *missing* something?

He looked at her, at her pregnant belly, and wondered.

Then he realized what it was.

Angel, I think I know what the problem is. But let's get you born before we worry about that. He paused. *You said that your Daddy is here. Why don't I see him?*

He could hear her melodic, telepathic laugh. *Silly! You won't see* him. *You have to notice him in other ways.*

He thought about that as he gently squeezed Phoebe's arm. "Phoebe? I… have a hunch that it might be about that time."

She opened her eyes, groggy, clearly wanting nothing more than to sleep longer, a symptom he now understood. Or thought he did.

On the positive side, she wasn't yelling at him. Yet.

"What makes you think…?" She broke off, her eyes widening, and she sucked in a deep breath. "Find… the anesthesiologist. *Now.*"

Acting like any frantic father-to-be—or grandfather-to-be, in his case—Adam raced from the room to the main desk, where a nurse looked up at him. "She's asking for the anesthesiologist."

The woman tapped a few keys on her keyboard and looked at the readings from the monitoring sensors in Phoebe's room. Her face registered deep surprise. "Well… that baby decided that now's the time. When they're ready, they're ready, aren't they?"

Adam nodded. "You have no idea."

He trotted back into the room, glancing around, expecting to see Will. Angel was confident that he was there, but Adam detected no visible sign of the man. Nor was there even a slight trickle of Energy. If Will was there, he'd proven that he could remain undetected by everything, save for his own daughter.

But Adam didn't doubt Angel's assertion. Will was here; it wasn't just his unborn daughter's wishful thinking and active imagination.

After the hours of waiting, the delivery process itself proceeded with little fanfare. Adam thought it rather straightforward, and then caught himself: he wasn't the one actually doing the work. But Phoebe looked to be in a nearly blissful state throughout. Adam had never delivered a child, but it seemed quite odd that she'd do so without the slightest apparent bit of strain or pain.

He wondered if Angel was somehow helping her mother.

Or… was Will?

Moments later, Angel was there, crying as any newborn would. Her thin hair was a white-blond color, as her mother's had long been. Her eyes were a deep violet, and seemed to sparkle with an internal light. The hospital staff was mesmerized, and fell in love with the little girl in an instant. None of them wanted to hand Angel back to her mother. But they did.

For the first time in recent memory, Phoebe looked genuinely happy and content. She gazed down upon her daughter, lost in the vision of the baby girl's face and eyes, stroking her cheeks and hair, amazed at the child now in her arms.

"He *is* here, isn't he?" Phoebe murmured to her daughter. "I know it as well."

A nurse wiped a tear from her eye at Phoebe's words, and glanced toward Adam with sympathy. He could read her face and thoughts well. The nurse believed Phoebe was recalling her dead husband, the baby's father, speaking to calm herself and instill in her baby the idea that her father would be watching out for her from beyond the grave.

That wasn't far from the truth.

They heard the skirmish outside, shouts and yelling, and the medical staff left the room quickly to investigate. A moment later, the door opened again. But it wasn't a doctor or a nurse, it was…

"Mommy!" Fil said. He looked at her conspiratorially, eyes twinkling with something other than Energy. "I convinced Aunt Eva and Uncle Aaron to bring me here. Uncle Aaron is… I think he called it 'keeping them occupied.'"

Eva glided into the room, an unusually sheepish grin on her normally regal face. "I do believe the boy has manipulated two people into doing what he wants, despite being told that what he wants is impossible."

Phoebe smiled. "Someone once told me that the word impossible is meaningless. It appears that my son learned that lesson at a far younger age than I did."

Eva nodded, unable to prevent the smile from covering her face. She held up a camera. "Fil would like to meet his sister and take a picture. We should do so quickly, before the diversion Aaron has set loses its effectiveness."

"What diversion?" Adam asked, curious.

"Sometimes it is best not to know. Plausible deniability. I did not ask him."

Adam snorted.

Fil moved toward his mother, his face beaming at the physical sight of the sister he'd known for months. She was now a real, tangible person, someone he could see and touch. "Can I hold her, Mommy?"

Phoebe smiled. "Of course, sweetheart."

Fil climbed up onto the hospital bed and nestled up against his mother. Phoebe gently placed the bundled child into his outstretched arms. A look of pure bliss covered Fil's face, and he bent down to gaze directly into his sister's violet eyes. "I will always protect you, little sister. That's what big brothers do."

Adam and Eva glanced at each other, both of their faces somewhat damp. Eva reached into her purse and removed a high resolution digital camera while Adam used his sleeve to dry his face. She worked to turn it on as Phoebe took Angel back from Fil. The little boy leaned over his sister, continuing to grin from ear to ear.

"Smile!" Eva said. When Phoebe and Fil looked in her direction, she snapped the picture, then powered off the camera and dropped it back into her purse.

"I'll need a copy of that picture," Adam told her in a low voice. "It's needed for… future communications."

Eva nodded. Adam would ensure that the picture made it into the diary… and that the diary would find its way into the time machine Will Stark would use to travel to the distant past. It was a photo that both Will and Hope would use, at various times, to maintain their motivation to go on: Hope, glowing and happy; Josh, beaming at his sister as if she was found under the tree on Christmas morning; and a healthy Angel, with her striking blond hair and violet eyes. More than anything else, that image was the one that said everything had come to fruition, that everything they endured and suffered through the centuries was all worthwhile because in the end, their children were born and healthy, that they were all there and happy and celebrating Angel's birth.

Adam's smile tightened. Images spoke volumes, but they couldn't speak. There was nothing in the picture to indicate that Will wasn't physically present, or that the family had been forced to move across the country to avoid detection by Aliomenti Hunters who would happily finish the murders they and the Assassin had failed to complete only a few months earlier. And there was nothing to suggest Phoebe's current mental health. But the picture would serve its purpose. Will's gift to his wife months earlier—helping her watch her grown children emerge from the time machine to do what they needed to do in their past—was her new version of the photo they'd just taken. When times were at their worst, she'd be able to recall those memories, recall their voices as they spoke to her, and realize that she'd made it through the process of raising her two children. She'd know her children would become the type of people she and Will had been. There could be no greater praise, or motivation, that she could receive.

Adam glanced at Eva. "It's probably best that Fil heads back home. I'm sure the hospital staff won't be happy to find that he's broken their rules. I'll take him to Aaron if you want to spend some time with Phoebe and little Angel."

Eva's smile didn't quite reach her eyes. "Of course."

Fil didn't want to go, but apparently got reassurances from his sister that she'd survive the next few hours in a hospital without him hovering over her. He took Adam's hand, and the two walked out the door.

The head nurse, now looking quite harried, spotted the little boy. "How did you get in there?" She glared at Adam. "Sir, I believe we've told *you* that children aren't permitted in here, haven't we?"

"You did," Adam agreed. "The child managed to sneak away from his guardians. I'll take him back and recommend that they take him home." He smiled. "Hard to fault a little boy wanting to see his sister so much, though, isn't it?"

The nurse pursed her lips. "Mmhmm."

They found Aaron pacing in the waiting room, looking around as if he'd lost something. He breathed a sigh of relief when Adam and Fil walked in. "Fil, you gave me quite a scare, running off like that!" Aaron exclaimed, frowning.

"Sorry," Fil said, bowing his head. "I just really wanted to see her."

Aaron sighed. "I understand." He glanced at Adam. "They're talking about… it?"

Adam nodded. "They are. I should probably get back up there. In theory, Eva should be leaving with you, right?" He tousled Fil's hair. "See you in a bit, Fil."

He made it back up to Phoebe's room, and was hit with a friendly telepathic burst from the Trask child still in the room before he walked through the door. *They're fighting. I don't like fighting.*

Nor do I, Angel.

He walked into the room and could feel the tension. Angel rested comfortably in her bassinet, or at least appeared to do so. Eva stood near the edge of Phoebe's hospital bed. Phoebe had folded her arms, a look of sheer defiance on her face, which she'd turned away from Eva.

Adam cautiously approached the bed, and glanced at Eva. "Problem?"

Eva's eyes flashed, though there was sympathy mixed in with the anger. "She resists my recommendations."

"I'm not a child, Eva."

"I have never claimed you were. Yet the fact remains that most of the concerning behaviors observed by those who care for you and your well-being began shortly after you became pregnant with Fil."

"I don't regret the decision, Eva, regardless of any 'observations' that might be made."

"There was no reason *not* to resume fruit consumption after his birth, Phoebe. You had the means necessary to enable Angel's birth, just as you did with his."

"You're wrong, Eva. There was only a single dose. We've been through this. Again. And again. And *again.*"

"There were two vials, Phoebe, for a reason. You still have the second, do you not?"

"What if it didn't work the second time, though, Eva?" Her head snapped around. "I'd never take chances with the *life* of my daughter. Even if all of you are correct, I'd never take that chance with Angel."

Adam held up his hand. "This conversation is upsetting Angel. Let's move beyond old arguments we've had many times." He paused. "Phoebe, I understand your rationale. You did not want to take chances with Angel's birth. You didn't want to take a fresh dosage while still pregnant, because while what happened to James and Elise might well have been pure chance, it might not be. Being risk-averse with your children's very existence is very commendable."

Phoebe sniffed. "Thank you." Her tone was heavy with

sarcasm.

"But she's here now, Phoebe. Angel is here, and she's healthy. The danger from possible side effects is in the past. Won't you reconsider?"

"Why do all of you act like something's *wrong* with me?" Phoebe snapped. "Stop trying to find something *wrong* with me!" And she burst into tears.

An alarm began to sound, and moments later two nurses raced in. "Her pulse rate and blood pressure just skyrocketed. What happened?"

"We were engaging in conversation about post-pregnancy nutrition," Eva replied.

"It appears that's a stressful topic for the new mother," the nurse observed. "Perhaps an alternative topic of conversation would be best going forward?"

"They were just leaving," Phoebe said, loudly. Her glare had an intensity they'd rarely seen from her. Adam and Eva exchanged worried glances.

"That might be best," the nurse said. "I'm sure you mean well, but she does need her sleep. Perhaps give her a few hours to rest and come back later?"

Adam nodded, slowly. "Take care, Phoebe. We'll be here when you need us."

In answer, Phoebe rolled to her side, facing away from them. They could see her sides rise in fall in staccato fashion, as she cried in silent heaves.

Eva and Adam moved to Angel's bassinet to give a parting touch to their "niece" and "granddaughter," and as Adam's hand made contact with the newborn, her frantic thought reached him.

My Mommy is sick. Please help her.

I know, Angel. And I will. I promise.

They moved down to the lobby, where Aaron and Fil were engaged in a high-stakes game of checkers. The prize for the winner—a chocolate bar—rested on the table near them. They glanced up, and Aaron frowned at the sight of Adam. "I thought you'd be staying with her."

"I got kicked out of the room."

"By the hospital staff? Sorry, that's probably my fault."

"No. By the mother."

Aaron frowned, but said nothing as they left the hospital building. Fil seized the chocolate bar, tore open the wrapper, and took a big bite before anyone could protest.

They stopped for dinner. Conversation was forced but light-hearted, focused mostly on the fact that Fil would be starting school on Monday. He'd done a bit of socializing with the children in the neighborhood, but Monday would be the first day he'd truly interact with others and be out of the direct sight of his mother or a member of the Alliance.

Fil's excitement over the birth of his sister and the prospect of school left him exhausted, and he didn't protest his early bedtime. Once he fell asleep, after hearing stories about his father battling the Hunters, the adults retired to the living room.

Eva looked at Adam. "You saw it, did you not?"

Adam nodded. "I did. This is getting serious. We may be forced into more drastic action."

Aaron glanced at both of them. "Care to fill me in?"

"We are fairly certain that what Phoebe is experiencing is due to her long-term withdrawal from the use of ambrosia after so many centuries of usage," Eva explained. "The moodiness, the fatigue, the tears, the unexpected bouts of anger… they have increased in frequency and intensity the longer she has gone without. She was correct to be concerned about the possibility that she might not be able to reverse the effects of ambrosia a second time. Or that taking it during her pregnancy with either child might have resulted in pregnancy issues, including miscarriage. We are fairly certain that is what happened with James and Elise centuries ago. Now, though, we must convince her to take ambrosia again, and soon, or the results… well, they are getting far more severe."

"Meaning?"

"Meaning as we left and she rolled away from us, we both noticed a clump of her hair on the pillow."

Aaron's eyes widened. "That's not good."

"It's worse than that, Aaron," Adam said. "It wasn't just that her hair had fallen out. It's that the clump left on the pillow wasn't jet black, the color she's using with her current public image. It also wasn't the platinum blond we're so accustomed to seeing."

Eva shook her head. "No. The hair she had lost was gray, Aaron. She's not just suffering the symptoms of what might be considered severe clinical depression. She's aging. Rapidly."

Adam turned a somber face away from them. "If we don't do something soon, she'll die of old age." He breathed deeply. "And she might take some of us out in the process."

●●●

He'd had nearly four decades of isolation to perfect every skill and technology he'd developed over his previous thousand years of life. He'd learned to alter the very signal of his Energy, so that it would appear to someone like Porthos that he was someone other than Will Stark. He'd enhanced the nanobots he'd owned for centuries to something beyond what they'd been, coating them with scutarium, and bolstering their strength and speed of transport. Those enhancements had enabled him to be present at, and prevent, many of the attempts on his own life. He'd been there to watch his son's birth, his own wedding, and he'd been there, watching, as the events of January 7th unfolded. Those nanos had turned his wife and son invisible to the Assassin without any telltale expenditure of Energy, deflected the flame and debris of the killer's anger-induced inferno, and choked the Assassin until he'd lost consciousness.

Today, they'd allowed him to witness the birth of the daughter he'd never truly known.

Her perception of him, her recognition of his presence, astounded him. She couldn't be fooled, not by his altered Energy signal, and not by the shield of nanos that made him invisible to three powerful Alliance members in that room... including his wife.

Only Angel, then, recognized his horror at Hope's decline.

He couldn't call her Phoebe, any more than he could call her Elizabeth. She would always be Hope to him. And watching Hope's descent over the past few years, watching as she crumbled before his invisible eyes, knowing he could do nothing but remain hidden and hope the others could help her... that was a pain that tore him apart. It was an agony much like Hope had suffered, knowing her suppression of Josh's Energy had rendered the boy mute to him until now.

The graying hair, the worsening mood swings and bouts of tears, the debilitating fatigue... they needed to take action, and quickly.

If not? If they weren't able to convince—or force—Hope to consume the ambrosia to reverse the withdrawal effects?

Will set his invisible jaw. If they couldn't succeed, then he'd be the one to take drastic action.

He'd kidnap his wife to ensure her survival.

FROM THE AUTHOR

Thank you for reading *Preserving Will*. I hope you enjoyed the story and are interested in continuing to read about Will Stark and the rest of the Aliomenti. As this goes to print, Book 6 in the series is being written. Please sign up for my mailing list to be notified when it becomes available.

If you enjoyed this book, please consider taking a moment to leave a review and rating on the site used to purchase it, or at sites like Goodreads and LibraryThing, which are dedicated to helping readers find books they'll enjoy. Others will be very interested in your thoughts, and as an author it's wonderful to see feedback from readers.

If you'd like to contact me or find out when the next book is due, the best bet is to visit my website, http://www.alexalbrinck.com. While there, you'll find links to my Facebook fan page and Twitter feed. You can also email me at alex@alexalbrinck.com at any time.

I thank you again for your support, and wish you every success in your endeavors.

ALSO BY ALEX ALBRINCK

THE ALIOMENTI SAGA

Prequel: *Hunting Will* (December 2012)

Book 1: *A Question of Will* (September 2012)

Book 2: *Preserving Hope* (December 2012)

Book 3: *Ascent of the Aliomenti* (April 2013)

Book 4: *Birth of the Alliance* (August 2013)

Boo 5: *Preserving Will* (November 2013)

To be notified of new book releases, sign up for my mailing list:
http://eepurl.com/o03Gv

ABOUT THE AUTHOR

Alex Albrinck is a lifelong Ohio resident, where he lives with his wife and three children. When he's not trying to be in three places at once with his active youngsters, he's following local professional and collegiate sports teams, or possibly unscrambling a Rubik's Cube. In lieu of sleep, he writes fiction.

His debut novel, *A Question of Will*, explores themes of technological advancement, human potential (good and bad), and the love bonding a family together. It reached the Amazon Top 100 in Science Fiction -> High Tech less than a week after publication.

The sequels—*Preserving Hope, Ascent of the Aliomenti, Birth of the Alliance,* and *Preserving Will*—follow Will Stark as he continues his epic quest to save and reunite his family against all odds, and continues the exploration of advanced technology and Energy skills.

He is currently working on the next novel in the series.

35899763R00214

Made in the USA
San Bernardino, CA
16 May 2019